D0518484

THE
SILVER
GRYPHON

Also available from Orion/Millennium

The Mage Wars
The Black Gryphon
The White Gryphon

The Mage Storms
Storm Warning
Storm Rising

THE SILVER GRYPHON

Mercedes Lackey & Larry Dixon

Book Three of *The Mage Wars*

Interior Illustrations by Larry Dixon

MILLENNIUM

An Orion Book

LONDON

Copyright © 1996 Mercedes R. Lackey and Larry Dixon

All rights reserved

The right of Mercedes Lackey and Larry Dixon
to be identified as the authors of this work has
been asserted by them in accordance with the
Copyright, Designs and Patents Act 1988.

This edition first published
in Great Britain in 1996 by
Orion Books Ltd
Orion House, 5 Upper St Martin's Lane
London WC2H 9EA

A CIP catalogue record for this book
is available from the British Library

ISBN: (Csd) 1 85798 440 4
(Ppr) 1 85798 441 2

Printed and bound in Great Britain by
Clays Ltd, St Ives plc

Dedicated to 'Dusty' Rhoades, Mike Hackett,
Scott Rodgers, and all the rest of those
who know the Infobahn is a tool
and not a religion.

OFFICIAL TIMELINE FOR THE

by Mercedes Lackey

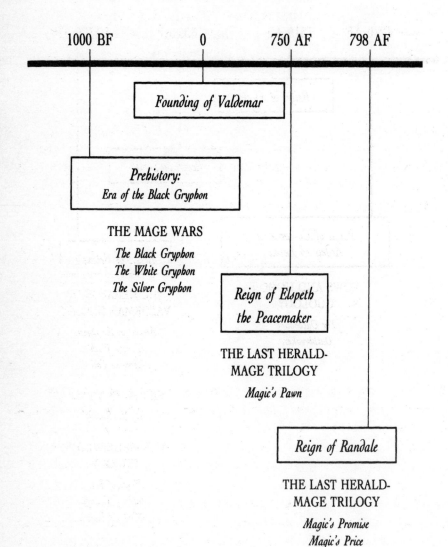

1000 BF   0   750 AF   798 AF

Founding of Valdemar

Prehistory:
Era of the Black Gryphon

THE MAGE WARS

The Black Gryphon
The White Gryphon
The Silver Gryphon

Reign of Elspeth
the Peacemaker

THE LAST HERALD-
MAGE TRILOGY

Magic's Pawn

Reign of Randale

THE LAST HERALD-
MAGE TRILOGY

Magic's Promise
Magic's Price

BF   *Before the Founding*
AF   *After the Founding*

HERALDS OF VALDEMAR SERIES

Sequence of events by Valdemar reckoning

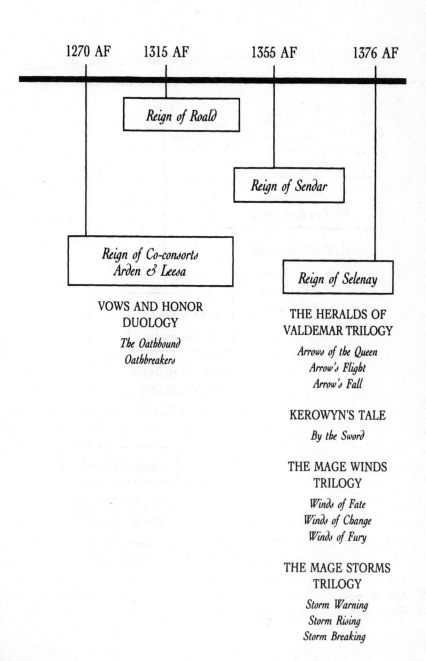

1270 AF   1315 AF   1355 AF   1376 AF

Reign of Roald

Reign of Sendar

Reign of Co-consorts Arden & Leesa

Reign of Selenay

VOWS AND HONOR
DUOLOGY

The Oathbound
Oathbreakers

THE HERALDS OF
VALDEMAR TRILOGY

Arrows of the Queen
Arrow's Flight
Arrow's Fall

KEROWYN'S TALE

By the Sword

THE MAGE WINDS
TRILOGY

Winds of Fate
Winds of Change
Winds of Fury

THE MAGE STORMS
TRILOGY

Storm Warning
Storm Rising
Storm Breaking

Skandranon

One

Freedom!

Tadrith Skandrakae extended his broad gray wings, stretching out his muscles to their fullest extent to take best advantage of the warm wind beneath him. *Freedom at last! I thought I'd never get away from that Section meeting.* He banked just slightly to his left, slipping sideways for the best line. *I know it wasn't my good looks or charm that were putting me under that old crow's watch! I swear, Aubri must get a special pleasure out of keeping people around him who desperately want to be somewhere else.* He half-closed his eyes against the glare of the sun on the water beneath him. He was conscious of two pressures, one tangible and one fanciful; the warm imagined push of the sun on his back, and the strong uplift of the thermal beneath him. Then again, maybe there were three pressures, or four; the warm air below, the hot sun above, and the twin desires to be away from the boredom of yet another Section meeting and the wish to be headed for something exciting.

The thermal tasted of salt and seaweed, and it gave him some welcome relief from rowing his wings against the breeze. Beneath and beyond his left wing, the great Western Sea shone green-blue and vast, the horizon a sharp line where the brilliant turquoise of the sky met the deep emerald green of the water farther out. To his right, the cliff-built city of White Gryphon sent back the rays of the sun in a dazzling display of snowy stone laced with growing things, drifts of trailing vines, and falling water. As had been planned a generation ago, the city itself was laid out in the shape of a stylized gryphon with his wings spread proudly against the mossy uncut stone of the cliff. By day, it glowed; by night, it glimmered, lit with candle, lantern and mage-light. Tadrith loved it; a proud, promising, beckoning city, home to thousands.

Beneath him, the olive-green waters of the cove rolled calmly against the base of the cliff and gurgled around the pillars of the dock, a delicate lacework of foam atop the swells. The moorings there were all empty except for light utility craft, for the fishing fleet of White Gryphon would be out at sea until sunset. Tadrith himself had served with the fleet in his first year as a Silver Gryphon; young gryphons acted as aerial scouts, spotting schools of fish from above, and then worked as catch haulers later in the day.

The only time that nets were used was when the catch haulers were taking the catch in to the shore. In their first years here, the fleet had fished with drag- and gill-nets, but did so no more. Their Haighlei allies had been horrified at the wastage caused by net fishing, for inedible sea life had been caught and wantonly destroyed along with the edible fish. They had rightfully pointed out that the Kaled'a'in would not have countenanced such wastage in *hunting*, so why should they allow it in fishing? Fishing was another form of hunting, after all; you did not kill creatures that were of no threat or use to you in the forest, so why do so in the sea? So now the fleets used only baited lines, allowing for the release of fish that were too young or unwanted. It took longer, and was more work, but that was a small matter compared with the fact that it ensured feeding the next generation, and the ten after that.

Ten generations to come. That's always the concern—the generations to come. Plan and work for ten generations' benefit, Amberdrake says. Even if we wear ourselves to wingsails and bones doing it!

Such thoughts tended to come to everyone at White Gryphon from time to time. Among the young, like him, they came to mind at least once an hour; in times of even harder work, they arose every few minutes. It was only natural, after all, that a day of bright sun and promise would hold a virile young gryphon's attention better than going over Patrol charts and Watch rosters with an elder gryphon, even one as likable as old Aubri.

I have places to go, things to do. I'm almost positive of it.

The landing platform that Tadrith had chosen was not untenanted, a factor that had played some little part in his choice. Not that he was *vain*, oh no! At least, not much. But there were three perfectly handsome young gryphon ladies spreading their wings to catch some sun on that platform, with their mothers in oh-so-casual attendance on the off-chance that a young bachelor might show some interest. He knew all three of them, of course; Dharra was a year older than he and a mage, Kylleen a year younger and still serving with the fleet, and Jerrinni a fellow Silver. *She* was already working with a partner on unsupervised assignments, and he particularly wanted to impress her if he could. She was by far the most attractive of the three, being of the same goshawk type that he was. But that was not the only reason for his interest in her; she was also his senior in the Silvers and her comments to her superiors might edge him up a little toward his long-delayed promotion to unsupervised assignments.

I wear the badge, but I am not yet allowed to bear the responsibilities the badge represents. He did not have to glance down at his harness to see that badge, made in the form of a stylized gryphon.

The Silver Gryphons, so named for that silver badge they wore, served in every kind of military and policing capacity that fighters, guards, scouts, and constables had in the old days. And in addition to those tasks, the gryphons in the Silvers—especially the young ones still in training—made themselves useful in a variety of other tasks.

Or to be more precise, their leaders *assigned* them to those so-useful tasks. Like hauling cargo, or carry-nets full of fish, or hoisting supplies, meat from the herds, and the fruits of the fields down from the top of the cliff, for instance.

Or sitting through boring meetings.

I have a hundred things that need to be done. Or as Father would say, "places to go, people to be." He makes a joke of it, but I live it, more than he ever did even after all of his adventures and missions and roles. Even more than he did at the Eclipse Ceremony.

He sideslipped and caught another thermal, one that would place him precisely where he wanted to be.

The thought of his father, as always, made him flinch internally. Not that Skandranon was a *bad* father—oh, no! He was an excellent teacher, provider, and friend. He was a fine father, but he was a very difficult person to *have as* a father. Trying to live up to the image of the Black Gryphon was. . .difficult and vexing. *He may be a living legend, but it makes being his son a living hell.*

But the platform and its attractive occupants loomed up before and beneath him, and Tadrith allowed himself a touch of smug satisfaction. He prided himself on his aerobatics, and most especially on his control. His mother Zhaneel was the gryphon who had been most revered for her flying finesse, and he had studied her techniques more than his father's. *At least the Great Skandranon can't do this as well as I can. . . .*

Tadrith banked in over the platform and pulled up, to stall in midair and then fall, wings cupped, to land standing on one foot, then two, and from then to all fours without any sound louder than the creak of the platform accepting his weight. The gryphon ladies all gazed on in approval, impressed by his display of control and dexterity, and Kylleen cooed aloud and smiled in his direction.

Yes! That worked out just the way I wanted. Tadrith stood rock steady and struck a momentary pose, wings folded crisply, crest up and gently ruffled by the breeze. *Just right. That will show them what I'm made of. Father never flew like that! He'd have powered straight in and knocked them half off their feet with the backwash of his wingbeats. I have finesse and style!*

Tadrith's self-congratulatory reverie was shattered a moment later when one mother said to another, "Did you see that? Why, he's the very image of his father, with aerobatics like that."

Crushed, Tadrith drooped his head and crest and stepped off the platform.

I'm doomed.

At least the younger ladies seemed oblivious to the effect that the casual remark had on him. They continued to bestow coy and admiring glances on him as he made as unhurried and graceful an exit as he could manage under the circumstances.

The platform jutted out over the cove below, and led directly to one of the balustraded "streets" that ran along the edge of the terrace. The Kaled'a'in who comprised the greater part of the population of White Gryphon were accustomed to being surrounded by greenery, and even in a city carved and built completely of cliff-stone had managed to bring that greenery here. Built into the balustrades were stone boxes filled with earth brought down a sackful at a time from the fields above; those boxes now held luxuriant vines that trailed down to the next terraced level. More stone boxes each held a single tree or bush, with flowering herbs planted at its base. There was water enough coming down from above to allow for the occasional tiny waterfall to trail artfully from terrace to terrace and end in a long fall to the sea. The greenery had been planned so that it actually formed feather-patterns, adding texture to the pure white of the stone gryphon. Part of the philosophy of White Gryphon, when the city was planned, had been "recovery with dignity." The leaders of the people—Skandranon included—used the survivors' artistry and style as a point of pride and unification. If a simple box would do, an ornamented box was better. This strategy of increased self-esteem, guided by the kestra'chern, worked in making the people feel less like beaten refugees and more like proud homesteaders.

The philosophy was simple. If an object could be made beautiful—whether it was a street, doorway, or garden—it was.

Homes were carved directly into the cliff behind the avenue, some going twenty or thirty gryphon-lengths back into the stone. The size of a family home or a gryphon aerie was limited only to the willingness of family members to dig (or pay for someone else to dig)—and to live in the windowless spaces beyond the main rooms. Gryphons tended to find such spaces disturbing and confining and preferred not to carve more than two rooms'-worth deep, but *hertasi* and *kyree* and even some humans actually liked the idea of such burrows, and sent their dwellings quite far back indeed. There were entire complexes of man-made caverns back in those cliffs, and Tadrith had to admit that the one advantage they had was that weather made little or no difference to the folk living in those rooms.

Amberdrake was one such. He and Winterhart had buried their personal chambers so far back into the living stone that no natural light ever reached there to disturb late sleepers. Tadrith shuddered at the very thought of so much rock on every side, cutting him off from the air and light. He had no idea how his partner Blade ever tolerated it, for she was another such as her parents.

Not that a gryphon ever needs to worry about being forced to live in such a place. Not while there are hertasi *and* kyree *vying for such mausoleums and eager to give up cliff-side residences to have one.* In the early days, when simply getting a dwelling carved out quickly had been of paramount importance, it had been faster and easier just to sculpt rooms side-by-side, often simply enlarging and improving existing caves. Mage-lights to aid in working deeper into the stone had been at a premium, and there were long stretches of time when magic could not be used to help work the stone at all, so that it all had to be done by hand. Workers tended to carve to a standard that happened to be preferred by most humans and all gryphons and *tervardi*. The *dyheli*, of course, needed the barest of shelters to be contented and all lived above, among the farms, but the *hertasi* and *kyree* who really were not comfortable with views of endless sky and long drops were forced to make do until there was time and the resources to create dwellings more to their liking. That meant there were always those who would happily trade an older, "precarious perch" for a newly-chiseled burrow. There were wider terraces, of course, that permitted real buildings and even small gardens, but those were all in the "body" of White Gryphon and most building space was reserved for public use. It was probably fair to say that three-quarters of the population of White Gryphon lived in glorified cave dwellings.

That was how Tadrith and his twin, Keenath, had gotten their own aerie, which allowed them to move out of their parents' home; they'd found a narrow stretch of unexcavated terrace down at the bottom of White Gryphon's "tail" and had claimed it for themselves, then hired a team of masons to carve out a long set of six rooms, one after the other, deep into the living rock. This sort of residence was precisely the kind preferred by den-loving *kyree* and burrowing *hertasi*. Once the dwelling had been roughed in and the twins made it known that they were willing to trade, there was a bidding war going on even before it was completed.

The result was that Tadrith and Keenath had their own bachelor suite of one main room, a food storage chamber, and two light and airy bedrooms on either side of the main room. Both bedchambers had windows overlooking the cliff, as had the main room. The *kyree* family that had gratefully traded this aerie for the dark tunnellike series of rooms pronounced themselves overjoyed to be leaving such a drafty, windswept perch, and had wondered why their parents had ever chosen it!

Which only proves that one creature's cozy nest is another creature's draft-ridden mess of sticks.

As Tadrith neared his home, which was out on what would

be the first primary of the White Gryphon's right wing, the "avenue" narrowed to a simple pathway, and the balustrade to a knee-high, narrow ledge of stone. Perhaps that had something to do with the *kyree*'s reluctance to live there—certainly such an arrangement would be dangerous for young, clumsy cubs. Tadrith and Keenath had been raised in an aerie virtually identical to this one, but on the first primary of the White Gryphon's *left* wing; that distance between them and their beloved parents had played no small part in their final decision as to which family would win the bidding war.

Tadrith could, if he had chosen to do so, actually have landed on the balustrade right outside his own door—but landing anywhere other than the public landing platforms was considered a breech of safety, for it encouraged the just-fledged youngsters, who were by no means as coordinated as they *thought* they were, to reckless behavior. No lives had been lost, but several limbs had been broken, when younglings had missed their landings and slipped off the edge or tumbled into a group of passersby. After a number of hysterical mothers demanded that the Council do something about the problem, the landing platforms were installed and gryphons and *tervardi* were "strongly encouraged" to use them. Tadrith and Keenath, with every eye in White Gryphon always on them, had been scrupulous in their use of the public landing platforms.

By daylight, anyway. And no fledge is allowed to fly after dark, so they'll never see us when we cheat.

In glorious weather like this, the doors and windows always stood wide open, so Tadrith simply strolled inside his shared dwelling, his claws clicking on the bare stone of the floor. The room they used for company was airy and full of light, with the rock of the outer wall carved into several tall panels with thin shafts of wood between them. Translucent panes of the tough material the Kaled'a'in used for windows were set into wooden frames on hinges, which in turn were set into the stone. The room itself was furnished only with cushions of various sizes, all covered in fabric in the colors of sandstone and granite, slate and shale. In the winter, thick sheepskins and wool rugs would cover that cold white floor, and the doors and windows would be shut tight against the gales, but in the summer all those coverings were whisked away into storage so that an overheated gryphon could lie belly-down on the cool rock floor and dump some of that body heat quickly. And, in fact, Keenath was doing just that, spread out on the floor, with wings fanned, panting slightly.

"I was just thinking about dinner," his twin greeted him. "I might have known that thoughts of food would bring you home."

Tadrith snorted. "Just because *you're* obsessed with eating it doesn't follow that I am! I'll have you know that I only just now escaped from yet another yawnsome Section meeting. Food was the very last thing on my mind, and escaping Aubri was the first!"

Keenath laughed silently, beak parted, as his tongue flicked in and out while his sides heaved. "That must have been a first, then," he bantered. "So who was she? The pretty young thing that your mind was *really* on, I mean. Kylleen, perhaps?"

Tadrith was not going to get caught in *that* trap. "I haven't made up my mind," he said loftily. "I have so many to choose from, after all, it hardly seems reasonable to narrow the field this early in the race. It wouldn't be fair to thc ladies, either, to deny my company to any of them. It is only polite to distribute my attentions over as wide a selection as possible."

Keenath reached out a claw and snagged a pillow, spun it twice as he raised up, and expertly hurled it at his brother's head. Tadrith ducked, and it shot across the room to thud against the wall on the other side.

"You should be careful doing that," he warned, flopping down on the cool stone himself. "We've lost too many pillows over the cliff that way. So what were you studying that has you panting so hard?"

"Field treatment and rescues under combat conditions, and specifically, blood stanching and wound binding," Keenath replied. "Why? Don't ask me; we haven't seen a state of combat since before you and I were born. Winterhart's idea. Probably because I take after Mother."

Tadrith nodded; Keenath *was* very similar in size and build to their mother, Zhaneel. Like her, he was technically a *gryfalcon* rather than a gryphon. He was small and light, most of his musculature in his chest and shoulders. His coloring and body type were that of a peregrine, his wings long and narrow, but most importantly, he had inherited Zhaneel's stub-taloned, dexterous claw-hands.

This was important, for Keenath was learning the craft of the *trondi'irn* from Winterhart herself, and he needed "hands" as clever as a human's. Before his apprenticeship was complete, he would be able to do anything a Healer with no Gift could do. The difference between him and an herb-, fire-, or knife-Healer was that, like all *trondi'irn*, his training was tailored to the needs and physiology of gryphons and other nonhumans.

Zhaneel had been trained as a fighter—and others had come to the realization that her small size and lack of fighting talons could be put to other uses too late for her to learn a new trade. At that point, she had opted to adapt her style of fighting to her body type rather than try to fit the accepted mold, and with Skandranon's help she had made the best of her situation with brilliant results. But when Keenath had shown early signs that he would resemble her physically, he was encouraged to think of a career in something other than the Silvers.

Nevertheless, it had surprised everyone when he had declared he wanted to train as a *trondi'irn*. Up until now, that had been an occupation reserved for humans and *hertasi*.

Tadrith stretched and yawned, turning his head so that the breeze coming in from the open door could ruffle his crest-feathers. "At least you were doing something!" he complained. "I sat there until I thought my hindquarters were going to turn to stone, and if any part of me is going to grow stiff on a day like this, that is *not* my primary choice. I

couldn't even take a nap; as usual, old Aubri had me con-
spicuously up front. Have to maintain the tradition of the
Black Gryphon, of course; have to pretend every Section
meeting is as important as a wartime conference. Have to
act as if every detail could mean life or death." He stretched
again, enjoying the fact that he could always vent his frustration to his twin. "You should be glad you look the way
you do, Keeth. It's bad enough being Skandranon's son, but
the fact that I *look* like him doesn't even remotely help! You
try living up to the legend, sometime! It's enough to make
anyone want to bite something!"

And to display the strength of his own frustration, he
snagged the poor, mistreated pillow Keenath had lately
lobbed at him, and bit at it savagely. It was a good thing they
had the cushions covered in tough linen-canvas, for the pillows had to take a great deal of punishment.

"Well, if you think it's hard living up to the legend, just
try breaking away from it!" Keenath retorted, as he always
did. Tadrith's twin groaned as he followed Tadrith's example, stretching. "Half the time I'm left wondering if Winterhart isn't pushing me so hard *expecting* me to fail, and half
the time I think she's doing it because everyone knows
Skandranon never failed at anything he tried."

Tadrith snorted and mock-scraped his hindfeet, as if burying something particularly noxious from a previous meal.
"He never let it be known how often he failed, which is the
same thing to legend-builders."

His brother snorted right back and continued. "And if it
isn't Winterhart, it's everyone else, watching, waiting to see
if the old Black Gryphon magic is strong enough in Keenath
to enable the youngling to pull off another miracle." He
parted his beak in a sardonic grin. "At least you have a path
to follow—I'm going through new skies in the fog, and I
have no idea if I'm going to run up against a cliff-face."

Naturally, Tadrith had his own set of retorts, already
primed, proving how much more difficult it was to have to
follow in the wake of the Black Gryphon. It was an old set of

complaints, worn familiar by much handling, and much enjoyed by both of them.

Who can I complain to, if not to my twin? For all that they
were unalike in form and temper, they were bound by the
twin-bond, and knew each other with the twin's intimacy.
There were other twins among the gryphons, and one or two
sets among the humans, and all the twin-sets agreed; there
was a bond between them that was unlike any other sibling
tie. Tadrith often thought that he'd never have been able to
cope with the pressure if Keenath hadn't been around, and
Keenath had said the same thing about his sibling.

Finally the litany of complaints wound to its inevitable
conclusion—which was, of course, that there was no conclusion possible. They ran through the sequence at least
once every day, having long ago decided that if they could
not change their circumstances, at least they could enjoy
complaining about them.

"So what has your tail in a knot this time?" Keenath
asked. "It wasn't just the meeting."

Tadrith rolled over on his back to let the breeze cool his
belly. "Sometimes I think I'm going to do something drastic
if Blade and I don't get assigned soon!" he replied, discon-
tentedly. "What are they waiting for? We've earned our freedom by now!"

"They could be waiting for you to finally demonstrate a
little patience, featherhead," Keenath said, and had to duck
as the pillow made a return trip in his direction.

There might have been more pillows than just the one flying, if Silverblade herself, Tadrith's partner, hadn't chosen
that moment to walk in their open door.

She stood in the doorway, posing unconsciously, with the
sun making a dark silhouette of her against the brilliant sky.
Tadrith knew it was not a conscious pose; it was totally out
of her nature to do anything to draw attention to herself unless it was necessary. Blade was the name the gryphons knew
her by, though her childhood name hadn't been the use-
name she wore now; it had been "Windsong," so dubbed by

her fond parents in the hopes, no doubt, that she would grow up to resemble one or the other of them. "Windsong" was a perfectly good name for a *trondi'irn* or even a *kestra'chern* or a Kaled'a'in Healer or mage. But "Windsong" hadn't had the inclination for any of those things.

The young woman who broke her pose and strode into the aerie with the soundless tread of a hunter was small by Kaled'a'in standards, although there was no mistaking her lineage. Her short black hair, cut in a way that suggested an aggressive bird of prey, framed a face that could only have graced the head of one of the Clan k'Leshya, and her beak of a nose continued the impression of a hunting hawk. Her golden skin proclaimed the lineage further, as did her brilliantly blue eyes. There was nothing of her mother about her—and very little of her father.

She fit in very well with those members of Clan k'Leshya descended from warrior stock, however. Despite her small size, she was definitely molded in their image. There was nothing to suggest softness or yielding; she was hard, lithe, and every bit a warrior, all muscle and whipcord.

Tadrith well recalled the first time he had seen her stand that way. The day she showed her real personality, one month after her twelfth birthday, a month during which she had suddenly turned overnight from a lively if undistinguished child to a rough and unpolished version of what she now was. Amberdrake had been holding a gathering of some sort, which had included the children, and of course Tadrith and Keenath had been in attendance. Winterhart had addressed her daughter as "Windsong" during the course of the meal, and the little girl had unexpectedly stood up and announced to the room in a firm and penetrating voice that she was *not* to be called by that name anymore.

"I am going to be a Silver," she had said, loudly and with total conviction. "I want to be called Silverblade from now on."

Silverblade had then sat down, flushed but proud, amidst gasps and murmurs. It was a rather dramatic move even for someone with an outgoing personality like Tadrith; for one as self-effacing as Blade, it must have taken an enormous effort of will—or assertion of the truth, as the k'Leshya believed. The willpower to do anything would come, the songs and writings said, if the motive was pure.

Nothing her parents could say or do would persuade her otherwise—not that Amberdrake and Winterhart had been so selfish as to attempt to thwart her in what she so clearly wanted. From that day on, she would respond to no other name than Silverblade, or "Blade" for short, and now even both her parents referred to her by that name.

It certainly fits her better than "Windsong." She can't carry a tune any better than I could carry a boulder!

"Keeth! I hear you didn't kill too many patients today, congratulations!" she said as she invited herself into the room and sat down on one of the remaining cushions.

"Thank you," Keenath said dryly. "And do come in, won't you?"

She ignored his attempt at sarcasm. "I've got some good news, bird," she said, turning to Tadrith and grinning broadly as he rolled over. "I didn't think it could wait, and besides, I wanted to be the one to break it to you."

"News?" Tadrith sat up. "What kind of news?" There was only one piece of news that he really cared about—and only one he thought Blade would want to deliver to him herself.

Her grin broadened. "You should have stayed after the meeting; there was a reason why Aubri wanted you up front. If you were half as diligent as you pretend to be, you'd know for yourself by now." She eyed him teasingly. "I'm tempted to string this out, just to make you squirm."

"What!" he burst out, leaping to his feet. "Tell me! Tell me this instant! Or—I'll—" He gave up, unable to think of a threat she couldn't counter, and just ground his beak loudly.

Now she laughed, seeing that she had gotten him aroused. "Well, since it looks as if you might burst if I don't—it's what we've been hoping for. We've gotten our first unsupervised assignment, and it's a good one."

Only the low ceiling prevented him from leaping into the

air in excitement, although he did spring up high enough to brush his crest-feathers and wingtips against the ceiling. "When? Where? How long till we can get in action?" He shuffled his taloned feet, his tail lashing with exuberance, all but dancing in place.

She laughed at his reaction, and gestured to him to sit down. "Just as quickly as you and I would like, bird. We leave in six days, and we'll be gone for six moons. We're going to take charge of Outpost Five."

Now his joy knew no bounds. "Five? Truly?" he squealed, sounding like a fledgling and not caring. "Five!"

Outpost Five was the most remote outpost in all of the territory jointly claimed by White Gryphon and their Haighlei allies. When this particular band of refugees had fled here, as they escaped the final Cataclysm of the Mage of Silence's war with Ma'ar the would-be conqueror of the continent, they had been unaware that the land they took for a new home was already claimed. They'd had no idea that it was part of the land ruled by one of the Haighlei Emperors (whom the Kaled'a'in knew as the Black Kings), King Shalaman. A clash with them had been narrowly averted, thanks to the work of Amberdrake and Skandranon, Blade's father and Tadrith's. Now White Gryphon jointly held these lands in trust with the Emperor, and its citizens were charged with the responsibility of guarding the border in return for King Shalaman's grant of the White Gryphon lands.

It was a border of hundreds of leagues of wilderness, and the Emperor himself had not been able to "guard" it; he had relied on the wilderness itself to do the guarding. This was not as insurmountable a task as it might have seemed; with gryphons to fly patrol, it was possible to cover vast stretches of countryside with minimal effort. Outpost Five was the most remote and isolated of all of the border posts. Because of that, it was hardly the most desirable position so far as the Silvers were concerned.

For *most* Silvers, perhaps, but not for Blade and Tadrith. This meant three whole months in a place so far away from

White Gryphon that not even a hint of what transpired there would reach the city unless he or Blade sent it by teleson. There would be no watching eyes, waiting to see if he could replicate his legendary father. There would be no tongues wagging about his exploits, imagined or real.

Of course, there would also be no delicious gryphon ladies for three months, but that was a small price to pay. Three months of chastity would be good for him; it would give him a rest. He would be able to use the leisure time to invent new and clever things to do and say to impress them. He would have all that time to perfect his panache. By the time he returned, as a veteran of the border, he should be able to charm any lady he chose.

Outpost duty was a long assignment, in no small part because it was so difficult to get people *to* the outposts. Even though magic was now working reliably, and had been for several years, no one really wanted to trust his body to a Gate just yet. Too many things could go wrong with a Gate at the best of times, and at the moment the only purpose anyone was willing to put them to was to transport unliving supplies. The consumables and their mail and special requests would be supplied to their outpost that way; a mage at White Gryphon who was familiar with the place would set up a Gate to the outpost. Workers would then pitch bundles through, and the mage would drop the Gate as soon as he could.

No one wants to leave a Gate up very long either. You never know what might go wrong, or what might stroll through it while it's up.

"You know, of course, that there's a great deal of uninhabited and poorly-surveyed territory in between Five and home," Blade went on with relish. "We're going to be completely on our own from the time we leave to the time we return."

"What, no lovely gryphon ladies and human stallions to wile away your time of exile?" jibed Keenath, and shuddered realistically. "Well, never mind. I can guarantee that in the case of the ladies, I can make certain that they will not notice your absence, twin."

"They are more likely to cry out in pain at your poor attempts at gallantry, Keeth," Tadrith told him, and turned back to Blade. "*You* realize that this shows a great deal of trust in our abilities, don't you? I mean, the usual first assignment is something like—"

"Like guarding the farms, I know," she replied smugly. "That must have been why they kept us behind the others, training and overtraining us. They wanted to be sure we were ready, and I bet they decided to send us out there because we're the only people who really *want* to go. In fact, I would bet my favorite armband that Aubri plans to send us out on long outpost duty every chance he can get!"

They grinned at each other with relish, for there was another aspect to outpost duty they both anticipated with pleasure. Those so posted were expected to do a certain amount of exploring, and sometimes the explorers found something valuable. The Emperor Shalaman got a share, of course, as did the treasury of White Gryphon, but the generous portion remaining went to the intrepid explorers who made the discovery. Not that Tadrith was *greedy*, of course, but he did have a certain love of ornamentation, a pronounced interest in the finer things of life, and finding something extremely valuable would make it possible for him to indulge his interests. And it didn't hurt to have the wherewithal to impress the ladies, either, and ornament them a bit now and then.

"Just how much exploring has been done up there?" he asked.

Blade's eyes widened knowingly. "Not all that much," she replied. "And there are more ways to explore than sailing over the tree-canopy, hoping something on the ground will show itself."

He nodded, following her thoughts. Probably most of the Silvers assigned to Outpost Five in the past had been gryphon teams; that made sense, although it probably wore them down terribly, not having humans and *hertasi* to tend to them. A human on station, though, could make a detailed survey of a particular area, including the smaller animals and plants living there, and take mineral samples. That was something a gryphon was ill-suited or, for that matter, ill-inclined, to do.

"There's been no trouble from that sector for years," she mused. "We should have plenty of time for surveys."

"But most of all, you'll be on your own," Keenath said enviously. "I wish I could find some way to escape for a few months."

Blade patted his shoulder sympathetically. "And miss all the benefits of *trondi'irn, hertasi* and *kestra'chern* fawning on you every spare moment? The horror! You could ask to be taken on by the Silvers once you've finished training under Winterhart," she suggested. "Then you'd get some assignments elsewhere. Down with the embassy at Khimbata, maybe; you could go as the *trondi'irn* taking care of the Emperor's gryphon-guards."

Keenath's eyes lit up at the idea, and Tadrith knew how he felt. For a chance to get out of White Gryphon he would have put up with just about anything.

The problem was that there was literally nothing that he said or did that Skandranon didn't eventually find out about. It wasn't that Skan was purposefully spying on his sons, or even deliberately overseeing them—

Well, not much, anyway. And not overtly.

—it was just that everyone told the Black Gryphon everything that went on in this city. A mouse couldn't sneeze without Skandranon finding out about it eventually.

Neither can we—except that it's guaranteed that if we sneeze, someone will go running to Father with the news. Not only that, but the report would be detailed as to how, when, and how well we sneezed.

It wasn't exactly tale-bearing, for people made certain to bring Skan the most flattering reports possible. Skan was a very proud father.

He can't get enough of hearing about all the marvelous things Keeth and I are doing, especially now that we aren't in the family aerie to bully into making reports on ourselves. The trouble is, he is fully capable of blowing the most minor accomplishment up into the equivalent of a brilliant piece of wartime strategy or heroism.

It was embarrassing, to say the least.

And, of course, anyone who wanted to curry favor with the Black Gryphon knew the fastest way to his heart was to praise his sons. Skan would go out of his way to see that someone who flattered the twins got a full hearing and careful consideration. That was *all* he would do, but often enough, that was sufficient.

As Keeth continued to look envious and a little pained, Tadrith preened his short eartufts in sympathy. "I wish there was a way to send you out of the city for *trondi'irn* training, Twin," he murmured.

Keenath sighed. "So do I. When we were all choosing the subject we wanted to study, I *tried* to think of some discipline I could enjoy that would also get me out of the city at the same time, but I couldn't. I think I'm going to be good at this, and it certainly feels right, but it means I'm stuck here."

Blade wore as sympathetic an expression as Tadrith.

"There is this, Keeth," the gryphon said to his twin. "You can just go on doing what you are doing and you will have earned every right to be considered unique and special. You're writing your own definition of a *trondi'irn*. You don't have to stand there, blushing at the nares with embarrassment when someone comes in acting as if running the obstacle course was the equivalent of stealing one of Ma'ar's magical weapons."

But Keenath ruffled his neck-feathers and clicked his beak. "That's true up to a point, but there is another problem. Father literally does not understand me. We have absolutely nothing in common. When I talk about what I'm doing, he gets this strange look on his face, as if I were speaking a foreign tongue." He laughed weakly. "I suppose I am, really. Well, I'll get my chance eventually."

"You will," Blade promised, but she made no move to rise to her feet. "I'm going to have to break the news to *my* parents, assuming that they don't already know, which is more than likely. Tad, you'd better figure out how to tell yours."

"They'll know," Tadrith replied with resignation. "Father is probably already telling everyone he thinks will listen how there's never been anyone as young as I am posted so far away on his first assignment."

Blade laughed ruefully. "You're probably right. And mine is probably doing the same—except—"

She didn't complete the sentence, but Tadrith knew her well enough not to pressure her. They each had their own set of problems, and talking about them wasn't going to solve them.

Only time would do that.

Or so he hoped.

Silverblade sat back on her heels when the twins began to argue over what Tadrith should pack. She was in no real hurry to get back home; since she was still living with her parents, she did not even have the illusion of privacy that her own aerie would have provided. The moment she walked in the door, the questions and congratulations— bracketed by thinly-veiled worry—would begin, and at the moment she did not feel up to fielding them.

She breathed in the scent of salt air and sunbaked rock, half closing her eyes. *I love this place. The only neighbors are other gryphons, quiet enough that the sound of the surf covers any noise they might make. And I love the fact that there are no other humans nearby, only* tervardi, *gryphons, and a few* kyree.

How she envied Tad his freedom! He really had no notion just how easy a parent Skandranon was to deal with. The Black Gryphon had a sound, if instinctive and not entirely reliable, knowledge of just when to shut his beak and let Tad go his own way. He also attempted to restrain his enthusiasm for the accomplishments of his twins, although it was difficult for him. But at least he showed that he approved; Amberdrake had never been happy with the path-choice his daughter had made, and although he tried not to let his disapproval color their relationship, it leaked through anyway. How could it not?

Perhaps "disapproval" was too strong a word. Amberdrake understood warriors; he had worked with them for most of his life. He respected them most profoundly. He liked them, and he even understood all of the drives that fueled their actions.

He simply did not understand why his child and Winterhart's would want to be a warrior. *He can't fathom how he and Mother produced someone like me. By all rights, with everything that they taught me, I should never have been attracted to this life.*

That was a gap of understanding that probably would never be bridged, and Blade had yet to come up with a way of explaining herself that would explain the riddle to him. "Blade, would you play secretary and write the list for me?" Tadrith pleaded, interrupting her reverie. "Otherwise I know I'm going to forget something important."

"If you do, you can always have it Gated to us," she pointed out, and laughed when he lowered his eartufts.

"*That* would be so humiliating I would rather do without!" he exclaimed. "I'd never hear the last of it! Please, just go get a silver-stick and paper from the box and help me, would you?"

"What else are gryphon-partners for, except doing paperwork?" she responded, as she rose and sauntered across the room to the small chest that held a variety of oddments the twins found occasionally useful, each in its appointed place. The chest, carved of a fragrant wood that the Haighlei called *sadar*, held a series of compartmentalized trays holding all manner of helpful things. Among them were a box of soft, silver sticks and a block of tough reed-paper, both manufactured by the Haighlei. She extracted both, and returned to her seat beside Tad. She leaned up against him, bracing herself against his warm bulk, using her knees as an impromptu writing desk.

As the twins argued over each item before agreeing to add it to the list or leave it out, she waited patiently. Only once did she speak up during the course of the argument, as Keenath insisted that Tad include a particular type of healer's kit and Tad argued against it on the grounds of weight.

She slapped his shoulder to get him to be quiet. "Who is the *trondi'irn* here?" she demanded. "You, or Keeth?" Tad turned his head abruptly, as if he had forgotten that she was there. "You mean, since he's the expert, I ought to listen to him."

"Precisely," she said crisply. "What's the point of asking his opinion on this if you won't take it when you know he's the authority?"

"But the likelihood that we'd need a bonesetting kit is so small it's infinitesimal!" he protested. "And the weight! I'm the one who's going to be carrying all this, you know!"

"But if we need it, we'll need exactly those supplies, and nothing else will substitute," she pointed out. "We don't know for certain that there's a bonesetting kit at the Outpost, and I prefer not to take the chance that the last few teams have been as certain of their invulnerability as you." Keenath looked smug as she added it to the list, unbidden. "I'm going to insist on it. And if it isn't in that basket when we leave, I'll *send* for one. We may be in a position of needing one and being unable to ask for one to be Gated to us."

Tad flattened his ears in defeat as he looked from one implacable face to the other. "You win. I can't argue against both of you."

Gryphons could not smirk like humans could, but there was enough muscular control of the beak edges at the join of the lower mandible that one could be approximated. More than a touch of such an expression showed on Keeth as they continued on to the next item. Part of the reason why Blade felt so comfortable in the Silvers and with the gryphons in particular was that their motives and thoughts were relatively simple and easy to understand. In particular, they made poor liars; gryphons were just too expressive to hold a bluff effectively once you knew how to read their physical cues, such as the lay of their facial feathers and the angle of their ears. Although they were complex creatures and often stubborn, gryphons were also exactly what they appeared to be. The *kestra'chern*, her father in particular, were anything but.

Their job was to manipulate, when it came right down to it. The whole point of what they did was to manipulate a client into feeling better, to give him a little more insight into himself. But she wasn't at all comfortable with the idea of manipulating anyone for any reason, no matter how pure the motive and how praiseworthy the outcome.

Oh, I know things simply aren't that black-and-white, but—

Ah, things were just simpler with the Silvers. Issues often *were* a matter of extremes rather than degrees. When you had only a single moment to make up your mind what you were going to do, you had to be able to pare a situation down to the basics. Subtleties, as Judeth often said, were for times of leisure.

She noted down another item, and let her thoughts drift.

I can't wait until we're away from here. I wish we could go without having to talk to my parents.

Once they were away from White Gryphon, she would finally be able to relax for the first time in several years. And once again, it was her father who was indirectly responsible for her unease of spirit.

He knows too much, that's the problem. When she had been a child, she had taken it for granted that Amberdrake would know everyone of any importance at all in White Gryphon. She hadn't known any reason why he *shouldn't*. But as she gradually became aware just what her father's avocation really entailed, she gained a dim understanding that the knowledge Amberdrake possessed was extraordinarily intimate.

Finally, one day it all fell together. She put the man together with the definition of *kestra'chern* and had a moment of blinding and appalling revelation.

Not only did her father know everyone of any importance,

he also knew the tiniest details about them—every motive, every desire, every dream and indecision. Details like that, she felt deep in her heart, no person should ever know about another. Such secrets gave the one who held them too much power over the other, and that would weigh as an unimaginable responsibility.

Not that Father would ever use that power. . . .

Or would he? If he had a chance to manipulate someone for a cause he thought was right, wouldn't he be tempted to do just that? And wouldn't the fear of having such secrets revealed to others be enough to make almost anyone agree to something that Amberdrake wanted?

She had never once seen any indications that Amberdrake had given in to the temptation to use his tacit power—but he was her father, and she knew that she was prejudiced on his behalf. For that matter, she was not certain she would know what to look for if he had misused his powers.

Oh, it's not likely. Father would never do anything to harm anyone, if only because he is an Empath and would feel their emotional distress.

She ought to know; she was something of an Empath herself, although in her case, she got nothing unless she was touching the person in question.

That was one of the reasons why Amberdrake was so confounded by the idea that she wanted to be a Silver. How could an Empath ever choose to go into a profession where she might have to kill or injure someone?

Easily enough. It's to prevent the people I must take care of from killing or injuring others.

He would never accept that, just as he would never accept the idea that she would not want to use her Empathic ability.

She shuddered at the very idea. *He knows every nasty little secret, every hidden fear, every deep need, every longing and every desire of every client he has ever dealt with. How he manages to hold all those things inside without going mad—I cannot fathom it. And that he actually* wants *to know these things—! I could never do that, never. It makes my skin crawl. I don't want to know* anyone *that intimately. It would be like having every layer of my skin peeled off—or doing it to someone else over and over.*

She loved her father and mother, she knew they were wonderful, admirable people, and yet sometimes the things that they did made her a little sick inside. All a Silver ever had to do was stop a fight, or break some bones once in a while, and apply force when words didn't work. That was just flesh, and flesh would heal even if it was shredded and bleeding—it wasn't as serious as getting into someone's heart and digging around.

From that moment of understanding of who and what her father was, she had been terrified that people would simply assume that she was like him—that she *wanted* to be like him. Her greatest fear had been that they would take it for granted that she would cheerfully listen while they bared their souls to her—

Gods. No. Anything but that.

For a while, until the Healers taught her how to control her Empathic ability, she had even shied away from touching other people, lest she learn more than she wished to. Even after she had learned to block out what she did not want to know, she had been absolutely fanatic about her own privacy.

At least as much as I can be while I still live with my parents.

She kept her thoughts strictly to herself just as much as she could; never confided anything about the things she considered *hers* alone. Even affairs of love or desire.

Especially matters of love and desire.

By now she wondered if both her parents thought she was a changeling. Here were two people who knew everything there was to know about the physical, and yet their daughter appeared to be as sexless as a vowed virgin.

She had made up her mind that she was not even going to give her father and mother the faintest of hints that she *might* have an interest in partnering anyone or anything. Unfortunately, they would not have been taken aback by *any* liaison she cared to make. They were, in fact, all too assiduous at suggesting possible partners, and would have been cheerfully pleased to offer volumes of advice on approach and technique once she even hinted at a choice!

And it would be advice of a kind she blushed even to contemplate. There was such a thing as too much information.

Why can't they be like other parents? she thought, rebelliously. *Why couldn't they have been surprised that I was no longer an innocent little girl, horrified by the idea that I might one day bed someone, and attempt to guard my virtue as if it were the gold mines of King Shalaman? Any of those would be so much easier to deal with!*

She had found out personally that it was much harder to deal with sunny cooperation than with outright opposition.

It's a great deal like the hand-to-hand combat styles we Silvers learn, she thought in frustration, noting down yet another item for Tadrith. *When your opponent moves against you, there are any number of ways you can counter him. You can block him, parry him, evade him, or use his attack against him. When he attacks, he gives you options, to counter him. But when he does nothing—when he actually flows with your moves, it is impossible to do anything to extract yourself from the situation.*

Ironic, to think of her outwardly serene life with her parents as a combat situation.

The only real escape from this ridiculous situation was to move away from White Gryphon altogether. As she had advised Keenath, there *were* positions available for Silvers in the Haighlei Empire. The ambassadors from White Gryphon needed a token guard of honor in order to convey the proper presence at the court of the Emperor; that guard was comprised mostly of humans, but always had at least four gryphons and two each of the *kyree* and *dyheli.* The *tervardi* preferred not to live in such a warm climate, and the *hertasi* took sly enjoyment in their roles of servants, ferreting out intelligence that would otherwise never have come to the attention of the ambassadors. The Emperor also had two gryphon-guards assigned to him, serving alongside the younger sons of the other Haighlei Kings.

I could ask to be posted there . . . I think I would enjoy the solitude of the outposts, but there are more things to consider here.

Tad would never be able to tolerate assignment after assignment to the lonely wilderness. He would go absolutely, stark, staring lunatic after a while. He was a very social creature, and their partnership would not last very long if she was the only other being around to talk to.

Not to mention what would happen to him without female gryphons about. He only thinks he's nothing like his father. He has as wild a reputation among the fair flyers as his father ever had, if not more so. I had better check in on him to make sure he gets some sleep before we leave.

She chuckled to herself, and Tad looked back at her for a moment in curiosity.

And as far as that went, *she* was no chaste virgin, untouched and unawakened. *She* might well go quietly insane if she lived too long away from civilization.

For one thing, after too long out there, some very disturbing things might begin to look attractive. Tension can do that. When I find myself eying snakes and fondling branches, I'll know I've been away too long. Still, that's only one thing to miss, and easy enough to simulate—it is far more difficult to replace a lover's concern. For another complication—well—there is Ikala.

She sighed. Ikala was important to Blade, and she had kept her parents from finding out about him only through plotting and planning that would have done a spymaster proud.

Haighlei Kings with more than one son—and most of them, ceremonially wedded to a new priestess-bride each year, had many children—sent those sons off to be the personal guards of other Kings. This ensured that there would be no warfare and no assassination attempts, for every King had hostages from every other King. Furthermore, every King had the opportunity to win the loyalty of the sons of his fellow Kings, giving him an ally in the courts of his neighbors. It was a good system, and in the highly structured and rigid culture of the Haighlei, it worked well.

Ikala was one of those younger sons, twentieth in succession behind the actual Crown Prince of Nbubi. But instead of being sent to serve in one of the other Courts, he had elected to come to White Gryphon instead, to be trained by Aubri and Judeth and serve in the Silvers.

The culture of the Haighlei was a strange one by Kaled'a'in standards. Every action was tightly bound up in protocol; every moment cemented with custom. The Haighlei lived in the most rigid society that the Kaled'a'in had ever seen or heard of; change was only permitted when decreed by the Emperor and his chief priests and then only at the Eclipse Ceremony. . . .

How anything gets changed at all is a mystery. There was a hierarchy for everything, from the gods to the poorest beggar, and no one was ever allowed to leave his place in that hierarchy except at approved times, under rigid circumstances. And that was why Ikala, son of a King, was here in White Gryphon.

Ikala cannot bear the constraints of his people any more than I can. Ikala had found relief here, as she hoped to find it in the wilderness. Perhaps that was why she had felt so drawn to him from the first. They were both trying to escape from lives that others wished them to lead.

Ikala was not the only Haighlei here; many found an escape in White Gryphon from the intolerable rigidity of their own culture. Although there were not as many as Blade would have expected, they were generally young, for the old were content to wait for their next lives to improve their lot. They were also more often female than male, even though there was no real difference in the way that men and women were treated by Haighlei law and custom. This was just as well, since there were more Kaled'a'in men in White Gryphon than women—an accident that Snowstar and Cinnabar thought might be due to one of the more subtle effects of the mage-storms following the Cataclysm that destroyed Ka'venusho. Perhaps that was the reason why so many more young Haighlei women came here than men; the perfectly ordinary reason of husband hunting!

The Kaled'a'in had been nearer the source of the blast than the lands of the Black Kings, and nearest when the storms were at their worst. Many other subtle changes had taken place during their migration here, not all of them as obvious as a superfluity of male children.

There were changes that affected the mages, for instance. We had more than half of the mages associated with Urtho's army. You'd never know that now.

The mage-storms had made it very difficult to practice magic, for the strength of spells literally varied from storm to storm. But once the last of the storms had passed, it became evident that they had not only affected magic, they had affected the mages as well. Some, formerly powerful, had lost much of their ability. One or two who had only been at the level of hedge-wizard before the storms were able to aspire to the rank of Master. Some had undergone personality changes so subtle that the effects did not come to light for months or years, growing slowly odder and less social, until at last they would gather their belongings and vanish into the wilderness alone. One had caused a great deal of damage before he left, both physical and emotional.

That one was *not* Hadanelith, though Hadanelith had caused a fair share of emotional damage himself. It was generally granted, however, that Hadanelith had *not* been warped into what he was by the mage-storms. All evidence seemed to indicate he had always been quite mad, and quite dangerous.

Only the mages of k'Leshya were so affected, at least, as far as anyone knew.

Then again, perhaps Shalaman's Nameless Brother was turned into what he became by the storms as well. We'll probably never know for certain.

At any rate, since now the rate of birth for boys and girls was about equal again, the next generation would not have the trouble finding mates that this one had until Haighlei women started coming in by curious ones and twos.

Ikala had intrigued Blade, however, because he was very much different from the other Haighlei that had drifted into the city. He had kept to himself and simply observed for several weeks, after accepting hospitality at the hostel set up for visitors. He had not made any secret of his lineage, but he had not attempted to trade on it either. He had gone about the city quietly watching everything and everyone— while the Silvers were watching him, as they watched all newcomers. Then, one day, he presented himself to Judeth and asked to be taken into the Silvers as a trainee.

Had he been making up his mind if he wanted to stay? Had he already known he intended to remain and was only looking for a place where he could earn his way? Not even Blade knew—unless he had told Judeth, which was possible—and he had spent more time talking to her than to anyone else.

This was a fact that she had taken great pains to conceal from her loving family, as was her growing affection for him. She wasn't certain what she was going to do about that yet. As with many things, it would have to wait until she returned from this assignment.

But having a Silver well acquainted with another court than Shalaman's would mean that White Gryphon could open up a second embassy in Nbubi. Ikala could prove invaluable there, as an expert in the background, able to advise the ambassador as Silver Veil had advised Amberdrake in Shalaman's court. And that would be a fine place for Blade and Tadrith to be posted—and perhaps even Keeth.

Unless, of course, Amberdrake managed to get himself appointed as Ambassador there—or Winterhart did—

No. No, that couldn't possibly happen, she reassured herself hastily. *Father's needed too much here. Mother wouldn't go without him, not after the mess that almost happened the last time. And he knows that there's no one here that could replace him.*

Of course he could always train someone as his replacement. . . .

Oh, why am I making up these stupid scenarios when I don't even know where I'm going after this, or whether Ikala and I would ever be more than close friends, or even if Judeth would consider Tad and me for posts with the Embassy! She realized that she was making up trouble for herself out of nebulous plans that weren't even a possibility yet!

Things must be going too well if I'm planning for opposition that doesn't exist and problems that would take a thousand variables to come up!

Just about then, Tad spoke to her. "I can't think of anything else," he said. "What about you?"

"I haven't had any great inspirations for the supply list, but then I haven't been really thinking about it," she confessed, and frowned at the scrawled document in her hands. "I'll tell you what; let's go talk to Judeth or Aubri, and see if either of them have any suggestions."

Tad clicked his beak thoughtfully. "Is that wise?" he asked. "Will it look as if we aren't capable of thinking for ourselves?"

"It will look as if we are not too full of ourselves to accept advice from those older and wiser than us, and if we tell them that, they'll adore us for it," she responded, and got to her feet, stamping a little to ease a bit of numbness. "Come on, bird. Let's go show the old dogs that the puppies aren't totally idiots."

"Not totally," Tadrith muttered, although he did get to his feet as well. "Only mostly."

Amberdrake

Two

"**O**utpost Five, heh?" Aubri stretched both his forelegs, one at a time, regarding the blunted, ebony talons on the end of each claw with a jaundiced eye. Wind rattled the wooden wind chimes harmoniously in the open window behind him, and Tad watched golden dust motes dance in the beam of clear sunlight lancing down to puddle on the floor beside the old gryphon. "Let me see if I remember anything about Outpost Five."

Tad sighed as Aubri went through the whole of his dry, impish, "absentminded" routine, first scratching his rusty-brown headfeathers meditatively (which made more dust-motes dance into the light), then staring up at the ceiling of the dwelling he shared with Judeth. His head moved again after a long moment, and Tad hoped he was finally going to say something. But no—he looked down at the shining ter-razzo floor, inlaid in a geometric pattern of cream and brown that to all outward appearances fascinated him. That is, he seemed to be staring at those places; like any raptor, a gryphon's peripheral vision was as good as his straight-on sight, and Tad knew very well that Aubri was watching them—well—like a hawk.

"Outpost Five," the elder gryphon muttered, shaking his

head so that the fragments of feather-sheath dislodged by his earlier scratch flew in all directions. A single headfeather, striped in brown and cream and as large as a human's palm, drifted down to lie in the pool of sunlight beside him. Its edges were outlined in light, and the white fluff at the base glowed with a nimbus of reflected sunshine. "Outpost Five . . . now why does that sound familiar?"

This could go on for some time if Tad didn't put a stop to it. He fixed Aubri with a look that said wordlessly, *I know just what you're doing and I'm not falling for it.* In tones of deepest respect, he told his superior "You and Commander Judeth took Outpost Five three years ago, sir, when we first took responsibility for it from the Haighlei. You said the tour of duty was a vacation from trainees who couldn't molt without explicit written instructions."

Aubri blinked mildly, but his great golden eyes were twinkling with hidden amusement. "Did I say that? I'm cleverer than I thought. Well, yes, I think I remember Outpost Five, now that you mention it. Pretty remote; it's hard to find volunteers to man it. Good place for a vacation if what you want is thunderstorms every evening, fog every morning, and just enough of the sun to taunt you about its existence. There's a reason why the Haighlei call that kind of territory a 'rain forest.' It is wetter than a swimming kyree."

Well, good. That's one thing that wasn't in our lessons on manning outposts. And there's nothing in the briefing Blade read me that says anything about the weather there. "Would you say the weather is difficult enough to become a hindrance to our duties, sir?" he responded politely.

"Hindrance? I suppose if you're the kind that thinks he's going to melt if he has to fly in the rain." Aubri's mild manner turned just a trifle sharp, as if giving Tad subtle warning that he'd better *not* be thinking any such thing. His pupils dilated and constricted rapidly, another sign of warning. "No one promised sunny beaches and half-day duty when you volunteered for the Silvers."

"It *is* dangerous to fly during thunderstorms, sir," Blade put in politely, verbally maneuvering Tad from under Aubri's talons. "And it can be dangerous to take off during heavy fog. We won't be doing White Gryphon any favors if we get ourselves bunged up doing something stupid and they have to send in replacements and a rescue party. If the weather can become difficult enough to be dangerous, we ought to know about it in advance and know what warning signs to watch for. We can always ground ourselves and wait out a dangerous storm."

"Well, now, that's true enough." Aubri was back to being the bumbling, genial old "uncle." "But I don't think I said anything to give either of you the impression that the weather was going to make it impossible to fly your regular patrols. You'll just have to be careful, the way you were taught, and be diligent in watching for developing problems, that's all. The thunderstorms aren't violent, just briefly torrential, and the fog is always gone an hour after dawn."

Both of which would have made his bones ache, if he's having the same problems as my father. Aubri might be the oldest surviving gryphon from Urtho's forces; he was certainly older than Skandranon. He looked it, too; his feathers were not as sleek or as perfectly preened as Tad's were; in fact, they were a bit ragged, a trifle faded from what must have been his original colors of dark, warm brown and tan. Now he was rusty-brown and cream, and even feathers just grown in looked a bit shabby. Like Skandranon, he was of the broadwing variety, hawklike rather than falconiform, but he was huskier than Skandranon. His raptoral prototype was probably the umber-tailed hawkeagle, rather than the goshawk. There were signs of age in the delicate skin around his beak and eyes, a webwork of faint wrinkles, though those wrinkles were not as pronounced as the ones that humans got with increasing age. There was *no* sign of age in the mind, although you could not have told that from the way he was acting now.

"Acting," indeed. It's all an act, first to last, the old fraud. He never forgets anything; I'll bet he remembers the

order in which every trainee finished the last run on the obstacle course two weeks ago.

Aubri and Judeth were adept at playing the ally-antagonist game, with Aubri playing the absentminded and easily-fooled ally and Judeth the sharp-edged antagonist. Tad had caught onto the game in his first day of training, but then he had seen both Aubri and Judeth all the time when he was growing up. In particular, he had watched "absentminded" and "bumbling" Aubri best Skandranon time and time again over a game of stones, so it wasn't likely that he would ever be fooled into thinking that Aubri wasn't as sharp as his human partner.

Not that Father would ever admit to losing a game to Aubri except on purpose.

"Where is Commander Judeth, by the way?" he asked, for the white-haired human co-Commander of the Silver Gryphons had not been in evidence when the two of them arrived a few moments ago. Aubri jerked his beak toward the door, still standing open, as it had been when they arrived. On warm, pleasant days like this, most of the inhabitants of White Gryphon preferred to keep all doors and windows open to the sea breezes, and Aubri was no exception.

"Meeting with the Haighlei; they're picking out the next set of Silvers to be in Shalaman's personal guard when Sella and Vorn come back." He preened a talon thoughtfully, chewing on the very end of it, his beak making little clicking sounds as he did so. "They'll probably take Kally and Reesk," he added. "They can't resist matched sets."

"You think so?" Blade asked skeptically; like Tad, she was aware that there were several pairs available for the duty whose skills were greater than the partners named.

Aubri snorted his contempt for anyone who would choose the looks of a set of guards over their ability. Not that Kally and Reesk were *bad;* no one was offered for Shalaman's guards who was bad. For that matter, anyone who wasn't up to Aubri's standards was generally asked to find some other vocation long before they got out of training—and exceptions had better prove themselves within six months or they would have to return that coveted silver badge. But by the yardstick of those that Judeth and her partner picked to represent White Gryphon in the service of the Haighlei Emperor, these two were just average.

Nevertheless, they were showy, their plumage of ruddy gold and bronze would complement the gold and lionskins of Shalaman's Grand Court, and they could stand at perfect attention for hours without moving a feather. Tadrith pointed out all of those attributes.

"The Emperor's Chief Advisor has other things to consider, sir," he finished politely. "It is very important, protocol-wise, for the Emperor's guards to be as still as carvings all during Court. That stillness implies *his* power and control."

"It's not as if they're ever going to have to *do* anything, sir," Blade said injudiciously. "Even assuming an assassin or madman got as far as the Emperor's Guard, he'd take one look at a pair of gryphons in full battle rage and pass out."

Tad winced. *That* was not a bright thing to say—not to a veteran of the Great Wars and the Migration. There was a slight grating as Aubri's talons reflexively scratched the terrazzo.

"Maybe," Aubri replied with a narrow-eyed glare in her direction that thoroughly cowed her. *"Maybe.* Never assume anything, young Silver. Assumptions get you killed. Either you know, or you make your plans for the worst-case contingency. Always. Never count on the best happening. I thought we taught you better than that."

The ice behind his words would have done his partner Judeth proud, and his tone was so sharp that even an idiot would have known he had made a mistake.

Blade flushed at the rebuke, and snapped stiffly to attention. Aubri waited a moment, to make certain that his words had taken effect, then waved a talon at her, and she relaxed, but warily.

That's one mistake she won't make again.

"Now, what was I saying? Outpost Five. . . ." He yawned, all trace of the Commander gone from his demeanor again.

He could have been any lazy old gryphon, without a single interest beyond a place in the sun to rest, a bit of good gossip, and the quality (and timely delivery) of his next meal. "Standard outpost, all the comforts of home if you happen to be a hermit, good hunting, always pretty damp, the nights are a bit chilly. Oh, and the area is largely unexplored." He gryph-grinned at Tad's ill-suppressed look of eagerness. "Figured that out, did you? If I were to guess, and it's *only* a guess, I'd say your best bet might be gold. Quartz pebbles in the river and streambeds that match the kind I've seen in the past where gold can be panned and separated out. We didn't bother looking when Judeth and I were there; we're too old to go wading around in cold water sloshing pans about. Since you've got a two-legger with you, it wouldn't hurt to do a little panning, just to see if there's anything there."

"No, it wouldn't," Tad agreed, as Blade grimaced, but nodded. That *would* be the easiest way to find gold, if Aubri was right and the area was sitting atop a vein or even a lode. Chances were, if they did find gold, panning would be the only way any of it would be taken out of the place for a long time. The Haighlei would first have to perform a divination to see if the gods approved of mining there, then they would have to wait for approval from Shalaman himself, *then* the priesthood and the Emperor would make a joint declaration that mining would be permitted. Even then, there would be no rush to sink mines; Shalaman himself would choose *one* person from among the handful born into the trade of mining expert to determine (with the help of the priesthood) where and when the first shaft should be sunk. That person, with the aid of his hereditary miners, would dig the first shaft while a member of the priesthood watched to be certain it was all done as the gods deemed fit and appropriate. If he struck the vein, the whole process might be gone through again, to see if the gods would allow a second mine in the forest. If not, it would be taken as a sign that the gods did not approve despite the earlier indications, and the whole concern would be packed up and moved home. Protocol.

And meanwhile, those citizens of White Gryphon willing to endure primitive conditions for the sake of the possibility of a fortune, would be industriously panning gold out of the streams, with Shalaman's blessing and his tax collectors monitoring. Panning involved nothing that would change the forest, the stream, or the earth beneath both, and so did not require the approval of the gods.

"What else?" he asked, and got the *figure it out for yourself, brat* look from Aubri. "I meant, what supplies would you suggest we take," he amended hastily. Blade took the hint and passed their list over to Aubri, who spread it out on the floor in front of him. "Other than the usual kit, I mean, the one we learned in training. This is what we'd thought of adding so far."

He was rather proud of the fact that he'd already put *prospecting pans* down; after all, if they didn't find any gold, they could always bake pies in them.

Aubri perused the list slowly, rumbling a little to himself. Finally, he looked up.

"This is all very well thought out," he said, "but it doesn't go far enough. That's not your fault," he added hastily, as both Tad and Blade's faces fell. "We train you fledges about *regular* outpost duty, but Five is almost twice as far away as any of the others. That was why Judeth and I went out there. If *we* couldn't handle it, we certainly didn't want to send any of you."

Aubri and Judeth shared the leadership of the Silvers as co-Commanders under Skandranon. Tad's father had turned over the actual working position to Aubri not long after the affair of the Eclipse Ceremony, more than twelve years ago. Skandranon had decided by then that he didn't *want* to be a leader, not unless it was a leader in name only. He much preferred to be the Black Gryphon (or White Gryphon, depending on whether he was at Khimbata and Shalaman's court or at home) with his talons into everything. The day-to-day trivia of leadership bored him; *doing* things made him happy.

Aubri, on the other hand, found himself, much to his surprise, to be quite good at the day-to-day trivia. Furthermore, it amused him. He said once to Skandranon that after all that he had been through during the Wars, dealing with requisitions and stupid recruits was a positive pleasure. The real truth was that he had long ago mastered the art of delegation and knew just who to saddle with the part of the job that he didn't care for. And now, with the able tutelage of his partner and co-Commander Judeth, he very much enjoyed being a leader. For the last three years or so, both of them had been claiming that they were going to retire "soon," but not one creature in the Silvers believed them. Neither of them was ever likely to enjoy retirement half so much as active duty.

It was Tad's opinion that what would probably happen was that a third co-Commander would be appointed, one in charge of the more physical aspect of the daily activities of the Silvers, and the minor decisions that didn't require an expert of the quality of either Aubri or Judeth. Judeth would remain in place as the overall Commander in charge of major decisions, and Aubri in charge of training, with which Judeth would assist him.

Now that, I can see happening. Judeth doesn't much like climbing all over the city all day, but they're both so experienced that it would be stupid to turn over complete control of the Silvers to someone younger—at least, not until they are comfortable with his competence. And Aubri loves bamboozling the trainees. Yes, that would make altogether too much sense, which is probably why that's what they'll do. They're the two creatures in the whole world that I can trust to act sensibly.

Tad couldn't imagine the Silvers without Aubri and Judeth in charge. It would have to happen someday, but he couldn't imagine what that day would be like when it came.

"Now look, you two," Aubri was saying. "You are going to be a long, long way from the city; it might be hard to get things to you if something wears out or breaks. Just because something minor like your water pump goes out, that doesn't mean we're going to rip open a Gate to send one to you. Gates

are expensive, and *you* have perfectly sound limbs for carrying water in buckets."

Tad was taken aback, and so was Blade. *That* simply hadn't
occurred to him; living among mages had made him think of
Gates being put up quite casually. Gryphons flew, mages
made Gates, it was that simple.

But now he realized that although a Gate went up just
about every two or three days, they didn't stay up for very
long, and what was more, they didn't even go up to the same
place more often than once every month or two. There were
just a lot of outposts and other far-flung ventures to supply,
and that was what had made it seem as if Gating was com-
monplace and simple.

Aubri's eyes twinkled. "Your Gates will be opened at the
scheduled times, not one moment earlier unless it's a *real*
emergency of a life-threatening nature. They will remain
open for *only* the scheduled times, so if there's more stuff
you've asked for than can be chucked through in a hurry,
that's too bad. You may have to wait through *several* resupply opportunities for your water pump. So what does that
mean, Silvers?"

"Manuals," Blade said with resignation, adding them to
the list. "We'll need repair manuals. All the repair tools
we'd need will be there already, right?"

"And the manuals, too, don't worry; that outpost's been
open a long time, and remember that Judeth and I were there
first. *We* had the rank to order whatever we thought should
be in place out there. Try again."

Blade chewed a nail and frowned as she thought. Her
brows furrowed, and her eyes darkened until they were
nearly blue-black. "Um. You said it's really damp. Humid?"

He nodded. "There's fog there, isn't there? Every morning.
And rain every evening."

She brightened. "Bladders. Seals. Anything made of
leather or wood—or metal that might rust. Repair parts that
can get ruined by damp! That would be for—the water
pump, the stove, the plumbing—" She began to scribble.

"Good!" Aubri turned to Tad, who fortunately had an answer waiting, because he already knew Aubri's prejudices. He'd heard the litany often enough, when he was still living at home.

"The kind of equipment that might go missing or get spoiled by damp that doesn't rely on magic to work," he said promptly. "Things like firestrikers, tinder boxes, trace sextant and compass for surveying . . . ah. . . ." He pummeled his brain. Aubri nodded.

"Don't strain yourself; since you've just shown me that you know the principle, I'll give you a list. It's basically a few common replacement parts and some old army gear; won't add that much to your load, but there isn't much you can't do with it if you put your mind to the problem."

He didn't even move; he just stretched out a claw and stabbed a piece of paper already waiting on the top of the goldenwood desk that stood just within snatching distance. He must have been ready for them, once again proving that he wasn't nearly as absentminded as he seemed.

Blade took it from him, and Tad noticed that she seemed a bit bemused. Probably because she had a tendency to take everything and everyone at face value, and every time Aubri went into his "senile old featherhead" act, she fell for it.

Well, she can't help it. This was her big weakness, and Tad had a good idea why she wasn't likely to cure it any time soon. Part of the problem was that she just didn't *want* to look past the surface masks that everyone wore, no matter how honest and genuine they were. Tad's partner just didn't want to know what surprises might lie beneath those polite masks; that Empathy thing of hers bothered her, and if she could have had it surgically removed, Tad had it figured that she would have done so no matter what the risk. And there were reasons behind that as well; she had realized a long time ago that she would never, ever be as good as her father at delving into people's hearts and souls. She was the kind of person who, if she couldn't excel at something, didn't want to try.

Silly. Not every mage can be a Snowstar, but the hedge-

wizards can do plenty of things he hasn't got the time for, or even do subtle things he can't do at all. Well, it'd be flogging pointlessly to take that up with her, at least now. Maybe after we've been out there a while, and we've had a lot of peace and privacy. That particular twitch of hers bothered him, though, and he wanted to have it straightened out before too very long. Any amount of mind-magic was useful, the more so in someone who might well be supposed to boast nothing of the sort. *Father always says that if you've got an ability, it's stupid not to train and use it, even if it isn't something that you'd use very often.*

Blade compared the two lists, and added several items to theirs before she handed the one Aubri had given her back to him. Tad was pleased to note that she had *not* needed to copy the whole thing down. So they hadn't done so badly on their own.

I wonder if there was a bonesetting kit on Aubri's list, though. It certainly fits his criteria of "nonmagical" and "spoiled by damp." But, oh, the weight! If only someone could come up with better splints and casting material! It seems so stupid to be hauling wood and powdered rock!

Aubri crossed his forelegs in front of him, and regarded both of them with a benign, almost paternal expression on his face. "Well. Two more of my fledges go out to prove their wings. I think you'll like the post; neither of you are the kind to pine after a city when you can thrash around in the forest and see things no one else ever has before." He sighed. "Adventures are for the young, who haven't got bone aches. Now me—I'm happy to be here in White Gryphon where I can sunbathe every day. But there should be enough new discoveries there to make even two youngsters like you happy."

He did not mention that he knew *their* personal prime reason for being so happy with this assignment; getting away from their beloved families. He had never acted as if he recognized them as Skandranon's and Amberdrake's offspring—

Well, he wouldn't; not while we were in training. But he's never even mentioned our parents casually. Maybe he is a little absentminded in that direction; maybe he doesn't recognize us now that we're grown.

"We're looking forward to it, sir," he said honestly. "And it'll be nice to be away from home for the first time."

Aubri nodded, then grinned. "Oh, you aren't the only ones who've been interested in long assignments outside the city, believe it or not. I told Judeth that she should never assign anyone to Five who didn't have a good reason for being there as well as a good reason for getting away from home. I've never seen anyone who fit those qualifications better than you two. And to tell you the truth, I had a third reason to want you out there—you're a two-and-four team. That's a good combination for an outpost."

That was a gryphon paired with a human. That particular team was not all that usual among the Silvers; people tended to team up with members of their own species. Usually the two-and-fours were default teams, made up of those who couldn't find a compatible partner among their own kind. Quite often they broke up after training, when a senior Silver could take a junior out of training as a partner. Those who were in default two-and-fours generally did just that.

"I like a two-and-four for these remote postings," Aubri continued, then got that twinkle back in his eye. "The teams are more flexible, more versatile. Even if some people think there's something wrong with a gryphon who doesn't team up with one of his own."

Tad stared back at his superior with his head held high and challenge in his gaze. He'd heard that one before, and it didn't ruffle his feathers. "Oh? Does that include you, too, sir?"

Aubri laughed. "Of course it does! Everyone *knows* I'm a twisted personality! All of us war veterans are warped, it comes with combat! What's your excuse?"

Tad grinned back as the perfect answer came to him. "Family tradition, sir," he responded immediately, prompting Aubri into another bray of laughter.

"Well said! And I can't wait to tell the Black Boy what

you just told me; if that doesn't make his nares redden, nothing will." He shook his head, and the feathers rustled. "Now, you two run along. Give that list to the supply officer; he'll see to getting your basket packed up. All you need to worry about is your own kit."

They both stood and snapped to attention. Aubri chuckled, and rose slowly to his feet to let them out—old, maybe, but not dead yet.

As Tad had expected, his father already knew about the posting, and was outwardly (and loudly) enthusiastic. If he had beaten every contender and been appointed as Judeth's sub-Commander, Skandranon could not have been more thrilled. It was positively embarrassing. As they gathered for the evening meal in the main room of the family aerie, with the sky a dark velvet studded with jewellike stars beyond the window, Tad wondered if he shouldn't have opted for a quiet bite alone—or perhaps have gone hungry.

"Outpost duty! And you fresh out of training!" he kept saying, all through dinner. "I can't ever remember any Silver as young as you are being put on remote duty!"

His tone was forced, though, and he hadn't eaten more than half his meal. At the least, this sudden change in his son's status had put him off his feed. Was he worried?

Why should he be worried? What's there to be worried about?

Zhaneel, Skandranon's mate, cuffed him lightly. "Let the boys eat," she admonished him. "You won't be doing Tadrith any favor by giving him no time to have a proper meal."

But her look of rebuke followed by a glance at Keeth made Skandranon's nares flush red with embarrassment. He *had* been neglecting Keeth the whole time, although Keeth didn't seem too terribly unhappy about that. "I hear fine reports about you from Winterhart," he said hastily to his other son. "You're training in things your mother and I dreamed of doing, but were never able to achieve."

Tad winced. Now, if *that* didn't sound forced, he'd eat grass instead of good meat!

"Well, if there hadn't been that annoying war, Father, you two would probably have invented the gryphon *trondi'irn*, the gryphon *kestra'chern*, and the gryphon secretary," Keeth said, with a sly grin at his brother. "And probably the gryphon seamstress, mason, and carpenter as well!"

Trust Keeth to know how to turn it into a joke, bless him.

Skandranon laughed, and this time it sounded genuine and a bit more relaxed. "And maybe we would have!" he replied, rousing his feathers. "Too bad that war interfered with our budding genius, heh?"

Tad kept silent and tore neat bites from his dinner, the leg of a huge flightless bird the size of a cow and with the brains of a mud-turtle. One of these creatures fed the whole family; the Haighlei raised them for their feathers, herding them on land that cattle or sheep would damage with overgrazing. The gryphons found these creatures a tasty alternative to beef and venison.

Tad was perfectly pleased to let clever Keeth banter with their father. *He* couldn't think of anything to say, not when beneath the Black Gryphon's pride lurked a tangle of emotions that he couldn't even begin to unravel. But he was more and more certain that one of them was a fear that Skandranon would never admit to.

Of course not. He doesn't want to cripple me with indecision or even fear of my own before I go out there with Blade. He knows that if he shows he's unhappy with this, I might be tempted to back out of it. And he knows that there's nothing to worry about; we're hardly the first team to ever take this outpost. We're just the first team that included one of his sons, and he's been thinking about all the accidents that could happen to us ever since he heard of the posting.

He was worrying too much; Tad knew that, and he knew that his father knew it as well. This was not wartime, and they were not going to encounter hostile troops.

But this is the first time I'm "leaving the nest." I suppose it's perfectly normal for parents to worry. I worry, too, but I know that it can be done. I wonder why parents can say they trust their young so much, yet still fear for them? He supposed that a parent's imagination could conjure up a myriad of other dangers, from illness to accident, and play them out in the space of a heartbeat. Parents had to be that way; they had to anticipate all the trouble youngsters could get into and be prepared to pluck them out of danger before they got too deeply into it.

But I'm an adult, and I can take care of myself! Isn't he ever going to figure that out? He has been an adult for ages longer than I have, and he has had to be rescued before—so why is it that adults regard trouble as the sole territory of the young? Do we remind them of their vulnerability that much?

Between bites, he cast a glance at his mother, surprising her in an openly concerned and maternal gaze at him. She started to look away, then evidently thought better of it, and nodded slightly.

Mother's worried, but she admits it. Father won't, which will make it worse on him. And there's no reason for either of them to worry at all! Maybe the more intelligent a parent is, the more they worry, because then they are able to see more of what could go wrong. The Kaled'a'in Quarters know that they could concentrate just as much on what could go right, but when it comes to children—or young adults—it could be smartest to have only grudging optimism. Still. . . .

He spared a thought for Blade, who was probably undergoing the same scrutiny at the hands of her parents, and sighed. He didn't know how Amberdrake and Winterhart would be reacting to this, but Blade had threatened to spend the night with friends rather than go home to face them. Tad had managed to persuade her to change her mind.

It could be much worse, he told himself. *They could be so overprotective that they refuse to let me take the post. Or, worse than that, they could be indifferent.*

A couple of his classmates had parents like that; Tad had heard mages speculating that the raptor instinct ran so strongly in them that it eclipsed what Urtho had intended. Those parents were loving enough as long as their young were "in the nest." They began to lose interest in them when they fledged, just exactly as raptor parents did. Eventually, when the young gryphons reached late adolescence and independence, their parents did their best to *drive* them away, if they had not already left. Such pairs were more prolific than those who were more nurturing, raising as many as six or eight young in a reproductive lifetime.

But those offspring were, as Aubri would say, "glorified gamehawks;" they lived mostly for the hunt and, while extremely athletic, were not very long in the intelligence department. Most of the gryphonic fatalities at White Gryphon had occurred among this group, which for the most part *were* assigned to hunting to supplement the meat supply of the city. They were very much like goshawks in focus and temper; they would fly into the ground or a cliff during a chase and break their foolish necks, or go out in wretched weather and become a victim of exposure. Some simply vanished without anyone ever knowing what happened to them.

Aubri had said once in Tad's hearing that a majority of the fatalities in gryphon-troops of the war—other than those attributable to human commanders who saw all nonhumans as expendable and deployed them that way—were also among this type of gryphon. Needless to say, the type had been in the minority among those that had reached safe haven here, and were not likely to persist into a third generation. Not at the rate that they were eliminating themselves, at least!

When they weren't hunting, they could usually be found lounging about on the sunning platform with others of their kind, either attempting to impress like-minded females or comparing wing-muscles. Granted, there was always a bit of that going on among young gryphons, but this lot acted like that *all the time!*

Very attractive, to look at perhaps. But as trysting mates or play-fighters, I don't think I could stand them.

So while Skandranon was probably thinking over how many young gryphons of Tadrith's generation had been lost, it was not occurring to him what those unfortunate fatalities had in common.

Say—an absolute dearth of brains. A squandering of what they had. And most importantly, a lack of decent parenting. Keeping a young one's body alive was one thing, but it only created more breeders to do the same with the next generation they bred. Even a charming young idiot can succeed with good parenting. I'm proof of that, aren't I?

His father had lost some of his self-consciousness and was now speaking normally to Keeth and Zhaneel about some modification Winterhart had made to the standard obstacle course in order to train *trondi'irn.* Tad took full advantage of their absorption to get some more of his meal down in peace.

Skandranon was an odd sight just now; halfway into a molt, he was piebald black and white. The white feathers were his natural color—now—and the black were dyed. He dyed himself whenever he was due to visit Khimbata in his capacity as special representative of White Gryphon. Ever since the Eclipse Ceremony, when he had come diving dramatically down out of the vanishing sun to strike down an assassin who would have murdered Emperor Shalaman, Winterhart, and probably several more people as well, he'd been virtually forced to wear his Black Gryphon "guise" whenever he visited. He had rescued Shalaman, the Black King, as the Black Gryphon—and in a culture that set a high value on things that never changed, he was mentally set in that persona whenever he returned to the site of his triumph.

The Gryphon King, beloved where e'er he goes. That was what Aubri had said to his face, mockingly.

But the real irony of the statement was that it was true. He never left Khimbata without being loaded down with gifts of all sorts. His jewelry collection was astonishing; if he and Zhaneel wore all of it at one time, they'd never get off the ground.

Between us, if we're lucky, Keeth and I might manage to be a quarter as famous as he is—and then most of it will be due to the fact that we're his sons.

That could have been a depressing thought, if Tad had any real ambition. But to be frank, he didn't. He'd seen the negative effects of all that adulation—how it was always necessary for Skandranon to be charming, witty, and unfailingly polite no matter what he personally felt like. How when the family visited Khimbata, Skandranon had barely a moment to himself and none to spare for them. And how even at home, there was always *someone* who wanted something from him. He was always getting gifts, and a great many of those gifts came with requests attached. Even when they didn't, there was always the chance that a demand, phrased as a request, would come later, perhaps when he wasn't expecting it and was off his guard.

There was no way for Skandranon to know whether someone wanted his friendship because of *what* he was or because of *who* he was—and the difference was critical.

No, thank you. I am very fond of obscurity, all things considered.

It would be no bad thing to be an obscure Silver, always assigned to the Outposts, hopefully collecting enough extra from his discoveries to finance a comfortable style of living. Let Keeth collect all the notoriety of being the first gryphon *trondi'irn;* Tad would be happy to donate whatever measure of "fame" fate had in store for him to his brother! Just as he had finished that thought, he noticed that the others were looking at him. Evidently Keeth had run out of things to say, and it was his turn again.

Oh, bother.

Skandranon cleared his throat. As always, the sound, an affectation acquired from living so much with humans, sounded very odd coming from a gryphon.

It sounds as if he's trying to cough up a hairball, actually.

"Well!" Skandranon said heartily. "Your mother and I are very interested in hearing about this outpost you're being sent to. What do you know about it?"

Tad sighed with resignation, and submitted himself to the unrelenting pressure of parental love.

Blade couldn't bring herself to sit, although she managed to keep from pacing along the edge of the cliff. The stone here was a bit precarious for pacing—how ignoble if she should slip and fall, breaking something, and force Judeth and Aubri to send someone else to the outpost after all! *Tad would never, ever forgive me. Or else—he'd take a new partner and go, and I would be left behind to endure parental commiserations.*

Ikala sat on a rock and watched the sunset rather than her. He'd asked her to meet him here for a private farewell; her emotions were so mixed now that she honestly didn't know what to say to him. So far, he hadn't said anything to her, and she waited for him to begin.

He cleared his throat, still without looking at her. "So, you leave tomorrow. For several months, I'm told?" Of course, he knew her assignment, everyone in the Silvers did; he was just using the question as a way to start the conversation.

The sun ventured near to the ocean; soon it would plunge down below the line of the horizon. Her throat and tongue felt as if they belonged to someone else. "Yes," she finally replied. Now she knew why people spoke of being "tongue-tied." It had been incredibly difficult just to get that single word out.

She wanted to say more; to ask if he would miss her, if he was angry that she was leaving just as their friendship looked to become something more. She wanted to know if he was hurt that she hadn't consulted him, or chosen him as her partner instead of Tad. Above all, she wanted to know what he was thinking.

Instead, she couldn't say anything.

"Come and sit," he said, gesturing at the rocks beside him. "You do not look comfortable."

I'm not, she said silently. *I'm as twitchy as a nervous cat.*

But she sat down anyway, warily, gingerly. The sun-warmed rock felt smooth beneath her hand, worn to satin-softness by hundreds of years of wind and water. She concentrated on the rock, mentally holding to its solidity and letting it anchor her heart.

"I am both happy for you and sad, Blade," Ikala said, as if he was carefully weighing and choosing each word. "I am happy for you, because you are finally being granted—what you have earned. It is a good thing. But I am sad because you will be gone for months."

He sighed, although he did not stir. Blade held herself tensely, waiting for him to continue, but he said nothing more. She finally turned toward him. "I wanted an assignment like this one very much," she agreed. "I'm not certain I can explain why, though—"

But unexpectedly, as he half-turned to meet her eyes, he smiled. "Let me try," he suggested, and there was even a suggestion of self-deprecating humor. "You feel smothered by your honored parents and, perversely, wish for their approval of a life so different from theirs. Additionally, you fear that their influence will either purchase you an easier assignment than you warrant, or will insure that you are never placed in any sort of danger. You wish to see what you can do with only the powers of your own mind and your own skills, and if you are not far away from them, you are certain you will never learn the answer to that question."

"Yes!" she exclaimed, startled by his insight. "But how did you—" Then she read the message behind that rueful smile, the shrug of the dark-skinned shoulders. "You came here for the same reason, didn't you?"

He nodded once, and his deep brown eyes showed that same self-deprecating humor that had first attracted her. "The same. And that is why, although I wish that you were not going so far or for so long—or that we were going to the same place—I wanted you to know that I am content to wait upon your return. We will see what you have learned, and what that learning has made of you."

"And you think I will be different?" She licked her lips with a dry tongue.

"At least in part," he offered. "You may return a much different person than the one you are now; not that I believe that I will no longer care much for that different person! But that person and I may prove to be no more than the best of friends and comrades-in-arms. And that will not be a bad thing, though it is not the outcome I would prefer."

She let out her breath and relaxed. He was being so reasonable about this that she could hardly believe her ears! "I don't know," she admitted. "I think I've spent so much time proving who I'm not that I don't know who I am."

"So go and find out," he told her, and laughed, now reaching out to touch her hand briefly. The touch sent a shivery chill up her arm. "You see, I had to come here to do the same thing. So I have some understanding of the process."

"Are you glad that you came here?" she asked, wondering if the question was too personal, and wishing he would do more than just touch her hand.

Now it was his turn to look away, into the sunset, for a moment. "On the whole—yes," he told her. "Although in doing so, it became impossible to follow the alternate path I might have taken. There was a maiden, back in my father's court—but she was impatient, and did not like it that I chose to go somewhere other than to the court of another emperor. She saw my choice as a lessening of my status, and my leaving as a desertion of her. I have heard that she wedded elsewhere, one of my more traditional half-brothers."

"Oh—I'm sorry—" she said quickly, awkwardly.

But he turned back to her, and did not seem particularly unhappy as he ran his hand across his stiff black curls. "There is not a great deal to be sorry about," he pointed out. "If she saw it as desertion, she did not know me; if I could not predict that she would, I did not know her. So. . . ." He shrugged. "Since it was not long before my sorrow was gone, I suspect my own feelings were not as deep as she would have liked, nor as I had assumed."

"It's not as if you were lacking in people willing to console you here!" she pointed out recklessly, with a feeling of breathlessness that she couldn't explain. She laughed to cover it.

"And that is also true." His smile broadened. "And it was not long before I felt no real need of such consolation, as I had another interest to concentrate on."

Her feeling of breathlessness intensified; this was the nearest he had come to flirting with her, and yet behind the playfulness, there was more than a hint of seriousness. Did she *want* that? She didn't know. And now—she was very glad that she was going to have three months to think about it.

"Well, I think, on the whole, it will be a good thing for you to have six months to learn what it is that Blade is made of," he said, in a lighter tone. "And I shall have the benefit of knowing that there will be no other young men at this outpost that may convince you to turn your attentions elsewhere. So any decisions you make—concerning our friendship—will be decisions made by you, only."

She snorted. "As if any young man could 'make me change my mind' about anything important!" she replied, just a little sharply.

"Which only proves that I cannot claim to know you any better than any other friend!" he countered. "You see? This much I do understand; you have a strong sense of duty, and that will always be the first in your heart. I would like to think that I am the same. So, whatever, we must reconcile ourselves to that before we make any other commitments."

It was her turn to shrug. "That seems reasonable . . . but it isn't exactly . . . romantic." That last came out much more plaintively than she had expected, or intended.

"Well, if it is a romantic parting that you wish—" He grinned. "I can be both practical and romantic, as, I suspect, can you." He took one of her hands, but only one, and looked directly into her eyes. "Silverblade, I crossed an empire, I left my land and all I have ever known. I did not expect to find someone like you here, and yet—I do not follow some of my people's reasoning that all is foredestined, but it sometimes seems as if I was drawn here because you were here. Now I know something of what I am. I believe that there is in you a spirit that would make a match for my own. If, in the end, a few months more will bring us together, such a wait will be no hardship." He patted her hand. "I trust that is romance enough for your practical soul?"

She laughed giddily. "I think so," she said, feeling as lightheaded as if she had just drunk an entire bottle of wine. "I— I'm not nearly that eloquent—"

"Neither is the falcon," he said, releasing her hand. "But she is admirable for her grace without need of eloquence. Go become a passage bird, Silverblade. When you return, we shall try out hunting in a cast of two."

Blade hadn't needed to do all that much packing last night, but she had pretended that she did—and as soon as she was done, she blew out her candle and willed herself to sleep. The need for rest was real, and if she had not torn herself away from her overly-concerned parents, she would not have gotten any. They would have kept her up all night with questions, most of which she didn't have any answers to, since all of them were fairly philosophical rather than practical.

She dressed quickly and quietly, and without relighting her candle. With any luck, only her mother would be awake; Winterhart, for some reason, seemed to be handling this better than her spouse. *Don't people usually complain that their mothers never see them as grown up?* she thought, as she pulled on a pair of light boots, then fastened the silver gryphon badge to the breast of her tunic. The Silvers had no regular uniform; Judeth thought it better that they wear the same clothing as those around them. Uniforms might remind people too much of the regular troops, and war, and even the most battle-hardened wanted to put warfare far behind them.

Now—if I can just walk quietly enough, I might be able to get out of here without another discussion of my life-view.

Her father Amberdrake was notorious for sleeping late—to be fair, it was usually because he'd been up late the night before, working—and she hoped by rising with the first light, she might avoid him at breakfast.

But no. When she carried her two small packs out to leave beside the door, she saw that there were candles burning in the rest of the house. Amberdrake was already up.

In fact, as soon as she turned toward the rear of the dwelling, she saw him; dressed, alert, and in the little nook at the back of the main room that they used for meals, waiting for her. But so was her mother, which might temper things a bit.

She sighed, while her face was still in shadow and he couldn't see her expression. Breakfast with Amberdrake was always a bit strained at the best of times, and this was not going to be "the best" of times.

He keeps remembering when he was the chief kestra'-chern and it was his habit to find out about his fellows when they all drifted in for breakfast. He keeps trying to do the same thing with me.

"Good morning, Father," she said, feeling terribly awkward, as she approached the tiny table. "You're not usually up so early."

She wondered if Amberdrake's smile was strained; he was too good at keeping a serene mask for her to tell. However, it was obvious that he had taken special pains with his appearance. *Silk tunic and trews, raw-silk coat, some of his Haighlei gift-jewelry, and Zhaneel's feather in his hair. You'd think he was having an audience with Shalaman.*

She regarded him objectively for a moment. He was still a strikingly handsome man. Despite the white streaks in his hair, her father scarcely looked his age in the low mage-light above the table, and the warm browns and ambers of his clothing disguised in part the fact that there were dark circles under his eyes.

Caused by worrying, no doubt.

"I didn't want to miss saying good-bye to you, Silverblade," he said, his voice quite calm and controlled. "If I slept until a decent hour, I knew that I would. You dawn risers are enough to make a normal person's eyes cross."

She knew that her answering laugh was a bit strained, but there was no help for it. "And you night prowlers are enough to make people like me scream when we think of all the perfectly good daylight you waste sleeping!" She slid into the seat opposite him, and helped herself to fresh bread and preserves. *He* reached across the table and added thinly-sliced cold meat to the plate quite firmly. She didn't really want anything that substantial first thing in the morning, but she knew better than to say so. Why start an argument? That would be a poor way to leave her parents.

What can it hurt to nibble a piece to please him? It can't, of course. Not that long ago, she would have protested; now she knew there was no point in doing so. She'd only hurt his feelings. He was only trying to help.

And after today he won't be able to be so meddlingly helpful for six whole months! I should be pitying the people, gryphon and human and hertasi alike, who will wind up as my surrogates for his concern.

She ate one slice of the meat, which was dry and tasted like a mouthful of salty old leather, and went back to her bread. Amberdrake pushed a cup of hot tea toward her, then made a move as if he was about to serve her a bowl of hot porridge from the pot waiting beside him.

"*Oh* no!" she exclaimed. Not for *anything* would she eat porridge, not even for the sake of pleasing her father! "None of that! Not when I'm flying! I do not want to decorate the landscape underneath me!"

Amberdrake flushed faintly and pulled his hand back. "Sorry. I forgot that you didn't inherit my impervious stomach."

"No, she inherited my questionable one. Stop badgering the child, dear." Winterhart emerged at last from the rear of the dwelling, putting the last touches on her hair. Blade admired the way she moved with a twinge of envy. Winterhart managed to combine a subtle sensuality with absolute confidence and a no-nonsense competence that Blade despaired of emulating.

Now if I looked like that. . . . Ah, well. Too bad I inherited Mother's interior instead of her exterior!

Unlike her mate, Winterhart had not dressed for a special occasion, which much relieved Blade. Her costume of a long linen split skirt, tunic, and knee-length, many-pocketed vest, was similar to anything she would wear on any other day. The only concession she had made to Amberdrake's sartorial splendor was to harmonize with his browns and ambers with her own browns and creams.

"I hope we won't be unwelcome, but we would like to see you and Tadrith leaving, Blade," Winterhart said, quite casually, as if they were only leaving for a few days, not six months. "We *do* know how to stay out from underfoot, after all. Yours is not the first expedition we've seen on its way."

Now it was her turn to flush. "Well, of course I want you there to see us off! Of course you won't be in the way!" she replied, acutely embarrassed. "I would never think that!"

The only trouble was, deep down inside, she had been thinking precisely that.

She gulped down her cooling tea to cover her embarrassment and guilty conscience, as Amberdrake toyed with a piece of bread, reducing it to a pile of crumbs.

He's trying to pretend that he isn't worried; trying to put on a brave face when I know he's feeling anything but brave. Why? Why is he so worried? If he's transparent enough for me to see through, he must be all of a knot inside.

Finally Amberdrake looked up at her, slowly chewing on his lower lip. "I know I probably seem as if I am overreacting to this situation, ke'chara," he said quietly. "I shouldn't be so worked up over the simple fact that you and your partner are going off on a normal, peaceful assignment. I realize that I am being quite foolish about this, and I can't even pretend that I have some mysterious presentiment of doom. It's all due to old—well, I suppose you'd have to call them habits, habits of feeling, perhaps."

Winterhart stood behind him and put her hands on his shoulders, gently massaging muscles that must have been terribly tense. Outside, seabirds cried, greeting the dawn and the winds that would carry them out to their fishing grounds.

Amberdrake reached up and covered one of his mate's hands with his own. "I have two problems with this assignment, really, and neither of them is rational. The first is that it is you, my daughter, who is going off for six months to a place that is unsettlingly far away. And you'll be all alone there, except for a single gryphon. If it were someone else, I would see him or her off with a cheerful heart, and go about my business."

"But it isn't," she stated.

"No." He sighed, and patted Winterhart's hand. "Your mother is handling this better than I."

"*I* have perfect confidence in Aubri and Judeth," Winterhart said serenely. "They wouldn't send anyone that far away who wasn't prepared for any contingency." Her tone turned just a little sharp as she looked down at him. "If you won't trust Blade, dearheart, at least trust *them*."

"Intellectually, I *do*," Amberdrake protested. "It's just— it's just that it's hard to convince the emotions."

He turned back to Blade, who was even more embarrassed at her parent's decision to bare his soul to her. She struggled not to show it. And underneath the embarrassment was exasperation.

Can't he learn that I am grown now, and don't need him to come haul me out of difficulties? Can't he just let me go?

"The other problem I have is very old, older than you, by far," he told her earnestly. "And it has absolutely nothing to do with your abilities; it's something I would still feel even if you were a warrior out of legend with magical weapons at your side. It doesn't matter to my heart that this is peace time, that you are simply going off to man a wilderness outpost. The point to my reaction is that you are going *out*. When—" momentary pain ghosted over his expressive features. "—when people used to go out, back in the days of the wars, they didn't always come back." She opened her mouth to protest; he forestalled her.

"I *know* this is peacetime, I *know* you are not going forth to combat an enemy, I *know* that there is no enemy but storms and accident. But I still have the emotional reaction to seeing people going out on a quasi-military mission, and that fact that it is my daughter that is doing so only makes the reaction worse." He smiled thinly. "You cannot reason with an old emotional problem, I am afraid."

She looked down at the polished wood of the tabletop, and made little patterns with her forefinger, tracing the grain of the wood. What on earth did he expect her to say? What *could* she say? *That was years and years ago, before I was even born. Can't he have gotten over it by now? He's supposed to be the great magician of the emotions, so why can't he keep his own trained to heel? What could possibly go wrong with this assignment? We'll have a teleson with us, we'll be reporting in, and if there is a life-threatening emergency and they can't get help to us quickly, they'll take the risk and Gate us back!*

But that wasn't what he wanted to hear, and it wouldn't help anything to say it. "I can understand. At least, I think I can. I'll try," she finished lamely.

True, it is nothing but wilderness between here and there—but when we get "there," we'll be in a fortified outpost built to withstand storm, siege, or earthquake. And, granted, no one has even tried to explore all the rain forest in between, but we'll be flying, not walking! What could possibly knock us out of the sky that our people or the Haighlei wouldn't have encountered a long, long time ago?

It was—barely—possible that some mage-made creatures of Ma'ar's survived from the Cataclysm. It was less likely that any of them could have made it this far south. And even if they did, there had never been *that* many of them that could threaten a gryphon. *The last makaar died ages ago, and there never was anything else that could take a flying gryphon down. We'll be flying too high for any projectile to hurt us, and even if we weren't, there'll be the mass of the carry-basket and all our supplies between us and a marksman.*

"Father, I promise you, we'll be fine," she only said, choking down a last dry mouthful of bread. "Makaar are extinct, and nothing less could even ruffle Tadrith's feathers. *You've* seen him; he's one of the biggest, strongest gryphons in the Silvers!"

But Amberdrake shook his head. "Blade, it's not that I don't trust or believe in you, but there is far more in this world than you or Tadrith have ever seen. There were more mages involved in the Mage Wars than just Urtho and Ma'ar; plenty of them created some very dangerous creatures, too, and not all of them were as short-lived as makaar. I will admit that we are a long distance from the war zones, but *we* got this far, so who's to say that other things couldn't?"

He's not going to listen to me, she realized. *He's determined to be afraid for me, no matter what I say.* There was more likelihood of moving the population of the city up to the rim of the canyon than there was of getting Amberdrake to change his mind when it was made up.

"What's more, as you very well know, the mage-storms that followed the Cataclysm altered many, many otherwise harmless creatures, and conjured up more." His jaw firmed stubbornly. "You ask Snowstar if you don't believe me; some of the territory we passed through was unbelievable, and that was only after a year or so of mage-storms battering at it! We were very, very lucky that most of the things we encountered were minimally intelligent."

"Sports and change-children die out in less than a generation," she retorted, letting her impatience get the better of her. "That's simple fact, Father. There're just too many things wrong with most magic-made creatures for them to live very long, if they've been created by accident."

He raised an elegant eyebrow at her, and the expression on his face told her she'd been caught in a mistake.

"Urtho was not infallible," he said quietly. "He had many accidents in the course of creating some of his new creatures. *One* of those accidents was responsible for the creation of intelligence in *kyree*, and another for intelligence in *hertasi*. And neither race has 'died out within a generation.' "

She had already spotted the flaw in his argument. "An accident may have been responsible for the intelligence of the creature, but not the creature itself," she countered. "Creature creation takes great thought, planning, and skill. An accident is simply not going to be able to duplicate that!"

He looked as if he were going to say something, but subsided instead.

"Besides," Blade continued, taking her advantage while she still had it, "people have been going to this outpost for years, and no one has seen anything—either there or on the way. Don't you think by now if there was going to be any trouble, someone would have encountered it?"

Amberdrake dropped his eyes in defeat and shook his head. "There you have me," he admitted. "Except for one thing. We don't know what lies beyond that outpost and its immediate area. The Haighlei have never been there, and neither have we. For all we know, there's an army of refugees from the wars about to swarm over you, or a renegade wizard about to take a force of his own across the land—"

"And *that*," Blade said with finality, "is precisely why we will be there in the first place. It is our duty to be vigilant."

He couldn't refute that, and he didn't try.

Blade extracted herself from her parents with the promise that she and Tad would not take off until they arrived. With one pack slung over her back and the other suspended from her shoulder, she hurried up the six levels of staircase that led in turn to the narrow path which would take her to the top of the cliff. She was so used to running up and down the ladder-like staircases and the switchback path that she wasn't even breathing heavily when she reached the top. She had spent almost all of her life here, after all, and verticality was a fact of life at White Gryphon.

Below, on the westward-facing cliff the city was built from, she had been in cool shadow; she ascended as the invisible sun rose, and both she and the sun broke free of the clinging vestiges of night at the same time. Golden fingers of light met and caressed her as she took the last few steps on the path. It would be a perfect morning; there were no clouds marring the horizon to presage storms to the east. Red skies were lovely—but red skies required clouds. *If I am going to be traveling, I prefer a morning like this one; not a cloud in the sky and the air dry, cool, and quiet.*

At the top of the cliff a great expanse of meadow and farmland composed of gently rolling hills stretched out before her. It was completely indefensible, of course; like Ka'venusho, Urtho's stronghold, there was no decent "high ground" to defend. This was why the city itself had been built into the cliff, with the only access being a single, narrow path. You couldn't even rain boulders down on White Gryphon from above, for the path had been cut into the cliff so cleverly that it channeled objects falling down from the edge away from the city entirely.

Judeth's idea, but it took some very clever stonecrafters to put her idea into solid form.

At the edge were large constructions of wooden frames and pulleys that could lower huge amounts of material down to the first level of the city; that was how food was brought down from the farms up here. Those could be dismantled or destroyed in mere moments by a very few people. Nothing that was up here would be left to be used by an enemy if there ever was an attack.

The farmers used to live in White Gryphon and travel up each day to tend their flocks and fields; now they didn't bother with the trip. There was a second village up here on the rim, a village of farmhouses and barns, a few warehouses and workshops, and the pens where herds were brought during the few days of each year that the weather was too bad to keep the herds in the fields. If severe winter storms came from the sea instead of the landward side, the herds could be driven into the shelter of the forest, and those who were not sent to watch over them could take shelter within the rock walls of White Gryphon.

The stockade and supply warehouse of the Silvers was up here as well. Space was too precious in the city for any to be wasted on bulk stores except in an emergency. And as for the stockade, most punishment involved physical labor in the fields with the proceeds going to pay back those who had been wronged. Since most crime in the city involved theft or minor damage, that was usually acceptable to the victims. There *had* been those—a few—who were more dangerous. Those were either imprisoned up here, under bindings, or— dealt with, out of the sight of the city. After Hadanelith, no one was ever exiled again. The possibility that another dangerous criminal might survive exile was too great to risk.

Just outside the stockade was a landing platform. Sitting squarely in the middle of it was what appeared to be a large basket, about the size of a six-person expedition-tent. There was a complicated webbing of ropes attached to it, and standing nearby was Tadrith, with a *hertasi* helping him into a heavy leather harness. As usual, he was carrying on a running dialogue with his helper, trying to get his harness adjusted perfectly. She knew better than to interrupt; her life would depend on that harness and whether or not he was comfortable in it.

This was the carry-basket that would take her and all their supplies to the Outpost. It looked far, far too heavy for Tadrith to fly with, and it was. Even the strongest of gryphons would not have been able to lift *her* alone in it unaided.

But magic was working reliably enough these days, and there would be a mage somewhere around who had made certain that the basket and anything that might be in it would "weigh" nothing, with a reserve for changes in momentum and speed. He would essentially have made the basket into a variant of one of the Kaled'a'in floating-barges. Tadrith would not be "lifting" the basket, only guiding it.

The spell was a complicated one that Blade couldn't even begin to understand. Anything *inside* the basket—like herself—would still have its apparent weight. If that wasn't the case, everything not tied down would be in danger of drifting off on a stiff breeze. But to Tad, although the basket had no up-and-down weight, it would still have a certain amount of side-to-side mass and momentum. He would not be lifting it, but he *would* have to exert some strength in pulling it, just as teams of *dyheli* and horses pulled the floating barges.

Blade hurried up to check the supplies lashed down inside the basket. As Aubri had promised, the supply sergeant had taken care of everything she and Tad would need except for their own personal gear. Most of the supplies they had requisitioned—the ones for after they reached the outpost—had already been sent on via Gate. So only what they would need for the trip, what there had not been time to send by the Gate, and what she had brought with her would actually travel with them.

That's certainly going to relieve Tad.

It had also relieved Tad when she told him that she was nothing like her father when it came to wardrobe. *She* could manage very simply, actually; but Aubri had once described Amberdrake's floating-barge and if gryphons could have blanched, Tad would have, at the thought of having to help move all that mass of clothing, gear, and furniture.

She tossed her two bags into the basket, and waited quietly beside the platform for the last of the adjustments to be made. The *hertasi* in charge was Gesten's daughter Chana; as thorough and meticulous as her father, she would not leave Tadrith's side until they were *both* satisfied with the fit of every strap. Blade knew that every buckle would be checked and rechecked, every rivet and every ring subjected to the most exacting scrutiny. Chana would leave nothing to chance, and there was no possible compromise with safety in her view.

Finally, she stepped back. "It'll do," she said, in her hissing *hertasi* voice. "Try to bring the rig back in one piece."

Blade suppressed a laugh, for the remark was so like Gesten that it could have been *he* who was standing there. Like her father, Chana would never admit to concern for the trainees she served, only to concern that the equipment return intact. But of course, it went without saying that if the equipment came back to the warehouse in pristine condition, the trainee would certainly have arrived at the landing platform in like shape.

Tad waved her over, as Chana began hooking up his harness to the basket itself. "We're waiting for the parents, I presume?" he said casually.

She sighed. "Much as I would like to simply slip away, if we leave without allowing them their fanfare, they may not let us come back."

"Or we may not want to," he groaned, and flexed his claws restlessly. "Because when we did, they'd make our lives sheer misery with guilt."

She laughed, and patted him on the shoulder. "Parents always know how to pull your strings," she advised him. "After all, they attached those strings in the first place."

"Do I hear someone borrowing my words?" The newcomer to the conversation was as elegant as Amberdrake in dress and demeanor, though far less flamboyant. Blade knew him too well to blush.

"Of course, Uncle Snowstar," she retorted. "You weren't using them, so why shouldn't I?"

He chuckled at her impertinence; next to Skandranon, she was the only person likely to take that tone with him. It was not wise to risk the anger of an Adept-level mage as powerful as Snowstar, as others, even his own underlings, had found out to their sorrow.

"I don't think you'll have any trouble with the basket-spells, Tadrith," he said, turning to the young gryphon. "They are as tight as any I've ever set."

Blade had assumed her "adoptive uncle" had come to see

them off, along with her parents; she was astonished to hear
him say that he himself had placed the magics on their
carry-basket that would make it possible to fly with it. "*You*
set them, uncle?" she said, making no secret of her surprise.
"Isn't that—well—?"

"Rather beneath me?" He laughed. "First of all, it is always a good idea for a mage to keep in practice on anything
he might be asked to do, and secondly, if something were to
fail, magically, on *your* basket—" He shrugged suggestively.
"Suffice it to say, it was easier and safer to do the work myself, than have to explain to your parents why I let some 'inferior mage' do it."

Blade nodded ruefully. "Only too true," she told him. She
would have said more, but at that moment she caught the
sound of familiar voices from below the edge of the cliff.

At nearly the same moment, Tad pointed warningly with
his beak at a trio of rapidly approaching gryphons, who
could only be his parents and sibling.

"All we need now are Judeth and Aubri to make this show
complete," Blade groaned, resigning herself to a long and
complicated farewell that would shave precious time off the
amount of daylight they *could* have used for traveling.

"Is that a complaint or a request?"

Commander Judeth stalked out of the door to the Silvers'
clifftop headquarters, but she was smiling rather than
frowning. She was not Kaled'a'in; her hair, before it turned
to snowy white, had been a dark blonde, and her eyes a clear
gray-green. Nevertheless she had been one of Urtho's gener-
als who understood the value of her nonhuman troops and
deployed them with care and consideration, and no one had
been unhappy to find her among the k'Leshya when the last
Gate came down. She had proved her worth over and over,
both during their retreat from lands racked by mage-storms
and at White Gryphon. With her partner Aubri, she had or-
ganized the first beginnings of the Silvers, and the Silvers in
their turn bore the stamp of her personality. She alone of all
of them wore anything like a uniform; a black tunic and

trews modeled from the tattered originals of her old dress uniforms. The gryphon-badge stood out proudly against such an elegant background.

She stopped just short of the platform and looked sardonically from Tad to Blade and back again. "Can I take it from that remark that you think I might be a hindrance to a timely departure?" she continued.

Blade flushed, and the old woman allowed a hint of a smile to steal across her lips.

"I assure you, Aubri and I came here solely to make certain that your loving relatives did *not* do any such thing," she said crisply, and cleared her throat.

"*All* right, troops!" she called out in a voice that had once commanded thousands, just as Amberdrake and Winterhart appeared at the end of the trail. "Let's get up here and get your good-byes said and over with! This isn't a holiday trip, this is a military departure! *Move your rumps!*"

"Thank the gods," Blade breathed, as her parents and Tad's scrambled to obey. "We just might actually get out of here before noon!"

"In a quarter-mark," Judeth replied sternly. "Or every one of you will be on obstacle-course runs before midmorning."

Blade chuckled; not because Judeth wouldn't make good on that promise—but because she *would.*

What had promised to be a difficult departure was already looking better, even with emotionally-charged families approaching. After this, things could only start looking up.

Zhaneel and Winterhart

Three

Skandranon continued to peer off into the blue, cloudless sky for a long time after Tadrith and Silverblade were out of even his extraordinary range of vision. Even after fooling himself several times that some speck or other was them, he gazed on, feeling his eyes gradually go out of focus as his thoughts wandered.

He was torn now between pride and anxiety. Their takeoff had been a very good one by anyone's standards; stylish, crisp, and professional. There had been no exhibitions of fancy flying, but not a single mistake in maneuvering either. With so many people watching, *he* would have been tempted to indulge in some theatrics, when he was Tad's age.

And the odds were fairly good that I could have pulled them off, too. But on the other hand, I did have my share of foul ups. With the rising sun in his eyes, though, it didn't make any sense to keep staring off after them. He suppressed a sigh, and told his knotting stomach to behave itself; a gryphon's bowels were irritable enough without encouraging cramps through worry.

Well, they're gone. My nestling really has fledged, gone past the brancher stage, and now—well, now he's on his way to have his own adventures. Real adventures, not just

*high scores on the obstacle course. He'll be making a name
for himself now, just like I did.*

He dropped his eyes to meet Zhaneel's, and saw the same
pride and worry in her gaze that he felt. She wouldn't show it
in front of the boy and, in fact, had kept up a brave and cheerful front, but he knew this sudden departure had her upset.

He tried to look completely confident for her, but it was a
struggle that he wasn't certain he had won. *Adventures.
Huh.* Now that *he* wasn't the one having the "adventures,"
he wasn't so sure whether or not looking for adventures was
such a good idea. Was Tad ready? With the war, there had
been no choice but to go and face the dangers—whether one
was ready or not—but this wasn't war, and it seemed to him
that they could all afford to be more careful of their young.

His wings twitched a little as the temptation to follow
them rose before him. *I could use some exercise. Lady
Cinnabar is always telling me to get more flying time in.
And if I happened to parallel their course—*

"You promised *not* to fly as the children's wingman all
the way to the outpost," Zhaneel whispered, quietly enough
that no one else could have overheard her. "Remember. You
did promise."

Drat. He had. And *she* could read him like a child's primer.
He twitched his wings again, ostentatiously settling them.
"I'm glad I'm not making that trip," he said, not precisely as a
reply, but to reassure her and to show her that he had heard
her and he remembered his promise. Granted, she had caught
him in a moment of extreme weakness and vulnerability last
night when she extracted that promise, but that did not
negate the fact that he had made the promise in the first
place. If the Black Gryphon's word to his mate wasn't good,
how could anyone trust him?

Aubri sniffed derisively. "You *couldn't* make that trip, old
bird," he retorted. "They're a lot younger than you, and in
better shape on top of that."

Skan bristled and started to retort, but paused for a moment to rethink his position. Aubri was not going to get him

going this time. "Oh, in theory I could," he replied, as mild as a well-bred matron. "*You* did, and I'm in better shape than you—what's more, Tad's towing that carry-basket, and that will slow him down to a pace even *you* could hold. But what would the point be? What would I have to prove? That I'm stupid enough to make a pointless journey to show I'm still the equal of a youngster? It would be a complete waste of time, and I don't have enough time to waste."

Aubri looked surprised and chagrined that he hadn't managed to egg Skan on to rash words or a rasher boast.

Zhaneel cast him a look of gratitude which promised another interesting evening, and more than made up for the faint blow to his pride administered by Aubri's taunts.

Judeth had listened to the conversation with a wry half-smile, and now put her own opinion. "So, now the next generation goes off hunting adventures," she said, combing her fingers through her hair, "while we stay home and see to it that when they come back, they won't find anything much changed. Personally, I don't envy them in the least."

"Nor I," Skan said firmly. "Adventures always seemed to involve impact with the ground at a high rate of speed, and ended in a lot of pain. Maybe my memory is faulty sometimes, but I haven't forgotten *that* part."

Amberdrake finally came out of his own reverie and sighed. "Your memory isn't faulty, old bird. I remember picking quite a few pieces of broken foliage and *not a few* rocks out of your hide, and more than once." He patted Skan's shoulder. "I don't know why you couldn't have picked a gentler way of collecting souvenirs."

Skan winced, and Aubri grinned at his discomfiture. From the look in his eyes, Aubri was about to make another stab at puncturing Skan's pride.

But Aubri had reckoned without Winterhart, who had been listening just as intently to the conversation as Judeth had.

"And I recall that rather than collecting souvenirs of enemy territory, Aubri specialized in attracting enemy fire," she said, with a little smirk and a wink at Judeth that was so fast

Aubri didn't catch it. "In fact, he did it so often that his wing used to refer to getting hit by flamestrike as 'being Aubri'ed.' As in, 'Well, I've been Aubri'ed out until my primaries grow back.' Or, 'Well, *you* certainly got Aubri'ed back there!'"

Aubri met this piece of intelligence with his beak open in a gape. "They did *not!*" he gasped indignantly.

Of course they didn't. Skan, who had known every piece of gossip there was to know back then, would have heard of this long before Winterhart ever had. In fact, Winterhart would probably not have heard any such thing, since before she was Amberdrake's lover, she had tended to treat the gryphons of her wing as little more than intelligent animals. Such an attitude was not likely to make anyone tell her *anything.*

But Aubri's reaction was so delightful that everyone fell in with the joke. For once, someone besides Skan was going to come in for a share of abuse.

Is it my birthday? Or has the Kaled'a'in Lady decided to bless me, however momentarily?

Judeth rubbed the side of her nose with her finger. "I'm afraid they did," she confirmed impishly, and then elaborated on it. "When I deployed your wing, they always liked to fly formation with you on the end since it just about guaranteed that no one else would get hit with lightning or mage-fire. Once or twice I heard them talking about 'Old Charcoal,' and I think they meant you."

Aubri's beak worked, but nothing came out; the muscles of his throat were moving, too, but he didn't even utter as much as a squeak.

"It could have been worse," Winterhart continued, delivering the final blow. "I did succeed in discouraging the nickname of 'Fried Chicken.'"

Aubri's eyes widened; his head came up and his beak continued to move, but all he could manage to say was, "Well!" over and over. Since he sounded exactly like a highly-offended old matron, he only managed to cause the entire gathering to break up into laughter. And if the laughter was somewhat nervous, well, there were four nervous parents there who drastically needed the release of laughter.

They laughed long enough to bring tears to the eyes of the humans and make Aubri's nares flush bright red. Before Aubri managed to have an apoplectic fit, though, Winterhart confessed that she had made it all up. "Not that you didn't deserve the nickname, after all the times you came back singed," she added. "But no one ever suggested pinning it on you."

Aubri growled, his hackles still up. "They wouldn't have dared," was all he said, and Judeth led him off to ease his ruffled feelings and ruffled feathers.

"I don't think he liked being on the receiving end of the teasing," Amberdrake remarked mildly.

"Then perhaps he will stop treating Skandranon to so much of it after this," Zhaneel responded, her voice quite tart. "A little is amusing, but he makes a habit of sharpening his tongue on Skandranon, and I am weary of hearing it! Skandranon does not deserve it; and if Aubri continues in this way, there may be trouble with younger gryphons believing in his so-called teasing. They will think that anything Skan says he has done is only wind and empty boast!"

Skan turned to her in surprise; she didn't often spring to his defense this way. "Aubri doesn't mean anything by it," he said on his old friend's behalf. "He's getting old and cranky, and he just likes to tease. And I don't think I'm going to lose any respect from the youngsters just because he tries to raise my ire now and again."

Zhaneel sniffed and twitched her tail with annoyance. "That might be, and I will not be rude by chiding him in public, but *I* have had enough of it, and he can expect to get as good as he has given from now on."

"I agree," Winterhart put in firmly, crossing her arms over her chest. "Skan deserves a great deal of respect, after all. Maybe not as much as you'd *like*, you vain creature, but more than Aubri gives you."

Skan cast a look at Amberdrake, who only shrugged. "Don't

get me involved in this," he said. "I don't think Aubri means anything of what he says, and I don't think anyone else takes him seriously either—but I think I'm outnumbered here."

Winterhart made a little face, and put her arm over Zhaneel's gray-feathered shoulders. "Come along, my dear," she said to the female gryphon. "I think we should discuss this at length, just the two of us, since the men don't seem to take this situation with the gravity we think it merits."

"I concur," Zhaneel said agreeably, and the two of them sauntered off toward the cliff rim and several pleasant lookouts that had been constructed there.

Skandranon turned a face full of astonishment on Amberdrake—who was gazing after the two females with equal puzzlement.

"What prompted all that?" he asked, trying very hard to get his thoughts back on track. Amberdrake shook his head.

"I haven't any more idea than you do," he confessed. "Maybe with their chicks gone from the nest, they both feel they have to defend *something*. I might be considered something of an authority on human emotions, but I have to admit to you that sometimes my lady Winterhart baffles me." He nodded with his chin toward the head of the trail. "Care to walk down with me so we can both worry about the youngsters together?"

Skan let out a deep breath; so Drake *was* just as troubled about Tad and Blade as he was! "Yes, I would," he admitted mournfully. "Zhaneel made me promise not to go with them, not to follow them, and not to talk about them with her unless she brings the subject up. I wish I had her confidence that everything is going to be all right, but I keep thinking of all the things that can go wrong."

Amberdrake followed his mate's example by draping an arm over Skan's shoulders. It felt very good there; the support of an old and trusted friend, even if the friend was just as much in need of support himself. Tradition spoke of an elegant half-arch being only a fallen pile of stones without its counterpart to make it whole.

"So much can go wrong, even in the most peaceful of times. I fear the worst, too," Amberdrake told him. "But as Blade very rightfully reminded me, their job is not to confront danger directly. They're only scouts, of a sort. If something dangerous appears, they are *supposed* to send a warning by way of the teleson, then keep themselves intact so that they can get home and brief us in detail."

Skandranon took care not to step on Amberdrake's feet, and snorted in reply to his statement. "And just how likely do you think that is to happen?" he demanded. "They're *our* children! Do you think there's even half a chance that they wouldn't see themselves as the front line of the White Gryphon defenses and go confront something dangerous if it appeared?"

He maneuvered Amberdrake into the inside position, between himself and the cliff, as they started back down toward the city. Drake needed to walk on the protected inside, since if one of them was to slip on the trail, it had better be Skan; he could fly and Drake obviously couldn't.

"I honestly don't know," Amberdrake admitted. "My daughter baffles me more often than my mate does. I sometimes wonder if the midwife switched babies with someone else when she was born. She doesn't seem anything like either of us, and believe me, I have *tried* to find common ground with her."

"I know what you mean," Skan replied with chagrin. "Although Keenath affects me more that way than Tadrith does. Still. Just because we've never seen either of them act the way *we* did at their age, it doesn't follow that they wouldn't. If you understand what I'm trying to say."

"I think so." Amberdrake picked his way over a rough spot in the trail before continuing. "Children tend to act differently around their parents than when they're on their own. At least, that's what I've observed, both professionally and nonprofessionally."

Of course he wouldn't remember himself being that way; he lost his own parents and all his family when he was hardly fledged. But he's right; I went out of my way to be the opposite of mine. They never wanted to be anything but followers, and I wanted to be the one others looked to for leadership. Sometimes I wonder if they weren't smarter than I was. "I wish we had some other way besides the teleson to keep track of them," he fretted. "It's very tempting to wish that Urtho was here to give us another Kechara. . . ."

He couldn't finish the sentence; the pang of loss he felt even when mentioning the name of the creator of his adoptive "daughter" was enough to still his voice for a moment.

"It's more than tempting to wish she was the way she used to be," Amberdrake sighed, "and not just because she'd be useful now. I'd gladly continue all the evasion and diplomatic garbage we had to concoct for the Haighlei if it meant she was still such a powerful Mindspeaker. She is such a cheerful little soul, though; I don't miss her powers at all if it means we get to see her alive and happy."

Kechara had been one of Urtho's rare "mistakes," although Skan had never discovered what his leader, mentor, and friend had intended when he created her. Had she simply been a first attempt at the "gryfalcon" type, of which Zhaneel was the outstanding example? Was it possible that she had been a deliberate attempt to create a gryphon with tremendous ability at mind-magic? Or had she simply been a "sport," something Urtho had not intended at all, an accident that Urtho saw and carried through, then hid away for her own protection?

Whichever the case had been, little Kechara had been what the other gryphons referred to as a "misborn." Severely stunted, slightly misshapen, with wings far too long for her dwarfed body, her mind had been frozen in an eternally childlike state. But her pure strength at mind-magic had been without equal. Adorable little Kechara had been able to reach her mind-voice as far away as the Haighlei capital of Khimbata, which was how she had discovered where Amberdrake and Skandranon had been made prisoners long ago. The madman Hadanelith and his two Haighlei allies had captured them in the last stage before the attempted assassination of Emperor Shalaman during the Eclipse Ceremony.

Without Kechara, Skandranon would never have been able to get away in time to save him, and Amberdrake most certainly would not even be alive at this moment. Impelled by danger to him that even she had been able to perceive, her mental "shout" had sundered magical shields and incapacitated Hadanelith's two allies across all that distance.

Urtho had known just how powerful her abilities were, and had kept her close-confined in his Tower for safekeeping. He had known that she might be viewed as a prize to be captured or a weapon to be used, and had thought to protect her from that fate. But in confining her, he had assumed that she would not live very long, an assumption that had proved incorrect.

Skan shook his head. "I agree. And I also know that I would never want to take the chance that another one with worse problems than hers might be born—we just don't have the skill and judgment that Urtho did. We all love her, but Kechara's flaws were too high a price to pay for her gifts, objectively speaking. Quite frankly, I think that it is only because she still doesn't understand most of what she saw in other people's minds that she hasn't been driven mad by it all."

He had done his best to make certain she never lost her trusting nature—and so had Judeth, Aubri, and anyone else in White Gryphon who ever came into contact with her. In her turn, she served the city and its people faithfully and joyously. She carefully relayed messages she barely, if ever, understood to and from all of the Silvers with even a touch of mind-magic of their own. It was a task they had all tried to ensure was never a chore for her, and she had loved the attention and approval.

Skan reflected that it was odd, the way the Haighlei had acted concerning her. For them, a creature with the mind of a child and the ability to read *anyone's* thoughts would have been a blasphemy. For a year or two after the Eclipse Ceremony, Skan was fairly certain the Kaled'a'in had been able to keep Kechara's existence secret from their allies—but eventually they *surely* had discovered just what she was. There had been many, many circumspect little hints, diplomatic tail-chases and discreet suggestions. Finally an official communique from High King Shalaman had come, advising the "permanent elimination of the long-range communicator of White Gryphon"—referring to Kechara—making it clear by its phrasing that it was not an idle request, and that not doing so would have grave consequences. Skandranon, Zhaneel, and Amberdrake went to Khimbata to appeal to Shalaman in private, and returned to White Gryphon with a delegation of mages led by Advisor Leyuet. Between various nervous ceremonies of state, "Papa Skan" explained to Kechara that it was time for her to rest from her work, and that they were going to make sure nobody was ever scared of her. Kechara trusted Skandranon completely, of course, and gleefully greeted the delegation. The grim-faced Haighlei, who were steeling themselves to meet a monster and fight against its horrible soul-invading power, instead faced a little creature who only thought they were very funny and demanded their absurdly elaborate and colorful hats to play with.

Well, that's the Haighlei for you. I suspect one could probably get away with just about anything, so long as it was wrapped in the proper historical protocol. Come to think of it, the reason Shalaman was so incensed about those murders in his Court was because the assassinations hadn't been done with the proper protocol! Perhaps if we could have found a way for Kechara to be put into Shalaman's service under their religion, she could have kept her powers—but that wouldn't really have been true to her, either, and it would only have made her into the tool, the bargaining chip that Urtho feared she'd be used as. It would have destroyed her loving innocence if she were used against one of us and realized it. At least this way she could stay at home and play. At least she can still talk to all the gryphons, as long as they're within the city limits.

"Well, what are we going to do, old friend?" the aging gryphon asked, as they picked their way steadily down to the topmost level of the city. This level was the receiving platform for everything lowered down from the cliffs above, or sent up from the city to the cliffs. Work crews were already unloading pallets of food from the farms, and would continue to do so all day. "What do we do about the children, I mean?"

"What *can* we do?" Amberdrake asked, with only the faintest hint of irritation. He led the way to the broad white-painted stairs that formed the back slope of the White Gryphon's "head." "Nothing. This is their job; the job they chose. They've been assigned to it by their superiors, who have judged them capable. Like it or not, they have grown up, and I'm afraid we had better start getting used to that."

Skan ground his beak and prowled after him, talons clicking on the stone ramp alongside the stairs, which was easier for a gryphon to handle than steps. "I don't like it," he said finally. "But I can't tell you why."

Amberdrake stopped suddenly, turned, and faced him, looking down at his friend with a troubled expression as the gryphon stopped a step later and looked up. "I don't either, and I haven't any real reason to feel this way. I wish I could say that I have a premonition about this—because this feeling that there is something *wrong* makes me look like a nervous old aunty—"

"But?" Skan prompted. "You're worried you don't have the correct dress to play aunty?"

Amberdrake chuckled, then sighed. "*But* I am afraid I haven't had anything of the sort, and there hasn't been a solid sign from anyone who does have Foresight that something is going to go wrong with Blade and Tad. I know what I would say to any of my clients who felt this way."

Skan looked into his friend's eyes, and shook his head. "Let me guess. What we are feeling is a combination of old war reactions, and unhappiness because this fledging of our youngsters is a sure sign that we are getting old."

"Too true. And who wants to know that he is getting old? Not I, I can promise you." Amberdrake's expression was as honest as it was rueful. "I've been keeping my body limber and capable for decades now, through all kinds of strain, as loose as a downfeather and as tight as whipcord as needed, but—it's all been to last as long as possible during the pace of time. One never bothers to think about growing old as one is *growing* older. Then suddenly it is *there*, looming in your face. Your bones and joints ache, youngsters are expressing concern that you are over-exerting yourself, and when you try to insist that your experience means you know more than they do, you find them exchanging knowing looks when they think you don't notice."

"Alas. It is life's cruelty, I say. One moment we are fretting because we are not considered old enough to do anything interesting, then we turn around and younglings barely fledged are flying off to do the interesting things we can't do anymore!" Skan shook his head, and looked out over the ocean. "And we are supposed to accept this gracefully! It is hardly fair. I protest! I believe that I shall become a curmudgeon. Then at least I can complain, and it will be expected of me."

"Too late for that."

Skandranon snorted, "Then I shall be an exceptional curmudgeon. I've earned the title. The Curmudgeon King."

"Endured Where E'er He Goes. May I join you, then? We can drive the youngsters to distraction together." Amberdrake seemed to have thrown off some of his anxiety and, to his surprise, Skan realized that he had relaxed a bit as well.

"Certainly," the Black Gryphon replied with dignity. "Let's go down to the obstacle course, and make loud comments about how we used to run it better and in half the time."

"And with more style," Amberdrake suggested. "Finesse and grace, not brutal power."

"Naturally," Skan agreed. "It couldn't have happened any other way—as far as they know."

"So, just how worried are *you!*" Winterhart asked Zhaneel as soon as they were out of the range of Skandranon's hearing. As a *trondi'irn* she had a very good notion of just how sensitive any given gryphon's senses were, but she knew Skan's abilities in excruciating detail. For all that he was suffering the onset of the ailments of age, he was a magnificent specimen with outstanding physical abilities, not just for his age, but for *any* gryphon male.

"About Skan, or about the children?" Zhaneel asked, with a sidelong glance at her companion.

"Hmm. Both, of course," she replied, returning Zhaneel's glance. *She's just as observant as I thought.* "Skan, first. He's the one we have to live with."

"As we must live with Amberdrake, heyla?" Zhaneel nodded shrewdly. "Well. Come and sit beside me here, where the wind will carry away the words we do not wish overheard, and we will discuss our mates." She nodded her beak at a fine wooden bench made of wave- and wind-sculpted driftwood, and sat down beside it on the cool stone rimming the cliff.

Winterhart sank gracefully down into a welcoming curve of the bench, and laid one arm along the back of it. "Drake is very unhappy about all this. I think he expected Judeth and Aubri to assign Blade to something like bodyguard duty, or city-patrol. I don't think it ever occurred to him that they might send her out of the city, much less so far away."

It didn't occur to me, either, but it should have. I've known that Blade wanted to get away from the city—and us—for the past year. Maybe if Drake hadn't been so adamant about her living with us until she was a full Silver. . . .

Keeth and Tad had been able to move out in part because Skan had lent them his resources to excavate a new home to trade for an existing one. Sensing Blade's restlessness, Winterhart had tried to persuade Drake to do the same for Blade, but he wouldn't hear of it.

"Why should she need to move out?" he'd asked at the time. *"It's not as if she has any need for a place of her own. We give her all the privacy she would have anywhere else, and it's not as if she could feel embarrassed to bring a lover here!"* Then he had sighed dramatically. *"Not that there's any interest in that quarter. The way she's been acting, a vow of celibacy would be an improvement in her love life. Where could we have gone wrong? It's almost like she doesn't want to listen to her body."*

Winterhart could have told him—that children were always embarrassed by the proximity of their parents when trying out the first tentative steps in the dance of amorous life, and inhibited by their parents when learning for the first time what kind of adults they would become—but she knew he wouldn't believe her. He would have, if Blade had been anyone else's child, but not when he was her father. *A parent can sometimes be too close to his child to think about her objectively.* When it came to seeing someone else's children, a parent could see a larger canvas, but with their own—all they would see were the close daily details, and not grasp the broad strokes. Amberdrake, brilliant as he was, couldn't grasp things like Blade not wanting to be around parents as she learned her body's passions. And if Blade had actually come out and *asked* him for a place of her own, he would probably have given in and made it possible. But she was too shy and too proud, and now, in retrospect, Winterhart could see that requesting assignment to outpost duty had probably seemed the only way she could get that longed-for privacy.

"Skandranon is fretting, but not to pieces, I think," Zhaneel said, after a long pause during which she gazed out seaward. She might have been watching the fishing fleet; her eyes were certainly sharp enough to make out details in things that were only moving dots to Winterhart. "I hope that as he realizes the children *are* capable, he will fret less. Part of it is inaction. Part of it is that he wishes to do everything, and even when he was young, he could not do half of what he would like to do now."

That observation surprised a faint chuckle out of Winterhart. "It is odd how our youthful abilities grow larger as we age, isn't it?" she replied. "I am absolutely sure that I *remember* being able to work for two days and nights without a rest, and that I could ride like a Kaled'a'in and shoot like a highly-paid mercenary, as well as perform all my duties as a *trondi'irn*. I couldn't, of course, but I remember doing so."

"Even so," Zhaneel agreed. "It will not be so bad with Skandranon as with Amberdrake; our children are male, and one is still left to us. Your little falcon was the only chick in the nest, and female. Men wish to protect their females; it is bred in the blood."

"And as much as Amberdrake would deny it, he is more worried because Blade is female, you are right." Winterhart stared out to sea, wondering how she could ever convince her spouse that their 'delicate little girl' was as fragile as tempered steel. "Perhaps if I keep comparing her to Judeth?" she wondered aloud. "I don't think Blade is doing it consciously, but I can see that she has been copying Judeth's manner and mannerisms."

"He admires and respects Judeth, and what is more, he *has* seen her in action; he knows that Judeth took special care in training your Blade, and perhaps he will take comfort from that," Zhaneel observed, then tossed her head in a gryphonic shrug. "I can think of nothing else you could do. Now, what am I to do with Skan? Concentrate on Keenath, perhaps?"

"Could we get him involved in Keeth's physical training?" Winterhart asked her. "I'm a bit out of my depth there—and you and Skan *did* invent obstacle-course training. I've started all the *trondi'irn* on working-under-fire training, but the Silvers' gryphon-course is set up for combat, not field-treatment. It isn't really appropriate, and I'm not sure how to adapt it."

"Ye-esss. I believe that might do. It will give him action, and something to think about. Or at least more action besides climbing my back to give him exercise." Zhaneel cocked her head to one side. "Now, what of Winterhart? And what of Zhaneel? What do we do to take our minds from our absent children?"

Winterhart shook her head. "You have me at a loss. I honestly don't know. And I'll probably wake up with nightmares every few days for the next six months. I suppose we should concentrate on our mates' worries instead?"

"That will certainly give *us* something to do, and give them the job of dealing with how we comfort them."

Zhaneel nodded, then turned, and reached out to touch Winterhart's shoulder with a gentle talon. She smiled, and her eyes grew softer as she met Winterhart's gaze. "And perhaps we can give each other the comfort of a sympathetic ear, now and again, sister-in-spirit."

One small problem with finally being on duty. Rising at unholy hours. Tadrith sighed, but inaudibly; his partner sometimes seemed to have ears as sharp as a gryphon's. As usual on this journey, Blade was up at the first hint of light. Tad heard her stirring around outside the tent they shared; building up the fire, puttering with breakfast, fetching water. She was delightfully fastidious about her person, bathing at night before she went to bed, and washing again in the morning. It would have been distinctly unpleasant to share a tent with anyone whose hygiene was faulty, especially now that they were away from the coast and into the wet forest. It was very humid here, and occasionally oppressively hot. Blade was not just being carried like living baggage; the basket shifted in every change of wind, and she had to shift her weight with it to keep it from throwing him off. This was work, hard work, and she was usually damp with sweat; by the time he landed for a rest, she was usually ready for one, too.

He, of course, was not burdened by the need to wash in order to get clean, and most humans expressed pleasure in a gryphon's naturally spicy musky scent. He couldn't fly with wet wings, and there usually wasn't time to bathe before night fell when they stopped. He had decided to forgo anything but dust-baths until they arrived at their outpost. So he felt perfectly justified in lying in warm and sheltered comfort while she went through her bathing ritual and tended to the camp chores.

There wasn't anything he could do to help her anyway. He couldn't fetch water; raptoral beaks were not well suited to carrying bucket handles. He shouldn't have anything to do with the campfire; gryphons were feathered and feathers were flammable.

He had done the larger share of work last night, when it

came to chores. He had brought up enough wood to feed the fire until this morning, and provided part of his kill to feed them both at breakfast. He would take the tent down, just as he had put it up; the fast way of erecting it required magic, and although he was no match for his father in that area, he *was* a minor mage in simple object-moving spells. So he had done his share of the camp chores; this was not lazing about, it was the just reward of hard work.

He closed his eyes, and listened to water splashing and Blade swearing at how cold it was, and smiled. All was well.

Because they were already working so hard, he was bending a personal rule and using magic to hunt with. He used it to find a suitable animal, and to hold that animal in place once he found it. They couldn't afford energy wasted in prolonged hunting, not now; he had to have the tent up, the wood in camp, and his kill made before dark. Back at White Gryphon, he could afford to be a "sportsman"; there were plenty of herd beasts and fish to feed the gryphons, and wild game was rightfully considered a delicacy. Once he arrived at Outpost Five, there would be time enough on each scouting patrol to hunt "properly". But he would consume more food than they could carry on this trip, and that meant hunting with absolute efficiency, using every trick at his disposal.

Finally, the sounds of fat sizzling into the fire made him open his eyes and bestir himself again. That was breakfast, and although he personally preferred his meat raw, there were other things to eat besides meat. Though primarily carnivores, gryphons did enjoy other delicacies, and Blade had found some marvelous shelf-fungi last night when he had been bringing in wood. A quick test had proven them to be nonpoisonous, and a quick taste showed that they were delicious. They had saved half for breakfast, still attached to its log just in case detaching it might make it decay.

Fresh venison and fresh mushrooms. A good night's sleep and a fine day of flying ahead of us. Life is good.

"If you don't come out of there, sluggard," Blade's voice

warned from beyond the canvas, "I'm going to have all of this for myself."

"I was simply granting you privacy for your bath," he replied with dignity, standing up and poking his beak out of the tent flap. "Unlike some other people I could mention, I am a gentleman, and a gentleman always allows a lady her privacy."

Perhaps it was technically morning, but out there under the trees it was gloomy as deepest twilight. Blade was slicing bits of fungus into a pan greased with fat; he saw that she had already set aside half of the remainder for him. It sat on top of his deer-quarter, from which she had sliced her breakfast steak.

She had dressed for the heat and humidity, in a sleeveless tunic and trews of Haighlei weave—though not of Haighlei colors. The Haighlei were quick to exploit the new market that White Gryphon provided, weaving their cool, absorbent fabrics in beiges, grays, and lighter colors, as well as black and white. The people of k'Leshya could then ornament these fabrics to suit their own cultural preferences. The results varied as much as the root-culture of the wearer. Those of Kaled'a'in descent embroidered, belled, and beaded their garments in a riot of shades; those who had been adopted into the clan, those outsiders who had ended up with k'Leshya and the gryphons, were usually more restrained in their garments. Blade, consciously or unconsciously, had chosen garments cut in the style of the Kaled'a'in, but in the colors of her mother's people. In this case, she wore a subdued beige, with woven borders in cream and pale brown. As always, even though there was no one to see it, the Silver Gryphon badge glinted on her tunic.

Around them, but mostly *above* them, the birds and animals of this forest foraged for their own breakfasts. After three days of travel, they were finally into the territory that the Haighlei called a "rain forest," and it was vastly different from any place he had ever visited before. The trees were huge, incredibly tall, rising like the bare columns of a sylvan temple for what seemed like hundreds of lengths until they finally spread their branches out to compete with each other for sun. And compete they did; the foliage was so thick and dense that the forest floor was perpetually shrouded in mysterious shadow. When they plunged down out of the sunlight and into the cover of the trees, it took some time for their eyes to adjust.

Despite that lack of direct sunlight, the undergrowth was surprisingly thick. As was to be expected, all kinds of fungi thrived, but there were bushes and even smaller plants growing in the thick leaf litter, and ropelike vines that wreathed the trees and climbed up into the light. Anywhere that a tree had fallen or the course of a stream cut a path through the trees, the undergrowth ran riot, with competition for the light so fierce that Blade swore she could actually see the plants growing larger as she watched them.

She was the team "expert" on plants, and half of the ones she had examined at their campsites were new to her. And they hadn't even done any exploring; the only plants she saw were the ones she found in the course of setting up camp! Tad couldn't even begin to imagine what she'd find when she began looking in earnest—and he began taking her up into the canopy.

He couldn't identify half of the calls they heard from above them. He couldn't even have told her if those hoots and whistles were coming from the throats of furred animals, birds, or reptiles. It was all just a further reminder of how little had been explored here. *Now* he understood why the Haighlei were so careful about what they did here; not only were there scores of completely unknown hazards in this forest, but careless handling of the woodlands could destroy a priceless medicinal herb or some other resource without ever knowing that it was there.

That's all very well, he reminded himself, as he eased himself out of the tent and ambled over to fall on his breakfast with famished pleasure. *But it is difficult to be philosophical on an empty stomach. Later, perhaps. . . .* He devoted himself single-mindedly to his meal. This would be the light one; he would eat heavily when they camped and he could digest while resting. A full gryphon could not fly very well.

A hungry gryphon did not take long to finish a meal, and Tad was famished. He polished off the last of his kill in short order, saving the tasty fungus for last. While he ate, Blade put out the fire, buried their trash in the wet ashes so that it would decay properly, and packed up the gear they had taken out as well as everything inside the tent. Tadrith would leave the bones of his meal for the forest scavengers, who would no doubt be glad of the windfall. When they took off, the only signs that they had been here would be ephemeral; the firepit, the bones, and the pressed-down foliage where they had walked and set the tent. In two days, three at the most, the forest would begin to reclaim the site. In a month, it would be gone. Not even the bones would remain.

No vultures, not in a place like this. Probably rodents, or perhaps some type of swine or canine. He preened his talons fastidiously, and stropped his beak on the log that had played host to their fungi. *Well, I believe it is time to do my part again.*

He strode over to the tent, concentrated for a moment, then extended his power with a deft touch. He let the mage-energy reach for the trigger point of the tent-spell where it lay just under the center of the canvas roof. Obediently, the canvas tent folded in on itself, starting from the top. The sturdy, flexible poles, once holding the canvas rigidly in place, now became the slightly stiffened ropes they really were. Without a hand to aid it, the tent folded, and refolded, as if it was a living creature. Within a few moments, where the tent had been, a boxy package of canvas sat ready to be put in the basket.

Now, as it happened, in accordance with Aubri's advice, the tent *could* be erected without magic, although new poles would have to be cut for it, since the rope supports obviously required magic to become "poles." Clearly, this was a great deal easier, however. Once the spell was triggered, the supports, which were nothing more than magically-bespelled pieces of thick rope sewn into special channels along the seams of the tent, stiffened in a particular order, unfolding the tent and setting it up at the same time. Since the shape of the supports was dictated by the shape of the channel, it was possible to have a tent that did not require a center-pole or guy-ropes, and only needed to be staked down in seven places to keep it from blowing away in a wind.

Of course, if there had been no mage about to trigger the spell, the tent *would* have required a center-pole as well as corner-poles, and guy-ropes at each corner.

This was standard issue among the Silvers now. Tad could never have set the spell himself; that required the hand of a Master. But even an Apprentice could trigger it, so any expedition coming out of White Gryphon that would be camping always had at least one mage along.

The spell that made the tent collapse and fold itself up was a more complicated one, but again, it only needed an Apprentice to trigger and feed it. Tad could handle that sort of spell easily, and enjoyed doing so. Perhaps it was analogous to the way that a human felt when whittling or chip-carving wood. There was an odd, suffused warmth of satisfaction at having created something by use of a tool, which was a different sensation from the visceral feelings of hunting by claw or flying by wings. Perhaps it was the ability to affect things outside one's own momentary grasp that made one feel civilized?

Tad picked up the neat bundle of canvas and rope and deposited it in the carry-basket. Blade was already stretching out and untangling the ropes of his harness. No matter how carefully they stowed the ropes the night before, in the morning they *always* seemed to have gotten tangled. How that could be was another of those mysteries he was certain he would never be able to solve. There were times when he suspected a supernatural explanation.

The harness had to be stowed out of reach of rodents or other creatures that might like to gnaw on leather—and it had to go somewhere where dampness would not get into it. There was only one place that answered that description, and that was the tent itself, so although the ceiling of their temporary dwelling was fairly high, enough of it was taken up with the harness resting in a net suspended from the corners of the roof that Blade could barely stand upright inside.

But if that minor discomfort meant that they could trust the harness not to have suffered damage in the night, it was a small price to pay. Both of them were agreed on that. "I'll share my bed with it if necessary," Blade had said firmly.

"I thought that sort of thing was your father's specialty," he'd jibed back, only to be flattened by a swung harness-girth. Apparently Blade was *not* amused!

Blade finally got the ropes sorted out; now she stood dangling the harness from one hand, beckoning with the other. It was time for Tadrith to go to work.

The harness took some time to get into, and Blade made certain that it was comfortable for him. This was not the token harness of soft deerskin every gryphon in the Silvers wore, displaying his or her badge, and carrying the pouch in which they kept small necessities. Every strap must fit snugly, but without chafing. Large feathers must be moved so that they lay on top of the leather, or they would be broken off. Tadrith could do none of this for himself; instead, he must stand as patiently as a donkey while Blade rigged him up.

The air warmed marginally, and now the usual morning fog began to wreathe among the trees. First, a few wisps formed and wafted through the forest of columns, disappearing and reforming again, like the ghosts of floating snakes. Then the ropes and swaths of fog thickened and joined together, until Tad and Blade were surrounded on all sides by it. Then, lastly, it began to thicken, until they could not see the trunks of trees more than two or three gryphon-lengths away.

Up above, the sounds of birds, animals, and insects continued unabated. Down below, under the cover of the fog, animal sounds increased. *Perhaps, now that they are con-*

cealed, they feel bold enough to call, Tad thought. *Or perhaps they are calling to one another* because *they cannot see each other. It is an interesting question.*

Neither the fog nor the heavy overcast that had shadowed them for the past two days had given them any great amount of trouble, but Tad felt a difference in the air today. Gryphons were supremely sensitive to changes in the weather, and he knew by the feeling behind his nares and the way his feathers felt against his skin that they were going to have a real storm today. Storms around here seemed to stretch for leagues, so there would be no moving out of its path unless they were very lucky. If he had been alone, he might have taken a chance and tried to climb above the clouds—but he dared not with the basket in tow. Unpredictable winds could catch it and send it and him tumbling; lightning could incinerate either him or Blade, or both, in a heartbeat.

No, if the storm threatened, they would have to go to ground quickly, before deadly updrafts or windshear caught them unaware. Then they would have to make a quick camp and get shelter before they were drenched. If the storm was over quickly and he was still dry, they could take to the air again to make a little more distance before nightfall; but if he was drenched, he would have to wait until his wings were dry, which would probably take all night.

He said nothing to Blade, but she must have felt the same urgency. Perhaps long association with him had made her weather-sensitive, too; at any rate, without skimping on her checks, she hurried through the preparations. Sooner than he had expected, she was done. She made a quick final check of the campsite as he shook himself, checking the harness for loose spots.

While she continued to police the campsite, he stretched and did wing-exercises, carefully loosening and warming up every muscle, even those he didn't normally use in flying. He faced away from the campsite, sunk his talons deeply into the ground, and energetically beat his wings as if he was trying to lift the earth itself. He twisted, writhed, and stretched, in a series of dancerlike movements designed to make sure every muscle was ready to do what he had asked it to. Then, when he finally felt no sense of strain no matter which way he moved, he looked at Blade.

"Ready?" she called, as she made her way back through the fog toward the basket.

He nodded. "Let's get in the air," he replied. "There's a storm coming."

"I thought so." She removed the stakes holding the basket firmly to the ground and tossed them in, then vaulted into the basket herself. She shifted a few things with a deft sensitivity to the weight and balance within it, then settled into place with both hands clutching the front of the basket.

That was his signal. With powerful wingstrokes, he rose slowly into the air. Leaves and dust scattered across the forest floor in the wind of his creation, and Blade narrowed her eyes against it.

He rose about three lengths into the air before encountering the momentary resistance of the basket beneath him. But the spell was still holding firm, and the pull against the harness was no more than if he had been hauling a deer-carcass instead of the massive basket.

Immediately, he felt something mildly wrong. The basket felt heavier, and now he noticed a stiffness in his muscles that had not been there when he finished his warm-ups.

Is it the damp and chill?

No matter; he was committed now, and he dared not abort the takeoff. He simply worked a little harder, made his wingbeats a little deeper, strained a little more against the harness.

Blade hung on as the basket lurched up off the ground; this was the moment when it was possible to overset the basket, or novice riders tumbled out. He and the basket rose together through the trees in a series of jerks, propelled by the powerful downthrust of his wings.

He was breathing harder than he should have. *What is the*

matter with me? Did I get less sleep than I thought? Or did I eat too much? The thought of the mushrooms hung uneasily in his mind; they were not poisonous, but what if they had some subtle weakening effect on him?

But if they had, wouldn't he have noticed it last night? Wouldn't he have noticed as he was warming up?

Not necessarily. . . .

In the next moment, they were above the layer of fog that clung to the earth and shrouded the leaf-littered ground, hiding it. He looked up, and the spreading branches of the canopy rushed to meet them.

He willed strength into his muscles, strained toward the light. A thousand birds screamed alarm to see them, then fell silent with shock, as the laden gryphon labored up through the branches. He threaded his way through the hole left in the canopy after the death of some millennium-old forest giant, while below him, Blade shifted and released her holds to fend off reaching branches that threatened to foul the ropes or catch on the basket itself. She used a long pole with a crosspiece tied to the far end, cut last night for this specific purpose. As they burst through the last of the branches into the open air, she dropped the pole. They would not need it for the next descent, and it was too long to carry with them without causing problems.

The contrast between the gloom below the trees and the overcast brightness above dazzled Tad until his eyes adjusted; he did not pause, however, for he needed more height. He might not be able to see clearly, but there was no doubt which way he had to go. "Down" was the direction of the dragging on his harness; he rowed his wings in great heaves in answer to that steady pull, and by the time his eyes cleared, he was as far above the canopy as the branches were above the forest floor.

That was enough. He angled out into level flight, taking his direction from his own inner senses, and now the basket hung true beneath him, no longer bobbing with every wingbeat. Blade did not release her hold on the edges, for she might have to shift her weight to compensate for sudden changes in the wind, but she did allow herself some relaxation.

As soon as they leveled out and he was certain that there were no strange winds to contend with, Tad took a survey of the weather. His weather-sense had not betrayed him; the clouds hung low, fat-bellied and gray with unshed water. He could not scent rain on the air yet, but it was just a matter of time. These were not yet storm clouds; the storm, when it came, would roar down at them out of clouds that would tower thousands of lengths above their slate-blue bottoms.

If they were extraordinarily lucky, they might manage to fly out from under this weather system before it developed into a storm, but he was not going to count on it. From the wind, they were flying in the same direction that this storm was going, which made it very likely that they would actually be flying into the teeth of it rather than away from it.

I'll have plenty of warning before we get into trouble. In fact, I'll see activity in plenty of time to land.

He might even feel it long before he saw it. *We aren't making the best time right now*, he noted ruefully. In spite of the careful warmup, he still felt—not stiff, not strained, but vaguely *achy.*

Am I coming down with something? Or did I just eat too much this morning? He drove westward, moving as quickly as he could, watching the horizon for the telltale flickers of the lightning that would herald the storm front. He hoped he was not coming down with a fever; although gryphons were not prone to such infections, they were not completely unknown. This would be a bad time and place to get sick—although, if it proved to be a real emergency, Blade could use the light teleson set they carried with them to call for help. Now that magic was working again, even rudimentary mind-magic like hers could be amplified by the teleson to carry all the way back to White Gryphon. It would be *work*, but she could get help.

It's probably just from sleeping in the damp. I've never had to sleep in a tent on damp ground before. Now, for the first time, he had a hint of how he might feel in years to come, when his joints began to ache and stiffen. No wonder his father moved so deliberately! And he had thought it was just an affectation, to increase his appearance of dignity!

I don't think I'm going to like getting old.

He flew on for some distance—and was very glad that they were not making this journey afoot. He had just traversed territory it would probably take *days* to cross on the ground, and all within a few marks. It wasn't even noon yet!

Now he scented water, and the air felt heavy and thick, and another explanation for his flying difficulties occurred to him. *This is not good air for flying. It may not be me at all; it may only be the atmosphere that is weighing us down.* It was as difficult to fly in thick air as in thin, though in different ways, and the extra exertion necessary would certainly be enough reason for the ache in his joints!

There was still no sign of the coming storm, but it could not be far off now. He strained his eyes, hunting for that elusive flicker of blue-white light among the clouds—

Tadrith had no real warning, just a sudden lurching sensation in the pit of his stomach, as if he had been caught in a burst of wind and been hurled up, then dropped. His head spun with disorientation for a moment, and he gasped.

Then—the magic on the basket was broken, like water draining out of a broken pot, all in the blink of an eye.

And the moment it vanished, the basket regained its real weight—the full weight of Blade, all their supplies, and the basket itself.

With nothing more holding it up than one very shocked gryphon.

It dropped like a stone, and pulled him, shrieking in strangled surprise, with it.

The harness cut into his shoulders; the sudden jerk drove the breath from his lungs and all thoughts from his mind. He pumped his wings frantically and with complete futility against the weight that hauled him down; below him, Blade shouted and sawed at the basket-ropes, trying to cut him free.

He had to slow their fall! She was *never* going to get him loose—even if the ropes were cut, *she* would still plummet to her death! He wouldn't leave her!

There was no time to try magic, no chance to concentrate enough for a spell, and what could he do, anyway? With his heart pounding in his ears, and his vision clouded with the strain, he tried to make his wings move faster, harder, scoop in more air. Surely, if he just tried hard enough, he could at least slow the basket! Fear sent him more energy, fueling the frantic wingbeats.

His wing-muscles howled in agony, burning with pain, as if a million tiny demons were sticking him with red-hot daggers. His foreclaws scrabbled uselessly at the empty air, as if some part of him thought he might be able to catch and hold something.

His mind jabbered as they plummeted down toward the forest canopy.

He did not even have enough control to pick where they were going to hit.

Below him, he thought Blade was screaming; he couldn't hear her through the pounding in his ears. His vision went red with the strain. . . .

Then they hit the trees.

That slowed them. As they crashed through the treetops, he felt the basket lighten a little; and for a moment he had hope that the springy boughs might actually catch and hold them.

But the basket was too heavy, and the branches not strong nor thick enough. As the basket dragged him down into the gloom, he realized belatedly that hitting trees with wings spread wide was not a good idea for a flying creature.

He was jerked a little sideways as the basket encountered more branches, which was not good for him; instead of dropping through the hole the basket made, he hit undamaged tree limbs with an open wing.

Pain shot through him like a bolt of lightning.

Then, there was only darkness.

Blade

Four

For some reason, Blade had never been the kind who sat frozen with shock when something dreadful happened. She had always acted; there was an even chance that whatever she did in an emergency, it would be the right thing. Without even thinking about it, Blade had her crossdraw knife out in an attempt to cut Tad free as they all plummeted toward the tree canopy below. She sawed frantically at the ropes holding him a helpless prisoner of gravity, but it was obviously of no use; they were falling too fast and there were too many ropes to cut.

We're dead, she thought absently, but her body wasn't convinced of that, and just before they hit the treetops, she dropped into the bottom of the basket, curled into a protective ball.

The basket lurched about as they hit tree limbs and broke through them. As wood crashed and splintered all around her, she was thrown around in the basket among all the lashed-down equipment like another loose piece of junk. Something hit her shoulder hard and she heard herself scream. The pain was like an explosion of stars in her head.

Then, mercifully, she blacked out.

*   *   *

Her head hurt. Her head hurt a *lot*. And her shoulder hurt even more; with every beat of her heart it throbbed black agony, and every time she took a breath or made the tiniest movement, it lanced red fire down her arm and side. She concentrated on that pain without opening her eyes; if she couldn't get that under control, she wouldn't be able to move. If she couldn't move, she, and probably Tad, would lie here until something came to eat them.

Surround the pain and isolate it. Then accept it. Stop fighting it. Don't fear it. Pain is only information, it is up to you how you wish to interpret it. You control it. Her father's lessons came back as she controlled her breathing; she hadn't ever used them on anything worse than a sprained wrist before, but to her surprise, they worked just as well on this serious injury.

Make it a part of you. An unimportant part. Now let the body numb it, let the body flood it with its own defenses. Blade knew the body could produce its own painkillers; the trick was to convince it to produce enough of them. And to convince it that at the moment, pain was getting in the way of survival. . . .

Slowly—too slowly—it worked. She opened her eyes.

The basket was on its side, a couple of wagon-lengths away from her. It looked as if she had been tossed free when, or just before, it hit the ground. Fortunately her lashings holding the cargo in place had held, or she probably would have been killed by her own equipment.

The basket lay in a mess of broken branches, wilting leaves draped everywhere. It didn't look like it was ever going to be useful for anything again.

Probably a fair share of the equipment is worthless now, too, she thought dispassionately. It was easy to be dispassionate; she was still in shock. *I'm alive. That's more than I thought a few moments ago.*

She sat up slowly, being very careful of whatever injury made her shoulder hurt so badly. With her good hand, her left, she probed delicately at her shoulder and bit her lip, drawing blood, when her fingers touched loose bone that grated.

Broken collarbone. I'll have to immobilize the right arm. No wonder it hurts like the Haighlei hells! Well, so much for doing any lifting or wielding any weapons.

Her questing fingers ran over her face and head without encountering anything worse than a goose-egg knot on her skull and more spatters of congealing blood. With the same care as before, she stretched out her right leg, then her left.

Bruises. Lots and lots of bruises, which just at the moment she couldn't feel at all.

I must be black and blue from head to toe. That could be bad; she'd start to stiffen up soon, and in the morning it would be worse.

She cradled her right arm in her left hand, and worked her legs until they were under her and she was in a kneeling position. She couldn't see anything but the basket at the moment, but from the direction that the ropes went, Tad should be right behind her.

She was almost afraid to look. If he were dead—

She turned, slowly and carefully, and let out a sob of relief as she saw him—and saw his sides heaving. He wasn't dead! He wasn't in good shape, but he was still breathing!

He lay sprawled atop a tangle of crushed bushes, still unconscious. His left wing was doubled up underneath him at an angle that was not natural, with his primary feathers pointing forward instead of back, most of them shredded and snapped. So he had one broken wing for certain, and that meant that he would not be flying off anywhere for help.

As she shifted again, trying to get to her feet, his eyes opened, and his beak parted. A thin moan came from him, and he blinked dazedly.

"Don't move," she called sharply. "Let me get over there and help you first."

"*Wing*—" That came out in a harsh whisper, and he panted with pain.

"I know, I can see it. Just hold still and let me get to you."

Gritting her teeth, she worked her right arm inside her tunic and belted the garment tightly, using only her left hand. That would do for immobilizing the shoulder for now.

She stood up with the aid of the debris around her, and worked her way over to Tad. Once there, she stared at him for a moment, deciding where to begin. The rain forest was unnervingly quiet.

"Can you wiggle the toes on your left hind foot?" she asked.

He did so, then repeated the gesture with his right, then his foreclaws. "The right rear hurts when I move, but not as if something is broken," he offered, and she heaved a sigh of relief.

"All right, your back isn't broken, and neither are your legs; that's better than we had any right to expect." The knife she had been trying to use to get him free was gone, but now she could reach all the snap-hooks holding the ropes to his harness. Hissing with pain every time her shoulder was jarred in the least, she knelt down in the debris of crushed branches and scratchy twigs and began unsnapping him.

"I think I'm one big bruise," he said, as she worked her hand under him to free as many of the ropes as she could without having him move.

"That makes two of us," she told him, straining to reach one last set of snap-hooks. He knew better than to stir until she told him to; any movement at all might tear fragile blood vessels in the wings where the skin was thinnest, and he would bleed to death before she could do anything to help him.

Finally, she had to give up on that last set. She moved back to his head, and studied his pupils. Was one a little smaller than the other? Without a light to make them react, she couldn't tell. "You might have a concussion," she said doubtfully.

"You might, too," he offered, which she really could have done without hearing. *I can't wait for the concussion-headache to set in.*

"Just lie there," she advised him. "I'm going after the medical gear."

If I can find the medical gear. If it's still worth anything.

It *had* been packed on top of the supplies, even though that meant it had to be offloaded and set aside every time they stopped for the night. Now she was glad that she had retained the packing order that the supply sergeant had ordained for the basket; they would have been in *worse* shape if she'd had to move foodstuffs, camping gear, and the tent to get at it!

The only question is, did everything fall on top of it?

She worked her way over to the basket again, to find to her great relief that the medical supplies were still "on top"—or rather, since the basket was on its side, they were still the things easiest to reach.

Although "easiest to reach" was only in a relative sense. . . .

She studied the situation before she did anything. The basket was lying in a heap of broken branches; the supplies had tumbled out sideways and now were strewn in an arc through that same tangle of branches. The medical supplies were apparently caught in a forked sapling at about shoulder height, but there was a lot of debris around that sapling. It would be very easy to take a wrong step and wind up twisting or even breaking an ankle—and she only had one hand to use to catch herself. And then, the fall could knock her out again, or damage her collarbone even worse—or both.

But they *needed* those supplies; they needed them before they could do anything else.

I'll just have to be very, very careful. She couldn't see any other way of reaching the package.

"Tad? Tad, can you concentrate enough to use a moving spell?"

All she got back was a croaked "No . . ." and a moan of pain.

Well . . . it wasn't a very good idea anyway. A delirious gryphon casting a spell nearby is more risky for me than if I tried running up that tree!

It looked like she would have to make it by foot. It was an

agonizing journey; she studied each step before she took it, and she made certain that her footing was absolutely secure before she made the next move. She was sweating like a foundered horse before she reached the sapling, both with the strain and with the pain. It took everything she had to reach up, pull the package loose, then numbly toss it in the direction of the clear space beside Tad. It was heavier than it looked—because of the bonesetting kit, of course. She nearly passed out again from the pain when she did so—but it landed very nearly where she wanted it to, well out of the way of any more debris.

She clung to the sapling, breathing shallowly, until the pain subsided enough that she thought she could venture back the way she had come. Her sweat had turned cold by now, or at least that was how it felt, and some of it ran underneath the crusting scabs of dried blood and added a stinging counterpoint to her heartbeat.

When she reached the spot beside her precious package, she simply collapsed beside it, resting her head on it as she shuddered all over with pain and exertion. But every time she shook, her shoulder awoke to new pain, so it was not so much a moment of respite as it was merely a chance to catch her breath.

With the aid of teeth and her short boot knife she wrestled the package open, and the first thing she seized was one of the vials of pain-killing yellow-orchid extract. She swallowed the bitter potion down without a grimace, and waited for it to take effect.

She'd only had it once before, when she'd broken a toe, and in a much lighter dose. This time, however, it did not send her into light-headed giddiness. It numbed the pain to the point where it was bearable, but no more than that. Another relief; the pain must be bad enough to counteract most of the euphoric effect of the drug.

There was another drug that did the same service for gryphons; she dragged the pack of supplies nearer to Tad, fumbled out a larger vial, and handed it to him. He tilted his head back just enough that he would be able to swallow, and poured the contents into his beak, clamping it shut instantly so as not to waste a single bitter drop.

She knew the moment it took effect; his limbs all relaxed, and his breathing eased. "Now what?" he asked. "You can see what's wrong better than I can."

"First you are going to have to help me," she told him. "I can't try to move you until this collarbone is set and immobilized. If I try, I think I might pass out again—"

"A bad idea, you shouldn't do that," he agreed, and flexed his forelimbs experimentally. "I think I can do that. Sit *there*, and we'll try."

He was deft and gentle, and she *still* blacked out twice before he was finished amidst his jabbered apologies for each mistake. When he was done, though, her arm and shoulder were bound up in a tight, ugly but effective package, and the collarbone had been set. Hopefully, it would remain set; they had no way to put a rigid cast on a collarbone. Only a mage could do that; the Healers hadn't even figured out a way to do so.

Then it was his turn.

It could not have been any easier for him, although he did not lose consciousness as she rolled him off the broken wing, set it, and bound it in place. This time she did use the bonesetting kit; the splints and bandages that hardened into rigid forms when first soaked, then dried. She was no *trondi'irn*, but she had learned as much as she could from her mother, once it became obvious to her that her old playmate Tad was going to be her permanent partner. Besides that, though, she guessed. She didn't know enough of the finer points of gryphon physiology to know if what she did now would cause lifelong crippling. Thin moans escaped Tad's clenched beak from time to time, however, and he did ask her to pause three times during the operation.

Finally they both staggered free of the ruins, collapsed on the thick leaf mold of the forest floor, and waited for the pain to subside beneath the ministrations of their potions.

It felt like forever before she was able to think of anything except the fiery throbbing of her shoulder, but gradually the potion took greater hold, or else the binding eased some of the strain. The forest canopy was still preternaturally silent; their plunge through it had frightened away most of the inhabitants, and the birds and animals had not yet regained their courage. She was intermittently aware of odd things, as different senses sharpened for an instant, and her mind overloaded with scent or sound. The sharp, sour smell of broken wood—the call of one insect stupid enough to be oblivious to them—the unexpected note of vivid red of a single, wilting flower they had brought down with them—

"What happened?" she asked quietly, into the strange stillness. It was an obvious question; one moment, they were flying along and all was well, and the next moment, they were plummeting like arrowshot ducks.

His eyes clouded, and the nictitating membrane came down over them for a moment, giving him a wall-eyed look. "I don't know," he said, slowly, haltingly. "Honestly. I can't tell you anything except what's obvious, that the magic keeping the basket at a manageable weight just—dissolved, disappeared. I don't know why, or how."

She felt her stomach turn over. *Not the most comforting answer in the world.* Up until now, she had not been afraid, but now. . . .

I can't let this eat at me. We don't know what happened, remember? It could still all be an accident. "Could there have been a mage-storm?" she persisted. "A small one, or a localized one perhaps?"

He flattened his ear-tufts and shook his head emphatically. "No. No, I'm sure of it. Gryphons are sensitive to mage-storms, the way that anyone with joint swellings is sensitive to damp or real, physical storms. No, there was no mage-storm; I would *know* if one struck."

Her heart thudded painfully, and her stomach twisted again. If it wasn't a "natural" event. . . . "An attack?" she began—but he shook his head again.

But he looked more puzzled than fearful. "It wasn't an *attack* either," he insisted. "At least, it wasn't anything I'd recognize as an attack. It wasn't anything offensive that I'd recognize." He gazed past her shoulder as if he was searching for words to describe what he had felt. "It was more like— like suddenly having your bucket spring a leak. The magic just *drained* out, but suddenly. And I don't know how or why. All the magic just—just went away."

All the magic just went away.... Suddenly, the chill hand of panic that she had been fighting seized the back of her neck, and she lurched to her feet. If the magic in the *basket* had drained away, what about all the other magic?

"What's wrong?" he asked, as she stumbled toward the wreckage of the basket and the tumbled piles of supplies.

"Nothing—I hope!" she called back, with an edge in her voice. *What's closest? The firestarter? Yes—there it is!* The firestarter was something every Apprentice mage made by the dozen; they were easy to create, once the disciplines of creating an object had been mastered. It was good practice, making them. They were also useful, and since their average life was about six months, you could always barter them to anyone in the city once you'd made them. Anyone could use one; you didn't have to be a mage to activate it—most were always ready, and to use one you simply used whatever simple trigger the mage had built in. The one in their supplies was fresh; Tad had just made it himself before they left.

It didn't look like much; just a long metal tube with a wick protruding from one end. You were supposed to squeeze a little polished piece of stone set into the other end with your thumb, and the wick would light.

You *could* manipulate it with one hand if you had to, and of course, she had to. Hoping that her hunch had been wrong, she fumbled the now-dented tube out of a tangle of ropes and cooking gear, and thumbed the end.

Nothing happened.

She tried it again, several times, then brought it back to

Tad. "This isn't working," she said tightly. "What's wrong with it?"

He took it from her and examined it, his eyes almost crossing as he peered at it closely. "The—the magic's gone," he said hesitantly. "It's not a firestarter anymore, just a tube of metal with a wick in it."

"I was afraid you'd say that." Grimly she returned to the tumbled supplies, and pawed through them, looking for anything that had once been magical in nature. Every movement rewoke the pain in her shoulder, but she forced herself to ignore it. The way that the supplies had tumbled out aided her; the last things into the basket had been on top, and that meant they were still accessible.

The mage-light in the lantern was no longer glowing. The tent—well, she couldn't test that herself, she couldn't even unfold it herself, but the canvas felt oddly limp under her hand, without a hint of the resistance it used to possess. The teleson—

That, she carried back to Tad, and placed it wordlessly before him. It wasn't much to look at, but then, it never had been; just a contoured headband of plain silver metal, with a couple of coils of copper that could be adjusted to fit over the temples of any of the varied inhabitants of White Gryphon. It was used to magically amplify the range of those even marginally equipped with mind-magic. All the gryphons, *kyree,* and *hertasi* had that power, and most of the *tervardi* as well.

Tad should have been able to use it to call for help. A shiver ran down her body and she suppressed the urge to babble, cry, or curl up in a ball and give up. She realized that she had been unconsciously *counting* on that fact. If they couldn't call for help—

He touched one talon to the device, and shook his head. "I don't even have to put it on," he said, his voice shaking. "It's—empty. It's useless." Unspoken words passed between them as he looked up mutely at her. *We're in trouble.*

"It wasn't just the basket, then," she said, sitting down

hard, her own voice trembling as well. *How could this happen? Why now? Why us?* "Everything that had any spells on it is inert. The mage-lights, the firestarter, the tent, probably the weather-proof shelter-cloaks—"

"And the teleson." He looked up at her, his eyes wide and frightened, pupils contracted to pinpoints. "We can't call for help."

We're out here, on our own. We're both hurt. No one at White Gryphon knows where we are; they won't even know we're missing until we don't show up at the rendezvous point where we were supposed to meet the last team that manned the outpost. That'll be days from now.

"It's a long way to walk," he faltered. "Longer, since we're hurt."

And there's something nearby that eats magic. Is it a natural effect, or a creature? If it eats magic, would it care to snack on us? It might; it might seek out Tad, at least. Gryphons were, by their very nature, magical creatures.

Don't think about it! Over and over, the Silvers had been taught that in an emergency, the first thing to think about was the problem at hand and not to get themselves tied into knots of helplessness by trying to think of too many things at once. *Deal with what we can handle; solve the immediate problems, then worry about the next thing.* She got unsteadily to her feet. "There's a storm coming. That's our first problem. We have to get shelter, then—water, warmth, and weapons. I think we'd better salvage what we can *while* we can before the rain comes and ruins it."

He got shakily to his feet, nodding. "Right. The tent—even if we could cut poles for it, I'm not sure we could get it up properly with both of us hurt. I don't think the basket will be good for much in the way of shelter—"

"Not by itself, but two of the sides and part of the bottom are still intact," she pointed out. "We can spread the canvas of the tent out over that by hand, and use the remains to start a fire." She stared at it for a moment. So did he.

"It looks as if it's supported fairly well by those two

saplings," he pointed out. "The open side isn't facing the direction I'd prefer, but maybe this is better than trying to wrestle it around?"

She nodded. "We'll leave it where it is, maybe reinforce the supports. Then we'll clear away the wreckage and the supplies, cut away what's broken and tie in more support for the foundation by tying in those saplings—"

She pointed with her good hand, and he nodded.

"Look there, and there," he said, pointing himself. "If we pile up enough stuff, we'll have a three-sided shelter instead of just a lean-to."

That, she agreed, would be much better than her original idea. In a moment, the two of them were laboring as best they could, her with one hand, and him with one wing encased and a sprained hind-leg, both of them a mass of bruises.

He did most of the work of spreading out the canvas over the remaining sound walls of the basket; he had more reach than she did. She improvised tent stakes, or used ones she uncovered in the course of moving supplies, and tied the canvas down as securely as she could manage with only one hand. One thing about growing up in the household of a *kestra'chern;* she had already known more kinds of knots and lashings than even her survival instructor.

She wasn't certain how Tad felt, but every movement made her shoulder ache viciously. *There's no choice,* she told herself each time she caught her breath with pain. *Rest once it starts to rain; work now.*

She wasn't sure what time it was. They hadn't gone very far before they had come crashing down, and they hadn't been unconscious for long, or else they would have awakened to find insects trying to see if they were dead yet. Scavengers didn't wait long in this kind of forest. That meant it was probably still early morning. If the rain threatened by those clouds held off, they had until late afternoon before the inevitable afternoon thunderstorm struck. *If our luck hasn't gone totally sour, that is. . . .*

Eventually, they had their three-sided shelter; the limp

tent canvas stretched tightly over the remains of the basket and the three young trees that had caught it. There were some loose flaps of canvas that she didn't quite know what to do with yet; she might think of something later, but this was the best they could do for now.

They both turned to the tumbled heaps of supplies; sorting out what was ruined, what could still be useful even though it was broken, and what was still all right. Eventually, they might have to sort out a version of what could be carried away in two packs, but that would be later.

She would fight to remain here, and so would Tad. Walking off should not become an option until they were certain no one was going to come looking for them.

Always stay with a wreck, if you can. That much she also remembered very well from their survival course. *The wreck makes the best target for searchers to find and the first place they'll look for you when they spot it.*

If they could stay here, they had a shelter they could improve more each day, plus what was left of the supplies. Even things that were ruined might be useful, if they had long enough to think of a use for them. If they were forced to leave, there was a lot of potentially useful and *immediately* useful gear they would be forced to leave behind.

If. That was the trick. She could not for a moment forget that something out there had drained away their magic without any warning at all. If the wreck made a good target for searchers to find, it also made a good target for other things to find—including whatever knocked them out of the sky. *Assume it's an enemy, and assume he attacked.* That was the wisest course of reasoning and the one she had to begin planning for.

For that matter, there was no telling what prowled the forest floor. Just because they hadn't *yet* run into any major predators, that didn't mean there weren't any. The longer they stayed in one place, the easier it would be for predators to locate them.

"Thank goodness for Aubri," came a muffled sigh from her

right, and Tad came up out of his pile of seeming-rubbish at the same moment. He held in his talon a nonmagical fire-striker, and Blade put aside the pile she'd been sorting to take it from him. Now she could make a fire with the dry, shellac-coated splinters of the basket and pile damp, green wood around that fire so that it could dry out enough to burn.

Tad remained with his pile; evidently he'd found the box that had held all of the nonmagical gear that Aubri had insisted they take with them. She eyed the improvised shelter for a moment. *Think first, plan, then move. If you ruin something, there's no one around to help with repairs. And not much to make repairs with.*

She wanted a way to shelter the fire from the rain, without getting too much smoke into the shelter. And she *didn't* want to take a chance on ruining the shelter they already had.

Right. There's the tent flap. I bend those two saplings over and tie them to the basket, then unfold the tent flap and tie it down—there. And I think I can do that with one hand. Then maybe we can create a wind barrier with long branches and some of those big leaves. Plan now firmly in mind, she one-arm manhandled the saplings into place, then pulled the flap of canvas out over the arch they formed to protect the area where she wanted to put the fire. Carefully she tied the end of the tent flap to another broken tree, fumbling the knot several times; if it wasn't caught by a big gust of wind, it would hold. At least they wouldn't be lacking in wood, even though it was very green. They'd brought down a two or three days' supply with them when they fell and they also had spare clothing to use for kindling. *Build the fire first, then see about that barrier.*

She scraped the leaf-litter away from the ground until she had a patch of bare earth, then carefully laid a fire of basket-bits, broken boxes, and some of the leaves she found that were actually dry. With the striker came a supply of tinder in the form of a roll of bone-dry lint lightly pressed together with tiny paper-scraps. She pulled off a generous pinch and put the rest carefully away, resealing the tinder box. The firestriker was a pure nuisance to operate, especially one-handed. She finally wound up squatting down and bracing the box with one foot, and finally she got a spark to catch in the tinder and coaxed the glowing ember into a tiny flame. Frowning with concentration, she bent over her fragile creation and fed the flame carefully, building it up, little by little, until at long last she had a respectable fire, with the smoke channeling nicely away from the shelter. At that point, *everything* ached with strain.

Breathing a painful sigh, she straightened, and looked over at Tad to see what he'd found. The thing that caught her eye first was the ax. That, she was incredibly glad to see! It was small enough to use one-handed, sharp enough to hack through just about anything. And right now, they needed firewood.

She got painfully to her feet and helped herself to the implement, then began reducing the debris around their improvised camp into something a bit more useful to them.

She tossed branches too small to be useful as firewood into a pile at one side. If they had time before darkness fell or the rain came—whichever was first—she'd make a brush-palisade around the camp with them. It wouldn't actually keep anything out that really wanted to get at them, but animals were usually wary of anything new, and they might be deterred by this strange "fence" in their path.

And anything pushing through it is going to make noise, which should give us some warning. Now just as long as nothing jumps over it. When Tad needs to urinate, we'll collect it and spread it around the perimeter, the scent of any large predator should scare most foragers and nuisance animals away. And other than that, it is a perfect day, my lord.

The branches holding huge leaves she treated differently, carefully separating the leaves from the fibrous, pithy branches and setting them aside. When she had enough of them, and some straight poles, she'd put up that sheltering wall.

Every time she swung the ax, her body protested, but it wasn't bad enough to stop her now that she had some momentum going. *If I stop, I won't be able to move for hours, so I'd better get everything I can done while I'm still mobile.*

Evidently Tad had the same idea; he was sorting through the supplies with the same single-minded determination she was feeling. He'd found her two packs of personal supplies, and his own as well and put all of them in the shelter; laid out next to them was the primitive "Aubri gear." In between swings of the ax she made out candles and a candle-lantern, a tiny folded cook-stove, canteens, two shovels, and three leather water bottles. Two enormous knives good for hacking one's way through a jungle lay beside that, also a neat packet of insect netting, fishing line and hooks, and a compass. He'd gotten to the weapons they'd carried with them as a matter of course, and she grimaced to look at them. They were largely useless in their present circumstances. Her favorite bow was broken; the smaller one was intact, but she couldn't pull it now. Nor could she use the sword Tad was placing beside the oiled-canvas quivers of arrows. Beside that he laid his set of fighting-claws—which might be useful, except that he couldn't walk while wearing them.

And what are we going to do if we're driven away from here and something attacks us on the trail? Ask it politely to wait while he gets his claws on?

But her heart rose in the next moment, because he had found a sling! He placed it beside his claws, and two full pouches of heavy lead shot beside it. Now *that* she could use, and use it well, even with only one hand!

That gave her a little more energy to swing, and his next find added to that energy, for it was a short spear with a crosspiece on it, like a boar-spear. It had broken, but mostly lengthwise with the grain of the haft, and what remained was short enough to use one-handed. *I can keep us fed with the sling; with the knife and the spear I can fight things off. He has his beak and talons, which are not exactly petty weapons. And he has some magic.*

All gryphons had at least a small command of magic; Tad

didn't have a *lot*, not compared to his father, but it might be useful. . . .

But she shivered again, thinking about what Tad's magic might attract, and decided that she had chopped enough wood. She ringed the fire with the green logs, stacked the rest at the back of the lean-to, and piled the remains of the basket that she had chopped up wherever she could under shelter. *I don't think I want him using any magic until we know for certain that whatever sucked the magic out of the basket isn't going to bother us.*

She joined Tad in his sorting, sadly putting aside some once-magical weapons that were now so much scrap. Unfortunately, they were shaped too oddly to be of any immediate use. The best purpose they could be put to now was as weights to hold pieces of canvas down to protect more useful items—like wood—from the rain.

She found the bedding at the bottom of the spill and took it all into the lean-to to spread on the ground, over mattresses of leaves and springy boughs. She made another trip with more assorted items and the weapons and gear she could actually use now. The rest, including some broken items, she laid under a piece of canvas; she might think of something to do with them later.

Most of the equipment was just plain ruined, and so was a great part of their food. The rations that survived the smash were, predictably, the kind a mercenary army normally carried; dried meat and a hard ten-grain ration-biscuit made with dried vegetables and fruit. This was not exactly a feast, but the dried meat would sustain Tad, and the hard ration-bread was something that a person could actually live on for one or two months at a time.

He wouldn't *enjoy* living on it, but it was possible to do so without suffering any ill consequences.

She paused, and took a closer look at the smashed and ruined food. At the moment, some of it *was* still edible, though it wouldn't stay that way for long.

Better save the rations for tonight, and eat what we can

of this. She gathered together enough of the food to make a very hearty meal, and placed it by the fire, then laboriously took the rest out into the forest and deposited it a goodly way away from the camp. Better *not* let the local fauna associate the camp with food. They could set snares another time, for the curious, to supplement the dried-meat ration.

Time for that windbreak-wall beside the fire. She stuck the ends of four of the long, whippy branches into the soil and tied the tops to whatever she could reach along the supported tent flap, using her teeth and her one good hand. Then she threaded the leaves on another of the long branches, overlapping them like shingles. When she came to the end of the branch, she tied *that* along the base of the four wall supports, about a hand's length from the ground, once again using teeth as well as her hand. Then she went back to threading leaves on another branch, and tied that one so that it overlapped the one below it. It didn't take very long, and when she finished, she thought that the result, like the shelter, would hold up fairly well as long as no violent winds came up, which wasn't too likely under the canopy.

When she left her completed wall, Tad was already sticking brush into the soft loam of the forest floor to make that brush-fence she had considered. She joined him, just as thunder rumbled threateningly in the distance. She took a quick glance over her shoulder, saw that everything worth saving was under some form of shelter and that the fire still burned well. *It'll survive, I hope. We'll just have to hope our luck has turned.* She joined Tad in constructing the "fence." Their new home wasn't much of one, but it was, after all, better than nothing. The work went quickly; the earth was so soft here that it didn't take much effort to thrust the thin branches down well enough to anchor them securely.

Thunder rumbled right above them; she glanced up just in time to catch one of the first fat drops right in her eye.

A heartbeat later, as they were scrambling back to the shelter of the tent, the sky opened up. Together they hud-

dled under the canvas; it was a very close fit, but no closer
than it had been when the tent was still a tent.

Water poured out of the sky at a fantastic rate. *Now* she
was glad that she had brought everything under the lean-to
that she could, as she found it; she'd seen waterfalls with
less water cascading down them! It all came straight down,
too, without a sign of any wind to blow it sideways. There
must have been some high winds at treetop level, though;
the trunks of trees nearest her swayed a little as she watched
them. The trees acted as a buffer between them and whatever wind the storm brought with it.

There was no moment when lightning was not illuminating some part of the sky, and there were times when she saw
the fat raindrops seemingly hanging in the air due to a trick
of the flickering light.

The rain knocked loose what branches hadn't come down
with them; one or two thudded against the shelter, and she
was glad that there was canvas *and* the basket between them
and the debris. Canvas alone would have caved in or torn.

She wondered if she should clear the fallen branches away
later. *If it isn't hurting anything, I'll leave it. If we look like
a pile of debris to animals, they might leave us alone. No—
what am I thinking? The native animals will know what is
right or wrong for their own area. I must be delirious.*

Tad gazed out at the powerful storm with his eyes wide and
his feathers roused against the cool damp. She wondered what
he was thinking. Every time one of the really big lightning-
bolts flashed across the sky, the back of his eyes glowed
greenly.

Her shoulder began to stab at her again, throbbing in time
to the thunder; the drugs she had taken must have worn off
a bit. If she was in serious pain, Tad probably was, too, and
there was no reason why they should endure it if they didn't
have to. The medical kit contained enough pain-relieving
drugs to last two people for two weeks—by then, they would
either be found or be in such serious trouble that a little
pain would be the least of their worries. She felt for the bag

of medicines and fished in it for two more vials of painkiller, handing him his. He took it, pierced the seal with a talon, and swallowed it down before she even had hers open. He took hers away from her and punctured the wax seal for her in the same way; she took it back gratefully, and downed it.

"Should we set a watch?" he asked. "I think we should. I think we should really try to stay awake even if we're taking painkillers. I don't like the idea of lying here helpless. It was different when we could set mage-wards, but now. . . ."

She thought about the question for a moment. *We probably ought to, even though it's not likely we could do much against a real enemy. Then again, if all that comes to plague us is scavengers and wild beasts, if we set a watch, whoever is awake can probably fend off any trouble.*

"I agree. If you can sleep now, go ahead," she said finally. "I can't, not even with this demon's brew in me. If you're rested by the time I can't stay awake any longer, then you can take second watch."

He nodded, and she draped some of the bedding over him to keep him warm. "I'll have something for you to eat when you wake up," she promised. "I think it's going to rain until well after dark; I'll wake you up when I can't keep my eyes open anymore." She had no idea how he did it, but he was actually asleep shortly after she finished speaking. *Must be exhausted,* she decided. *He was trying so hard to slow our fall; that must have taken an awful lot out of him. I ought to be surprised that he didn't just collapse completely after his wing was set.*

She ought to feel a great deal more than she did; it was hard to sustain anything, even fear, for very long. *That's shock, and maybe it's just as well. As long as I plan everything and concentrate, I can carry it out.*

Later, perhaps, she would be able to feel and react; now she was oddly grateful for the peculiar numbness.

Since the supplies she had salvaged were pretty much mixed up together already, she used the hodgepodge of food-stuffs to make a kind of giant pancake with meat, vegetables, and spices all baked into it. She made as many of these cakes as she had supplies for; ate one herself, and saved the rest for Tad. After that, she just stared out into the rain. It was growing darker by the moment, although that simply could have been thickening clouds and not oncoming night-fall. A dull lethargy settled over her, and the rain lulled her into a state of wary weariness.

There was no sign that the rain was going to collapse the roof, and no sign that it was going to stop any time soon. Be-latedly, she realized that *here* was a good source of fresh wa-ter for them, and she began to rummage through the supplies again. As she found things that could hold water, she stuck every container she could find into the streams of run-off along the front edge of the canvas. Before long, she had all their canteens and storage-bottles full, and had re-filled the rest of their containers a second time, *and* she'd washed and rinsed the dishes.

I can get a wash! That revived her somewhat; she felt sweaty, grimy, and the mere idea of being able to wash her-self revived her a little. She put a potful of water beside the fire to warm up; if she didn't have to wash herself in cold water, she wasn't going to! They might not have magic, but they still had other resources.

Besides, there were some remedies for bruises in that medical gear that had to be steeped in warm water. When she finished washing, she could do something about her mi-nor injuries. They probably wouldn't feel so minor when she tried to sleep.

Poor Tad; I don't think my remedies will work on his bruises; he hasn't got bare flesh to use them on. No point in soaking his feathers either; that would only chill him and make him feel worse.

Rain continued to pound the canvas; the falling rain was the only sound in the whole forest, at least to her limited ears. She sat with her knees drawn up to her chest and her good arm wrapped around them, watching the silver water continue to pour out of the sky, sent into a trancelike state by the steady, dull roaring. The flash of lightning and the pounding of thunder were the only things that kept her from completely succumbing and falling asleep a time or two. She caught herself with a sudden shock and a pounding heart, jerking herself awake.

When her water warmed, she clumsily stripped off her tunic, fished out a scrap of ruined cloth and bathed her bruises with gratitude in lieu of soap. How good a simple thing like a warm, damp cloth on her aches felt! And how good it felt to be clean! Her sense of being grimy had not been wrong.

Oh, how I wish I had one of those hot pools to soak in. . . . Well, while I'm at it, why don't I wish for rescue, a soft bed in a deep cave, and enough painkiller to keep me asleep until this shoulder is healed! More such thoughts would only depress her or make her frantic with worry; she should concentrate on *now*, and on doing the best she could with what she had.

Just being clean again made her feel a great deal better; time to put on clothing that was equally clean. The air had cooled considerably since the rain began; now it was getting positively chill as well as damp. She pulled out a tunic with long sleeves—and realized as she started to put it on that it would be impossibly painful to get her arm into the sleeve without ruining the tunic.

Well, who was there to see her? No one.

She slit the front of the tunic with her knife; she could belt it closed again. But before she put on any clothing, she wrapped a blanket around her shoulders, and went back to the medical kit. She should treat the bruises first, then get dressed.

She found the herbs she needed in the kit, and put them into the pot of remaining warm water to steep. Now the rain did show some signs of slacking off, but it was also getting much darker out there. This wasn't just thickening cloud cover; it must be just past sunset.

She reached for the shortened spear, and pulled out a selection of knives that could be thrown in a pinch, then considered her next move.

Do I build the fire up to discourage night prowlers, or bank it so as not to attract attention?

After some consideration, she opted for the former. Most animals were afraid of fire; if they smelled the smoke, they might avoid this area altogether. She had to burn green wood, but that was all right, since the smoke it made drifted away from the lean-to and not into it. A bigger fire warmed the interior of their shelter nicely, and beside her, Tad muttered drowsily and settled into deeper sleep.

When the herb-water was a deep, murky brown, she stripped off her blanket; soaking bandages in the potion until the bowl was empty, she wrapped the soaked cloth around the areas most bruised, curling up in the blanket until they dried.

The heat felt wonderful—and the medicines actually began to ease the dull throbbing ache wherever some of the worst bruises were. The scent of the potion arose, bitter and pungent, to her nose.

Good. At least I don't smell like anything edible. I wouldn't want to eat anything that smelled like me. Even the bugs won't bite me now. Maybe.

It wasn't long before the bandages were dry enough to take off; she pulled on her breeches with one hand, then got her tunic on over her good arm and pulled it closed. Fortunately the belt fastener was a buckle with a hook instead of a tongue; she belted the slit tunic so that it would stay closed, more or less.

The rain stopped altogether; insects called out of the gloom in all directions. As the last of the light faded, odd whoops and strange, haunted cries joined the buzzing and metallic chirping of insects. Bird, animal, reptile? She had no way of knowing. Most of the calls echoed down from high above and could come from any throat.

It was very damp, cold, and very dark out there. The only other spots of light were foxfire off in the distance (probably from a decaying stump), and the mating lights of wandering insects. No moon, no stars; she couldn't see either right now. Maybe the cloud cover was still too thick. Maybe the cover of the leaves was too heavy.

At least they had a fire; the remains of the basket were burning very well, and the green wood burning better than she had expected.

Perhaps the most frustrating thing of all about their situation was that neither she nor Tad had done a single thing wrong. They hadn't been showing off, nor had they been in the least careless. Even experienced campaigners like Aubri and Judeth would have been caught unaware by this situation, and probably would have found themselves in the same fix.

It wasn't their fault.

Unfortunately, their situation was still a fact, and fault didn't matter to corpses.

Once Blade had immobilized Tad's wing, it hadn't hurt nearly as much as he had expected. That might have been shock, but it probably wasn't; the break was simple, and with luck, it was already knitting. Gryphon bones healed quickly, with or without the services of a Healer.

It probably didn't hurt nearly as much as his partner's collarbone either; his wing was not going to move no matter what he did, but if she had to move and work, she *was* going to be jarring her shoulder over and over again.

I wish the teleson wasn't gone. I wish I could fix it! He could fix the firestarter and the mage-light, and probably would after he slept, but the teleson was beyond him, as was the tent and the cook pot. If they had the teleson, help could be here in two days, or three at the most. Now it might be two or three days before anyone even knew they were in trouble.

He had volunteered for the second watch because he knew that she was going to have to be *very* tired before she could sleep—but once she was, those painkillers were going

to hit her hard. Once she fell asleep, it was going to be difficult to wake her until she woke by herself.

For his part, although the painkiller helped, Keeth had
taught him a fair amount about taking care of himself; he
could self-trance pretty easily, and he knew several pain-
reduction and relaxation techniques.

Lucky I have a trondi'irn *for a brother.*

He made himself comfortable, and once Blade draped a
blanket over him so that he was warm, he fell asleep quickly.

Strange images, too fleeting to be called "dreams," drifted
with him. Visions of himself, visiting a trading fair in Khimbata, but as an adult rather than a child trailing after his
Haighlei nurse, Makke; moments of flying so high above the
earth that even with his keen eyesight, humans below him
were no more than specks. There were visions that were less
rational. He thought, once, that the trees were talking to
him, but in a language he didn't recognize, and that they
grew frustrated and angry with him because he didn't understand what they were trying to tell him.

None of this was enough to actually disturb his rest; he
roused just enough to dismiss the dreams that were unpleasant without actually breaking his sleep, then drifted back
into darkness.

He was just about on the verge of waking all by himself—
half-dreaming that he ought to wake, but unable to really
get the energy to rouse himself—when Blade shook him
slightly, enough to jar him completely out of his half-sleep.

He blinked up at her; her face was a bizarre mask of pur-
pling bruises and dancing golden firelight. If it had been a little more symmetrical and less obviously painful, it would
have been oddly attractive. He tasted bitter herbs in the air
as she yawned, and guessed that she had bandaged herself
with some of her human medicines.

"I took more painkillers, and I can't stay awake anymore," she confessed, yawning again. "I haven't seen or
heard anything that I can confirm, although my imagination
has been working away nicely."

"Fine, then get some sleep," he said, a little thickly, and blinked to clear his eyes. "I'll take over until dawn."

She settled herself between the wall of the tent and him, lying against him. He let her curl up in such a way as to take the most advantage of his warmth; she needed it. *And she probably needs the comfort just as much,* he thought, as she tried to arrange herself in a way that would cause the least pain to her broken collarbone. *It can't have been easy, sitting here, staring into the dark, and wondering what was out there, with your partner a great snoring lump beside you.*

Granted, he wouldn't have stayed a great snoring lump for long if there'd been trouble, but that was no comfort when you were straining your ears trying to tell if that was a nightbird, a bug, or a maneating whatever out there.

Gryphons were not noted for having powerful night vision, but both Skandranon and his two offspring were better than the norm at seeing in the dark. They weren't owls—but they weren't half-blind, either, and they *were* better than humans. He let his eyes adjust to the darkness, and mentally marked the shadows so that he knew where everything was. Some, he could even identify, by matching the general shape with his memory of the objects surrounding the camp; the place that looked like a crouching bear was really a stump over-grown with inedible fungi. And the bush that seemed to have a deeper shadow at the heart of it really *did;* it had grown around what remained of a snag, which could have passed for another crouching creature. Deep in the distance, a phospho-rescent shape was a rotting tree with a patch of foxfire fun-gus in it—and it wasn't really moving, that was an illusion brought on by eyestrain. Things that might have been pairs of eyes reflecting the firelight were nothing of the kind; if he watched them until they moved, it was clear that they moved independently of one another, which meant they were only a couple of light-bearing insects, probably flying in pairs because they were in the middle of a mating dance. A swift and silent shape passing from branch to branch above his head was an owl; one that flew with a faint fluttering just out of range of the firelight was a bat.

Once he identified things in his range of vision, he began cataloging sounds. The obvious buzzes and whirs were insect calls; likewise there were croaks and cheeps he knew were frogs. There were some calls he recognized from around White Gryphon; not *all* the creatures here were new to him. The occasional sleepy twitter or mutter from high above meant that something had mildly disturbed a bird's rest—nothing to worry about, birds bumped into each other while they slept all the time.

Then there were the howls, barks, and growls. He took note of all of them, keeping track of where they were coming from and under what circumstances. Most of them originated from up in the tree canopy; that meant that, barring something completely strange, whatever made them wasn't going to bother the two down below. The things living in the trees would, for the most part, be prey rather than predator; life in the tree tops was difficult, with the most difficult task of all being how to get to water. Anything living up there had a reason not to want to live on the ground. Any creature up there would probably be relatively small, no bigger than Blade at the most, with a disproportionately loud call, because in the thick leaf cover up there, it would be hard to keep track of herd- or flock-mates. And if you yelled loudly enough when something grabbed you, there was a chance that you might startle it into letting go.

Predators in the tree canopy would either be snakes or winged; four-footed predators would hunt on the ground. While it was certainly possible that there could be a snake up there large enough to swallow Blade or even Tad, it would not be able to seize both of them at once, and it would not be very fast except when it struck. That left winged predators, and Tad was confident that he would be a match for anything that flew, even grounded.

No, what they had to worry about was what lay down

here, so sounds up above could be dismissed unless and until they erupted in warning or alarm calls.

While his vision was incredibly keen by human standards, it was even more suited to picking up tiny movements. So once he had identified everything that lay in front of the shelter, he did not need to sit and stare into the darkness as Blade did. He need only relax and let his eyes tell him when something out there had changed its position. No matter how clever a predator was at skulking, sooner or later it would have to cross a place where he would spot it moving through the shadows, even on a night with no moon.

His hearing was just as good, and now that he knew what the normal noises were, he could listen through them for the sound of a grunt, a growl, or the hiss of breath—or for the rustle of a branch—or the crack of a twig snapped beneath a foot.

That was the other reason why he didn't mind taking second watch. When all was said and done, he was much better suited to it than Blade was.

Now, if anything decided to come up *behind* them, he wouldn't see it, and he might not hear it either. But it wouldn't get through the canvas and basketry of their shelter quickly, and they should have time to defend themselves.

Or so I tell myself.

He stared out into the darkness, watching winking insect lights, and finally acknowledged to himself that, far from feeling competent, he was feeling rather helpless.

We're both crippled and in pain, we can't use most of the weapons we have left, we aren't entirely certain where we are, and we're too far from home to get back, and that's the honest truth. I don't like it at all.

They had to hope that in three days or so, when they didn't make the appointed rendezvous, they'd be missed, and that White Gryphon would send out a search party looking for them. They had to hope that they could survive long enough to be found!

Oh, stop feeling sorry for yourself and eat! he scolded himself. *You aren't going to get a chance at a better meal for a while, and starving yourself is hardly going to do any good. Whatever Blade fixed, it probably won't keep past morning.*

Slowly, to make them last, he ate the meat-and-vegetable cakes that Blade had concocted. They weren't bad, considering how awful they could have been. Blade was not noted for being anything other than an indifferent cook, and these had actually been one of her best efforts. The two of them would probably joke about the incongruity of cooking a gourmet meal in the middle of a disaster, after they had escaped this stranding and healed. *Of course, to hear the stories about Father, you would think he was so dashing that he would fight off two hundred makaar, seduce his wingleader, arrange a tryst, fight off another hundred makaar, and then pause for tea from a silver cup.*

Blade had placed the odd cakes close enough to the fire that they kept warm without burning or drying out much. They would probably stay with him for a while, which was a good thing, since he wasn't going to be doing much hunting for the next couple of days. And even then, in order to take down the size of prey he was used to, he'd have to somehow surprise it on the ground.

Father's claims about being able to slip through enemy lines unseen might be true, but deer have keener noses and ears than human soldiers. I'm going to have to be very lucky to catch anything larger than a squirrel.

He was satisfied before finishing the cakes, so he covered the last four of them with a leaf followed by a layer of hot ashes, burying them next to the fire. He would leave them for breakfast; they should keep that long. Then he rested his chin on his foreclaws and resumed his interrupted thoughts.

The trouble is, I have no idea just what it was that knocked us out of the sky.

Obviously, he had several options. It *could* have been a purely natural phenomenon—or, if not natural, simply an anomalous and accidental creation of the mage-storms.

The trouble with that theory is that there have been a

*number of folk through here, Haighlei included. So that pre-
cludes it being stationary or ground bound.* If it was something natural or accidental, it *had* to be stationary, it seemed,
so why didn't anyone discover it before this? The Haighlei in
particular, suspicious as they were of anything magical that
was not under the direct control of one of their Priest-Mages,
made a point of looking for such "wild" magic, using broad,
far-ranging sweeps. They had established the outpost; they
would have come this way, though perhaps not this exact
route. They should have found something this powerful.

*Granted, we were a bit off the regular route. I wasn't
watching the ground that closely for landmarks, I was
watching the sky for weather. I think I was even veering off
a bit to avoid the worst of the storm.*

Still, a "bad spot," even a null area, should show up to any
skilled mage who was looking for it. It should be obvious to
any mage looking for oddities.

*I wasn't looking; I have to think about using mage-sight
in order to see things. I'm not like Snowstar, who has to remind himself* not *to use it.*

That left the next possibility; it was something new, or
else something that was outside his knowledge. He inex-
orably moved his thoughts toward the uneasy concept that
something had brought them down intentionally, either in
an attack or as a measure of preventive defense.

*But if it was a defensive measure, how did they ever see
us from the ground?* The attack couldn't have come from
the air; there hadn't been anything in the air except birds
and themselves. It hadn't come from the tree canopy, or he
would have seen something directly below. It *had* to have
come from ground level, below the tree canopy, so how had
"they" seen the basket, Blade, and Tad?

Still, so far, whatever brought them down hadn't come after them; that argued in favor of it being a defensive, perhaps
even a reflexive, answer to a perceived threat.

But it happened so quickly! *Unless "they" had a spell ac-*

tually ready to do something like that, I can't see how "they" could have done this before we got out of range!

That argued for an attack; argued for attackers who might actually have trailed them some time before they landed last night, and waited for them to get into the sky again before launching a spell that would send them crashing to the ground.

So why didn't they come see if they'd killed us? Could they have been that sure of themselves? Could they simply not have cared?

Or could they be better at hiding themselves than he was at spotting them?

Could they be out there right now?

It was certainly possible that the attackers had struck from some distance away, and had not reached the site of the crash before he and Blade were up, alert, and able to defend themselves. The *kind* of attack certainly argued for a cowardly opponent, one who would want to wait until his prey was helpless or in an inescapable position before striking.

Unless, of course, he is simply a slow opponent; one who was making certain of every inch of ground between himself and us before he initiated a confrontation.

He sighed quietly. There was only one problem; this was all speculation. None of this gave him any hard evidence for or against anything. He just didn't have any facts beyond the simplest—that they *had* been the victim of something that destroyed their holds on magic and brought them tumbling helplessly down out of the sky.

So, for the rest of the night, he continued to scan the forest and keep his ears wide open, starting at every tiny sound, and cursing his unending headache.

Dawn was heralded by nothing more obvious than a gradual lightening of the darkness under the trees. Tad knew that his partner was about to waken when her breathing speeded up and her heartrate increased—both of which he could hear quite easily. At his side, Blade yawned, stirred, started to stretch, and swore under her breath at the pain that movement caused her.

Tad hooked a talon around the strap of the medical supply bag and dragged it over to her so she could rummage in it without moving much. She heard him, and shoved her hand in and pulled out one of the little vials; without being asked, he pierced the wax seal with his talon, and she drank it down.

Blade lay quietly for many long moments before her pain-killers took effect. "I assume nothing happened last night?" She made it an inquiry.

"Nothing worth talking about—except that I think there was some squabbling over the remains of the foodstuffs." He hadn't heard anything in particular except a few grunts and the sound of an impact, as if one of the scavengers had cuffed another. "We ought to consider putting out snares, especially whip-snares that would take a catch out of reach of the ground. It would be very frustrating to discover we'd trapped something, but a scavenger beat us to it."

She sat up slowly, rubbing her eyes with her good hand. "I should have thought of that last night," she said ruefully.

"They wouldn't have worked last night," he pointed out. "It was raining until well after dark. Chances are, the lines would have been ruined, or stakes pulled out of the mud. If it doesn't rain that badly today, we can put them out *after* the afternoon rains are over."

She yawned again, then grimaced and gingerly rubbed her bruised jaw. "Good idea," she agreed. "Snares are a more efficient means of getting us supplemental rations than hunting. We'll trap the area where I dumped the ruined food. Even if there's nothing left, animals still might come back hoping there will be. Oh, *gods*, I am stiff and sore!"

"I know precisely how you feel. I saved us some breakfast." He scraped away the ashes and revealed the cakes, now a bit crisper than they had been, and a bit grimier, but still edible. *I wish I had some bruise medicine that would work as well on me as hers does on her.*

"Did you!" She brightened, and scratched the back of her

neck with her good hand. "Well, that puts a better complexion on things! And my bruise remedy seems to have the additional value of keeping away bugs; for once I haven't got any new bites. Do you think you want another dose of your painkillers?"

He shook his head. "I took one as soon as it was light enough to see which vial was which." He handed her a cake, and ate the remaining three, neatly but quickly. One cake seemed to be substantial enough to satisfy her, though he noted that she did devour every crumb and licked her fingers clean afterward. Thanks to the fact that she had filled and refilled every container they had, he had even been able to get a drink without her assistance from a wide pot.

He waited until she ate, washed her face and hands, and looked a bit more alert. "Now what do we do?" he asked, as she dried off her face on her ruined tunic of yesterday. He made a mental note to have her set that out when the rains started, to give it a primitive wash.

She sat back on her heels, wincing as she jarred her shoulder. "Now—we discuss options," she said slowly. "What we do next, and where we go."

He stretched, taking care with his bandaged wing, and settled back again. "Options," he repeated after her. "Well, we both know that the best thing we can do is stay here. Right?"

"And build a beacon." She squinted past the canvas up through the treetops, at the tiny patches of sky visible, now and again, winking through the greenery like bright white eyes. "A very smoky beacon. It's going to take a lot of smoke to trickle up through that cover."

"It's going to take two or three days before they know we're missing," he said aloud, just to make certain he had all of his reasoning straight. "We have a shelter, and we can make it better and stronger, just by using available wood and leaves. I saw what you did with that windbreak, and we could certainly add layers of 'wall' that way over the canvas and wicker. If you look at the fallen leaves, you'll see that the ones you used dry up a lot like light leather; they'll hold up as shelter material."

She nodded, although she made a face. "It won't be easy, one-handed," she warned. "And I'm still the only decent knot tier in this team. You can bite holes, I can tie cord through them, but it is still tedious."

"So we take it slowly. I can do quite a bit, I just have to be careful." He paused for a moment, and went on. "We're injured, but I'm *still* a full-grown gryphon, and there aren't too many things that care to take on something my size, hurt or not."

"In that two or three days, whatever brought us down can find us, study us, and make its own plans," she countered, falling easily into the role of opposition—just as he would, when she proposed a plan. "We have to assume we were attacked and plan accordingly to defend ourselves. This place isn't exactly defensible."

He nodded; that was obvious enough. There was cover on all sides, and they didn't have the means to clear it all away, not even by burning it down.

Assuming they could. He wasn't willing to place bets on anything. Chances were, if they tried, nothing would happen; after all, they had no way to take down trees with trunks big enough for two and three men to put their arms around. But there was always the chance that they would succeed "better" than they anticipated—and set fire to the whole forest, trapping themselves in an inferno. He had not forgotten that the green wood around the fire last night had certainly burned more efficiently than he had anticipated. No, setting fire to this place to get a defensible clearing was not a good idea.

"We ought to be someplace where our beacon has a chance of being seen at night," she went on. "I don't think we made *that* big a hole in the tree cover when we went through it."

"We didn't; I checked." Too bad, but she was right. Half the use of the beacon was at night, but there wasn't a chance that a night flyer would see a fire on the ground unless it was much larger than one that two people could build and tend alone.

"The last problem is that there's no source of water here," she concluded, and held up her good hand. "I *know* we've had plenty of rain every afternoon ever since we entered this area, but we don't dare count on that. So—we're in an undistinguished spot with no landmarks, under the tree canopy, with nothing to put our backs against, and no source of water."

He grimaced. "When you put it that way, staying here doesn't seem like much of an option."

"We only have to go far enough to find a stream or a pond," she pointed out. "With luck, that might not be too far away. We'll get our break in the cover, and our water source, and we can worry about making it defensible when we see what kind of territory we're dealing with. But I think we ought to at least consider moving."

"Maybe," he said, doubtfully, "but—"

What he was going to reply was lost in the rumble of thunder overhead—and the spatter of rain on leaves.

"—not today," he breathed, as the rain came down again, as torrential as yesterday, but much earlier in the day.

Blade swore and stuck her head out to get a good look at the rain—a little too far, as she managed to jiggle the canvas and wicker of their roof just enough to send a cascade of cold water down the back of her neck. She jerked back, and turned white with pain.

The stream of oaths she uttered would have done a hardened trooper proud, but Tad didn't say anything. The cold water was insult enough, but when she lurched back, she must have really jarred her bad shoulder.

"I'll get wood," he offered hastily, and crawled slowly out of the shelter, trying not to disturb it any more.

Getting soaked was infinitely preferable to staying beside Blade when several things had gone wrong at once. She was his partner and his best friend—but he knew her and her temper very, very well.

And given the choice—I'd rather take a thunderstorm.

Tad

Five

"Wet gryphon," Blade announced, wrinkling her nose, "is definitely *not* in the same aromatic category as a bouquet of lilies."

"Neither is medicine-slathered human," Tad pointed out mildly. "I'll dry—but in the morning, you'll still be covered with that smelly soup."

Since he had just finished helping her wrap her limbs and torso in wet, brown bandages, he thought he had as much right to his observation as she had to hers.

In fact, he had shaken as much off his feathers as he could before he got into the tent, and he was not *wet* anymore, just damp. "And it could be worse. You could be sharing this shelter with a wet *kyree*," he added.

She made a face. "I've been stuck in a small space with a wet *kyree* before, and you are a bundle of fragrant herbs, if not a bouquet of lilies, compared to that experience."

Supper for her had been one of the pieces of travel-bread, which she had gnawed on rather like a *kyree* with a bone. They had been unbelievably lucky; Blade had spotted a curious climbing beast venturing down out of the canopy to look them over, and she had gotten it with her sling. It made a respectable meal, especially since Tad hadn't done much to exert himself and burn off breakfast.

He *had* gone out to get more wood, searching for windfall and dragging it back to the camp. Then he had done the reverse, taking what wreckage they were both certain was utterly useless and dropping it on the other side of their brush-palisade where they wouldn't always be falling over it.

Blade had gone out in the late afternoon to chop some of the wood Tad had found, and bathe herself all over in the rain. He had been a gentleman and kept his eyes averted, even though she wasn't his species. She was unusually body-shy for a Kaled'a'in—or perhaps it was simply that she guarded every bit of her privacy that she had any control over.

At any rate, she had gathered up her courage and taken a cold rain bath, dashing back in under the shelter to huddle in a blanket afterward. She claimed that she felt much better, but he wondered how much of that was bravado, or wishful thinking. She was a human and not built for forceful—or bad—landings. Although the basket had given her some protection, he had no real idea how badly hurt she was in comparison with him. Nor was she likely to tell him if she was hurt deeper than the skin-obvious. To his growing worry, he suspected that her silence might hide her emotional wounds as well.

After she was dry, she had asked his help with her bruise-medicines. There was no doubt of how effective they were; after the treatment yesterday, the bruises were fading, going from purple, dark blue, and black, to yellow, green and purple. While this was not the most attractive color-combination, it did indicate that she was healing faster than she would have without the treatments.

He finished the last scrap of meat, and offered her the bones. "You could put these in the fire and roast them," he said, as she hesitated. "Then you could eat the marrow. Marrow is rich in a lot of good things. This beast wasn't bad; the marrow has to have more taste than that chunk of bread you've been chewing."

"Straw would have more taste," she replied, and accepted the larger bones.

"I can bite the bones open later, if they don't split, and you can carve out the cooked marrow. We can use the long bone splinters as stakes. They might be useful," Tad offered.

Blade nodded, while trying unsuccessfully to stretch her arms. "You try and crunch up as much of those smaller bones as you can; they'll help your wing heal." She buried the bones in the ashes and watched them carefully as he obeyed her instructions and snapped off bits of the smaller bones to swallow. She *was* right; every gryphon knew that it took bone to build bone.

When one of the roasting bones split with an audible *crack*, she fished it quickly out of the fire. Scraping the soft, roasted marrow out of the bones with the tip of her knife, she spread it on her bread and ate it that way.

"This is better. It's almost good," she said, around a mouthful. "Thanks, Tad."

"My pleasure," he replied, pleased to see her mood slowly lifting. "Shall we set the same watches as last night?" He yawned hugely. "It's always easier for me to sleep on a full stomach."

"It's impossible to keep you awake when your belly's full, you mean," she retorted, but now she wore a ghost of a smile. "It's the best plan we have."

His wing did hurt less, or at least he thought it did. Gryphon bones tended to knit very quickly, like the bones of the birds that they were modeled after. Just at the moment, he was grateful that this was so; he preferred not to think about the consequences if somehow Blade had set his wing badly. Not that his days of fancy aerobatics would be over, but having his wing-bones rebroken and reset would be very unpleasant.

He peered up at the tree canopy, and as usual, saw nothing more than leaves. And rain, lots of it.

"I'm afraid we're in for another long rain like last night," he said ruefully. "So much for putting out snares."

"We can't have everything our way." She shrugged. "So far, we're doing all right. We could survive a week this way, with no problem—as long as nothing changes."

As long as nothing changes. Perhaps she had meant that to sound encouraging, but as he willed himself to sleep, he couldn't feel any encouragement. *Everything changes eventually. Only a fool would think otherwise. We might think we know what we're doing, but it only takes one serious mistake out here and we're dead. Even a minor mistake would mean that everything changes.*

The thought followed him down into his sleep, where it woke uneasy echoes among his dreams.

He slept so lightly that Blade did not need to shake him awake. He roused to the sound of water dripping steadily from the leaves above, the crackling and popping of the fire, and the calls of insects and frogs. That was *all.* It was very nearly silent out there, and it was a silence that was unnerving.

The forest that he knew fell silent in this way when a large and dangerous predator—such as a gryphon—was aprowl. He doubted that the denizens of this forest knew the two of them well enough to think that they were dangerous. That could only mean that something the local creatures *knew* was dangerous was out there.

Somewhere.

"Anything?" he whispered. She shook her head slightly without taking her eyes off the forest, and he noticed that she had banked the fire down so that it didn't dazzle her eyes.

He strained both eyes and ears, testing the night even as she did, and found nothing.

"It isn't that everything went quiet, it was that nothing much started making night-sounds after dark," she whispered back. "I suppose we might have driven all the local animals off—"

"Even the things that live up in the canopy? I doubt it," he replied. "Why would anything up there be afraid of us?"

She shrugged. "All I know is, I haven't heard or seen anything, but I have that unsettling feeling that something is watching us. Somewhere."

And whatever it is, the local creatures don't like it either. He had the same feeling, a crawling sensation at the back of his neck, and an itch in his talons. There were unfriendly eyes out there in the night, and Tad and Blade were at a disadvantage. *It* knew where they were and what they were. They had no idea what *it* was.

But if it hadn't attacked while he was asleep, hopefully it wouldn't while Blade took her rest. "Get to sleep," he told her. "If there's anything out there except our imaginations, it isn't likely to do anything now that I'm on watch. I look more formidable than you do, and I intend to reinforce that."

Under the packs holding Blade's clothing were his fighting-claws. He picked up her packs with his beak and fished them out. The bright steel winked cruelly in the subdued firelight, and he made a great show of fitting them on. Once Blade had fastened the straps, he settled back in, but with a more watchful stance than the previous night.

If there's nothing out there, I'm going to feel awfully stupid in the morning, for putting on all this show.

Well, better to feel stupid than be taken unaware by an attacker. Even if it was just an animal watching them, body language was something an animal could read very well. Hopefully, in the shiny claws and the alert stance, it would read the fact that attacking them would be a big mistake.

Blade pulled blankets around herself as she had the night before, but he noticed that she had a fighting-knife near at hand and her crossdraw knife under her pillow.

I just hope she can make herself sleep, he fretted a little. *She's going to be of no use if she's exhausted in the morning. If there was the slightest chance of convincing her to drink it, I'd offer her a sleeping tea.*

He waited all night, but nothing happened. Drops of water continued to *splat* down out of the trees, and frogs and insects sang, although nothing else moved or made a sound.

He began to wonder, toward dawn, if perhaps they *had* frightened away everything but the bugs and reptiles.

It wasn't likely, but it was possible. . . .

By the time the forest began to lighten with the coming of dawn, every muscle in his body ached with tension. His eyes twitched and burned with fatigue, and he could hardly wait for Blade to wake up. But he wouldn't awaken her himself. She needed her rest as much as he needed his.

Finally, when dawn had given way to full daylight, she stirred and came awake, all at once.

"Nothing," he said, answering her unspoken question. "Except that nothing larger than a gamebird made a sound all night, either, near the camp."

Now he moved, removing the fighting-claws, getting stiffly to his feet, and prowling out into the rising fog. He wanted to see what he could before the fog moved in and made it impossible to see again, shrouding in whiteness what the night had shrouded in black.

He was looking for foot- or paw-prints, places where the leaves had been pressed down by a body resting there for some time.

This was the area of which he was most proud. He wasn't just a *good* tracker, he was a great one. Blade was good, but he was a magnitude better than she.

Why a gryphon, who spent his life furlongs above the ground, should prove to be such a natural tracker was a total mystery to him. If Skandranon had boasted a similar ability, no one had ever mentioned it. He only knew that he had been the best in his group, and that he had impressed the best of the Kaled'a'in scouts. That was no small feat, since it was said of them that they could follow the track of the wind.

He suspected he would need every bit of that skill now.

He worked his way outward from the brush-fence, and found nothing, not the least sign that there had been anything out in the darkness last night except his imagination. He worked his way out far enough that he was certain no one and nothing could have seen a bit of the camp. By this time, he was laughing at himself.

I should have known better. Exhaustion, pain, and too many drugs. That's a combination guaranteed to make a person think he's being watched when he's alone in his own aerie.

He debated turning and going back to the camp; the fog was thickening with every moment, and he wouldn't be able to see much anyway. In fact, he had turned in his tracks, mentally rehearsing how he was going to make fun of himself to Blade, when he happened to glance over to the side at the spot where he had left the wreckage he had hauled out of the camp yesterday.

He froze in place, for that spot was not as he had left it. Nor did it look as if scavengers had simply been rummaging through it.

Every bit of trash had been meticulously taken apart, examined, and set aside in a series of piles. Here were the impressions he had looked for in vain, the marks of something, several somethings, that had lain in the leaf mold and pawed over every bit of useless debris.

His intuition, and Blade's, had been correct. It had not been weariness, pain, and the medicines. There *had* been something out here last night, and before it had set to watch the camp it had been right here. Some of the larger pieces of wreckage were missing, and there were no drag marks to show where they had been taken. That meant that whatever had been here had lifted the pieces and carried them off rather than dragging them.

And except for this one place, there was no trace of whatever had been here. The creature or creatures that had done this had eeled their way through the forest leaving nothing of themselves behind.

This couldn't be coincidence. It *had* to be the work of whatever had brought them crashing down out of the sky. Now their mysterious enemies, whatever they were, had spent the night studying him, Blade, and as much of the things belonging to them as had been left within their reach. They now had the advantage, for he and Blade knew nothing of them, not even if they ran on four legs, six, eight, two, or something else. All that he knew was that the creature— or creatures—they faced were intelligent enough to examine things minutely—and cunning enough to do so without clear detection.

He turned and ran back to the camp, despite the added pain it brought him. It was not simple fear that galvanized him, it was abject terror, for nothing can be worse to a gryphon than an opponent who is completely unknown.

As Tad spoke, Blade shivered, although the sun was high enough now that it had driven off the fog and replaced the cool damp with the usual heat and humidity. The pain, weariness, the drugs—all of them were taking their toll on her endurance. Her hands shook; her pale face told him that it wasn't fear that was making her shake, it was strain. This just might be the event that broke her nerve.

Tad had tried to be completely objective; he had tried only to report what he had seen, not what he had felt. Out there, faced with the evidence of their watchers, he had sensed a malignant purpose behind it all that he had no rational way of justifying. But Blade evidently felt the same way that he did, and rather than break, this new stress made her rally her resources. Her face remained pale, but her hands steadied, and so did her voice.

"We haven't a choice now," she said flatly. "We have to get out of here. We can't defend this place against creatures that can come and go without a sign that they were there. If we're lucky, they're territorial, and if we get far enough out of their territory, they'll be satisfied."

Once again, the wildlife of this place was mysteriously absent from their immediate vicinity; only a few birds called and cried in the canopy. Did they know something that the two below them did not?

"And if we're not, we'll be on the run with *no* secure

place to hole up," he argued. His focus sharpened, and he felt the feathers along his cheeks and jaws ripple. "If they can come and go without our seeing them, they can track us without our knowing they're behind us! I don't want some unseen enemy crawling up my tail. I want to see whoever I am against." That unnerved him, and he was not ashamed to show it. The idea that something could follow them, or get ahead of them and set an ambush, and he would never know it until it was too late. . . . It just made his guts bind and crawl.

Blade was quiet for a moment, chewing on her lower lip. All around them, water dripped slowly from the leaves, making the long fall to splash into puddles below, and the air was thick with the perfumes of strange flowers. "Look," she said, finally. "We didn't fly all that far before we were brought down. Twenty, maybe thirty leagues at most. We can go back in the direction of our previous campsite. *That* was defensible; remember, there was a cliff nearby? And remember the river that ran alongside it?"

Nervously, Tad flexed his talons into the loam. New scents rose to his nostrils, of earth and old leaves, dampness and the sharp aroma of a torn fungus. "You have a point." He thought about her suggestion, mentally trying to figure out how long it would take two injured people to walk the distance that two uninjured people had flown. *It isn't so much the distance, as what we have to cross to get there.* "It might take us as much as four days," he pointed out. "We don't have any real way of getting good directions other than the north-needle, and we're going to be crawling through leagues of this—" He waved his claw at the tangled undergrowth. "We're going to be carrying packs, we'll have to guard our backtrail and watch ahead for ambushes, and we're both injured. All of that will delay us; in fact, we probably ought to assume that we're going to be creeping through the forest, not hiking through it."

If we're going to do this, I want to creep. I want to go

from bit of cover to bit of cover; I want to walk so that we leave no sign and little scent. I want to leave traps behind.

"But when we get there—we'll be at a cliff face, Tad. That means caves, probably at least one waterfall; even if we don't find the river at first, we can work our way along the cliff until we do find the river. We'll at least have something we can put our backs against!" She looked unbelievably tense, and Tad didn't blame her. Of the two of them, she was the most vulnerable, physically, and the least able to defend herself, knife skill or not.

Not that either of us will be particularly good at it. In terrain like this, I'm at a distinct disadvantage. If anything gets in front of me, I can probably shred it, but at my sides and rear I'm badly vulnerable at close quarters.

If they left this camp, their choice of how to proceed was simple; pack out what they could, or try to live off the land with very little to aid them. Take the chance that they could improvise, or—

Or find out that we can't. We're hurt; we are going to need every edge we can get. That means tools, weapons, food, protection.

"The one advantage that we have is that whatever these creatures are, they don't know us, so they can't predict us," she persisted. "If we move now, we may confuse them. They may linger to look over what we left. We aren't going to lose them unless they lose interest in us, but we may leave them far enough behind that it will take them a while to catch up."

If only they had some idea of what kind of creature they were up against! The very fact that they would be trying to slip quietly through the forest rather than running might confuse their foes.

Or it might tempt them into an attack. They might read that as an admission of weakness. There was just no way of knowing.

He nodded, grinding his beak a bit. "Meanwhile, if we stay, they can study us at their leisure," he admitted. "And that makes us easy targets."

Go or stay? Remain where they were or try to find some place easier to defend?

Either way, they were targets. The only question was whether they made themselves moving targets or entrenched targets.

Aubri and Father always agreed on that; it's better to be a moving target than a stationary one. "All right, I agree," he conceded. "Let's make up two packs and get out of here. You might as well load me down; it isn't going to make a great deal of difference since I can't fly anyway."

She nodded, and wordlessly turned to rummage through the supplies cached in the tent. In a few moments, she handed him a pack to fill.

He joined her in picking through all the supplies they had salvaged. It was obvious what they were going to leave behind; just about everything they had saved. They would have to abandon everything that wasn't absolutely essential.

Their discards went everywhere, now that there was no point in sheltering them. If their foes *did* come to rummage through what they left behind, the confusion of belongings might gain them a little more time.

Clothing, personal items, those joined the rejected items; it was easier to decide what to leave than what to take. The piles of discards grew larger, with very few items making it into the packs. The medicine kit *had* to come along; so did the weapons, even though the pouches of lead shot were heavy. So far, there hadn't been anything around that Blade could use in the sling instead of lead shot. This was the wrong time of the year for fallen nuts; the soil here wasn't particularly rocky, and they couldn't count on a cairn of pebbles turning up at a convenient moment. The only distance-weapon she could use one-handed was the sling, so the shot had to come, too.

The food had to come with them, and some of the tools, and just enough bedding and canvas to keep them warm and dry at night. All of that cloth was bulky and heavy, but if they got soaked, they could easily die of cold-shock, even with a fire to keep them warm and dry them out. Then again—if they got soaked in another long rainstorm and they were caught without shelter, there would be no way to build a fire to warm them. No, the canvas half-shelter and a blanket apiece had to come along.

They were leaving a great deal for their opponents to look over, and Tad hoped that it would keep them very, very busy. *And if only I knew something, anything about "them," I'd be able to think of a way to keep them even busier!*

Part of their training included this sort of selection process, and they had learned just what was truly essential to survive. It didn't take long before they had two packs put together, one large, and one small. Blade would carry two spears and use them as walking sticks; that way she would have both aid and weapon in one. It had taken some ingenuity to rig her pack so that it would stay on with a minimum of pain—there couldn't have been a worse injury than a broken collarbone when it came to carrying a pack. Much of the weight was going to fall on her hips, now, and would probably cause bruises and abrasions. Both Tad and Blade had come to accept that pain was going to be an omnipresent part of their immediate future, and their concern regarding it was more a case of figuring out ways to lessen its immediate impact, since eliminating it was impossible. 'Endure now, heal later' was the philosophy that would serve them best.

The morning fog was just beginning to lift when they took a bearing with the north-needle and headed into the west. Blade led in more open areas. She was small—they both had the feeling that if an attack came, it would come from the rear. *He* was better suited to bearing the brunt of an attack from the front than she, and in open areas he could turn around quickly to help Blade. In close quarters, he led, with Blade guarding his tail. They were still vulnerable from the sides, but it was better than a completely unguarded rear. They had discussed booby-trapping the camp, but decided against it. If their foes were kept nicely busy with what remained, that was good, but if one of their number was hurt or killed by a booby-trap, it might make them angry and send them hot on the trail, after revenge. Also, discovery of one trap might make whatever it was give up on a search of the camp entirely and go straight into tracking them, which would lose them valuable distance.

As they left the area, Tad paused once for a look back at the camp, wondering if they were making a dreadful mistake. They were leaving so much behind, so much that they might need desperately in the next few days! But their pathetic little shelter looked even more vulnerable now, and rationally, he knew that it couldn't withstand a single determined blow, much less a coordinated attack by several creatures at once. In fact, with its canvas-over-wicker construction, it *could* become a trap for both of them. It wouldn't take much to drive the supporting saplings through the wicker-work. . . .

A shiver ran along his spine at that thought, for it was all too easy to picture something slamming the cup of wicker down on top of them, trapping them inside, where they would be helpless to defend themselves. . . .

With a shudder, he turned away, and followed after Blade as she picked her way through the tangled growth of the forest floor.

There was still fog in the treetops, just high enough that there was no real way for them to tell precisely where the sun was. In a little while, the last of the fog would burn off completely, and then they might be able to cross-check their bearings with the angle of the sun—although so far, they hadn't been able to manage that yet.

We'll know where we are exactly, but only if we can find a hole big enough to see the sun through. And then it will only be possible if the sun is high enough to shine down through the hole at the time we find it.

Living in this forest was like living inside an enormous, thick-aired cave. How could anything that lived here know where it was? It was very disorienting for Tad not to be able to see the sky, and somewhat claustrophobic; he wondered if Blade felt the same as he.

She seemed determined to concentrate on the forest

ahead, slipping carefully through the underbrush in such a way that she disturbed as little as possible. The kind of leaf litter that served as the forest floor didn't hold tracks very well, and if their enemies could just hold off following until the afternoon rains started, it wouldn't hold a scent very well either. If she found their surroundings claustrophobic, she wasn't letting the feeling interfere with what she was doing.

But he kept swiveling his head in all directions every time they paused to pick a good route. Those frequent pauses as she pondered her route to the next bit of cover gave him ample opportunity to feel the forest closing in on him. His nerves were afire with tension; he couldn't imagine why she wouldn't feel the same.

But maybe she doesn't; maybe this doesn't bother her. Maybe she doesn't even need to feel sky and wind. He had always known that humans weren't like gryphons, and that thought made her seem positively alien for a moment.

But, then again, she lived in a veritable burrow back in White Gryphon, so maybe this landscape felt cozy to her, rather than constricting. But oh, how he longed for enough room to spread his wings wide, even if that longing reminded him pointedly that he *couldn't* spread them at the moment!

As Blade eeled her way between two bushes that were barely far enough apart to let him through, he realized something else that was very strange. There weren't any game trails here.

That realization was just as disconcerting to him as not being able to see the sky. He *knew* there were some large animals that lived down here on the forest floor, so why didn't they leave regular trails? There should be deer trails, going to and from water. Deer couldn't collect rainwater in vessels to drink, obviously; they had to have a water source. He had never in all of his life encountered a deer herd that didn't make paths through their territory just by virtue of the fact that there were a lot of them going in the same direction.

Was there something living down here that was so dangerous that it was suicidal to *have* a regular trail, foolhardy to move in groups large enough to make one?

Could that something be what had brought them down, and what had been examining their ruined belongings?

That's altogether too logical, and is not a comforting thought. I know there are large cats like lions here, and bears, because the Haighlei told us there were—yet I have never seen deer and wild pigs afraid to make game trails in lion or bear country. If there is something else living here that makes creatures who regularly face lions afraid to leave a game trail. . . .

The answer could be that whatever this putative creature was happened to be so fierce, so bloodthirsty, that it wasn't safe for herbivores to travel in herds. That it was the kind of creature that slaughtered everything within its reach, whether or not it was hungry. He swallowed, his throat feeling tight and dry.

But he might be overreacting again. He didn't *like* this place; perhaps his imagination was getting the better of him. *Maybe we just are in a bad place in the forest. Maybe there's nothing here worth foraging for to bring deer and other browsers into this area. There certainly doesn't seem to be anything tasty for a plant eater to feed on; all these bushes are extraordinarily tough and we've seen precious little grass. Maybe that's why there aren't any trails through here; it simply isn't worth a deer's time to come here.*

And perhaps that was the reason for the unnatural silence all about them.

There might be an even better explanation for the silence—they were dreadfully *obvious* to anything watching and listening. Despite the fact that they were trying very hard to be quiet, the inevitable sounds they were making were an unholy racket in contrast with the silence surrounding them. Try as they might, as they passed from one spot of cover to the next, they rattled vines and rustled bushes, and none of those noises sounded natural.

*And anything living up in the trees is going to have a fine
view of us down below. I doubt that Blade looks harmless
to what's up there, and I know I don't. I look like a very
large, if oddly shaped, eagle.*

Tree dwellers might not recognize Blade as a predator, but
they would certainly recognize Tad. There were eagles here,
they knew that for a fact, for he had seen them flying below
him, hunting in and above the forest canopy. Anything that
looked like an eagle was going make a canopy dweller nervous.

And yet. . .there hadn't been a silence this wary and pro-
found since they had felt as if they were being watched. For
that matter, the tree dwellers hadn't been particularly quiet
in any of the other places that they had camped before they
had crashed.

*This is exactly like the silence that falls when an eagle-
owl is hunting, and everything stays absolutely quiet and
motionless until the moment it makes a kill, hoping that
whatever it is hunting, it will not find one of them.*

There weren't even the sounds made when other animals
hunted . . . *but when a greater predator prowls, the lesser remains silent and hidden. Are we the greater predators, or is
something else?*

Perhaps he should put his mind to thinking of ways to delay pursuit.

*If whatever-it-is does come after us, it wouldn't matter
now if I laid booby-traps behind us. Would it? How much
worse could I make things, if I hurt something that was following us?*

Well, the answer to that could well be—much worse. Why
anger something that was following only out of curiosity?

Perhaps not booby-traps then, at least not yet. Perhaps
just things to confuse the trail. The first thing to confuse
would be scent, because that was of primary importance to a
ground-dwelling predator in an environment like this one.
There wasn't much of a line-of-sight, but scent would hold
and cling until the next rain washed it away. And by then, a
trail would more than likely be too cold to follow anyway.

He began watching for a vine with leaves veined with purple and red; it had a pungent, peppery smell. He'd noticed that they were fairly common, and when he finally spotted one, he hissed at Blade to stop for a moment.

When they next moved on, it was with the thick juice from those leaves rubbed all over their feet and hands—and they were going to have to remember not to rub their eyes until they washed it off, for it burned just like real pepper! There were other plants, less common, that had equally distinctive odors, and as he came across them he intended to gather generous samples. Every time the current scent was about to wear off, he'd change it. If anything came hunting them depending on its nose, he'd have handed it a surprise. And maybe one of these plants would have the effect of numbing a sensitive nose.

He had to hope this ploy would work, for they were certainly proceeding at a crawl to begin with, and their progress only slowed as the day progressed. His pack was awkward, heavy, and made his bad wing and all his bruises ache; he wasn't suited to walking in the first place, and his injuries combined with the pack only made it worse. Fortunately for his own feelings, Blade wasn't doing any better, so he wasn't in the position of knowing that he was the one impeding their progress.

The longer they walked, the worse it got. Eventually the fog burned off, and the temperature rose, so that he was overheated as well as in pain. Blade's shirt stuck to her, dark with sweat. He couldn't sweat, so he panted. Neither sweating nor panting brought any relief in the humid air; it must have been nearly as sultry as a Kaled'a'in steambath. There wasn't a breath of breeze down here to stir the heavy air. If he had been left to his own devices, he'd have called a halt and flung himself to the ground for a rest.

As he had predicted, their progress was measured in furlongs, not leagues, with no discernible differences in the territory that they crossed. He could only be certain that they were not walking in circles by virtue of the fact that Blade kept checking the north-needle every time they stopped moving. They stopped for a brief break and something to eat. The sun actually penetrated the canopy in a few places eventually, but it was not much help in showing them where they were. There wasn't enough of it visible to help them get a bearing from it, either by using a measuring stick or by taking the angle of it.

In fact, the sunlight proved to be something of a new hazard. The beams of sunlight lancing down through the dark green leaves *were* very pretty, very picturesque, but they were also to be avoided at all costs. Pinned even for a moment in such a bright light, they would be extremely obvious as something that didn't belong there.

There were still no signs of any watercourses, either, which probably meant that this forest depended on rain rather than ground water for the trees to thrive. That was not precisely a surprise, given the daily thunderstorms.

But a creek or a small stream would have given them a path to a river, and a way to break their trail completely. If they were ever able to wade for some distance along the path of a creek bed, they would completely lose anything that hunted by scent. He had been hoping for a stream, in fact, for that very reason.

That, and stream water would certainly be cooler than the water in my water skin. The tepid liquid he was carrying had not been particularly refreshing, although he had drunk his ration dutifully. *And it would taste better. Much better.*

But there was no sign of any sort of a stream, and eventually the beams of sunlight faded, the light all about them dimmed, and a distant rumble heralded the afternoon storm approaching. At that point, despite their lack of progress, he was almost grateful to hear it. Now they would have to stop and rig a shelter for the night, because it wouldn't be long before the rain started to fall and made it impossible to get anything constructed.

Blade stopped, held up her hand, then motioned him up beside her.

"We've got to stop and get our canvas up," she said, weariness in every syllable. He felt instantly sorry for her; she sounded even more tired than he was.

She pointed ahead, to one of the few distinctive places he'd seen in this forest. There was a break in the cover, through which the fat, gray bellies of the clouds were clearly visible; at some point in the past few years one of the forest giants had toppled here. They edged forward to a place where the hollowed-out carcass of an ancient snag stood, half-covered with vines, the remains of the rest of the tree lying on the ground beside it, smothered in vines and plants. "That snag is big enough to hold both of us. We'll use that for the base of our shelter; it's the closest thing I've seen today to something that we can count on to protect us overnight."

And she doesn't mean from the rain. He nodded. Abandoning any pretext at moving quietly, they thrashed their way through the undergrowth to the giant snag. It stood a little taller than Blade's head, and as she had stated, was just large enough to hold both of them in its hollow interior. There was no room for a fire, but in confines that close, they would keep each other warm with the heat of their bodies.

And I'm not certain that I want a fire to advertise our presence tonight.

They *were* going to need one initially, though—otherwise they were going to be sharing this shelter with a wide variety of multi-legged guests. Rotten wood meant insects, and some of them could be noxious or even poisonous.

They didn't have much time before the storm broke, though; perhaps not enough time for Blade to use the fire-striker to start a fire in the hollow. But he *was* a mage, and the easiest spell in the lexicon was to call fire.

Dare I? It could have been the mere presence of magic that got us attacked. . . . Well, if I don't, she might not get a torch going before the rain comes. And the fire-spell is so very small, so limited in scope and duration—I'd better chance it. "Move back," he ordered her; as soon as she had obeyed, he closed his eyes, concentrated—and called fire into the midst of the hollowed-out trunk.

There was enough in the way of dry leaves and dry, half-rotted woodchips on the floor of the snag to start an enthusiastic and very smoky fire. The smoke had the immediate effect of driving out everything that could leap or fly; Blade bundled other burnables together into two torches and they lit both at the fire and proceeded to char the interior. Smoke rose all about them in a thick fog; he coughed and backed out to get a breath of cleaner air more than once. Half-rotten wood did not give off the kind of pleasant smoke that made sitting beside a campfire a pleasure. It was a pity they hadn't come upon this place earlier; some of the grubs might have been very tasty, especially cooked. Now their only concern was to rid the tree of all other inhabitants before the rains came.

He coughed again, as a new and more acrid set of odors joined the heavy smoke. *We must have hit a nest of something nasty. Ugh. Or maybe we've just incinerated a crop of unpleasant fungi.* He hoped that whatever they burned off didn't give off poisonous fumes. *A little late to worry about that now.*

They didn't quite beat the downpour completely. They were in the process of roofing the snag with their canvas and tying it down when the first cloudburst descended, wetting them both to the skin.

At that point, Blade gave in to the inevitable and stood in the downpour until she and her clothing had been flushed clean, and he let the rain wash all of the soot and dirt from his own feathers before shaking himself partially dry under the shelter of a nearby tree. It was too bad that Blade's clothing didn't sluice clean so easily, nor could she shake herself dry. He made a dash to the snag and squeezed himself into the downed tree with the supplies. She had already gotten out blankets and bread and dried meat. He tucked the packs up in a way that she could sleep on them, and put her blanket on top of the pile. He had to put the dried meat out into the stream of water pouring off the canvas and soak it until he could eat it. Meanwhile, Blade emptied and refilled their water skins, then joined him in their shelter.

Their combined body heat did do something to warm the interior; with blankets over each of them, they weren't completely miserable, and Blade's clothing actually began to dry out. And the strong smell of smoke wasn't too bad after a while—though they must not have gotten all of the bugs out of their shelter, since periodically he would feel a small one taking a trip under his feathers, or Blade would slap at something. Once again, the rain persisted until after nightfall, though once it stopped, it was—again—uncannily silent beneath the trees.

"Damn," Blade whispered. "I was hoping. . . ."

"That we'd left them behind?" Tad was altogether glad of the thick wood at his back, and of the deep shadow of the interior of their shelter. Not even an owl would be able to see them in here. "It might not be *them* that's making everything so quiet. It might just be the smell of smoke; you know how most wild things fear fire."

"And I might be the Haighlei Emperor. No, they're out there. They followed us, I'm sure of it." She stared out into the darkness fiercely, as if willing her eyes to be better than they actually were.

"Well, they can't get us in here," he said, and meant it. "It's safe enough for you to sleep if you want to take second watch this time."

"You can't sleep?" she asked. He shook his head.

It was true, he *wasn't* going to be able to sleep for a while; he was horribly tired, but not sleepy. His muscles kept twitching and jumping with accumulated fatigue. His nerves all felt strung as tightly as a Kaled'a'in horse-bow, and every tiny sound out there had him peering into the darkness as fiercely as she. It was going to be some time before he relaxed enough to fall asleep.

"Well, I think I've reached the limit on my nerves," she replied, punctuating the sentence with a yawn. "Believe it or not, I'm going numb. Right now, I hurt so much that all I want to do is drink my medicine and drop off as soon as the pain stops. In fact, right now, *they* could come kill me as long as they did it while I was asleep; I just can't get up the energy to care."

"I know how you feel." Awkwardly, he managed to pat her leg in sympathy. "You go ahead. I'll take the first watch as long as I can."

She sounded fatalistic; he wasn't quite ready to share that emotion, but there was something else to consider. *I'm not sure it would matter if we both fell asleep tonight. So far, we haven't any evidence beyond the fact that something probably dangerous is probably following us. They haven't actually done anything. Even assuming that they intend to attack us, as cautious as they have been, I don't think they're ready to try and pry us out of some place like this.* "I think we're as safe as we can be under the circumstances. Get some sleep while you can."

She didn't need a second invitation. In an instant, she had downed her vial of medicine and curled up against his side in her blanket, propped up by the packs to save her shoulder. Provided she didn't get a kink in her neck from sleeping this way, or stiff muscles from a chill, she ought to be more comfortable tonight than she had been since the accident.

He stared out into the darkness until his eyes burned— and just as he was contemplating waking her to take her watch, the forest itself woke. But not with sounds of alarm—to his intense relief, these were *normal* night sounds, the same they had heard every other night of this journey.

The *whoop* of something up above startled Blade awake. She came alive with a jerk and a thin gasp of pain. "What?" she demanded, then relaxed as she recognized the noises outside their shelter for what they were.

The sudden onset of normal night sounds had been the trigger that let all of his own fatigue catch up with him. Suddenly, he could not keep his eyes open, no matter how hard he tried. He was actually nodding off even as he stared into the dark.

"Can you take over?" he whispered, and felt her nod. That was all he needed; a moment later, not even the scream of a makaar would have awakened him.

For the second time that morning, Blade motioned to Tad to freeze. Obedient to her hand gesture, he went rigid, and for something as huge as he was, he blended into the forest surprisingly well. His eyes were fixed on her, not on the forest around him; that was because she hadn't used the gesture that meant *danger*, just the one that meant *wait*.

In fact, there was no danger, only an opportunity. She had spotted another of the long-limbed tree dwellers climbing cautiously down out of the canopy, in pursuit of something it had dropped. This must be a young one; the elders never were so foolish as to risk coming down into the danger zone just because they wanted something they had lost. If she was lucky, this one would not survive a lesson in *why* they did not.

Although this hunting was delaying them, it was a necessary delay.

Her quarry dropped down off the tree trunk and took two cautious steps on the forest floor, reaching for the bright object it had lost. It had four long limbs, a pointed snout, and large eyes set on the sides of its head. If it had been up in the canopy, she would never have been able to spot it, for its brown fur blended in beautifully with the bark of the tree. Not that she could have reached it with her puny weapon, either. Nothing short of a very powerful bow would put a missile up into the canopy with force great enough to kill.

She whirled her sling twice and let fly.

The beast barely had time to register the movement and start to turn his head. Then the lead shot struck it squarely on the skull with a wet *crack*, and it dropped to the ground, instantly dead.

Grinning with elation, she ran forward anyway, just to make certain of it with her knife; fresh meat was too precious a commodity for her to take any chances that it might

simply be stunned. When she finished, she stood up and motioned Tad to come up and join her.

She straightened and walked over to see what it had
dropped. The brightly colored object that had exerted a fatal
attraction for this tree dweller proved to be absolutely
unidentifiable. It was bladderlike, and a bright blue and red.
It could have been a flower, a seed pod, a fruit, even an insect carapace or a portion of some other unfortunate animal.
She ignored it at that point; perhaps it was edible, but this
was not the time nor the place to experiment.

Tad, meanwhile, had made short work of her prey. It hadn't
been very large, and he had dismembered it and eaten it almost whole. This was the second such catch she'd made this
morning for him, and he looked much the better for the fresh
meat. The first had been a rodent, both rabbitlike and rat-like;
bigger than a rat, but small for a rabbit. This one was about
the size of a large rabbit, though the long limbs had made it
look bigger. If her luck kept up, she'd be able to keep *him* in
fresh-killed prey, mouthful by mouthful. That would take
one worry away from her; how to keep him from starving.
Gryphons weren't big eaters just by choice.

Although the forest sounds had by no means returned to
normal, there were more signs of other living things now,
which made her feel a bit better. Maybe they were outdis-
tancing their invisible trackers. Or maybe those trackers
were just waiting until nightfall to move in on them.

At least this meant that she could actually *see* some game
to take down.

*I can probably get enough small animals and birds over
the course of the day to keep Tad in good shape,* she decided,
retrieving the bit of lead shot and pocketing it before checking her north-needle. Tad had cautiously taken the downed
creature into the shelter of a bush to eat it; she pressed herself
against the bole of the tree and picked the next landmark they
would head for. That was how she was navigating, in line-of-
sight increments; checking her north-needle, picking a particular bit of distant cover that was farther west, and moving in

toward it. Not only were they—hopefully—avoiding being spotted by their foe, they were not frightening the game.

She made two more such moves when she spotted another one of the rat-rabbits, nosing about on the forest floor in search of something edible. She warned Tad to freeze and potted it, too. That made three pieces of small game in about three marks, or one piece per mark, and she was beginning to feel very proud of herself. That was not at all bad for someone hampered by a bad shoulder, with a primitive weapon, in unfamiliar territory. *If I remember my gryphon-rations correctly, he should actually prosper on that amount of food. Granted, it's like feeding a hawk by tidbitting it, but beggars can't be choosers. If he isn't exactly full at any one time, he isn't going hungry, either.*

He looked faintly annoyed at being asked to swallow another bit of game every mark or so, but he didn't say anything. He was used to eating once lightly, and once hugely, then sleeping on that larger meal. He probably wondered why they were stopping so frequently just so he could eat.

But if she carried the game until they had enough for him to have that single large meal, she'd be weighing herself down for no good purpose. Let the game ride in the most efficient way possible; inside Tad.

If he hasn't figured out what I'm doing, he will soon, she decided, moving on ahead.

She was worried about him; in spite of the fact that she was the one with the worse injury—as her shoulder reminded her sharply of just how badly hurt she was, every time she moved a bit too quickly—in some ways he was the more vulnerable of the two of them.

She knew, only too well, just how vulnerable he was. Trapped on the ground as he was, he had as many weaknesses as she did. Unless he could get his back up against something to protect it, he could not only be attacked from the rear, but from below. Most of what he had learned about fighting was meant for aerial combat, not ground fighting. Granted, he could improvise, and granted, he had four sets of very nasty "knives" on the end of each limb, not to mention the weapon in the middle of his face, but he was made for another element. Faced with the need to fight on terms and terrain he was not suited to, he was vulnerable in ways even he probably didn't realize.

His other weakness was the sheer volume of food he had to consume in order to stay in decent physical shape. If she couldn't get that into him—well, too many days of rain-soaked dried meat, and he wouldn't be in good condition at all.

Too many days of that kind of ration, and we'll have to find a permanent place to hole up, because he won't even be able to travel.

Walking was much harder on him than flying; he wasn't built for it. Intellectually, of course, she had known that; watching him try to move through the underbrush had driven it home to her in a more concrete form.

He was *not* clumsy; he was a great deal more graceful at this sort of travel than his classmates had ever been. He was, in fact, as adept at it as some humans—but he tired easily, and occasionally his wings got caught up on some obstacle or other. It would be some time before his legs strengthened and gained the endurance for steady walking, and until then, he was handicapped.

If they ever ran across a large browser like a deer, he *should* be able to bring it down so long as they surprised it, but until then she was the better ground hunter. He was going to be depending on her for something he was normally self-sufficient at.

She was just grateful that he was as good a tracker as he was. He'd done a fair amount to confuse their scent and backtrail, and that could only help right now.

That might be one of the reasons I'm spotting game today; that muck he had us rub all over ourselves is probably hiding our scent and confusing the tree dwellers. Scent rose, especially in *this* heat; a wary canopy beast would not come anywhere near the ground with the scent of a large predator coming up to meet his nose, but at the moment all that they smelled like was crushed plants.

And that might very well be the explanation of why they had been surrounded by silence until lately. Quite frankly, Tad was damp, and he smelled like—well—damp raptor, a combination of wet feathers and the heavy musk that was peculiar to gryphons and birds of prey. He hadn't been able to dry out properly since the accident, and that made his scent more obvious. *Could be that when we first camped, not only was he not as fragrant, but we simply weren't on the ground long enough for the scent to rise into the canopy. Now we are.*

That speculation made her feel a little better; and the current state of affairs did seem to offer support for that speculation. Tad didn't smell like raptor, wet *or* dry, at the moment. The juicy plant he had her rub all over both of them imparted a peculiar, sharp, mossy scent to their respective hides. It made a hideous mess of her clothing, streaking it a mottled green, but she wasn't particularly worried about stains.

Besides, the stains make a fairly good impromptu camouflage.

She ought to start looking for a good place to go to ground for the night. As she kept an eye out, she tried to mentally reckon up the time it would take for them to be missed. They ought to start putting up some sort of signal if there was any chance that the White Gryphon people might be looking for it.

We should have made our rendezvous today or tomorrow, so by tomorrow or the day after, the Silvers we're relieving will know there's something wrong. They have a teleson; they'll let Judeth know, but it would take a team of rescuers coming at full speed another two or three days to reach here. So—what does that make it? Another two or three days before help will have a chance of being here at best. More likely a week.

So there was no point in looking for a shelter *and* a place where they could set up a good signal fire. Shelter alone would do for today and tomorrow.

Nothing presented itself for another mark—except the first signs she had seen yet of large animals on the forest floor. She came across a place where a pig had clearly been rooting at the base of a tree, searching for underground fungi, and with regret she saw that the trail went off into the north and not the west. A pig would have been very welcome to both her and Tad.

But she was not going to risk going off in a different direction on just the chance that they might be able to bring one down.

The heat was oppressive; when the rains came again, she had every intention of soaking herself and her clothing. If she didn't, by tomorrow morning her tunic and trews would be able to stand by themselves, they were so saturated with sweat. She was grateful to Tad for his subterfuge with the plant scent for more reasons than the obvious; without the pungent aroma of crushed leaf hanging around her, she would be smelling herself by now.

On the other hand, maybe if I smelled bad enough, our trackers would be offended and leave us alone. Hah!

Sweat trickled steadily down the back of her neck, and her hair itched unbearably. For that matter, so did her feet, shins, armpits. . . any number of tiny forest insects were finding her tasty fare, and she was covered with itching, red welts. Something she had forgotten was that their original tent not only set itself up and took itself down, the spells on it protected them from insects. Without that protection, she seemed to be the only source of food for every bloodsucker for furlongs about, except for the ones buzzing about poor Tad's eyes and ears. Her bruise-medicine eased the itching enough for her to sleep, but she would have given a great deal to discover a plant that rendered her inedible to bugs. Every time she paused, she found herself reaching inside her clothing to scratch at another itch.

She kept reminding her herself to *rub*, not scratch. If she broke the skin, she opened herself up to infection—if she bled, she added a particularly tasty scent to her own, and one the plant juice would not cover.

Something near her ear buzzed, landed, and bit. She slapped and swore, as Tad crept into cover beside her.

We may not need stalking beasts to finish us off. The insects may nibble us to death.

"Ants," Tad muttered in her ear.

"Is that what just got me?" she asked without turning her head.

"No. That had wings and a long nose. I am reminding myself to lie on an anthill, if we can find some of the small brown ones. It will be irritating, but they will rid me of any passengers I may be carrying. Their secretions, when the ants are angered, drive away mites and other small pests."

She felt a twinge of raw envy; if only it could be that easy for her! But lying on an anthill would do her no good since most of the bugs that plagued her were winged, and the subsequent ant bites would be just as irritating as her current crop of bites and stings.

She couldn't wait for the afternoon rain; sweat made the bites itch worse, and standing in the pouring cold water gave her the few moments of complete relief she got from the incessant itching.

Time to move. Maybe we'll find a stream today, and I can go to sleep lying in it! Then again, given our current luck, if we found a stream it would be infested with leeches.

Never mind. The one thing they had to do was keep moving, and cope with whatever came up. It couldn't be more than a week until help came.

All they had to do was to survive that long.

Ikala

Six

Ah, hells. This isn't easy, one-handed. A bit off-balance because of her injured shoulder, Blade threw her final bundle of branches over the canvas of tonight's shelter just as the first rumbles of thunder began in the distance.

Ah, damn! That hurt!

Blade doubled over despite herself. Her chest felt constricted, as if cinched tight with rope. Thunder rumbled again, nearer. She'd finished just in time, though not too soon so far as she was concerned; she was ready for the rain, more than ready by now. As she straightened up, she had no doubts that she was ready for rest as well.

This shelter was both superior and inferior to the last one; like last night's, it was also based on the remains of a fallen tree, but this tree had fallen quite recently. The splintered wood of the trunk shone fresh and pale against the greenery, which was how she had spotted it in the first place. Although there were no hollow places in the trunk or snag to shelter in, the tree had taken down another right next to it in its fall, and there was an intersection of the two trunks, providing a triangular area with two man-high "walls" of wood. Stretching the canvas over the top of this place made a roof; piling branches on top of the canvas disguised their presence. A further barricade of brush hid the entrance, and they would even have the luxury of a small fire tonight, screened from view by the brush. More branchlets over a pile of big leaves made a springy floor, giving them more comfort tonight than they had enjoyed since the accident.

Now if only she could find something in her medicines to numb these damned insect bites!

Thunder rumbled again, overhead this time. In the course of gathering their branches, she had stirred up many tiny animals; mice, lizards, snakes, and frogs. She had caught and killed as many of those as she could, and tonight she and Tad would supplement their dinner with these tidbits. Individually, they weren't impressive, but she had collected an entire sack of them, enough to give Tad much-needed supplements. She'd probably appropriate a couple of snakes to roast and give some flavor to her flavorless bread, but the rest would go to Tad.

She would be adding insects to her ration, for she had found grubs of a wood-borer that she recognized, ant pupae, and crickets, all of which she could choke down so long as they were toasted. When she had been going through survival training, she had never *really* pictured herself putting any of her training into practice!

Well, I have this much revenge; if the bugs are eating me, I'm eating the bugs! Insects were really too small to do Tad any good, so by default they went to her.

Tad was inside the shelter arranging things and getting the fire going, and she thanked the Star-Eyed that he had enough magic to light fires again. With the help of magic, even the greenest, wettest wood could be coaxed to burn. Without it—they'd have a poor fire, or none, and she could not bear the thought of eating untoasted bugs.

I'd rather go hungry a bit. I might get hungry enough to consider it, but not now.

Their shelter lay underneath a long slit of sky, cleared by the falling tree. It had shown gray when they first arrived here, gray with those fat, round-bellied clouds, and had been growing steadily darker ever since, as the inevitable afternoon storm gathered strength. Was it her imagination, or were those storms coming earlier every afternoon?

She remained standing where she was, watching the clouds overhead, while the dark gray went bright white periodically and thunder followed the lightning. As the sky darkened steadily, the ambient light dimmed, stealing the color from the leaves, softening the edges of the shadows, and painting the clearing in shades of indigo blue. White light suddenly flooded the entire area, not just the clouds. Lightning lanced across the raw sky and thunder cracked right overhead, making her jump and yelp involuntarily— and jolting her shoulder again, which made her swear.

She forced herself to hold still, to wait for the pain to ebb. *I ought to be used to this by now—* But she wasn't; every time she jerked her shoulder, the pain lanced down her arm and up her neck. It wasn't getting any better. She could only hope that she was just being impatient, and that this didn't mean that it wasn't healing.

Two breaths after the lightning came the rain. As always, it poured down in a torrent. She held out her good arm and tilted her head up, letting the sweet, cool water wash away all the sweat and grime she had accumulated, opening her mouth and drinking the fresh, clean liquid. It actually eased her thirst and did not taste of warm leather. As sweat washed away and her skin cooled down, her insect bites stopped itching.

With walls of trunk on either side of her, she felt secure enough to stand out in the open and indulge herself; the only thing that would have improved the situation would have been a bar of soap! But even with nothing but water, she was getting reasonably clean, and that always made her temper improve. She stood out in the downpour until the dark green stains on her tunic faded to match the others already there, until she was as chilled as she had been overheated the moment before, until the swollen welts of her insect bites stood out against her cold, pallid arms and the bites themselves no longer bothered her at all. There was something very exhilarating and elemental about standing out in a storm like this one; powerful storms back home had always been too cold and dangerous to "play" in, something that had disappointed her ever since she was a child. But here—there wasn't much chance that she would be struck by lightning when everything else around her was so very much taller than she, and to be able to stand out in rain so heavy that it literally stole the breath was an intoxicating experience. It was enough to make her forget her pain, almost enough to make her forget their danger.

Is this what Tad feels when he flies? If so, I envy him. Is this the way it feels to not face people, not be in a building or cave, and be encompassed by the elements? To stand alone and alive as a living creature only, and not as Someone's Offspring? Is this the moment that makes all the pettiness of everyday living worthwhile?

Only when she was so chilled she had begun to shiver did she duck her head and scuttle back to the heap of branches that covered their shelter.

She pushed past the brush and almost went back out into the rain when she encountered a thick cloud of eye-watering smoke.

"What—what *is* this?" she demanded as, coughing, she fanned her hand in front of her face and dropped to the ground where the air was marginally clearer.

"Sorry," Tad said apologetically. "I'm trying to get rid of the bugs, both in here and on me. It's working; I certainly got rid of my little plague."

"You almost got rid of me," she grumbled, crawling all the way inside to settle beside him. More thunder punctuated her statement. "I suppose it'll be worth it if this smoke-weapon of yours allows us to get a good night's sleep." Then she laughed. "But if I'd known that this was how you were going to interpret my wish for an herb to repel insects, I might have been more careful in what I asked for!"

He gryph-grinned at her, his beak gaping wide. "You didn't

remember Drake's favorite proverb—'Be careful what you ask for'—"

"I know, I know," she groaned.

Tad had been snacking, and the bag was almost empty, but he had saved her two of the biggest snakes—though they weren't very big, being no longer than her forearm. One was brown, one was green, and both looked vaguely orange in the uncertain light. Tad carefully scraped some hot coals to one side with a stick, then added drier wood to the rest of the fire.

She skinned out the snakes with Tad's help, then arranged her snakes, along with her harvest of crickets, grubs, and pupae, on the blade of their shovel and placed that on top of the glowing coals. There wasn't much aroma, but her bugs did toast quickly, and she was very hungry by now. She picked them gingerly off the hot metal and ate them, trying not to think too hard about what she was doing. They weren't too bad, though; she could almost imagine that she was eating toasted grain if she didn't pay too close attention to the shapes.

The snake was better, and made it possible to finish her ration-bread. Tad, meanwhile, had placed his dried meat out in the rain to soak; he wolfed it down with no expression of pleasure when it was soft enough to eat.

"Do you take first watch, or shall I?" he asked. She put a pan of water on the fire to steep her bruise-remedy in, then made up her potion with the addition of a couple of recognizable, foraged herbs known to numb sore throats. If they soothed a sore throat, perhaps they would make her bites stop bothering her.

"I'd appreciate it if you would," she replied. "I'm hoping this stuff will let me fall asleep without clawing my skin off, but it's bound to wear off before daybreak. If I'm going to be itching, I might as well be awake so I can control myself."

He nodded. "The smoke worked as well as an ant hill, and my passengers are no longer with me to bother either of us. At the moment, I'm feeling fairly lively. You might as well get to sleep while you still can."

By now her clothing and her hair were both dry, though only her gryphon-badge was as pristine as it had been when they set out. Besides being stained, her tunic and trews were torn in several places, and the hems were beginning to fray. *I look like a tramp,* she thought ruefully. *I hope Ikala is not with a search party . . . oh, that's ridiculous. He would hardly expect me to look like a court lady, and I would be so happy to see a rescuer that the last thing I would be thinking of would be my clothing!*

Tad helped her wrap her herb-steeped bandages around the worst of her bruises, and to dab the remainder of the mixture on her insect bites, as best as his large, taloned hands would allow. At first, she thought she was going to be disappointed again in her attempt to heal her bites, but as the mixture dried, she noticed that her itching had ebbed, at least temporarily. The tenderness of her flesh was perhaps in some way eased by the tenderness of the gryphon's care of her, as well.

Tad looked at her, disheveled feathers slightly spiked from the moisture, with inquiry in his expression.

She sighed with relief. "It's working," she said. "I'll have to make more of this up and keep it with me in one of the waterskins. If I keep putting it on, I might find it easier to freeze in place without being driven mad."

Tad chuckled. "Good. Now we just need to find something that will keep the bugs off us in the first place—without driving *us* crazy with the smell!"

With her mind off her itching, she turned a critical eye on Tad, and without warning him what she was about to do, reached over to feel his keelbone, the prominent breastbone that both gryphon and bird anatomy shared. That was the first place that a bird showed health or illness, as muscle-mass was consumed by a gryphon or bird that was not eating enough.

It was a bit sharper, the muscles on either side of it just a little shrunken. Not something an ordinary person would notice, but Tad was her partner, and it was her job to do as much for him as she could. "You've lost some weight," she said thoughtfully. "Not a lot, but it has to be either the short rations or the fact that you're using up energy in healing. Or both."

"Or that I'm building leg-muscle and losing wing-muscle because I'm not using it," he pointed out. "I don't remember walking this much before in my life. Much more of this and I'm going to look more like a plowhorse than a hawk."

She granted him a skeptical look, and crossed her legs and rested her chin on her good hand. "I wish we'd find the river," she replied fretfully. "No matter *what* is following us, if we just had the river, we could fish; I'd get some decent food into you. Even if there's something following us and scaring off the game, I doubt that fish would be frightened off by a land predator." The river, the promise of the river, it now seemed to embody the promise of everything—food, shelter and rescue as well. Perhaps she was placing too much hope on a strip of water, but at the moment it was a good goal to concentrate on.

He heaved a huge sigh and scratched at one bug-bitten ear. "I really have no idea where we are in relation to the cliff and the river," he confessed. "And this kind of forest is very strange to me. If this place were more like home, I could probably find a river, but I can't see the sky and the ground cover is ten or twelve layers thick here. . . ."

"I know, and I'm not blaming you," she assured him hastily. "How could you know anything about this kind of forest? We never trained here. We expected we'd be going to an established outpost, with shelter, a garden, food stores, and weapons."

"Emphasis on the food stores," Tad said hoarsely, as if the momentary thought of all the food he was used to eating made him homesick. He rubbed at his throat a moment and then swallowed. He'd been gulping more air for days than was healthy for him.

She frowned with frustration. "I'm sure there are plenty of things to eat growing all around us, if only I knew what they were! Roots, stalks, leaves—even some things you might be able to eat, too!" She waved her hand, helplessly. "We haven't the luxury of experimenting, since we don't dare make ourselves sick, so we're stuck. Only a native would know how to find his way around a place like this."

"A native like Ikala?" Tad replied shrewdly, and chuckled when she blushed involuntarily. "Well, I wish he was with us."

"I do, too—" she began, intending to change the subject, quickly.

"And probably for more reasons than one!" he teased, not giving her a chance to change the subject, and sounding more like his old self than he had in days. "I can't blame you; he's a handsome fellow, and he certainly accounted well for himself in training. It wouldn't be a bad thing to get to know him better."

"I suppose," she said, suddenly wary. There was nothing that Tad liked better than to meddle in other peoples' love lives. "If we'd had a chance to ask him more about forests like these, we might be faring better now."

He saw what she was trying to do. "Oh, come on, Blade!" he coaxed. "Stop being coy with me! Am I your partner, or not? Shouldn't your partner know who you're attracted to?" He gave her a sly, sideways look. "I know *he's* attracted to *you*. It's obvious, if you're watching."

"And you were watching, I suppose," she grumbled, giving up on her attempt to distract him to something more serious. He laughed.

"I'm supposed to watch out for you, aren't I? You'd be happier with a male friend to share some—hmm—pleasant moments with, and I know it would be easier dealing with you if you were happier." He tilted his head comically to the side.

"Oh, thank you," she said sarcastically. "Now you sound like both my parents. They can't wait to get me—attached."

Into bed with someone, you mean, she thought sourly. *And Tad knows it. He should know better than to echo them! He knows how I feel about that!*

"They're obsessed with it, and have built much of their

lives around pleasures of flesh. They think of it as a means to all happiness, even if it is by a strange, obscure path! Seeing you bedded with someone is not my goal. I simply want to see you content in all areas of your life," Tad said persuasively. "He's certainly a fine prospect. Good-looking, intelligent, and open-minded enough that you wouldn't get all tangled up in Haighlei custom with him. Good sense of humor, too, and that's important. And being trained as a prince, he knows that you have to be able to concentrate on your duty, you can't just devote yourself slavishly to a man. Hmm?"

Blade fixed her partner with a stern and fierce gaze, neither agreeing nor denying any of it. "You're matchmaking," she accused. "Don't try to deny it; I've seen you matchmake before, you're as bad as an old woman about it! You want to see everyone paired off and living—well, if not happily ever after, at least having a good time while the affair lasts!"

"Of course!" Tad replied smugly. "And why not?"

She growled at him. "Because—because it's invasive, that's why not! I repeat—I get enough of that kind of nonsense from my parents! Why should I put up with it from you?"

He only snorted. "I'm your partner, I have to know these things, and I have to try to help you get what you want and need, whether or not you know what it is! I'd tell *you*, and I'd expect you to help me. We both have to know if there's something that is going to have us emotionally off-balance, because that's going to affect how we do our job. Right? Admit it!"

She growled again, but nodded with extreme reluctance. He was right, of course. A Silver's partnership was as close as many marriages, and partners *were* supposed to confide in each other, cooperate with each other, in and out of the duty times.

And for some reason, what seemed so invasive from her parents didn't seem so bad, coming from Tad. Perhaps it was because Tad was a gryphon, and not human. Despite the gryphons' abilities to see things like a human did, Tad would always be one step removed from complete empathy with Blade, and that gave her a barrier of safety.

"So tell your partner how you feel about it." He settled his head down on his foreclaws. "What *do* you think of Ikala, then?"

Rain drummed down outside their shelter and pattered through the branches they had piled on the roof. Lightning made patterns of the branches screening the front of the shelter, reflecting whitely off Tad's eyes and the silver gryphon-badge on her tunic. As usual, rain and thunder were the only sounds that *could* be heard outside.

Inside—the smoke had finally cleared away and the fire burned brightly. She was dry, full, and warm. Her shoulder didn't hurt too much, and she was in a well-camouflaged shelter with two very solid walls on either side of her and a cushioning of springy boughs between her and the cold, damp ground. In short, there was nothing to distract her from her thoughts, which were confused to say the least.

"I suppose I don't really know," she said slowly, as Tad's dark eyes watched her with that intensity that only a raptor could display. "He *is* very handsome, he's very charming, he's quite intelligent . . . but I just don't know. Part of the time I think I like him for himself, part of the time I think I'm attracted to him just because he's so exotic, and part of the time I think it's because he's the only person in White Gryphon that my father *doesn't* know everything about!"

Tad chuckled heartlessly. "There is that. I've noticed that Ikala has never once had the occasion to patronize a *kestra'-chern*. Amberdrake should find him more of an enigma than you do."

"That would certainly be an improvement," she said acidly. "It would be very nice for once to have a conversation with someone without the person wondering if Father was going to tell me all the things he'd really rather I didn't know."

"And it would be very nice for you," Tad commented, "to talk to your father without wondering if he *was* going to tell you things you'd rather not know." Blade nodded, and Tad shrewdly added, "I don't go to *kestra'chern*, so you are doubly safe talking to me about how you feel; word will not reach your father. May I give up all my hedonism if I lie."

Blade smiled despite herself. Depend upon a gryphon male to count *that* as the ultimate oath.

"He's under control," she added. "He's a very controlled person. I like that."

I like it a great deal more than unbridled passion, truth to tell.

Tad coughed. "Still," he prompted helpfully. "Some might say that argues for a certain coldness of spirit?"

She snorted. "You know better than that, you've worked with him. He loses his temper about as often as anyone else, he just doesn't let it get away from him. And—so far as not visiting a *kestra'chern*—"

"And?" Tad's eyes sparkled with humor.

She blushed again. "And he hasn't exactly been—well—chaste. He's had female friends while he's been here. They just weren't *kestra'chern*. Even if they were casual. Recreational."

And I could almost envy Karelee. I wish she hadn't been so enthusiastic about his bed abilities.

"Oh?" Tad said archly. "He hasn't been chaste? I suppose you were interested enough to find out about this."

She coughed and tried to adopt a casual tone. "Well, one *does*, you know. People talk. I didn't have to be *interested*, people gossip about that sort of thing all the time. I only had to be nearby and listen." She favored him with a raised eyebrow, grateful to feel her hot face cooling. "Winds know that *you* do enough talking, so you ought to know!"

"Me? Gossip?" His beak parted in silent laughter and he squinted his eyes. "I prefer to call it the 'gathering of interpersonal information,' for 'management of sources and receivers of pleasure.'"

"Well, *I* call it gossip, and you're as bad as any old woman," she retorted. "You are just as bad when it comes to matchmaking. And as for Ikala—he is attractive, and I don't deny it, but I think you're getting way ahead of yourself to tie the two of us together in any way. I don't even know how

I feel, so how could I even speculate about how *he* feels? And anyway, you and I have our missions to run, and when we get out of here, we have a long tour of duty at a remote outpost to take care of. If we don't die of embarrassment at having to be rescued."

If we are rescued, if we do get out of here. . . . The unspoken thought put a chill in the air of the tent that the fire could not drive away. All frivolous thoughts faded; this was the change in subject she had tried to make, but not the new subject she would have preferred. Reflexively she glanced out through the screening branches. It was getting darker out there, and it looked as if—once again—the rain was going to continue past nightfall.

That might not be so bad, if it keeps our unseen "friends" away.

"Well," she said, as lightly as possible, which was not very, "now you've got my brain going, and I'm never going to be able to get to sleep. I'll just lie awake thinking."

He yawned hugely. "And I am warm and sleepy. I always get worn out listening to people's reasons why they won't be happy. Shall we switch watches?"

He didn't wait for her to answer, settling his head back down on his foreclaws. She shrugged. "We might as well," she replied, and edged over until she was in a position where she could see through a gap between two of the branches hiding the front of their shelter. She memorized the positions of everything in sight while the light was still good enough to identify what was visible through the curtain of rain. The flashes of lightning helped; if she concentrated on a single spot, she could wait until the next lightning bolt hit to give her a quick, brightly-lit glimpse of what was there, and study the afterimage burned into her eyes.

Tad hadn't been lying about his fatigue; within a few moments, she heard his breathing deepen and slow, and when she turned to look behind her, she saw that his eyes were closed. She turned back to her vigil, trying to mentally review what she had done when she constructed the shelter.

She had tried not to take too many branches away from any one place. She had tried to pile the ones she brought to the shelter in such a way that they looked as if they were all from a single smaller tree brought down by the larger. *With all this rain, every trace of our being here should have been washed away. No scent, no debris. . . .*

Smoke, though—the smoke Tad had used to drive out insects had been very dense and odoriferous, and she wondered if the rain had washed all of it out of the air. If not—how common would smoke be in a forest that experienced thunderstorms every day? Common enough, she would think. Surely lightning started small fires all the time, and surely they burned long enough to put a fair amount of smoke into the air before the rain extinguished them.

Well, there wasn't anything she could do about the smoke—or the shelter itself—now. If there was anything looking for them, she could only hope that she had done everything she needed to in order to cover their presence. Last night it would have been difficult for their possible followers to find them; she hoped tonight it would be impossible.

The rain turned from a torrent to a shower, and slowed from a shower to a mere patter. Then it wasn't rain at all, but simply the melodic drip of water from the canopy above, and the sounds of the night resumed.

She breathed a sigh of relief, and checked the fire. No point in letting it burn too high now; the inside of the shelter was at a good temperature, and with two walls being the trunks of trees, it should sustain that level without too much work. She rebuilt the fire, listening to the hoots and calls from above, tenting the flames with sticks of green fuel and banking the coals to help conceal the glow. This should let the fire burn through the night without needing too much more fuel or tending. It would burn slowly now, producing a bed of deep red, smokeless coals instead of flame. That was precisely the way she wanted it.

With the level of light in the shelter down to the point

where Tad was nothing more than a large, dark shape, she turned her attention back to the outside.

Nothing had changed; the creatures of the canopy continued to go about their business with the accompanying noise, and now the luminescent insects she had noted before began to flit about the foliage. She allowed herself to relax a little further. It just might be that whatever had been following them had decided to leave them alone.

But don't count on it, she cautioned herself. *Assume the worst. Assume that they're still—*

Something moved out in the darkness.

Just a shape, a shifting of shadow, but she knew that there should not have been a shadow in that place, much less a moving one. Instantly she was on the alert.

Whatever it was, it was big. Bigger than the tame lion she'd seen in Shalaman's menagerie. She knew to within a thumb's breadth just how wide a distance lay between each bush, how tall a young tree was. The head of the shadow would rise a little above hers, she thought, though she had the impression of a very long, slender neck; the chest briefly obscured one bush while its hindquarters still lay behind another. Altogether, that would make it about the size of a horse, perhaps a little smaller. She couldn't quite tell how bulky it was, but the fluid way in which it moved and the fact that it melted in with the other shadows so well suggested that it had a slender build.

Her view was a narrow one, limited to the wedge of forest between the two long walls of log—yet in a moment, as she concentrated further, she knew that there was more than one of those creatures out there. One shadow flitted as another froze; further flickering in the distance suggested that either they were incredibly fast, or there might be a third.

Two, at least, for certain. But they don't seem to know we're here.

The first of the shadows darted suddenly out of sight; a heartbeat later, and a bloodcurdling scream rang out into the night.

Blade's heart leaped into her throat, and she felt as if she had been plunged into ice water. Tad only wheezed in his sleep. It took all of her control to remain frozen in place. She had an impression that those shadows possessed extremely sharp senses, and that if she moved, even obscured by branches as she was, they might spot the movement, or hear it.

Silence descended, as Blade tried to get her heartbeat started again. It was a good thing that she had heard the death scream of a rabbit before, or she would have thought that one of those *somethings* had just killed a child.

Now, as if the canopy dwellers had only just noticed the shadows' presence, the silence extended up into the treetops. Only the insects and frogs remained unaffected, chirping and trilling as calmly as they had a moment before.

She blinked—and in the time it took her to do so, the shadows vanished, at least from her view.

She did not breathe easier, however. From the silence, she knew that *they* were still out there, and she had no intention of letting them know her location.

I can only hope that they haven't had the bright idea to come take a walk on top of the sheltering logs.

The very idea made her want to shiver. The back of her neck crawled as she imagined one of those creatures sniffing around the brush piled above her head. There was nothing between her and these hunters stronger than a layer of canvas and a pile of flimsy branches and leaves. Surely if one of the hunters got close, no amount of brush and herb juice would obscure their scent. Surely the scent of the fire alone would tell the creature that they were here—

But I'm assuming that the thing is intelligent, that it would associate a fire with us. I'm assuming that it's hunting us—it could simply be here, we could have wandered into its territory. We haven't seen any large predators nor any sign of them; this could simply be the local equivalent of a lion.

And yet . . . something about the way it had moved had suggested intelligence and purpose. That could be her imagination, but it might be the truth. It was wary; it moved carefully, but when it did move, it was quick and certain. That was an indication of something that either had incredible re-flexes, or something that decided very precisely what it was going to do before it acted.

In any case, there was no reason to take any chances, and every reason to be painfully cautious. No matter what else, these creatures were hunters, predators. The behavior of the canopy dwellers showed that, and demonstrated that the animals that lived in the treetops recognized these beasts and feared them.

Even if those things are just the local equivalent of a lion, they're still big, they're still carnivorous, and they're hunting. There's no reason to put myself on their menu.

A new thought occurred to her; what if they were not dealing with one enemy, but two? One that had brought them down, and a second that was hunting them? In that case, there were two possibilities; the shadows were either wild hunters that had nothing to do with what brought them down—or they were allied with it. In the second case, the shadow shapes out there could be the equivalent of a pack of hunting hounds, trailing them for some unknown master.

It was not something that was unheard of; that was the problem. *Urtho wasn't the only mage that created living things. Ma'ar did, and so did others who never participated in the wars. The ability to create a new species was a mark of prestige or a symbol of ability above and beyond the status of being an Adept. Among the higher mages there were a handful that had created new creatures for centuries before the war with Ma'ar.*

That gave her yet another possible scenario; a mage who hunted other intelligent creatures, and had chosen them for his next prey. Their chasers were his dog pack—

Ma'ar had been one such, and she'd heard tales of others, both from her own people and from the Haighlei. That, in fact, was one of the reasons why the Haighlei restricted magic use to the priests; they had a tale of a sadistic, powerful mage who captured men and brought them to his estate to hunt them like beasts. A brave young priest had suspected what was happening and allowed himself to be taken, thus giving his fellows an agent within the spell-protected walls through which they could channel their own power to destroy the mage.

That was how the story went anyway.

She grew cold all over again, and restrained herself from running her hand through her hair nervously. Her imagination went wild again, taking off all on its own. She had never had any difficulty coming up with scenarios for trouble. *So—suppose that one of the neutral mages came down here to hide before the Cataclysm. Even if he wasn't Urtho's equal, he could have guard-beasts and birds to warn him when anything was in the area. The Haighlei never travel through the wilderness in groups of less than ten, and that includes a priest, but all he'd have to do would be to stay quiet while they passed by. Unless they actually stumbled over him, they wouldn't find him. Then he could hunt individuals at his leisure.*

There was just one problem with that hypothesis; no one had ever been reported missing from here. Unless a Haighlei was so antisocial as to sever all familial and clan ties and go off wandering the wilderness, *someone* would have raised a fuss by now if anyone had vanished, wouldn't they? Woodcutters, explorers, trappers, hunters—they all told friends, neighbors, and fellow workers *where* they were going, what route they intended to take, and when they should be back. They did so especially if they were going off into poorly-explored lands; if something happened, they would want others to mount a rescue as soon as possible.

Perhaps there had been a few Haighlei hermits who had wandered in here only to vanish—but not enough to provide sport for a maniacal manhunting mage.

Well, all right, then—what if he came here to escape all the conflict. What if he wants to be left alone, and he brought us down to keep us from revealing his presence?

But that didn't make any more sense than the first hypothesis. There had been others through here; they had all flown overhead on the same route. Why hadn't *they* been brought down?

Because we were the only gryphon-human pair?

But there had been Aubri and Judeth. . . .

Oh, winds. I should be a storyteller.

She gave it up as a bad notion. It was getting too complicated, and usually, the more complicated a hypothesis was, the more likely it was that it was incorrect.

Stick to the two possibilities that work best. Simple answers work best and are more likely. First: we hit some kind of accidental—thing—that brought us down, and now we're having to guard ourselves from the local predators which are following us because we're hurt and look like easy prey. Second: something down here brought us down for reasons of its own and now is hunting us. And the first is more likely than the second.

That didn't mean they were in any less danger. Wolves and lions had been known to trail wounded prey for days, waiting for it to die. And if her guess about the size of the shadow-creatures was right, they were a match for Tad, which would make them formidable opponents indeed. If the shadows knew that she and Tad were hurt, that might well put them in the category of "wounded prey."

A bird called; another answered. And as if that tentative call had been meant to test the safety of the area, or to tell other creatures that the menace had gone for the moment, the canopy above began to come to life again.

She sighed, and let her shoulders relax. She cast a wry glance at her slumbering companion.

Somehow, Tad had managed to sleep through it all.

Tad yawned, and stretched as best he could, blinking in what passed for light in their shelter. When Blade woke him for his watch, she had looked tired, but that was to be expected. She also looked nervous, but how could she not be? He would be nervous on his watch, too. Nervous sentries remained living sentries; relaxed ones had short epitaphs.

"I saw something out there that might account for the way everything goes silent every so often," she offered. "It was pretty big, and I think there were two or more of them. I didn't see anything more than a shadow, though. One of them caught a rabbit, and every bird and beast in the canopy shut up and stayed that way for a long time."

Well, that accounts for the nerves, and for the fact that she looks tired. Nerves wear you out and she didn't have much of a reserve when she began her watch.

"Huh." He glanced out into the darkness, but didn't see anything—and some of the local creatures were acting as if they were in the middle of a singing competition. "Well, if silence means that there's something out there we should be worried about, I'd say you can sleep in peace until dawn. I'm surprised I slept through it. I must have been more tired than I thought—or my medicine is stronger than I supposed."

She managed a ghost of a chuckle. "It got my hackles up, I can tell you that much. It's quick, very quick, and I didn't hear a rustle of leaves or a single broken twig. I'd say the one I saw was about the size of a horse, which would make it a formidable predator in a fight. It might have been my imagination, but I thought that it acted fairly intelligent."

"So do the big cats, hunting," he reminded her. "Everything acts intelligent in its own realm. Drink your painkillers, get some sleep. We'll see what's out there in the morning. I set some snares before the rain—"

She chuckled again. "Don't count on there being anything left. I think you were robbed. That may have been where our shadows found their rabbit."

He sighed. "Probably, but it was worth doing. And we'll know how intelligent they are by how the snares were robbed. If it was just snatch-and-eat, then they won't be any more intelligent than the average lion."

"Good point." She settled herself down at the back of the shelter; he was certain she was going to get a good rest for the rest of the night, so long as things stayed noisy up in the canopy. The mattress of boughs and leaves he'd made was very comfortable, and she should be able to lie cradled in a way that permitted her to sleep soundly, rather than fitfully. With her shoulder supported so that pressure was off her collarbone, she should be in less pain.

He had not wanted to mention it before this, but he had already seen signs on their backtrail that something was following them. It could have been anything, and he hadn't seen any signs that their follower was particularly intelligent—just alert and incredibly wary. The trouble with telling her now was that there was nothing to prove whether or not the shadowy creature that was following them was something they had just picked up today, or if it had been following them all along and only now was feeling bold enough to move in where he might catch a glimpse of it. It could certainly match the description that Blade had given him of the creature she saw tonight.

That basically was all that he *knew* as a fact. This, of course, had nothing to do with what his own imagination could conjure up.

In his imagination, the sighting confirmed the fear that he'd had all along, that they were being followed for some specific purpose. The only question in his mind now was if the purpose was a simple one—kill and eat the prey—or something more complicated than that. If it was simple, then these creatures were simple predators, and relatively "easy" to deal with. If, however, there was a larger purpose in their minds—if his imagination was right, and in fact these creatures had something to do with their accident— then he and Blade were in very deep trouble.

Such extreme caution combined with curiosity as these "shadows" had exhibited was very unlike most predators he was familiar with. In general, large predators tended to shy completely away from anything that was not familiar, at the most watching it from a distance. Only if the unfamiliar object continued to remain in a predator's territory would it gradually move in closer to investigate it.

Predators are very nervous, very jumpy. They have a lot

of competition, and normally they can only take down large creatures if their prey is old, sick, very young, or wounded. Prey that fights back is to be avoided, because the predator can't afford to be injured in the struggle. Being a carnivore is an expensive business, as I well know. When your dinner can run away from you, you're going to spend a lot of energy hunting and killing it. Vegetarians have it easy. Their dinner can't move, and they don't have to do anything other than walk up and open their mouths.

That meant that the predators following them were not following "normal" behavior; the gryphon and the human were strange, they might be dangerous, hence there was no reason to follow them. In fact, there was every reason to *avoid* them—unless he and Blade were giving off signals that fit the profile of "sick, old, very young, or wounded," or had become familiar enough for their pursuers to investigate.

Either the territory these shadows claimed was so very large that he and Blade had been within its boundaries all along, or these creatures were something out of the ordinary.

The fact that one of them had killed and eaten a rabbit did not tend to make him believe that they would not attack him or Blade. Wolves made very good meals of mice, yet did not hesitate to pull down deer. For that matter, *he* was eating mice this very night! No, a predator's prey on a given night did not necessarily define what it *could* take. Something as big as a horse could very easily consider something as big as a gryphon to be reasonable prey. Top predators often pulled down animals very much larger than they themselves were; the only exceptions were birds of prey, who would ideally not kill anything larger than they could fly off with—generally much less than half the bird's own body weight. The only eagles that had ever carried off lambs were Kaled'a'in-bred bondbirds, who had the required wingspread and muscle mass, and carried them off at the behest of their bondmates.

I think we are going to have to set traps around our camps at night, he decided reluctantly. *Even if these creatures manage to escape from a trap, there is a chance that we will make them hesitant to attack us by frightening or even injuring one or more. If they are nothing more than animals, the mere fact that one of them is hurt should make them give up on making us into dinner.*

They would just have to also take the chance that in frightening or injuring one of those shadows, they would not make an attack more likely.

Well, if we anger them, at least we'll know that they have the intelligence to connect a trap outside the camp with the people inside it—and the intelligence to want revenge for an injury.

There was one point on which he felt Blade was incorrect; he was fairly certain that the creatures she saw had been very well aware of the presence of the camp, and its precise location. They had also probably thought that they would not be seen where they were. They must have very keen senses to hunt at night, and their sense of smell, at least, had clearly not been deceived by his subterfuges with the plant juices. They must have been able to scent the fire. Where the fire was, there the camp would also be. And no matter how well-banked the fire had been, some hint of it was surely visible out there in the darkened forest. No, those creatures knew exactly where the camp was; the only encouraging part was that they had not felt it necessary to surround the camp and place it in a state of siege. Nor had they decided to rush the camp to try and take the occupants by surprise.

So they don't feel ready to try and confront us yet. I hope that their interest is only curiosity.

Noise was priceless; an indicator that the shadows had gone elsewhere to hunt for food.

At least, I hope that's the case. I hope the canopy dwellers are better at spotting these creatures than we are.

All this was enough to give a gryphon a headache.

Wait until morning, and I'll see to it that we're more careful. And I'll try and make the best time afoot that I can, since I'm the slower of the two of us. Maybe we can lose them. Maybe we'll find a river and really be able to hide our scent and our trail. And tomorrow night, if they follow us again, maybe we can find a way to discourage them from continuing to do so.

And maybe horses would fly, and maybe they would stumble upon a lost enclave of amorous female gryphons, and maybe this was all just a bad dream.

Tad surveyed the remains of his snare—pulled up out of the ground, and left carelessly tangled, but all in a heap, as if it had been examined closely, then dropped. It looked very much the same as the debris back at the crash site that had been so carefully examined.

"Well, as I warned you, this is where our friends found their rabbit last night," Blade said with resignation. "See over there?"

He'd already noticed the few bits of fur and the drops of blood on a dead leaf. "I should have known better than to expect that anything would leave a snared rabbit alone," he sighed. "It doesn't look as if they found any of the other snares—but neither did any rabbits. Then again, if any rabbits *had*, they'd probably have gone the way of this one."

At least the shadows hadn't gone *looking* for other snares. Or had they? They'd examined this one that had been sprung; had they gone looking for others, found them, and left them alone once they saw how the snares were set?

Or was he ascribing far too much in the way of intelligence to them?

He regarded the scraps of fur ruefully. *Hardly fair to stalk me and then eat my breakfast.* He thought wistfully of how nice that rabbit would have tasted, and resigned himself to a tasteless meal of dried meat, but Blade had been out and prowling before he was, and had a surprise for him.

"Maybe your snares didn't work, but my sling did," she said, with a tiny smile. She pulled a decent-sized rabbit out of the game bag at her side, and his mouth watered at the mere sight of it.

"Thank you," he said, doing his best not to snatch it out of her hand. He took it politely, but his hunger was too great for more than that. Fortunately she was quite used to watching him eat, for his growling stomach made it impossible for him to wait long enough for her to go elsewhere while he dined. Nor was he able to do anything other than devour his meal in a few gulps.

"What about you?" he asked belatedly, a moment later, when the rabbit was a mere memory and a comfortable feeling in his crop.

At least I managed to resume civilized behavior without a rabbit leg still sticking out of my mouth.

"I'm appropriating a bit of your dried meat," she replied, "And I can eat that as we move. Let's get the packs on and get out of here; I don't want to stay here a moment longer than we have to."

"Agreed," he said firmly. "Especially after last night. Luck permitting, we *should* find the river today or tomorrow."

The canopy dwellers had gone silent once more on his watch, although he had not seen anything. That had given him a very strange feeling; his hackles had come up, as he wondered if the shadowy hunters had decided to take a walk on the great tree trunk and come at them from the rear. He'd never know until the moment that they came crashing down through the branches and canvas. . . .

But they hadn't, and the noises had resumed within a very short time, remaining at a constant level until dawn. Blade had made another batch of her herb concoction and had poured it into one of her waterskins after dabbing her itching bites liberally with it. He hoped it worked as well for her in the heat of the day as it had last night.

He put some effort into confusing their backtrail, while Blade set the course. This time he laid some false, dead-end trails, even taking one up a tree. That made him think; if they had trouble finding a place to shelter tonight, perhaps *they* ought to go up a tree—

Oh, no. Blade can't climb with only one hand. Well, so

much for that good idea. I could perhaps pull her up by rope if it came to that, but the risk of hurting her further would be too great.

Once again, however, they were in luck. This time, in late afternoon, they came upon another good site to hole up. It was another fallen tree, but this time it was one with a large den dug out underneath it. Whatever had dug it originally wasn't home, and from the look of things, hadn't been resident for some time. It *did* have some current occupants, far too small to have dug the den originally, and between them, he and Blade bagged the entire family of five. He wasn't certain quite what they were; something like a beaver with no tail, and about the same size. He didn't even know what species they were, and it really didn't matter. They had rodent teeth, and that was enough for him. Rodents were always edible.

This bit of good fortune more than made up for the fact that Blade had not been as lucky with her sling; the rabbit she had gotten for his breakfast was the only kill she'd made all day. She'd had targets, but had missed her throws. She was so crestfallen about it that he had done his best to reassure her that it was all right.

Well, tonight he would have a truly full stomach for the first time since the crash. The fresh meat had made a great deal of difference to him; he felt much more energetic and lively after having it.

With his help she made a fire outside their den. While she built it up into something respectable, he excavated the den quite a bit more. His talons weren't well suited to digging, but he did have determination, and the earth was soft. When he finished, he knew that it would be a tight fit for both of them, but that they would manage. To keep them off the raw earth, he lined it with branches and packed the dirt he'd dug out into a little dam to prevent water from coming in during the rain. He took a torch and charred the underside of the log to prevent "visitors," then went out to collect a tangle of vines to conceal the entrance. Blade roasted her share of the catch, made up her medicine, then put out the fire and buried the ashes, doing her best to obliterate any traces of their presence that might persist through the afternoon downpour. Like the hollow snag, there would be no room in this den for a fire tonight. As long as the den stayed dry, he didn't think they'd need one.

Need and want, why are they so far apart sometimes?

By the time Blade was done tidying things, he was ready to eat; she took over, clumsily weaving the vines with one hand and both feet into a rough mat that they could pull over the hole. Last of all, she collected a lot of leaves from that peppery plant and tucked them into the mat to kill their scent.

As soon as the rain started, they would climb into this hole and pull the mat over the entrance. There they would remain until dawn. In his opinion, this was their most vulnerable camp yet, but he had an answer to that.

Although she couldn't climb, *he* could, and since the den was barely big enough for the two of them without their packs, he had an idea.

"Help me with this," he said, as soon as he'd finished gulping down his meal. "I want to make some decoys." He dragged in some more vines and began making them into bundles that resembled a human and something with four feet. She was puzzled, but gave him a hand, as the clouds began to gather for the afternoon rain.

"What are you planning on doing with these?" she asked, as the bundles began to take shape. "They aren't going to fool anything for long."

"Not if they're on the ground—but what if they're up *there?*" He nodded up at the canopy. "I'm thinking of taking the packs and these up to a good branch and tying them there. Maybe our trackers will see 'us' up there, and decide we're becoming too much work to pursue. Provided, of course, that they can't climb."

Somehow, I don't think they can, even though the canopy creatures are afraid of them. I think they're too big;

there's a maximum size that a tree-climbing predator can be and still hunt successfully, and I think they're bigger than that maximum size.

"If you really want to, it's worth trying." She didn't look convinced, but at least she wasn't too negative. He was just as glad that she didn't object to him taking the packs elsewhere to store; although the tree he had in mind was a dwarf by the standards of the ones around him, he was not looking forward to the climb, and that was giving him enough qualms without having to argue with her.

He accomplished the feat by clamping all four sets of talons into the bark and hitching himself up like an inchworm. This used an entirely new set of muscles, as well as awakening a new set of pains in his broken wing, and by the time he reached a suitable place to cache the packs and the two decoys, he wished with a strength beyond telling that he would have been able to glide down instead of climbing. He was *not* looking forward to retrieving the packs in the morning!

He had taken a rope with him, rather than the packs and the decoys themselves. Once he got himself securely in place, he dropped the end down, and Blade tied it to the first pack as best she could with one hand. When he had hauled that up and tied it successfully in place, he dropped the end back down. The second pack came up next, and following that, the two decoys.

And now, if there is a disaster, Blade will at least have a rope she can try to escape by. If there is any time to escape, I can come back up here and pull her up. Maybe.

It did not take long to secure the items in place, but this was not the best of perches, nor was it a place where he would have wanted to spend the night. The packs would remain dry through the storm, but not the decoys. If they had been up here instead of the decoys, it would have been a soggy and most uncomfortable night for them.

He lowered himself down, inching backward and no doubt giving Blade an interesting view all the while. He dropped off the trunk the moment he thought that he'd be able to land safely. "There!" he said, more briskly and brightly than he actually felt. "Now, we have just enough time to rig a deadfall and a couple of other traps before the rain starts!"

Blade groaned at the idea of so much work, but nodded. They both knew that the more distractions they could offer the hunters, the better.

And the more challenge we give to their intelligence, the more we'll learn about them.

He let her lead, though, so that she wouldn't see how tenderly he was walking. His fear was rising again.

By the time the rain started, their traps were in place and concealed, placed in hiding around the tree rather than around their real den, to lend verisimilitude to the decoys in the tree. He and Blade scrambled for their shelter as the first drops started falling, but as was her custom, she stayed outside long enough to get a good sluicing down by the rain before coming in.

She was soaking wet when she came in, but since he had lined the den with branches, they weren't lying directly on the soil; the water she brought in dripped through their bedding and from there into the earth. There wasn't a lot of room to move, and by the time he had snaked out a claw and pulled the mat of vines over the entrance, there was even less. By dint of much squirming, she managed to anoint both herself and him with her bruise-cum-bug-bite medicine. He squinted his eyes at the bitter scent, but decided that he could live with it. With any luck, they *had* to be getting near the river, and he could wash it all off rather than attempting to preen it off tomorrow.

They had deliberately made the entrance as small as possible, just barely large enough for him to squeeze inside. That meant that there wasn't enough room for anyone to stand watch except Blade, because she was the one near the entrance, and he was crammed so far back that he really couldn't see anything. As thunder roared and the rain fell down mere hand-lengths away from their noses, they looked at one another in the semidarkness.

"There's no point in really standing watch," he ventured. "I mean, one of us should try and stay awake, just in case one of us can *hear* something, but there's no point in trying to look out. We made that mat too well; I can't see anything from where I am."

"I can't see that much," she admitted. "Are you sleepy? Your ears are better than mine; if you could take second shift, I can take first."

"I have a full stomach, of course I'm sleepy," he retorted, forbearing to mention the fact that he was afraid that if he didn't try to sleep *now*, his stiffening muscles would make sleep impossible. In fact, he fully expected to wake up about the time she was ready to sleep. His sore legs and back would see to it that he didn't oversleep.

That was precisely what happened. By that time, she was ready for sleep, warm and relatively cushioned, with him curled around her. She dropped off almost immediately, while he concentrated on keeping his muscles relaxed so that they didn't go into cramps. That was *quite* enough to keep him awake all by itself, but the position he was in did not agree with his broken wing either. It probably wasn't causing any damage, but the wing twinged persistently. He caught himself nearly whining in pain once, reducing it to a long wheeze and shiver.

So he was fully awake and wary when the usual silence descended outside in the canopy, signaling the arrival of the shadowy hunters.

Of all of the nights so far, this one was perhaps the most maddening and the most frightening. He was essentially blind, and he and Blade were curled in an all-too-accessible hole in the ground. If anything found them and really was determined to dig them out, it could.

But as he strained his ears, he heard nothing in the way of movement outside the mat of vines. He hoped that if anything heard them, their breathing and tiny movements might be taken for those of small animals that were too much effort to dig out, and which might have a rear entrance to this den through which they could escape.

I wish I'd thought of that and dug one. That might have been a smarter thing to do than rig those traps.

As the moments stretched out unbearably, he became acutely sensitive to every sound, more so than he ever remembered being before. So when he heard the deadfall "go," it sounded as loud as a peal of thunder.

And what was more, he clearly heard the very peculiar cry of pain that followed.

It wasn't a yelp, and it certainly wasn't a shout. There were elements of both a hiss and a howl in it, and it was not a cry he had ever heard before in his life. It startled him, for he could not for a moment imagine what kind of animal could have made such a sound. It cut off rather quickly, so quickly that he wondered if he had managed to actually kill something with his trap.

Possible, but not likely, not unless our "friend" out there was extraordinarily unlucky.

Then he heard more sounds; another thud, tearing and breaking noises, something being dragged briefly, another hiss. Then nothing. His skin crawled under his feathers.

More silence, while his beak ached from being held clamped shut so tightly that his jaw muscles locked, and then, when he least expected it, the canopy sounds returned.

He waited, on fire with tension, as the faint light of dawn began to appear in the tiny gaps in their covering. When he couldn't bear it any longer, he nudged Blade with his beak.

She came awake instantly, her good hand going to her knife.

"I heard the deadfall go," he whispered. "I think we got *something*. Whether it was one of them, whether it's still there—I can't tell. If it *is* still there, I don't think it's still alive, though."

She nodded, and cocked her head to listen to the sounds of

the forest. "I'd say we're safe to come out," she said. "Are you ready?"

"As ready as I'm likely to be." They'd discussed this last night; she was going to come out in a rushing attack, just in case there was something lying in wait for them, and he was supposed to follow. It had all seemed perfectly reasonable and appropriate last night. Now, with his muscles so sore, stiff, and cramped, he wasn't certain he was going to be able to crawl out, much less rush out.

She drew her knife and wriggled around until she was crouched in place. With a yell, she threw off the mat and leaped out—inadvertently kicking him in the stomach as she did so.

His attack-cry was considerably spoiled by this. Instead of a fierce scream of defiance, all he could emit was a pitiful grunt, remarkably similar to a belch. But he managed to follow her out, if not in a rush, at least in a hurry.

There wasn't anything there, which, although an anticlimax, was also a relief. "Sorry," she said, apologetically. "My foot slipped."

What could he say? "It happens," he managed, as graciously as possible—not very, but he doubted that she blamed him at the moment for not speaking with an Ambassador's tact and dissimulation. "Let's go check that deadfall."

When they got close to where the trap had been, it was quite clear that it was going to be empty, for the remains of the vegetation they had used to conceal it were scattered all over the area. The trap itself was quite empty—though there *was* a trace of blood on the bark of one of the logs.

"We marked him," Blade said, squatting down beside it to examine it further. "How badly—well, probably not too badly. Maybe a scrape, or a minor cut. Possibly a broken bone. But we did hurt him a little."

She stood up and looked toward the tree where the decoys were hidden. "We'd better go see how they reacted."

When they reached the base of the tree, they finally saw

something of what their trackers could do, and some clues as to their nature.

Persistent. And ... possibly angry. But not foolishly persistent.

There *were* scratches, deep ones, in the bark of the tree, about twice as high up on the trunk as Blade was tall. So the decoys had worked, at least for a while, and the hunters had been unable to resist trying to get at the quarry when it was openly in sight.

Or else they were so angry when one of their number got caught in the deadfall that they tried to get to us no matter how difficult it was going to be.

Now they knew this much: the hunters could leap respectable distances, but they *couldn't* climb the tree trunk, which at least meant that they were not great cats. The ground at the foot of the tree was torn by claws, either as the hunters tore at the ground in frustration, or when they tried to leap up to drag their prey down out of the tree.

On the other hand, there wasn't a lot of damage to the tree trunk itself; the hunters had made several attempts, but it didn't look as if they had tried mindlessly, over and over, until they were exhausted.

That meant that they were intelligent enough to know when their task was impossible.

Or intelligent enough to recognize that the decoys were just that. In that case, they might well have reasoned that we would have to come back to get the packs before we left, no matter where we hid ourselves overnight.

And if it had been anger that motivated their attack, their anger did not overcome them for long.

Blade looked around, shivering, as if some of the same thoughts had occurred to her. "Let's get the packs and get out of here," she urged. "Fast. They haven't shown themselves by day before, but that doesn't mean they won't now. We might have given them a reason to."

He swarmed up the tree far more quickly than he had thought possible a few moments before, and this time he didn't notice his sore muscles. There was no need to concern himself with ropes on the way up, which made things simpler. He untied the packs when he got there, and dropped them and the rope that held them in place down to the ground, leaving the decoys stuck in the forks of the branches. If the shadow-lurkers were still deceived by the decoys, they might linger, giving him and Blade that much more of a head start.

He went down the tree twice as fast as he had gone up. Every nerve in his body jumped whenever an unexpected sound occurred, and the quicker they left, the happier he would be. There was just a moment more of delay during which they stowed the rope and donned the packs, and then they were on their way without even a pause for a meal.

He wasn't hungry, and he suspected that Blade wasn't either. His insides were all knotted up with tension, and he kept hearing old gryphon proverbs in the back of his mind, about well-fed gryphons and the inability to fly out of danger.

Not that I can fly out of danger now—but it's better to run or fight on an empty stomach than a full one!

It was barely dawn by the light, and the morning fog had not yet lifted. The entire world was painted in dim grays and blues, vague gray shapes and columns appearing and vanishing in white mist. In a way, that was all to the good, for rather than using the trees as cover, they counted on the fog itself for primary concealment. They were able to make much better time that way, and since they were taking their bearings from the north-needle rather than the sun, it didn't matter that everything was obscured and enshrouded.

The fog itself had an odd, bitter aftertaste to it, nothing at all like the sea mists Tad was used to. The air felt heavier and thicker, although that was probably his imagination. The fog condensed on his feathers, and he kept shaking himself so that it didn't soak in. Poor Blade had no such ability; her hair was damp, and she would probably be shivering if they weren't trotting along fast enough to stay warm from exertion.

He found himself trying to think what kind of creature the hunters could be. *Those stories about Ma'ar and all the creatures he made—what sort of things did he do? Father said that most of what he did was to make copies of the creatures that Urtho developed. . . .*

The makaar had been analogs of gryphons; had there been analogs of *hertasi* and *kyree?* The *tervardi* and *dyheli* were natural creatures, surely Ma'ar had not bothered to make analogous creatures to them; why would he? But then again, why not? Ma'ar had never hesitated to do or try anything he considered might give him an edge.

He made cold-drakes and basilisks, but those weren't analogs of anything Urtho made, so there goes Father's theory. There were smaller creatures, but I can't remember anything that might correspond in size to the hunters. Did he do flightless makaar? But why would he, when a makaar on the ground would be more helpless than I am? The shadow-hunters can't be analogs of hertasi, *because I'm certain that what we've been seeing is four-footed, not two-footed.*

Had anyone else involved in the Mage Wars made a four-footed hunter the size of a horse?

I just can't remember anyone ever going into a lot of detail about the mage-made creatures. Maybe Snowstar would know, but he's rather effectively out of reach at the moment.

He kept his ears trained on the trail behind them, and his eyes on Blade's back. She was a ghost in the fog, and it was up to him to keep track of her and not lose her. Her pale beige clothing blended in beautifully with the fog—but so would his own gray plumage. For once, it would probably be harder for the hunters to see *them* than vice versa.

Whatever is behind us is clever, very clever. They weren't deceived by my false trails, and they either gave up on the decoys or recognized them as false, and if they gave up temporarily, there's no guarantee that they won't realize what's going on when they come back. They didn't find us, but they might not have bothered to look. Or they might have needed to hunt and feed, and they couldn't take the extra time to figure out where we were. Why should they? They knew we'd come out in the morning, and all they have to do is wait for us to come out and get on our way and they could trail us again. They could even be hoping we will stay put in that campsite, since it has been proven to protect us once.

He wanted rock walls around him; a secure place that these shadow-hunters couldn't dig into. He wanted a steady food source that the shadows couldn't frighten away. Once they had both, they could figure out ways to signal the help that must be coming.

And he wanted to *see* them. He wanted to know exactly what was hunting them. Traps might give him more of a chance to see one, provided that any injured or dead hunters remained in the trap. And there was no guarantee of that, either.

They freed the injured one from the deadfall. That was what I heard last night; they were freeing him.

That meant cooperation, which meant more intelligence. Wolves might sniff around a trapped fellow, might even try to help him gnaw himself loose, but they would not have been able to remove parts of a deadfall trap except by purest accident, and then only after a great deal of trial and error effort.

He had *heard* them last night. It had not taken them long at all to free the trapped one. And they had done so without too many missteps, if there were any at all.

The snare—they didn't just chew the leg or head off the rabbit it caught and then eat the rest. The noose of the snare was opened. They killed the rabbit, pulled the snare open and removed it, then pulled up the snare and looked it over.

That was evidence of more intelligence, and certainly the ability to manipulate objects. What that evidence meant to their survival, he couldn't yet tell.

But he had his fears, and plenty of them. He could only wonder right now if Blade shared those fears. Maybe it was time to stop trying to shelter her and start discussing things. Maybe it had been time to do that a couple of days ago.

Blade stopped in the shelter of a vine-covered bush.
Is that what I think it is?

She frowned with concentration, and motioned to Tad to remain where he was so she could hear without distraction. There was something in the distance, underneath the chatter of the four-legged canopy creatures, and the steady patter of debris from a tree where some of the birds were eating green fruit—a sound—

Tad shifted his weight impatiently. "Shouldn't we—" he began.

"Hush a moment," she interrupted, and closed her eyes to concentrate better. Was that really what she thought it was? She began to isolate it mentally from the rain of bits of leaf, twig, and half-eaten fruit.

"I think I hear running water," she said at last. "Come on!"

She abandoned all attempts at secrecy, trotting as quickly as she could through the tangle of underbrush, with Tad hot on her heels. If that *was* the long-sought river she heard, then their safety lay more surely in reaching it than in trying to hide themselves or their trail. Above them, a few canopy creatures barked or chattered a warning, but most of them seemed to regard her and Tad as harmless.

Well, they would. Now we're running openly, not stalking. We can't be hunting, so we're not a danger to them directly. The sounds above kept on, and the fruit eaters didn't even pause in their gluttony. That was comforting; it meant there was nothing else around that aroused the tree dwellers' alarm. If there *had* been something trailing them closely, when they broke cover, it would have had to do the same to a certain extent, just to keep up with them. And if that had happened, the treetops should have erupted with alarm or once again gone silent, or both.

There was sunlight pouring down through a huge gap in the trees, off in the distance; it shone green-gold through the leaves, white between the trunks of the trees. The closer they got, the clearer the sound of water running rapidly over rocks became.

They literally burst through the luxuriant curtain of brush at the river's edge, teetering on the rocks lining the banks. She wanted to cheer, but confined herself to pounding on Tad's shoulder enthusiastically.

The river at their feet was wide, but so far as she could tell, it was deep only in the middle. More to the point, across the river lay the cliff they had been looking for, with a wide beach made of rocks and mud lying between the rock cliff face and the river.

Caves, waterfalls—even a crevice that we can fortify. Any of those will do very nicely just now!

"Let's get across," Tad urged. "If they're following us, we'll be able to see them, and there's going to be water between them and us."

Water between them and us. Right now, that was the best protection she could imagine. Tad was right; with an open space of water between their enemy and themselves, they would certainly be able to see the mysterious hunters coming. *We can look for a cave as soon as we're across.*

For the first time in four days, they should be able to find a safe and secure place to wait for rescue, a place too difficult to dig them out of, with walls of rock instead of flimsy canvas.

And they might be able to actually *see* the creatures that were following them—assuming that the shadow-hunters were bold enough to go this far. They might give up. She wasn't going to count on it, but they might. This was certainly more trouble than most predators wanted to go through for a meal.

Now she grinned, and it was heartfelt. "Let's go get wet," she said. "We both need a bath anyway!"

Snowstar

Seven

Blade peered through the curtain of rain, looking a few lengths ahead to see if there was anything like a cave in sight, then looking back down at her feet to pick out her footing among the slippery mud and river rocks. Here, out in the open, the rain came down in sheets, making footing doubly treacherous. More rain sluiced down the cliff face, washing across the rocks at her feet. This time, they hadn't gone to ground when the rains came; they didn't even look for a shelter. Instead, they continued to make their way along the cliff-side bank of the river. For one thing, the only shelter from the rain lay back on the other side of the river, and she didn't really want to take her chances back there. For another, every moment they spent in huddling away from the rain was a moment that they could not spend in looking for *real* cover, the protection of a place from which they could not be extracted by force.

By now poor Tad was a wet, sodden mess, and after this, she was certainly going to have to figure out what they could spare to make him a new bandage for his wing. The bandages he wore were soaked and coming loose, and wouldn't be any good until after they had been rinsed clean and dried. *Sacrifice some clothing, maybe, if we don't have enough bandages. I could shorten the legs of my trews for cloth, since they don't seem to be much protection against the bugs. That and some rope might make a decent sling.*

She was going to have to get him dried out before they slept; allowing a gryphon to go to sleep wet was a sure prescription for illness.

We need a cave, or at worst, a cleft. This rain is going to go on until nightfall, and we won't be able to see anything then.

The water level in the river didn't seem to be rising much, if any, which suggested that it was probably as high now as it ever got, except in the occasional flood. *And I hope we don't happen to be in the midst of flood season!* There was evidence aplenty for a flood, in the form of flotsam, mostly wood, washed up and wedged among the rocks. It would make admirable firewood, if they could ever find a place where they could build a fire!

It would be just our luck to have pinned our hopes on finding this cliff only to discover that there is less shelter here than there was in the forest. If they didn't find a place to hole up before dark, they might have to spend the night exposed on this rocky shore, where they would have the grim choice of lighting a fire and attracting attention or shivering, cold and damp, wrapped up in wet blankets all night.

The gods, or fate, were not to be so unkind, however. After a few more furlongs of picking their way across the rocks and sliding through the mud, the cliff receded somewhat to her left and the river opened up before her. A white, roaring wall loomed up out of the rain, as if someone had torn a hole in the clouds and let all the water out at once. After a moment of blinking and trying to get her dripping hair out of her eyes, she realized that she was not staring at a torrent in the midst of the downpour, she was looking at a waterfall, and just on their side of the waterfall, there was a series of darker holes in the cliff wall that must be caves.

Tad spotted them at the same time, and shouted into her ear. "If any of these are deep enough, this is where we should stop! We may not be able to hear anything coming, but whatever tries to come at us from ahead won't be able to get past the falls! We'll only have to guard in one direction!"

She winced at the bellowing, since she was right beside the excited gryphon, but saw at once that he was right. That overcame her misgiving at camping in a place where the sound of an enemy approaching would be covered by the roar of the water. And as if to emphasize just what a good spot this was, a stunned fish came floating to their very feet to lodge among the rocks, flapping feebly. It had obviously been knocked silly by going over the falls, and Tad, who was probably starving, was on it in a heartbeat. Two gulps, and it was gone, and Tad had a very satisfied look on his face.

"See what else you can forage!" she shouted at him. "I'll check out these caves!"

"Wait a moment!" he shouted back. Picking up a milky-white, smooth pebble from the rocks at his feet, Tad stared at it in concentration that she found very familiar. Then he handed it to her, gryph-grinning with open beak. The pebble glowed with mage-light.

She accepted it with relief; at least he had enough magic back now that he could make a mage-light again!

She didn't have to go far to find their new shelter; the very first cave she entered proved to be perfect. It went back a long way, slanting upward all the time. For a few lengths, the floor was covered with soft, dry sand. Then there was a pile of driftwood marking the high-water line that past floods had also left behind; that was where the sand ended and dirt and rock began. A thin stream of water ran down the center of the cave, coming from somewhere near the back, cutting a channel through the sand and rock alike.

She made her way past it, holding the blue-glowing rock over her head to cast the best possible light ahead of her without dazzling her eyes. The cave narrowed, the farther she went back, then abruptly made a ninety-degree turn upward. This was where the stream of water originated. She put her head inside the hole and looked up. Besides getting a faceful of rain, she clearly saw the cloud-filled sky a great distance above. At one time, a real stream of water, perhaps a branchlet of the river that tumbled down the cliff further on, had cut a channel through here, forming the cave. Now, except perhaps during rain, that channel was dry. But it formed precisely what *they* needed; a natural chimney to carry the smoke away from their fire. Provided that nothing acted to funnel more water down that ancient outlet, this would be a perfect shelter. She could not have asked for anything better. Even the chimney was too small for anything threatening to climb down it, except perhaps snakes and the like. There were signs that other creatures had found this place just as congenial, a collection of small bones from fish and other creatures, and a cluster of bats toward the rear of the cave. She did not mind sharing this cave with bats; after her constant battles with insects, she was altogether happy to see them. They didn't seem disturbed to see her.

"Blade?" Tad called from behind her, and she realized that although the sound of the waterfall did penetrate in here, it was much muted by the rock walls.

"Coming!" she responded, turning her back on the chimney and climbing back down to the driftwood pile. She smelled smoke, and indeed, a plume of it, ghostlike in the blue light of the bespelled pebble, drifted toward her and the chimney outlet. A warmer light up ahead greeted her; Tad had already started a fire with the driftwood, and she joined him there.

"The fish around here must not be terribly bright," he said cheerfully. "Quite a lot of them ended up on the rocks a few moments ago. I got you some." He pointed with his beak at a pair of sleek shapes at his feet.

"After you ate your fill, I hope?" she admonished. "You need the food more than I do; I manage quite well on that travel-bread."

His nares flushed, and she judged by that and the bulging state of his crop that he had been perfectly greedy. Not that she blamed him, especially not after going on short rations for so many days. "You might as well put this under something, so we can sleep," she said, handing him the pebble and shrugging painfully out of her pack. "If I'd ordered up a cave, I couldn't have gotten a better one than this. We can even make a really smoky fire back there—" she pointed to the rear of the cave, "—there's a natural chimney that'll send it up without smoking us out. The only thing we don't have is a nighttime signal. We need to talk about that."

He ground his beak as he thought, his good wing half-spread in the firelight to dry. "I can't imagine them flying at night—" he began, then laughed. "Well, on the other hand, since it's me and you who are lost—"

"Skandranon will have night flights out if he has to fly them himself," she finished for him, with a wry chuckle. Then her humor faded. She could not forget, even for a moment, that they were still being hunted. Until they knew by what, and for what reason, they should not assume they would be here to rescue when rescue came. Yes, they had good shelter now, and it would be very difficult to dig them out of it. But not impossible; not for—say—a renegade mage and his followers, human or created.

Tad, however, was going to take the moment as it came; he shrugged out of his pack and nudged a fish over to her with one talon. "You eat," he said. "There's enough wood in here already to easily last the night. While you cook and eat that, I'll go back out and see what I can see."

She hesitated a moment, then gave a mental shrug and bent to pick up the fish. *I might as well eat and make myself comfortable. He's right about that.* While the rain fell, it was unlikely that anything would try to find them. If the creatures trailing them were semi-intelligent, they would assume that the two castaways had followed their usual pattern, and had taken shelter *before* the rain started. The hunters would probably be looking for them on the other side of the river first, especially if the hunters had not traced them as far as the river when the rain began. Any trail would end short of the river itself, and the mud and rock of the riverbank would not hold any scent or footprint through the rain. The trail on the other side of the river would be completely obliterated, and if they could keep their fire out of sight, it was possible that they could keep their presence in this cave a secret for a day or more. By the time smoke got up the rock chimney and exited above them, it would be very difficult for anything scenting it to tell where it originated.

After that, of course, it would become increasingly harder to stay hidden. Every time they left the cave, which they would have to do to catch fish, wash, and get firewood, they stood a chance of being seen. Watchers on the other side of the river could spot them without being seen themselves.

But I'll worry about that after I eat, when I can think better, she decided. It was wonderful to be able to have enough space to properly open the packs and spread everything out. Once again though, she found herself attempting a task one-handed that was difficult enough using two; scaling and gutting a fish. She wound up slipping off her boot and using a foot as a clumsy "hand" on the tail to hold it down.

She saved the head and the guts for later use as bait; they could not count on having the kind of luck that sent a harvest of fish down over the cliff to their feet every day. That was all right; they had fishing line and hooks with them, and if the fish guts didn't work, she could try a bug, a bread-ball, or a bit of dried meat. Once again, her shovel came into play as an impromptu grill; it probably would have been better if she'd had something to grease it with, but at the moment, she was too hungry for trifles like that.

The fish burned a little and stuck to the shovel, but that didn't matter in the least—she could scrape the fish meat off and eat, and some blackened fish meat stuck to it wouldn't adversely affect the use of the shovel as a shovel. She was hungry enough, in fact, that she very nearly burned her fingers, picking flaky bits of meat off the hot carcass before it had properly cooled. She alternately swore softly and ate, making a happy pig of herself.

Tad reappeared, dripping wet again, and regarded her thoughtfully. "Clay," he said. "Next time, wrap it up in clay and bake the whole thing. When you break the clay open, the skin comes off with it, but the rest of the fish is fine."

"Where did you learn that one?" she asked, looking up at him in surprise.

"Mother. She loves fish, and even though she likes it best fresh, she's been known to accept baked fish if it wasn't straight out of the sea." He gryph-grinned at her again, and cocked his head to one side. "You know how she is—unlike father, she'll wish for the ideal, but *not* complain when it isn't given! What do you want to do about the firelight? Move the fire back farther into the cave? The cave bends enough that I think that will make it harder to see from across the river. Or does it matter?"

So, he *had* been thinking about their stalkers. "I'm not sure it matters; sooner or later they're going to see us, or see signs of where we are. I'd rather put some thought into defenses."

"I've set up some simple line snares on the path, so watch out for them," he said. "Not much, there's not much I can do in the rain, but some. It should help, I would think. I can do better tomorrow."

"So that's why you're wet!" She signed to him to sit beside the fire, as she devoured the cooked fish. It didn't taste like much, a bit bland, which in itself made it an improvement over the dried meat, which tasted like old boots. It was hot and satisfying and *cooked*, which made all the difference, and she ate every scrap, using her knife to scrape the burned bits off the shovel and eat them too. Then she settled back on her heels, sucking her slightly-burnt fingers to get the last of the juices, and gave him all of her attention.

"Right, then. Let's settle the short-term first, then the long-term. First watch?" she asked.

"Yours," he said promptly. "As full as I am, I'm going to doze off no matter what. I can't help it; it's the way I'm built. And I have marginally better night-vision than you do. I also have better hearing," he added, "but with that waterfall out there, that isn't going to matter. I can run our fishing line from one of the snares into here, and stack some stones over the light pebble to make a sort of alarm."

Well, that seems pretty reasonable to me. "Good enough. If I see anything tonight, should I take a shot at it? Across the river is in the range of my sling, and with all these rocks around I can afford to miss now, and we won't have to go after my ammunition to get it back." That was another source of easing tensions. Now she was no longer limited to the pouches of lead shot for ammunition. The rocks might not fly as true, but she could lob as many of them around as she needed to. "My vote is that we not provoke anything tonight," he said instantly. "Let's not give them the answer to the question of where we went. If they can't find us tonight, we *might* get lucky and they'll go away."

"Probably not, but it's worth giving ourselves the chance. Agreed. Do we trap the other side of the river?" That was another good question. It might well be worth it to try—or it might make them targets when they crossed the river to check the traps. The river wasn't all *that* deep even at its deepest; barely chin-high on Blade. Anything energetic enough could cross it easily. After all, *they* had, and neither of them was in the best of shape. A stealthy swimmer could cross it and never betray himself by sound, what with the waterfall out there pounding away.

He shook his head. "No; we trap this side of the river, but not the other. We'd be too vulnerable on that side, and why bother? We really don't *want* to catch these things, do we?" He didn't look as if *he* did, and she agreed with him. After all, what could they do with one if they did catch it, alive or dead? All that would do would be to tell them what the hunters looked like, and there were easier ways to do that.

"Not unless we have to start whittling down their numbers," she murmured, thinking that this cave was both a good and a bad place to be. They could defend it—but it would be hard for rescuers to spot, and it would be very easy to place them in a state of siege from which there was no escape. The narrowness of the chimney that made it impossible for anything to climb down also rendered it impossible for them to climb up.

"Right. Then tomorrow, if it looks clear, we go get some green wood and leaves from across the way to make a smoke signal with. We get all the dry driftwood we can and stock it in here." He cocked his head to one side, and waited for her contribution.

"Water we have, finally; I might just as well start fishing and as long as we're running a smoke-signal fire, it can do double duty and I can smoke what we don't eat." *That way if we're trapped in here we'll have something to eat.* "We ought to go back down the way we came in and decide what kind of traps we can lay."

"At least one rockfall, right at the entrance, with a release one of us can trigger from in here," he said promptly, and yawned. "With a lot of work and cleverness we can even barricade the opening of the cave with wood and rocks; we're certainly clever enough, so all we need is the work. And that is about all of the thinking that I'm good for. I have *got* to get some sleep. I don't need a blanket; it's plenty warm enough in here next to the fire." He winked at her. "I can even lie down on this nice, soft sand so that I'm between the fire and the entrance, and screen it with my body. I shall sacrifice staying near the cold and water to do this duty."

"Big of you. Help me spread out the bedding so it can dry," she responded dryly. "Then you can sleep all you like—at least until it's your turn on watch!"

And may there be nothing to watch for—except a search party, and that soon, she thought, as he chuckled and moved to help her with the damp blankets. *By now they'll have missed us back home. We didn't make the rendezvous, and the other patrol should have sent word back with their teleson. How long until we're missing instead of overdue? And will they look for us when they think we're only late? I wish I knew.*

I only know one thing. Father's going to go out of his

*mind when he hears of this. I'm glad I'm not the one to
tell him!*

Amberdrake stared at Commander Judeth; for a moment
her words made no sense.

Then suddenly, they made all too much sense.

"They're *what?*" All of Amberdrake's hard-won equanim-
ity deserted him. He rose out of the chair in his office as if
he'd sat on a hot coal. Indeed, that was very much the way
he felt.

"Calm down, Drake, the youngsters are only overdue by a
day," Judeth told him. She looked outwardly calm, but he
knew more than enough about her and the tiny telltale signals her body showed to know that she was seriously worried. And yet, that was simply *not good enough.* "The patrol
they were relieving got to the rendezvous point expecting
them to be there yesterday, and they weren't there."

She's worried. She's only *worried. And she still hasn't
done anything.* "And they haven't shown up yet." He held
both the arms of his chair in a strangle grip, and stared at her
with unveiled accusation in his eyes. "So why aren't you doing anything? You *know* those two are as by-the-book as any
trainees you've ever had! They have never, *ever* violated orders. If they had a reason to be late, if they knew they were
going to be delayed, they'd have sent a teleson message! If
they haven't, it's because they can't, because something
happened to them!"

His voice was rising, and he knew it, and what was more,
he didn't care that he was making a blatant display of his
emotions. For once in his life he *wanted* someone to know
how upset he was. Judeth made soothing motions, as if she
thought he could somehow be propitiated by a few words.
As if she thought he could be "reasoned out of his hysteria."

She was certainly going to try. "We *are* doing something,
Drake; the patrol has left the rendezvous and they are going
on out to see if they can't find some sign of Blade and Tad.
It's too early to get in a panic about this—"

Too early to get in a panic? Who does she think she's talking to? He held himself back from exploding at her only by great effort of will. "You tell me that when it's *your* child that's missing!" he snapped at her. "Or have you gotten so wrapped up in being a *commander* that you've forgotten this isn't wartime? Instead of telling me not to panic, I suggest you tell me what else you're doing *right now*. And if you aren't doing anything right now, I am not interested in hearing why you can't! I'll pull in every resource I have to see that something *does* get done, and without any nonsense about *not getting into a panic* because one person thinks it's *too early!*"

That was the closest he had ever come in his life to saying that he was actually going to use all the power and influence he held and had never used before, for any reason. *And I will, I'll do it, if I have to blackmail everyone in this city. Even her.* It was a threat, a real one, and he was not bluffing. But he felt he owed it to Judeth to warn her that lightning was going to fall on her before it came. If he used all his influence, it would be worse than lightning, and Judeth's position as commander might not survive the storm.

Her eyes darkened dangerously at his words, but her voice remained calm and even, which was something of a testament to her own control. Judeth did not like threats, but she was a realist, and she must know that he was not bluffing. "Right at this moment, the original patrol is flying out about a day in the right direction to see if they can find anything. If they don't, they'll go north of the track, then south, to see if they somehow went off course. Meanwhile, we're working on it. We're not just sitting around, waiting to see what happens. We're trying to find some way of locating them from here, and—*and*—" she finally raised her own voice as he got ready to explode again. "—*and* we are putting together search parties. Those will leave in the morning, since we can't *possibly* get one together before then. There is no point in grabbing unprepared people and sending them out at random. Now, if you can think of anything I might have missed, I'd like to hear it." The truth was, he couldn't, but that didn't stop him from wanting some action right that very moment, something besides merely "readying a search party." "I can't think of anything, but I'm—this is difficult. It's hard to think," he admitted grudgingly. "Does Skan know yet?"

"Aubri's telling him." *Poor Aubri,* her tone said, but *Poor Skan,* was what *he* was thinking.

He was afraid of this. He didn't want Tad to go off on this assignment any more than I wanted Blade to. I know he thought about going to Judeth and asking them to be reassigned to something else, and didn't do it. And now he must be wondering if he is to blame for them being missing.

"I'll tell Winterhart—" he began, his throat tightening at the thought. *Gods, how do I tell her! This was my fault, if it all comes down to it; something I said or did made Blade want to be in the Silvers in the first place, all my interference made her want to be assigned somewhere far away from here—if I hadn't tried to meddle in her life so much, she would still be here—maybe even doing something else with her life. And Tad would have a different partner, one that wouldn't have urged him to ask for assignment out of the city.* He desperately wanted someone else to take on the burden of telling her, so that he did not have to face her accusing eyes. Cowardly, yes, but—

"No, I'll tell her," Judeth said firmly. "I already know where she is, and I'm Silverblade's commander; that's part of my job. You go to Skan; I'll send her to you there."

There, as everyone in White Gryphon knew, was "Kechara's nursery" this time of the day. Skandranon spent at least an hour with her and the other children, human and otherwise, every afternoon. He loved to spend time with them, telling stories, playing games. Once again, Amberdrake got to his feet and headed for the door; this time Judeth didn't stop him.

As soon as the White Gryphon Council Hall was finished, the spouses of every city official had demanded the addition of real offices to it—Winterhart included. "We're tired of you people bringing work home, and we're tired of having work *follow* you home," she had said, both in her capacity as "spokes-spouse" and in her capacity as a city official herself. "Home is where you go to get away from idiots who couldn't find the public latrine without a map and a guide! And *every* official gets an office, even if it's no bigger than a closet!" she had added. "I don't care if the post of k'Leshya Clan chief has never had a physical office before, the k'Leshya Clan chief has also never lived in anything other than a tent before, and if he can break tradition by living in a cave, he can break it a little more by having an office and regular hours, and he can bar the door when his office hours are over!" She had glared at Amberdrake, and her eyes had said, *And that goes twice as much for you, my dear and overobliging spouse!*

Since Lionwind's wife had been standing behind Winterhart, nodding her head at every word and with one hand on her knife, he and every other city official had readily agreed.

The offices were all built into the cliff behind the Council Hall, small and private, and close to the other public buildings. The administrative building for the Silvers was not that far away from Amberdrake's office, and in that building was the nursery they had made for Kechara when she was still acting as the communication center for the Silvers. She shared it with the youngsters of anyone else in the Silvers or in city administration who needed to have someone tend their little ones while they worked. It was a good arrangement for everyone, and it gave Kechara a never-ending stream of playmates who were all her mental age, even if she was chronologically six or more times older.

Even though Kechara's powers were severely limited, she could still "talk" to any gryphon within the city territory. That alone was useful to the Silvers, and a very good reason to keep her right where she always had been.

As Amberdrake hurried toward the building, every muscle and nerve writhing with anxiety, he couldn't even begin to imagine how Judeth had thought that Aubri could break something like this gently to Skan. She must have been so upset by the news that her ability to reason had flown right out the door! *Aubri hasn't the tact of a brick. When Skan—*

"DRAKE!" The bellow of a gryphon enraged could probably be heard all the way up to the farms, and the gryphon that burst out of the door of the Silvers' headquarters looked perfectly ready to chew up iron and spit out nails. *Burst* was indeed the correct term; the white-and-black gryphon erupted from the door flying, his head swiveling in all directions, presumably looking for his friend as he gained altitude. *"Drake!"* Skan bellowed again, from a height of about three lengths above him. "These *idiots*! They've lost—"

"I know, I know," Amberdrake shouted back, waving his hands frantically. "That's why I'm—"

Skan folded his wings and landed heavily, as if he were pouncing on something, every feather on end. "I want every mage in this city working on a way to find them!" he said wrathfully. "I don't care what they're doing! This is an emergency! I want everybody pulled in off of whatever they're doing, and I want search parties out there *now!* I want messengers sent to Shalaman! I want every man the Haighlei can spare out there looking, too! I want—"

We have to work this together, or they're not going to listen to us. Amberdrake seized his friend's head in both hands, hooking his fingertips into the gryphon's nares. He pulled Skan's beak down so that the gryphon was looking directly into his eyes. "I *know*," he said forcefully. "Believe me, I feel the same! We have to call the Council to authorize this, Skan, but I don't think anybody on it is going to disagree with us, and if they do—"

Skan growled wordlessly at the very idea.

"If they do, we—we both know things they wish we didn't," he pointed out.

"We do. And I'll use that." There it was; Skan agreed with him. It wasn't *right*, but it was better than arguing with shard-counters until it was too late to do anything.

"But there's no point in scattering everybody like a covey

of frightened quail," Drake persisted, trying to convince himself as much as Skandranon. "All right? Let's get things coordinated. Judeth told the original patrol to look for them; right now that's all that anyone can do *out there*. We have to organize, and get people out there, talk people into using Gates again if we have to. We have to get Council backing for all that before anything else can be done, and that isn't going to happen if we're both standing here and wasting precious time screaming like outraged parents!"

"We *are* outraged parents!" The gryphon kicked clods of dirt in flurries of rage. "I don't want to have to follow procedure!"

Amberdrake put his fists on his hips and leaned toward Skandranon. "We will get Council approval, by whatever means necessary."

I hate it, but that's the case. If we want to have more than just "the usual effort" from the Silvers, we have to get Council authorization. And that's where the threats of blackmail come in.

Skan growled again, but without as much force behind it. "Damn it, Drake, why do you have to be so right?" he snarled. "All right then, I'll go back in there and have Kechara call in the Council members so we can authorize all of this."

Amberdrake wanted to add *don't frighten her*, but he held his tongue. Of all of them, Skan knew best how not to do anything that would make Kechara unhappy. He was her "Papa Skan," and she loved him with all of her heart—which was as large as her poor brain was small. He would no more do anything to frighten her than he would allow Blade and Tad to languish in the wilderness, unsought-for and unrescued.

He headed back toward the Council Hall, certain that if Winterhart and Zhaneel were not already on the way there, after Kechara's call, they would be.

Skan came stalking in shortly after Drake, and within moments after that, the rest of the Council members came

hurrying in. Judeth was one of the first, looking very surprised and taken aback, and just a little annoyed; and although Skan leveled an icy glare at her, his tone was civil
enough.

"I've called this meeting," he said. "Since this *is* an emergency situation."

He waited only until there were enough Council members present to constitute a quorum, and until everyone was
seated before nodding to Judeth.

"You're the commander of the Silvers, so I think it best
that you explain the emergency to the rest of the Council,"
he said crisply. Judeth looked as if she wanted to say something scathing to him, but held her tongue, which was probably wise.

Amberdrake had a good idea of what she was thinking,
however. She was, first and foremost, a military commander, and under any other circumstances, the fact that two of
the most junior members of the Silvers were missing—or
overdue—should not have been considered an emergency
the Council should be concerned with. Only an hysterical—
but powerful—parent could have thought that it was.

And Amberdrake would have cheerfully throttled her for
suggesting any such thing, if she dared.

*Throttled her, then revived her so I could throttle her
again.* Part of him was appalled at this capacity for violence
within himself; the rest of him nodded in gleeful agreement
at the idea. *Then I'd revive her so that Skan could have
a turn.*

But she evidently knew better—or the threat of his influence made her think twice about suggesting any such thing.
Judeth explained the situation, coolly and calmly, while the
other members of the Council listened without making any
comments. Skan kept glaring around the table as if daring
any of them to say that this was not the sort of emergency
for which the Council should be called.

No one did, but Snowstar did have something to say that

put the entire situation into a perspective that Amberdrake greatly appreciated.

"Has anyone ever gone missing this way before?" he asked, without looking either at Skan or at Amberdrake. "I know that there have been a handful of accidents among the Silvers, but I don't ever recall any of our Silvers on Outpost Duty ever *disappearing* before. Judeth, you haven't even had any fatalities in the Silvers since we encountered the Haighlei, and all of *those* were on the trek to find the coast. If this is a new development, I think it is a very serious one."

Aubri opened his beak, then looked at Judeth, startled. She was the one who replied.

"Actually—you're right," she said, sounding just as surprised as Aubri looked. "The fatalities among young gryphons since we founded the city have all been among the hunters, *not* the Silvers, and the accidents causing injuries among the Silvers have all been just that—accidents, usually caused by weather, and not a single death from something like a drunkard or fight. To date we haven't had a single case of Outpost Patrols going missing. They've broken limbs, they've gotten sick, we've had to send help out to them, and one set of humans even got lost once—but they had a teleson and we knew they were all right, we just couldn't find them for a while. We've never had anyone just vanish before. . . ."

Her eyes were the only part of her that showed how alarmed this new observation made her, but Amberdrake was savagely pleased at the way that her eyes went blank and steely. He knew that look. That was General Judeth, suddenly encountering a deadly enemy where she had been told there was open ground with no threats.

"I kept thinking this was—sort of one of the hazards of duty—but that was under war conditions or while we were making our way here," Aubri muttered, so shamefaced that his nares flushed a brilliant red. "Snowstar, you're right! We've *never* lost a Silver since—since we allied with the Haighlei!"

You two have been making the mistake of thinking that the Silvers were the extension of the old army—but they aren't and our situation is completely different than it was before the wars. And how could I have been so blind not to have seen your blindness?

"Then I believe this does qualify as a full-scale emergency," Snowstar said firmly. "When two highly-trained individuals drop completely out of sight, for no reason and with no warning, it seems to me that the danger is not only to them alone, but possibly to the entire city. What if they were removed so that they could not alert us to some enemy who is moving against us? How can we know that if we don't mount a rescue, in strength and numbers?"

Heads nodded all around the table, and Amberdrake exchanged stricken glances with Winterhart, who had come in just in time to hear that. He felt cold all over, and she had paled. He could have done without hearing that. He was perversely glad that Snowstar had thought of it, for it certainly swayed even the veterans on the Council to their cause, but he could have done without hearing it.

Either Snowstar really believes that, or the self-proclaimed nondiplomat Snowstar just made a shrewd play in our support. Or both.

A heavy and ominous silence filled the Council Hall, and no one seemed prepared to break it. Skan was as frozen as a statue, and beside him, Zhaneel simply looked to be in too much shock to be able to think. Winterhart stood beside her Council seat, unable to sit, clutching the back of it; her knuckles were as white as her namesake. Amberdrake himself felt unable to move, every limb leaden and inert.

Judeth cleared her throat, making all of them jump. "Right," she said briskly, silence broken. "We have the original pair flying a search pattern; we're putting together more search teams. Does anyone have any further suggestions?"

Skan opened his beak, but Snowstar beat him to it. "I'll organize the mages and start distance-scrying," he said immediately. "We're probably too far away, but those who *can* scry for them should at least try. We'll look for the traces of the magic on all the items they had with them; even if something made them crash, those traces will still be there. I'll also pick out mages for the search parties."

Once again, Skan opened his beak—then glared around the table, to make certain that he wasn't interrupted this time. "We should send a message to Shalaman," he said belligerently. "His people know that forest better than we do. We should make him—I mean, *ask* him—to send out parties of his hunters."

"That's good," Judeth approved, making a note of it. "I can put anyone who's been posted to that area on search parties, but if we can field Haighlei who are trained to hunt the forest in addition to our own people, that will be even better. Anything else?"

Search parties, magic, the Haighlei. . . . Thoughts flitted through Drake's head, but he couldn't make any of them hold still long enough to be examined. Judeth looked around the table to meet shaking heads, and nodded.

"Good. We've got a plan," she said firmly. "We should assume that whatever has happened to these Silvers could endanger the city, and make finding them a top priority. Let's get to it."

She stood up and was halfway to the door before anyone else was even out of his chair. He didn't blame her. If the situation was reversed, *he* wouldn't want to be in the same room with four frantic parents either.

And he wouldn't want to face two people who had just threatened to blackmail him for not taking the loss of their children seriously enough.

Everyone else deserted the hall as quickly. Only Aubri paused at the door, looking back with uncertainty in his gaze. He opened his beak, then swallowed hard, shook his head, and followed the others.

Skandranon wanted nothing more than to rush off to the rescue of his son. Failing that, he wanted to tear the gizzard out of those who were responsible for his disappearance. Right now, so far as his heart was concerned, the ones responsible were right here in White Gryphon.

Judeth and Aubri. It was all *their* fault. If they hadn't assigned the children to this far-flung outpost, both his beloved son and his dear friend Amberdrake's daughter would still be here.

"I *knew* that this was a mistake all along!" he seethed at Zhaneel as he paced the length and breadth of the Council Hall. "I knew they were too young to be sent off on Outpost Duty! No one that young has ever been sent off alone like that before! They should have been posted here, like everyone else was! Judeth's getting senile, and Aubri was already there to show her the way—and—"

"Please!" Zhaneel suddenly exploded. *"Stop!"*

He stared at her, his mouth still open, one foot raised.

"Stop it, Skan," she said, in a more normal tone. "It is not their fault. It is not the fault of anyone. And if you would stop trying to find someone to blame, we would get something done." She looked up at him, with fear and anxiety in her eyes. "You are a mage; I am not. You go to work with Snowstar and the others, and I shall go to the messenger-mage and send a message in your name to Shalaman, asking for his help. At least I can do that much. And Skandranon— he is *my* son as well as yours, and *I* am able to act without rages and threats."

With that, she turned away from him and left him still standing with his foot upraised and his beak open, staring after her in shock.

Alone, for Amberdrake and Winterhart had already left.

Stupid, stupid gryphon. She's right, you know. Blaming Aubri and Judeth won't get you anywhere, and if you take things out on them, you're only going to make them mad at you. The Black Gryphon would be remembered as an angry, overprotective, vengeful parent. And what good would that do? None, of course.

What good would it do?

All at once, his energy ran out of him. He sat down on the floor of the Council Hall, feeling—old.

Old, tired, defeated, and utterly helpless, shaking with fear and in the grip of his own weakness. He squinted his eyes tightly closed, ground his beak, and shivered from anything but cold.

Somewhere out there, his son was lost, possibly hurt, certainly in trouble. And there was nothing, *nothing* that he could do about it. This was one predicament that the Black Gryphon wasn't going to be able to swoop in and salvage.

I couldn't swoop in on anything these days even if I could salvage it. I'm an anachronism; I've outlived my usefulness. It is happening all over again, except this time there can't be a rebirth of the Black Gryphon from the White Gryphon. The body wears out, the hips grow stiff and the muscles strain. I'm the one that's useless and senile, not Judeth and Aubri. They were doing the best they could; I was the one flapping my beak and making stupid threats. That is all that is left for a failed warrior to do.

For a moment, he shook with the need to throw back his head and keen his grief and helplessness to the sky, in the faint hope that perhaps some god somewhere might hear him. His throat constricted terribly. With the weight of intolerable grief and pain on his shoulders, he slowly raised his head.

As his eyes fell on the door through which Zhaneel had departed, his mind unfroze, gradually coming out of its shock.

What am I? What am I thinking?

I may be old now, but I am still a legend to these people. Heroes don't ever live as long as they want to, and most die young. I've lasted. That's all experience. I'm a mage, and more skilled than when I was younger—and if I'm not the fighter I used to be, I'm also a lot smarter than I used to be! And what I'm feeling—I know what it is. I know. It was what Urtho felt every time I left, every time one of his gryphons wound up missing. I loved him so dearly, and I breathe each breath honoring his memory—but he was a great man because he accepted his entire being, and dealt with it. I am not Urtho—but I am his son in spirit, and what I honor I can also emulate. There's plenty I can do, starting with seeing to it that Snowstar hasn't overlooked anything!

He shook himself all over, as if he was shaking off some dark, cold shadow that was unpleasantly clinging to his back, and strode out of the Council Hall as fast as his legs would carry him.

What I honor in Urtho's deeds, others have also honored in me. Urtho could embrace every facet of a situation and handle all of them with all of his intellect, whether it angered him personally or not. That was why he was a leader and not a panicked target. He could act when others would be overwhelmed by emotion. If I think of this disappearance in terms only of how I feel about it, then I will miss details that could be critical while I fill my vision with myself, and that could cost lives. Let the historians argue over whether I was enraged or determined or panicked on this day! I can still be effective to my last breath!

It was not clear at first where the Adept had run off to, and by the time Skan tracked him down, Snowstar had managed to gather all of the most powerful mages together in his own dwelling and workshop. Skan was impressed in spite of himself at how quickly the Kaled'a'in mage had moved. It was notoriously difficult to organize mages, but Snowstar seemed to have accomplished the task in a very limited amount of time.

There were seven mages at work including Snowstar. They had been divided into pairs, seated at individual tables so that they didn't interfere with each other, each pair of them scrying for something in particular. One pair looked for the teleson, one for the tent, one for the basket. Snowstar was working by himself, but the moment that Skan came near him, he looked up and beckoned.

"I'm looking for Tadrith myself," he said without preamble, "I was waiting for you to help me; the blood-tie he has with you is going to make it possible to find him, if it's at all possible. You will both feel similar magically, as you know."

"If?" Skan said, growing cold all over. *Is he saying that he thinks Tad is—dead?* "You mean you feel he is already dead—"

Snowstar made a soothing gesture. "No, actually, I don't. Even if Tadrith was unconscious or worse, we'd still *find* him under normal circumstances. The problem is that I'm fairly certain that they're quite out of our range." The white-haired Kaled'a'in Adept shook his head. "But 'fairly' isn't 'completely,' and under the impetus of powerful emotions, people have been known to do extraordinary things before this. As you should know, better than any of us! I'm more than willing to try, if you are."

Skan grunted in extreme irritation, but reined it in. "Stupid question, Snowstar. I'd try until I fell over."

Snowstar grimaced. "I know it was a stupid question; forgive me. Fortunately, that won't matter to the spell or the stone." He gestured at a small table, and the half-dome of volcanic glass atop it. "Would you?"

Skan took his place opposite the chair behind the table; he'd done scrying himself before, once or twice, but always with another mage and never with Snowstar. Each mage had his own chosen vehicle for scrying, but most used either a clear or black stone or a mirror. He put his foreclaws up on the table, surrounding his half of the stone with them. Snowstar placed his own hands on the table, touching fingertip to talon-tip with Skan.

After that, it was a matter of Skan concentrating on his son and supplying mage-energy to Snowstar while Snowstar created and loosed the actual spell. Some mages had a visual component to this work, but Snowstar didn't. It took someone who was not only able to see mage-energy but one who was sensitive to its movement—like a gryphon—to sense what he was doing.

Skan felt the energy gathering all around them and condensing into the form of the spell, like a warm wind encircling them and then cooling. He felt it strain and tug at the restraints Snowstar held on it. And he felt Snowstar finally let it go.

Then—nothing. It leaped out—and dissipated. It wasn't *gone*, as if it had gone off to look for something. It was *gone* as if it had stretched itself out so thin that a mere breeze had made it fragment into a million uncoordinated bits.

Snowstar jerked as if a string holding him upright had snapped, then sagged down, his hands clutching the stone. *"Damn,"* he swore softly, as harsh an oath as Skan had ever heard him give voice to. "It's no good. It's just too far."

Skan sagged himself, his throat locked up in grief, his chest so tight it was hard to take a breath. *Tad. . . .*

A few moments later the others had all uttered the same words, in the same tones of anger and defeat—all except the pair trying to reach the teleson.

They simply looked baffled and defeated, and they hadn't said anything. Finally Snowstar stopped waiting for them to speak up for themselves and went over to them. "Well?" he said, as Skan followed on his heels.

Skan knew both of them; one was a young Kaled'a'in called Redoak, the other a mercenary mage from Urtho's following named Gielle. The latter was an uncannily lucky fellow; he had been a mere Journeyman at the beginning of the mage-storms following the Cataclysm, but when they were over, he was an Adept. He was more than a bit bewildered by the transition, but had handled it gracefully—far more gracefully than some would have.

"I can't explain it, sir," he said, obviously working to suppress an automatic reaction to authority of snapping to attention and saluting. "When I couldn't reach Tadrith's device, I tried others, just to make certain that there wasn't something wrong with me. I've been able to call up every teleson we've ever created, including the one out there with the patrol looking for the missing Silvers. I got the one we left with the garrison at Khimbata, which is farther away than Tadrith is. I got all of them—except the one we sent out with Tadrith and Silverblade. It's—" he shook his head. "It's just gone, it's as if it was never there! It hasn't even been retuned or broken, that would leave a telltale. I've been working with telesons most of my life as a mage, and I've only seen something like this happen once before."

"Was that during the Wars?" Snowstar asked instantly.

Gielle nodded. "Yes, sir. And it was just a freak accident, something you'd have to have been an Adept to pull off, though. Some senile old fart who should never have been put in charge of anything was given an unfamiliar teleson to recharge and reversed the whole spell. Basically, he sucked all the magic out of it, made it just so much unmagical junk." Gielle shrugged. "The only reason he *could* do that was because he was an Adept. Senile, but still an Adept. We make those telesons foolproof for a good reason. Tadrith couldn't have done that, even by accident and a thousand tries a day, and even if someone actually smashed the teleson, I'd still be able to activate it and get a damaged echo-back. If it had been shattered by spell, the telltale would still mark the area magically. I don't know what to think about this."

Snowstar pursed his lips, his forehead creasing as he frowned. "Neither do I. This is very peculiar. . . ."

Skan looked from one mage to the other, and back again. He caught Redoak's eye; the Kaled'a'in just held up his hands in a gesture of puzzlement.

"The signature of an Adept is fairly obvious," Redoak said slowly. "All Adepts have a distinctive style to even a moderately-trained eye. Urtho's was his ability to make enchantments undetectable—his mark was that there was no mark, but as far as I know, he could only veil spells he himself had crafted. The Haighlei would have seen something like this situation, I wager, by now. An Adept usually doesn't refrain from doing magic any time he can, especially not one of the old Neutrals. They were positively flamboyant about it. That was one of the quarrels that Urtho had with them."

"I have an idea," Snowstar finally said. "Listen, all of you, I'll need all your help on this. We're going to do something very primitive, much more primitive than scrying." He looked around the room. "Redoak, you and Gielle and Joffer put all the small worktables together. Rides-alone, you know where my shaman implements are; go get them. Lora, Greenwing, come with me." He looked at Skan. "*You* go to the Silvers' headquarters and get me the biggest map of the area the children were headed into that you can find or bully out of them. They might give me an argument; you, they won't dare."

"They'd lose a limb," Skan growled, and he went straight for the door. He did his best not to stagger; he hadn't used that much mage-energy in a long time, and it took more out of him than he had expected.

All right, gryphon. Remember what you told yourself earlier. You have experience. You may fall on your beak from fatigue and tear something trying to fly in and save the day, but you have experience. Rely on experience when your resources are low, and rely on others when you can—not when you want to, vain gryphon. Work smarter. Think. Use what you have. And don't break yourself, stupid gryphon, because you are running out of spare parts!

He saw to his surprise that it was already dark outside; he hadn't realized that he had spent so long with the mages, trying to find the children. No wonder he was tired and a bit weak!

The Silvers' headquarters was lit up as if they were holding high festival inside, which made him feel a bit more placated. At least they were *doing* something, taking this seriously now. *Too bad Snowstar had to convince them there was a threat to their own hides before they were willing to move. They should have just moved on it. Wasn't that the way we operated in the old days?* He barged in the front door, readied a foreclaw and grabbed the first person wearing a Silver Gryphon badge that he saw, explaining what he wanted in a tone that implied he would macerate anyone who denied it to him. The young human did not even make a token protest as the talons caught in his tunic and the huge beak came dangerously near his face.

"S–stay here, s–sir," he stammered, backing up as soon as Skan let go of him. "I'll f–find what you w–want and b–bring it right here!"

Somehow, tonight Skan had the feeling that he was *not* "beloved where e're he went." That was fine. In his current black mood, he would much rather be feared than beloved.

People have been thinking of me as the jolly old fraud, the uncle who gives all the children pony rides, he thought, grating his beak, his talons scoring the floor as he seethed. *They forgot what I* was, *forgot the warrior who used to tear makaar apart with his bare talons.*

Well, tonight they were getting a reminder.

The boy came back very quickly with the rolled-up map. Skan unrolled it just long enough to make certain that they weren't trying to fob something useless off on him to make him go away, then gruffly thanked the boy and launched himself out the door.

Despite the darkness, he flew back with his prize. When he marched through Snowstar's door, he saw at once that the workroom had already been transformed. Everything not needed for the task at hand had been cleared away against the wall. Other projects had been piled atop one another with no thought for coherence. It was going to take days to put the workroom back into some semblance of order, but Skan doubted that Snowstar was going to be thinking about anything *but* Blade and Tad until they were found.

At least we have one friend who took all this seriously without having to be persuaded.

The several small tables were now one large one, waiting for the map he held in his beak. The moment he showed his face at the door, eager hands took—snatched!—the map away from him and spread it out on the table. Redoak lit a pungent incense, filling the room with smoke that just stopped short of being eye-watering. The mage that Snowstar had called Rides-alone, who came from one of the many odd tribes that Urtho had won to his cause, had a drum in his hands. Evidently he was going to be playing it during— whatever it was they were going to do.

"Right." Snowstar stood over the table, the only one who was standing, and held a long chain terminating in a teardrop-shaped, rough-polished piece of some dark stone. "Redoak, you watch what the pendulum does, and mark what I told you out on the map. Rides-alone, give me a heartbeat rhythm. The rest of you, concentrate; I'll need your combined energies along with anything else I can pull up out of the local node. Skan, that goes for you, too. Come sit opposite me, but *don't* think of Tad or Blade, think of me. Got that?"

He was not about to argue; this looked rather like one of those bizarre shamanistic rituals that Urtho used to try, now and again, when classical spellcasting failed. He simply did as he was told, watching as Snowstar carefully suspended the pendulum over the map at the location where the youngsters had last been heard from. Rides-alone began a steady drum pattern, hypnotic without inducing slumber; somehow it enhanced concentration. How *that* was managed, Skan could not begin to imagine.

For a long time, nothing happened. The stone remained quite steady, and Skan was afraid that whatever Snowstar had planned wasn't working after all. But Snowstar remained impassive, and little by little, he began to move the pendulum along a route going north and east of the point of the youngsters' last camp.

And abruptly, without any warning at all, the pendulum *did* move.

It swung, violently and abruptly *away* from the spot Snowstar had been trying to move it toward. And in total defiance of gravity, it hung at an angle, as if it were being repelled by something there.

Snowstar gave a grunt, although Skan could not tell if it was satisfaction or not, and Redoak made a mark on the map with a stick of charcoal. Snowstar moved his hand a trifle.

The pendulum came back down, as if it had never exhibited its bizarre behavior.

Snowstar moved it again, a little at a time, and once again came to a point where the pendulum repeated its action. The strange scene was repeated over and over, as Redoak kept marking places on the map and Snowstar moved the pendulum back.

It took uncounted drumbeats, and sweat was pouring down the faces of every mage around the table, when Snowstar finally dropped the pendulum and signaled to Rides-alone to stop drumming. There was an irregular area marked out in charcoal dots on the map, an area that the pendulum avoided, and which the youngsters' flight would have bisected. Redoak connected the dots, outlining a weirdly-shaped blotch.

"I would lay odds that they are in there, somewhere," Snowstar said wearily. "It's an area in which there is *no* magic; no magic and no magical energy. Whatever is given off in the normal course of things by animals and plants is immediately lost, somehow, and I suspect magic brought into that area is drained away as well. I can only guess that is what happened to their basket when they flew over it."

"So the basket became heavier, and they couldn't fly with it?" Redoak hazarded, and whistled when Snowstar nodded. "That's not good. But how did you know what to use to find all this?"

Snowstar shrugged modestly. "It was Gielle that gave me the idea to look for a negative, and I remembered shamanic dowsing; you can look for something that is there, like metal, or something that is *not* there, like water. Urtho taught it to me; we used to use it to make certain that we weren't planting our outposts atop unstable ground." He looked across the table at Skan, who was trying very hard to tell himself that it wasn't likely for all the magic infused into the basket to drain off at once. He did not want to think about what that would have meant for poor Tadrith if the basket regained its normal weight in a single moment while aflight.

"Take that map with you, and tell Judeth what we've found," the Adept told Skan. "I'll work with the mages I'm sending out with the search teams. There's probably something about the area itself that we can shield against. I doubt that a mage caused this. It might just be a freak of nature, and the Haighlei would never have seen it, because they were looking *for* magic, not for its absence."

Skan nodded, and Redoak brushed a quick-drying varnish on the map to set the charcoal. The fumes warred unpleasantly with the lingering scent of the incense, but the moment the map was dry, the younger mage rolled it up and handed it to the Black Gryphon. Skan did not wait around to see what the rest of the mages were going to do; he took the map and fled out the door for the second time that evening.

This time he went straight to the planning room—which Judeth still referred to as the "War Room" out of habit. And it looked very much as if they were planning for a wartime situation. Judeth had a map spread out over the table, there were aides darting everywhere, Aubri was up on his hindquarters tracing out a line with one talon when Skan came in through the door.

"Snowstar thinks he has a general area," Skan said, as silence descended and all heads but Judeth's swiveled around at his entrance. "That's what he wanted the map for. *Here.*"

He handed the map to the nearest aide, who spread it out on the table over the existing one at Judeth's nod.

"What's that?" she asked, pointing at the blobby outline on the map.

"It's an area where there isn't magic," Skan replied. He repeated what Snowstar had told him, without the details about shamanic dowsing. "That would be why we can't raise the teleson. Snowstar thinks that anything that's magical gets all the mage-energy sucked out of it when it enters that area."

"And if the spell making the basket into something Tad could tow lost its power—" Judeth sucked in her lower lip, as one of the aides coughed. "Well, no matter how they landed, they're stuck now. No teleson, no magic—they'd have to hole up and hope for rescue."

Aubri studied the map for a moment. "The only teams we've sent out there were gryphon pairs, with one exception," he pointed out. "You and me, Judeth. We used a basket, and our flight path took us over that area. Nothing happened to *us*, so where did this come from?"

"Maybe it's been growing," offered one of the aides. "Maybe the more it eats, the bigger it grows."

"Well, that's certainly cheerful," Judeth said dryly, and patted the girl on the shoulder when she flushed a painful red. "No, you have a point, and we're going to have to find out what's causing this if you're right. If it's growing, sooner or later it's going to reach us. I did without working magic long enough and I'm not in the mood to do it again."

"That's a lot of area to cover," Aubri pointed out. "They could be anywhere in there, depending on how far they got before they had to land."

Land. Or crash. Skan's imagination was all too clever at providing him with an image of the basket plummeting down out of the sky. . . .

"We can probably cover it with four teams including a base camp," Judeth said, at last. "But I think we're going to have to do a ground search, in a sweep pattern. Those trees are bigger than anything most of us here have ever seen before, and you could drop Urtho's Tower in there and not see most of it. Gryphons may not do us a lot of good."

"They can look for signal smoke," Aubri objected.

Judeth did not say anything, but Skan knew what she was thinking, since it was something that he was already trying *not* to think about. The youngsters might be too badly hurt to put up a signal fire.

"Right, then the two already in the area can look for sig-nal smoke," she said. "I'll fly in a mage *here*, to set up a match-Gate terminus, and I'll call for volunteers for four teams who are willing to trust their hides to a Gate—"

"I shall go," said a deep voice from the doorway.

Skan swiveled his head, as Ikala moved silently into the room. "With all respect, Commander, I must go. I know this forest; your people do not. Forget my rank and my breeding; my father would say that you should, in a case like this. These two are my friends and my sworn comrades, and it is my honor and duty to help them."

"You are more than welcome, then. I'm going, you can count on it," Skan said instantly. "Drake will probably want to go, too. Judeth, that'll give you one mage and a field-Healer, along with a fighter."

Judeth sighed, but made no objections, probably because she knew they would be futile. "All right, but these are go-ing to be *big* teams. I don't want tiny little patrols running around in unknown territory. I want two mages, so you have one for each night watch on each team, and I want at least as many fighters. Ikala, you go call for volunteers among the hunters and the Silvers. Skan, go back to Snowstar and ex-plain the situation and what we need." She glared at both of them. "Don't just stand there, *go!*"

Skan went, but he was a fraction slower than Ikala and reached the door in second place. By the time he was out-side, Ikala was nowhere in sight.

But he was overjoyed that Ikala was still willing to volun-teer, even with the need to trust to a Gate for transport. The young Haighlei was precisely what they needed; someone who knew the ordinary hazards of such a forest, and how to meet them.

Snowstar had already anticipated Judeth's decision about a Gate. "As if any of us would be afraid to trust our own Gates!" he replied scornfully. "We've been perfectly willing to use them for the last five years, it's been the rest of you who were so overly cautious about them!"

"Not *me!*" Skan protested, but Snowstar was already on to other things. "Gielle will fly out with a gryphon as soon as it's light; I'll have Redoak head one of the other three teams after you all get through the Gate," the Adept was saying. "I have more mages willing to volunteer than Judeth needs, but not all of them are suited to this kind of mission. Tell her I'll be choosing combat experience over sheer power; we can't take the chance that this dead zone is a freak of nature. No matter what she thinks, it might have a traceable cause, and that cause might be one of the mages who escaped the Wars."

Skan nodded; he was certain that Judeth had already thought of that.

"I'll go find Drake," he said. It was going to be a long night, and one he was certain none of them would be able to sleep through. They might as well start getting ready for deployment.

At least *that* was something useful.

Aging and hedonistic you may be, stupid gryphon, but you're also effective.

Aubri and Judeth

Eight

Amberdrake did not sleep that night. Despite the feeling that he was working at a fever pitch, he got precious little accomplished. Most of what he did was to go over the same scenarios, in his mind, on paper, in fevered conversation with whoever would listen—usually the long-suffering Gesten. But no matter how tired he became, the weariness was never enough to overcome him, not even for a moment.

Insomnia was only one of the physical effects he suffered. He simply could not be still; he would sit or lie down, only to leap to his feet again as another urgent thought struck him. The muscles of his neck and back were so tense that no amount of soaking would relax him—not that he stayed long enough in a hot pool to do any good. He had not eaten since the news. His throat was too tight to swallow, his stomach a tight, cold knot, and as for his nerves—if he'd had a client as wrought up as he was, he would have recommended immediate tranquilization by a Healer. But if he had submitted himself to a Healer, he would be in no condition to accomplish anything thereafter. He could not do that.

Amberdrake recalled Zhaneel's words of so long ago, as if they were an annoyance.

Who heals the healer?

Skan and Snowstar had not commandeered all of the
mages in the city—there was always one whose sole duty
was to oversee magical communications. Those communications were between both White Gryphon and the Silvers
posted outside the city—in Shalaman's bodyguard, for instance—and with Shalaman himself, via his priests. There
could be no speaking with Shalaman directly, of course.
There was no such thing in Haighlei society as a direct link
to anyone important. The messages would have to go
through the priests, who were the only people permitted the
use of magic, then to Shalaman's Chief Priest Leyuet, and
only then to Shalaman. Amberdrake tracked down the mage
in question and had him send his own personal plea for help
to the Haighlei in addition to Skan's—but after that, he was
at loose ends.

There was only so much he could do. He was no mage, he
could not possibly help Skan in trying to locate the children.
He could pack, and did, for a trek across rough, primitive
country, but that did not exactly take much time, even with
Gesten coming along behind him and repacking it more efficiently. He certainly couldn't do anything to help the rescue
parties of Silvers that Judeth and Aubri were organizing.

Even if he could have, it might only have made things
worse. He suspected that after his threats, overt and covert,
Judeth would not appreciate seeing his face just now. Aubri
would be more forgiving, but Judeth had lived long under
the comfortable delusion that she no longer had to cope
with the vagaries of "politics." As with most true military
leaders, she had always hated politics, even while she used
political games to further her own causes. She had thought
that without a King, a court, or a single titular leader among
them, she was at last free to do what she wanted with a
policing branch. She tried to keep the Silvers autonomous
from the governing branch, and that was largely what she
had accomplished.

Now Amberdrake had made it very clear to her that there

was no such thing as an environment that was free of politics, that under duress, even friends would muster any and all weapons at their disposal. And she had just learned in the harshest possible way that no one is ever free of the politics and machinations that arise when people live together as a group.

No one likes to have their illusions shattered, least of all someone who holds so few.

Judeth would be very difficult to live with for some time. He only hoped that her good sense would overcome her anger with him, and that she would see and understand his point of view. Hopefully Judeth would see Amberdrake as having used a long-withheld weapon at a strategic time, rather than seeing him as a friend who betrayed an unspoken trust to get what he wanted. If not—he had made an enemy, and there was nothing he could do about that now. Nor, if he'd had the chance to reverse time and go back to that moment of threat, would he have unsaid a single word. He had meant every bit of it, and Judeth had better get used to the idea that people—even the senior *kestra'chern*—would do anything to protect their children. That was one thing she had never had to deal with as a military commander before, because a military structure allowed replacement or reassignment of possible mutineers. Parental protectiveness was a factor that was going to be increasingly important as the children of the original settlers of White Gryphon entered the Silvers. Perhaps it was for the best that the precedent had been set in this way.

And no matter what happens, knowing myself, I will have simultaneous feelings of justification as a concerned and desperate parent, as well as guilt over not having done better and had more forethought.

So there was nothing more he could do, really, except to wait. Wait for morning, wait for word from Shalaman and from the mages, wait, wait, wait. . . .

Just as it was when he had served in Urtho's ranks, waiting was the hardest job he had ever held. He had been in control of at least part of the life of this city for so long that, like Judeth, he had gotten accustomed to being able to fix problems as soon as they arose without anyone offering opposing force. Now, as the number of emergencies died down and new people came into authority, his control was gone. All of his old positions of influence were in the hands of others, and he was back to the old game of waiting.

Finally he returned home, since it was the first place where anyone with news would look for him. As he paced the walkway outside the house, unable to enter the place that now seemed too confining and held far too many memories of his lost daughter, his mind circled endlessly without ever coming up with anything new. Only the circling; anger and fear, fear and anger. Anger at himself, at Judeth, at Blade—it wasn't productive, but it was inevitable, and anger kept his imagination at bay. It was all too easy to imagine Blade hurt, Blade helpless, Blade menaced by predatory animals or more nebulous enemies.

And once again, he would be one of the last to know what others had long since uncovered. He was *only* Blade's father, as he had *only* been a *kestra'chern*. Yet hanging about in the hope that someone would take pity on him and tell him something was an exercise in futility. So he alternately paced and sat, staring out into the darkness, listening to the roar of the waves beneath him. In the light falling gently down onto the harbor from the city, the foam on the top of the waves glowed as if it was faintly luminescent. A wooden wind-chime swung in the evening breeze to his right, and a glass one sang softly to his left. How often had he sat here on a summer evening, listening to those chimes?

Caught between glass and wood, that which breaks and that which bends, that which sings and that which survives. So our lives go.

Winterhart joined him long after the moon had come out. He turned at her familiar footstep, to see her approaching from the direction of the Council Hall, the moonlight silvering her hair. In the soft light there was no sign of her true age; she could have been the *trondi'irn* of Urtho's forces, or the first ambassador to the Haighlei so many years ago. Only when she drew close were the signs of anxiety and tension apparent in her face, her eyes, the set of her mouth.

"They're putting together the last of the supplies," she said, before he could ask. "Skan and the mages haven't come out of Snowstar's work area yet, and Shalaman hasn't replied. Don't worry, he will before the night is over; remember how long his court runs at night."

He did remember; in the tropical heat of the climate around Khimbata, Shalaman's people all took long naps in the afternoon, and then continued their court ceremonies, entertainments, and duties until well after midnight. And he had no fear that Shalaman would refuse help; the Emperor could send off a hundred hunters or more from his forces, and they would never be missed. No, the only question was how soon the hunters could be somewhere that they could do some good. First the priests would have to approve the departure, then they would have to travel across many leagues of forest before they were anywhere near the place where the children had vanished. All that would take time, precious time. . . .

Blindly, he held out his arms and Winterhart came into them. They held each other, seeking comfort in one another's warmth and presence. There was no point in talking; they would only echo one another, each saying what the other was thinking. They both knew that, and knew that talking would ease nothing, soothe nothing.

So they simply sat down on the smooth, cool stone bench outside their home, and held each other, and waited beneath the stars. Neither of them were strangers to waiting.

That did not make waiting any easier—except that it removed the additional pain of loneliness.

Judeth must have gotten over her own anger by dawn, for she showed no signs of it when a messenger summoned both Amberdrake and Winterhart to what the young Silver called a "planning session." The two of them had bathed and changed clothing, hoping that clean bodies would restore their minds a little. Amberdrake had shunned his usual finery in favor of something very like Winterhart's practical working garb, hoping that there might *possibly* be something he could *do* once the sun rose. When the summons came, both of them had been sitting over a breakfast neither of them had been able to touch, and it was a relief to rise and follow the youngster back to the Council hall.

Skan and Zhaneel and their other son Keenath were already there, showing just as much strain as Amberdrake felt, although only someone who knew gryphons well would have recognized the signs of strain in overpreened feathers, plumage lying flat against the body, posture that showed their muscles were as tense and knotted as Amberdrake's. He doubted that they had slept, but the sight of Keenath made a moment of intense anger flash through Amberdrake's heart.

He still has *a child. And if his other had not been so intent on leaving the city, mine might not have gone either!*

But that was irrational and entirely incorrect, and he knew it. He suppressed it immediately, and he and Winterhart maneuvered through the group crowded in here so that they could form a united block with the other set of parents.

Judeth did not look as if she had slept either. Deep shadows touched the swollen pouches under her eyes, and she looked twice her real age. Aubri didn't even pretend to be calm; he chewed incessantly on one of his old, shed feathers, presumably to keep from shredding his current plumage.

There were thirty or forty people in the group; Amberdrake noticed that at least six of them were mages and he, Winterhart, Skan, Keenath and Zhaneel were the only non-Silvers. Ikala was among the Silvers gathered here, and Amberdrake was irrationally pleased to see him, as if the tall young man represented more than just a local expert on the rain forest.

The Council Hall was the only room large enough to hold

all of them, and Judeth had completely taken it over, strewing maps and other documents all over the table. It looked as if she had been here for some time. "Snowstar and the mages have uncovered something damned peculiar," she said, when they had all gathered around the map-covered table. She tapped a darkened, irregularly shaped blob on the map in front of her. "This area here has no signs of magic. *None,* and they tell me that's practically impossible. The missing patrol was due to pass along this line—" She drew a swift mark with a piece of charcoal which crossed the southern end of the irregular-shaped area. "—and if there's something in there that's negating mage-energy, you can imagine for yourself what that would mean for both their carry-basket and their teleson."

Amberdrake was all too able to imagine what that would do to a carry-basket; and from the way Winterhart suddenly clutched his arm, her fingers digging into the muscle, so was she. In his mind, he saw the two figures he had watched fly off into the distance suddenly stricken for a moment, then plummeting to their deaths on the unforgiving ground below.

"That means we're going to have to come in somewhere near the edge and walk in," Judeth continued, without any hint that *she* had envisioned the same disaster that had played itself out behind Amberdrake's eyes. "Our Gate probably won't work inside this area, and we'll have to suppose for now that nothing else magical in nature will work either. We'll have to operate by the old rules of working without magic, although yes, we *will* be taking mages, just in case magic does work after all. Though—if there's no local mage-power available, Snowstar tells me that the mages will be just like Journeymen and Apprentices, and limited to their own personal power. That's going to put a serious crimp in their activities, and any mages that go along had better start thinking in terms of budgeting themselves before they act."

She leveled a sharp glance across the table, to the point where the mages of the Silvers had bunched together.

"What about the gryphons?" someone wanted to know. "Can't they just fly overhead and scout the way they always do?"

She closed her eyes for a moment, and sighed. "If I wanted a sign that our luck has turned truly wretched, I could not have conjured up one more certain. This *is* the rainy season for that part of the world—and the weather-mages tell me that storms will be unceasing over this particular area for the next several days to a week. Thunderstorms have already grounded the original pair that was out looking for our missing Silvers; they are on the ground and we know where they are. It might well be a side effect of the loss of magic over the area; we just don't know for certain. But what that means is that there won't be any flying going on. I'm not going to ban any gryphons from the search-parties, but they'll be strictly on foot unless the weather improves drastically."

"I'm still going, and so are Zhaneel and Keeth," Skan spoke up firmly. Judeth nodded, as if she had expected as much. "In that case, since I'm going to divide the searchers into three parties, each gryphon can go with one. I've already sent out a gryphon with a Gate-mage; but he'll be coming straight back, and so will the two still out there while weather cooperates." Judeth cocked an eyebrow at Skan as if she expected him to object to this, but he didn't. Amberdrake could certainly understand why. A gryphon on the ground was severely handicapped; Skan, Zhaneel, and Keenath would be as much a hindrance as they were a help. The two who had been on patrol would be exhausted, and the one who had ferried the Gate-mage even more so.

Judeth continued. "Now, here's the current plan. We'll Gate in here—that's the closest I want to get to this area with anything that depends upon magic."

She stabbed down with her index finger. *Here,* the point where her finger indicated, was on the line that Blade and Tad had been expected to fly.

"The Gate-mage and a small party will stay here, at a base camp, holding the area for the rest of you. We'll divide up; the party with Skan and Drake in it will go north, up to the top of the area, and then in. The one with Ikala leading it, including Keenath, will go straight in. The one with Winterhart and Zhaneel will go south, then in. That way we'll cover the maximum area in the shortest possible time." Judeth straightened, and looked straight at Skan again. "And in case you're wondering why I haven't put you two in on the expected line, it's because the two gryphons out there already flew that line and didn't see anything before weather forced them down. So either the missing patrol *didn't* fly that line, or it's going to take an expert in that kind of territory to find signs of them. That's Ikala, not you; he'll be leading a party of people all used to moving quickly, and after he scouts the line on the ground, he'll be covering the areas north and south of that line. I'm putting you two on the likeliest alternate track; Tad always had a tendency in training to stay on the northern side of a given flight line. My guess is, if they're anywhere off the line, it's in the north."

"But that's just a guess," Skan stated. "They could be south."

She nodded. "And the gods know I've guessed wrong before; that's why the third party. The parties are going to number eight; one gryphon, one Healer or *trondi'irn*, or whatever comes close—that's you, Drake—two mages, and five fighters, all *experienced* Silvers. Any smaller is dangerous, any larger is unwieldy. Don't bother to pack at all; you'll be taking standard Silver kits including medical supplies, and you aren't going to have time to change clothing. Besides, by the time you make a camp at night, you and your clothing should be sluiced clean."

Her stare at Amberdrake said, as clearly as words, *And if you don't like that, you don't have to go.*

He stared right back at her. *Try and keep me from going and you'll have a fight.*

She waited for him to say something, staring into his gaze

with challenge in her stance, but it was she who finally dropped her eyes. "This is an in-and-out mission, the faster the better. As of this moment, consider yourself facing a real enemy, a powerful one, if he can drain all the mage-energy out of a place. I don't *know* what's caused magic to leach out of that area, but I have to assume it's a hostile, and it isn't going to like having twenty-four people traipsing all over its territory. As soon as the mage gets to the Gate-point, we'll be bringing it up, and I don't want it up for longer than it takes to pitch all of you through it. Is that understood?"

Once again, she stared at him as if her words were meant for him alone. Her tone of voice implied that, given the opportunity, she *would* "pitch" Amberdrake through the Gate. He simply nodded, as did everyone else.

"Good. From now until you leave, you are all sleeping, eating, and everything else right here." She smiled thinly at their surprise. "That'll be quicker than trying to gather all of you up once the mage gets into place. I don't intend to waste a single minute on any dallying. I'll have sleeping arrangements brought in; the mage I sent out is being carried by Darzie, so I expect to hear that they've made their landing within the next full day."

Amberdrake was impressed, as much by the identity of the gryphon as by the speed with which the duo expected to reach their destination. He wondered what Judeth had promised to get Darzie to fly a carry-basket at all, much less try to do so breaking a record and in bad weather. Darzie was *not* a Silver; he was one of a new class of gryphons who were primarily athletes. Whether as aerobats, fast couriers, or actual racers, these gryphons earned a very fine, even luxurious, living by serving the Haighlei appetite for speed and spectacle. Darzie was *the* best of the fast couriers and one of the fastest racers—he was a more consistent flyer than gryphons who actually clocked the occasional faster time. It was hard to imagine what hold Judeth could have over him to induce him to risk injury and strain in this way.

But maybe he was being uncharitable; maybe Darzie had actually volunteered. . . .

Not without blackmail.

It didn't matter, so long as Judeth had gotten him, whether it was through bribery or blackmail, or a combination of both.

Maybe she's following my example. The gods know she has enough power of her own to leverage just about anyone in this city into doing her bidding at least once.

"Any questions?" Judeth asked, and looked around the room. "No? Right. Fall out, and for those of you who haven't slept, I'm calling Tamsin in to make you sleep." There was no doubt who she was targeting with the daggers of her gaze, and both Amberdrake and Skan flinched; but she wasn't finished. "That includes me; we won't be any good to anyone if we aren't rested when the call comes. Right, Drake?"

Her question came as a surprise, and he was doubly surprised to sense the compassion and sympathy—and worry of her own—behind the words. It penetrated even his defensiveness.

"Ah, right," he admitted sheepishly, relaxing just a trifle. *So she does understand, and she's forgiven us. . . .* He had not hoped for it so soon, but he welcomed it as a tiny bright spot of hope in the midst of too much grief.

"Good. Glad you agree, because you're going to be one of the first to go to sleep." A commotion at the door proved to be bedding, food, and Tamsin all arriving simultaneously. "Now, stand down, all of you, and get yourselves taken care of. I'll be watching to see that you do."

And she did; standing over them all like a slavemaster, to see that every member of the three search parties ate, drank, and submitted to Tamsin's touch. As Judeth had warned, Amberdrake was one of the first, and after one look at Judeth's expression, he knew better than to protest.

So he crammed down a few mouthfuls of food as dry and tasteless as paper, drank what was given him, and laid himself down on a standard, military-style sleeping roll. He closed his eyes as Tamsin leaned over him, and that was the last thing he knew until the rally-call awakened him.

Rain. Why did it have to be rain? Even snakes would be better. Skandranon tried to keep his thoughts on his purely physical discomfort, but try as he might, he couldn't. His skin crawled, and the rain had nothing to do with it. If Skan's feathers hadn't been plastered flat to his body, they'd have been standing up in instinctive alarm.

He did not like this place, and his dislike was not connected in any way whatsoever with the miserable weather.

It could have been that this bizarre, claustrophobic forest had swallowed Blade and Tad without a trace, but that wasn't the reason his soggy hackles were trying to rise either. The other mage of the party felt the same, and if there had been any choice in the matter, he'd have gone back to the base camp because it just plain felt *wrong* here.

The two of them, after some discussion last night before the human took the first sleep shift, had decided that the problem was that lack of mage-energy in this place. Presumably an Apprentice-level mage or Journeyman would not be affected in this way; they were not used to sensing and using energies outside themselves, unless those energies were fed to them by a mage of greater ability. But a Master (as Skan and the human Silver, Filix, were) was as accustomed to the all-pervasive currents of mage-energy as a gryphon was to the currents of the air. Skan could not remember a time in his adult life that he had not been aware of those currents. Even when the mage-storms had caused such disruptions in magic, the energy had never *vanished*, it just hadn't worked or felt quite the same. But having no mage-energy about—it felt wrong, very wrong. It had him disoriented and off-balance, constantly looking for something that simply wasn't there.

It feels as if I've suddenly lost a sense; something subtle, like smell.

Nevertheless, a quick trial had proved to his satisfaction that magic still *worked* here, and furthermore, those magi-

cal items that they had brought in with them were still em-
powered. Further checks proved that, at the moment at
least, there was no ongoing drain of mage-energy. The power
that built up in any area naturally was slowly rising back up.
So whatever was wrong in this forest, whatever had caused
this anomaly, it had not completely negated magic, just removed it. Whether that drainage had been gradual or all at
once was anyone's guess. And there must be something
coming along to drain mage-energy again as it built up, or
there would be some areas that had at least a *little* power
available.

As for what *that* could be, he had no idea. He did not
care to think about what must have happened if the basket
had also had all of its empowering mage-energy drained—all
at once.

Skandranon mentally worked on a few new phrases to use
when he finally complained about it all to someone whom
he could corral into listening sympathetically. He had a reputation for—colorful—language to maintain after all. He
would much rather concentrate on that, than how miserable
his soggy feathers felt, how cold he was, how sore his muscles were after two days of walking. *That* was something he
simply hadn't considered, and it was galling to realize that
Drake was in better physical shape than he was! Drake had
been climbing the stairs and ladders of White Gryphon for
almost twenty years; *he* had only been flying. He could not
think of more than a handful of times that he had actually
climbed *up* rather than down, and none of those times had
been in the last three years. At least Keeth had been working
out on the obstacle course lately, and Winterhart had made
certain that all muscles were exercised. Poor Zhaneel must
be as miserable as he.

But she has the best trondi'irn *in the city to tend her. Keeth
is a* trondi'irn. *I only have Drake, who does his best, but still
. . . he's preoccupied.*

Rain dripped into his nares and he sneezed to clear them,
shaking his head fiercely. He and Drake were at the rear of

the party; with his keener sense of hearing than the humans possessed, it seemed a good idea to have him at the back where he might be able to detect something following them. Now he wished he had thought to ask Judeth for a couple of *kyree* scouts for each party; they would have been much more effective than any of the humans.

Rain poured down out of the sky, as it had since the fog lifted that morning. This was a truly lovely climate; fog from before dawn to just after, followed by rain until well past darkness, followed by damp chill until the fog came again in the morning. Judeth had been absolutely right in grounding them, and he would have grounded himself once he saw the weather; there was no way for a gryphon to fly safely in this muck, even if he could get his wings dry long enough to take off. Darzie had managed to bring his mage in safely only because he was insanely self-confident and lucky enough for four gryphons, and because the weather changed abruptly to something more like a "normal" rainy season outside of the "no-magic" area.

That, and Darzie is young enough to think he's immortal, and good enough to fly as if he were. Like another stupid, stupid gryphon I used to know. In spite of the fact that the rainy season was normal back at the base-camp, "normal" still meant a raging thunderstorm every afternoon. Darzie had flown *and landed* in one of those thunderstorms, blithely asserting that it was all a matter of timing and watching where the bolts hit. His passenger had been white-lipped, but remarkably reticent about discussing the flight.

Drake had found out what had tempted Darzie into making the trip; a challenge. Judeth had asked the young gryphon if he knew of anyone who might be persuaded, and had hinted broadly that she didn't think *he* could do it. That had been enough for Darzie, who had insisted that he and only he could manage the trip. And he had, in record-breaking time, and without damaging himself or his passenger. For sheer speed, audacity, and insane courage, that flight had surpassed even some of the Black Gryphon's legendary accomplishments.

Some, but not all. Darzie will just have to take his own time to become a legend, and if he is wise, he will do it in his own way, and not try to emulate me. I think that my life must have used up the luck of twenty gryphons.

Skan, the base-camp crew, and the other twenty-three rescuers had piled through the Gate in a record-setting time of their own. Although no people had been "pitched" through, all the supplies had been; hurled in a mass by a small army of Judeth's support crew. Not even during a resupply had Skan ever seen a Gate go up and down again so quickly.

Darzie flew home to receive his justly-earned accolades and the admiration of every unattached female in the city; the results of that would likely be more exhausting for him than the great deed itself. The Gate-mage and his helpers and guards remained to set up a base camp; the rest of them had shouldered packs and moved out under the beginnings of a rainstorm. No one had told them, however, that they were going to have to climb down a cliff to get into the forest where the children were lost. The three gryphons had shaken themselves dry and flown themselves down, but the humans had been forced to get to the bottom the hard way. That experience, in a worsening thunderstorm, had been exciting enough to age even the most hardened veteran in the lot. Absolutely everything they touched was slippery, either with mud, water, or substances they were probably better off not knowing about.

Once at the bottom, the three parties had formed up and gone their separate ways—and Skan had been amazed at how quickly the forest had swallowed the other two search parties. In an amazingly short period of time, he couldn't even hear the faintest *sound* of the others; only the steady drumming of the rain, and the whistles, chirps, and calls of creatures up in the tops of the trees.

Each day had been much like the one before it; only the navigator knew for certain that they were going in the right direction and not in circles. The only time that Skan was ever dry was just before he slept; the moment he poked his beak out of the tent he shared with Drake and the other mage, he was wet. Either fog condensed on his feathers and soaked into them, or he got soaked directly by the usual downpour.

Just at the moment, the downpour had him wet to the skin.

And he was depressed, though he would have been depressed without the rain.

How can we ever hope to find any sign of them? he asked himself, staring up at the endless sea of dripping leaves, and around at the dizzying procession of tree trunks on all sides, tangled with vines or shrouded with brush. There wasn't a sign of a game trail, and as for game itself—well, he'd had to feed himself by surprising some of the climbing creatures in the mornings, while he could still fly. *They could be within shouting distance of us, and we would never know it!* This forest was not only claustrophobic, it was uncannily enveloping. One of the fighters swore that he could actually *see* the plants growing, and Skan could find it in his heart to believe him.

How long would it take until vines and bushes covered anything left after a crash? A few days? A week? It had been a week since the children went missing, maybe more than a week; he lost track of time in here.

And they could have been down for three or four days before that. Gloomy thoughts; as gloomy as their surroundings. And yet he could not give up; as long as there was any chance, however minuscule, that they would find the children, he would search on. No matter what, he had to *know* what had happened to them. The uncertainty of not knowing was the worst part.

Drake looked like Skan felt; the *kestra'chern* was a grim-faced, taciturn, sodden, muddy mess most of the time. He spoke only when spoken to; tended to the minor injuries of the party without being asked, but offered nothing other than physical aid, which was utterly unlike him. He hiked with the rest of them, or dealt with camp chores, but it was obvious that his mind was not on what he was doing. It was out *there*, somewhere, and Skan wondered if Drake was trying to use his limited empathic ability as a different kind of north-needle, searching for the pole star of pain and distress hidden among the trunks and vines. With the blood tie between himself and his daughter, he should be especially sensitive to her. If she were alive, he might be able to find her where conventional methods were failing.

More power to him; he's never tried using it that way, but that doesn't mean it won't work. Skan only wished he had a similar ability he could exercise. As it was, he was mostly a beast of burden, and otherwise not much help. He couldn't track, he couldn't use much magic without depleting himself, and as for anything else—well, his other talents all involved flying. And he could only fly for a short time in the mornings.

Regin, the leader in their party, held up a hand, halting them, as he had done several times already that day. There didn't seem to be any reason for this behavior, and Skan was getting tired of it. Why stop and stand in the rain for no cause? The more ground they covered, the better chance they had of finding something. He nudged past Filix, and splashed his way up to the weather-beaten Silver Judeth had placed in charge.

"Regin, just what, exactly, are we waiting for?" he asked, none too politely.

Fortunately, the man ignored the sarcastic tone of his voice, and answered the question by pointing upward. Skan looked, just in time to see their scout Bern sliding down the trunk of a tree ahead of them with a speed that made Skan wince. "Bern's been looking for breaks in the trees ahead," Regin said, as Bern made a hand signal and strode off into the trees. "We figure, if the basket came down it had to make a hole; that hole'll still be there. He gets up into a tall tree and looks for holes all around, especially if he can see they're fresh. You might not believe it with all these clouds around, but if there's a break in the trees more light gets in, and you can see it from high enough in the canopy. That's what we're waiting on."

Bern reappeared a moment later, and rejoined the party, shaking his head. Skan didn't have to know the Silver's signals to read that one; *no holes.* He and Regin had a quick conference with the navigator, and the scout headed back off into the forest on a new bearing. The rest of the party followed in Bern's wake.

So far, there had been no sign of anything following or watching them, much less any attacks. Skan was beginning to think that Judeth's insistence on assuming there was a hostile entity in here was overreaction on her part. There hadn't been any signs that *anything* lived in here but wild animals; surely whatever had drained off all the mage-energy here must be a freak phenomenon. Maybe that was what had caught the two children. . . .

Skan dropped back to his former place beside Amberdrake, but with a feeling of a little more hope, brought on by the knowledge that at least they weren't totally without a guide or a plan.

Drake still seemed sunk into himself, but he revived a bit when Skan returned and explained what the lead members were up to. "I've heard worse ideas," he said thoughtfully, wiping strands of sodden hair out of his eyes, and blinking away the rain. "It's not a gryphon eye view, but it's better than nothing."

Once again, the leader signaled a stop. Skan peered out and up through the curtains of rain, but he couldn't see anything. Wherever the scout was this time, not even Skan's excellent eyes could pick him out. "I have no idea how Bern is managing to climb in this weather, much less how he's doing it so quickly." Skan moved up a few feet and ducked around a tangle of vines, but the view was no better from the new vantage. "He must be as limber as one of those little furry climbers that Shalaman keeps at his Palace as pets. For all we know, this sort of place is where those come from."

Drake shrugged dismissively, as if the subject held no interest for him. "I—"

"*Hoy!*"

Skan looked up again, startled, and just caught sight of the tiny figure above, waving frantically. He seemed to be balanced on a thick tree limb, and clung to the trunk with only one hand. The other hand waved wildly, and then pointed.

"*Hoy!*" the call came again. "*Fresh break, that way!*"

Fresh break! The same thought occurred to all of them, but the Silvers were quicker to react than Skan or Drake. They broke into a trot, shoving their way through the vegetation, leaving the other two to belatedly stumble along in their wake.

Skan's heart raced, and not from the exertion. He longed to gallop on ahead, and probably *would* have, except that it was all he could do to keep up with the Silvers. And much to his embarrassment, just as he developed a sudden stitch in his side, Bern, the scout who had been up in the tree, burst through the underbrush behind them, overtook them, and plunged on to the head of the column.

Show-off. . . .

Another shout echoed back through the trees, muffled by the falling rain. The words weren't distinguishable, but the tone said all Skan needed to know. There was excitement, but no grief, no shock.

They've found something. Some*thing* and not some*one*— or worse, bodies. . . .

From some reserve he didn't know he had, he dredged up more strength and speed, and turned his trot into a series of leaps that carried him through the underbrush until he broke through into the clearing beneath the break in the trees. He stumbled across the remains of a crude palisade of brush and onto clear ground.

A camp! That was his first elated thought; if the children had been able to build a camp, they could not have been too badly hurt. Then he looked at the *kind* of camp it was, and felt suddenly faint. This was no orderly camp; this was something patched together from the remains of wreckage and whatever could be scavenged. Regin looked up from his examination of the soggy remains of the basket as Skan halted inside the periphery of the clearing.

"They crashed here, all right." He pointed upward at the ragged gap in the canopy. "They're gone now, but they did hit here, hard enough to smash two sides of the basket. They both survived it, though *I* can't guess how. Maybe there was enough in the way of branches on the way down to slow their fall. The medical kit's gone, there's signs they both used it."

They were here. They were hurt. Now they're gone. But why? "Why aren't they still here?" he asked, speaking his bewilderment aloud.

"Now *that* is a good question." Regin poked through a confusion of articles that looked as if they had just been tossed there and left. "Standard advice is to stay with your wrecked craft if you have an accident. I'd guess they started to do that, were here for maybe two days, then something made them leave. It looks to me as if they left in a hurry, and yet I don't see any signs of a fight."

"They could have been frightened away," Amberdrake ventured. "Or—well, this isn't a very *good* camp—"

"It's a disaster of a camp, that's what it is," Regin corrected bluntly. "But if all I had was wreckage, *and* I was badly hurt, I probably wouldn't have been able to do much better. It's shelter, though, and that isn't quite enough. I wish I knew how much of their supplies got ruined, and how much they took with them." He straightened, and looked around, frowning. "There's no sign of a struggle, but no sign of game around here either. They might have run out of food, and it would be hard to hunt if they were hurt. There's no steady water source—"

Amberdrake coughed politely. "We're *under* a steady water-source," he pointed out.

Regin just shrugged. "We're taught not to count on rain. So—no game, no water, and an indefensible camp. Gryphons eat a lot; if their supplies were all trashed, they'd be good for about two days before they were garbage, unfit to eat. After that, they've *got* to find game, for Tadrith alone. My guess is, they stayed here just long enough to get back some strength, and headed back in the direction of home. They're probably putting up signals now." He grimaced. "I just hope their trail isn't too cold to follow—but on the other hand, if they headed directly west, we should stay pretty much on their trail. That's where I'd go, back to the river. It's a lot easier to fish if you're hurt than to hunt."

Skan groaned. "You mean we could have just followed the river and we probably would have found them?"

Regin grinned sourly. "That's exactly what I mean. But look on the bright side; now we *know* they're alive and they're probably all right."

Skan nodded, as Regin signaled to Bern to start hunting for a trail. But as Bern searched for signs, Skan couldn't help noticing a few things.

For one thing, the piles of discarded material had a curiously ordered-disordered look about them, as if they had been tossed everywhere, then gathered up and crudely examined, then sorted.

For another, there were *no* messages, notes, or anything of the sort to give a direction to any rescuers. Granted, the children might not have known whether anyone would find the camp, but shouldn't they have left *something?*

And last of all, there was no magic, none at all, left in any of the discarded equipment. So the surmise had been correct, something had drained all of the magic out of their gear, and from the signs of the crash, it had happened all at once. And yet none of the search-party gear had been affected—yet.

So what had done this in the first place? What had sorted through the remains of the camp?

And what had made the children flee into the unknown and trackless forest without even leaving a sign for searchers to follow?

Was the answer to the third question the same as the answer to the other two?

Tad entered the cave, sloshing through ankle-deep water at the entrance, carefully avoiding Blade's three fishing lines. Blade held up some of her catch, neatly strung, and he nodded appreciatively.

"Water's higher," he told her. "In places it covers the trail here."

That was to be expected, considering how much is falling out of the sky. "Well," Blade said with resignation. "At least we have a steady water supply—and we don't have to leave the cave to fish anymore."

It had not stopped raining for more than a few marks in the middle of the night ever since they had arrived here. She'd wondered what the rainy season would be like; well, now she knew. The stream of water running down the middle of the cave had remained at about the same size, only its pace had quickened. The river had risen, and now it was perfectly possible for them to throw lines into the river itself without going past the mouth of the cave, with a reasonable expectation of catching something.

That was just as well, since they were now under siege, although they still had not seen their hunters clearly. The flitting shadows espied in the undergrowth had made it very clear that there was no getting back across the river without confronting them.

Tad nodded, spreading his good wing to dry it in front of the fire. He had gone out long enough to drag in every bit of driftwood he could find, and there was now a sizable store of it in the cave. He'd also hauled in things that would make a thick, black smoke, and they had a second, extremely nasty fire going now. It stood just to one side of the stream at the rear of the cave, putting a heavy smoke up the natural "chimney." Whether or not there was anyone likely to *see* it was a good question; this was not the kind of weather anything but a desperate or suicidal gryphon would fly in.

On the other hand—-how desperate would Skandranon or Tad's twin be by now? Desperate enough to try?

Blade both hoped so and hoped that they would have more sense; their pursuers were getting bolder, and she hadn't particularly wanted Tad to go out this afternoon. The stalkers were still nothing more than menacing shadows, *but* she had seen them skulking through the underbrush on the other side of the river even by day, yesterday and this morning.

"I think *they* might try something tonight," Tad said, far too casually. "I know I was being watched all the time, and I just had that feeling, as if there was something out there that was frustrated and losing patience."

"I got the same feeling," Blade confessed. She hadn't enjoyed taking her shields down and making a tentative try at assessing what lay beyond the river, but it had felt necessary. In part, she had been hoping to sense a rescue party, but the cold and very alien wave of frustrated anger that met her tentative probe had made her shut herself up behind her shields and sit there shivering for a moment. "I—tried using that Empathic sense, and I got the same impression you did. They would like very much to get a chance at us."

She hoped that Tad wouldn't make too big a fuss about that confession; he'd been at her often enough to use *everything* she had. Now she'd finally given in to his urgings, she was not in the mood for an "I told you that was a good idea." She wasn't certain that it *was* a good idea; what if those things out there had been able to sense her just as she sensed them?

Then again, what would they learn? That she was hurt, and scared spitless of them? They already knew that.

Fortunately for him, Tad just nodded. "It's good to know that it's not just my own worry talking to me," he said, and sighed. "Now I don't feel so badly about setting all those traps." .

"What—" she began. At that moment, one of her fishing lines went tight, and she turned her attention to it long enough to haul in her catch. But after rebaiting the hook and setting the line again, she returned to the subject.

"What other traps do you think would work?" she asked. "On our side of the river, that is. Where could we set more?"

Thus far, they hadn't had any luck with deadfalls like the one that had marked one of the shadows before. It was as if, having seen that particular sort of trap, the hunters now knew how to avoid it. Large snares hadn't worked either, but she hadn't really expected them to, since there was no way to conceal them. But perhaps now, with water over the trail, trip-wires *could* be hidden under the water.

"I tended to that during my 'walk' earlier. There's only one good place, really," he told her. "The river's gotten so deep and fast that there's only one place where I think they might try to cross—that's downstream, past where we crossed it when we first got here. I didn't set a trap right there, though—what I did was rig something that's harmless but looks just like the rockfall I rigged later on." He gryph-grinned at his own cleverness, and she could hardly blame him.

"So they'll see the harmless decoy, and then walk right into the rockfall?"

He nodded, looking very proud of himself. "It's a good big one, too. If they actually try coming after us, at least one of them is going to be seriously hurt or killed, unless they've got lightning reflexes and more luck than any one creature deserves to have."

"Just as long as you don't hurt someone coming to rescue us!" she warned. Yesterday she might have argued with him about the merits of setting something meant to kill rather than discourage—but that was before she had opened herself to the creatures across the river. She still might not know what they looked like, but now she knew what they were. Killers, plainly and simply, with a kind of cold intelligence about them that made her wish for one good bow, two good arms, and three dozen arrows. She would debate the merits of permitting such creatures the free run of their own territory some other time; and if they gave up and left her alone, she would be perfectly happy to leave *them* alone. But if they came after her or Tad, she would strike as efficiently and with the same deadly force as they would.

There was still the question of whether or not these creatures were the "hunting pack" of someone or something else; she did not have the ability to read thoughts, even if these creatures had anything like a thought. But she hadn't sensed anything else out there with them; all of the creatures had been of the same type, with a definite feeling of *pack* about them.

Which could simply mean that their master was off, lounging about at his ease somewhere, watching all of this in a scrying-mirror. That would certainly fit the profile of a sadistic Adept; she couldn't picture Ma'ar, for instance, subjecting himself to mud and pouring rain.

If that was so, if there was an Adept behind all this, and she ever got her hands on him. . . .

"That wasn't the only trap I built," Tad continued proudly, oblivious to her dark thoughts. "I have trip-tangles under the water that will throw them into the stream, I balanced boulders to roll at a touch and trap feet and legs, and I put up some more snares. Between all that and the rock barricade we have across the front of the cave, I think we can feel a little safer."

"Just as long as we can continue fishing from in here," she corrected. "And as long as *you* can stand to live on fish."

"All I have to do is think about eating any more of that dried meat, and fish takes on a whole new spectrum of delight," he countered. "I'm learning to tell the difference between one fish and another, raw. Some are sweeter, one has more fat—"

And they all taste the same to me. "Fine, I believe you!" she interrupted hastily. "Listen, I wonder if we could rig some kind of a net or something to haul in driftwood as it comes down over the falls. There's a lot of stuff getting by us that we could really use."

There was nothing that Tad liked better than trying to invent a new way to do something, and the idea of a driftwood-net kept him happily occupied for some time. And more importantly, it kept him *restfully* occupied; no matter how cheerful and energetic he seemed—or tried to appear—he was tired, and so was she. The ever-present roar of the falls would cover the sounds of anything approaching them, and most especially would cover the sounds of anything bold enough to try swimming across the river at this point. They both knew that, and she suspected that *he* was staying half-awake even through her watch, as she was staying through his. Not especially bright of either of them, but neither of them were able to help themselves. Their imaginations supplied the creatures out there with every kind of supernatural attribute, especially in the dark of the night. It was easier to dismiss such fears by daylight, except that she kept reminding herself that just because their hunters hadn't done something *yet*, that didn't mean they weren't capable of a particular action. It was hard to strike a balance between seeing threats that didn't exist and not being wary enough, especially when you didn't know everything the enemy could do.

"Not long until dark," Tad observed, after a long discussion of nets and draglines and other ways of catching runaway driftwood. He pointed his beak toward the river. She nodded; although it was difficult to keep track of time without the sun being visible, the light did seem to be fading. Another one of her lines went taut; this fish was a fighter, which probably meant that it was one of the kinds Tad liked best. *Any* fish seemed pretty tasteless to her, wrapped in wet clay to bake and without any herbs to season it with. She'd thought about using some of the peppery leaves just to give her food some spice, then thought better of the idea. Although they had not had any deleterious effect rubbed on the skin, there was no telling if they were poisonous if eaten. You could rub your skin all day with shadow-berries and not get anything worse than a purple stain, but eat a few and you would find yourself retching up your toenails. . . .

She fought the fish to exhaustion and reeled it in, hand over hand, taking care not to tangle the line. That was enough for tonight; she pulled in the other lines, and by the time she was done, there was no doubt; it *was* darker out on the river.

She took the fish back behind the rock barrier to the fire, where Tad still basked. Each day they added a few more rocks, but they were rapidly approaching the point where they wouldn't be able to use river clay as mortar anymore. It just wasn't strong enough.

There was another advantage to this cave; no bugs. Enough smoke hung in the air from their signal-fire to discourage insects of all sorts. Her bites had finally begun to heal and didn't bother her too much anymore. In fact, if it hadn't been for those watchers out there, she would be feeling pretty pleased with the state of things. They had fire, excellent shelter, and plenty to eat, and sooner or later *someone* from White Gryphon or even Khimbata would see or smell the signal-fire, and they could go home. And in the meantime, while they were not comfortable, they were secure.

She took one of the big, sluggish bottom feeders from her string, gutted it, wrapped it in wet clay, put it in the firepit and raked coals and ashes over it. The rest she handed to Tad as they were.

No longer as famished as he was when they first got here, he ate them with gusto. And if he lacked fine table manners, she was not going to complain about the company. *I can think of worse people to be stranded with.*

"How's the wing?" she asked, as she did at least once a day.

"It doesn't hurt as much as it did yesterday, but I still don't want to unwrap it," he replied. "Whenever I move in an unusual way, it hurts."

In Tad-language, that meant "it hurts enough that my knees buckle and I almost pass out." She knew; she'd seen it happen. Tad was so stoic. He tried very hard to be cheerful, and it was likely for her benefit alone. By moving very carefully, she had managed to keep the same thing from happening to her, but that meant a lot of restriction on her movement.

If *only* she had two good hands—or he had two good wings! If either of them could manage to get to the top of the cliff, she was sure they could think of a way to bring the other up afterward. Up there, they wouldn't have to worry about pursuit anymore; if the hunters couldn't climb a tree, they sure as stars couldn't climb a cliff!

Might as well wish for three or four experienced Silvers with long-range bows, she thought grimly. *I have the feeling that there is something about all of this that I'm missing completely, something that should be obvious, but isn't. I just wish I had a clue to what it is.*

"Do you really think they're going to try something tonight?" she asked, more to fill the silence than because she thought he'd changed his mind.

For an answer, he nodded toward the cave entrance. "Rain's slackening early. The current isn't bad in that one wide, shallow spot. Not that hard to wade across, if you've got claws to hang onto the rock with. And we already know they do have claws."

She wondered if she ought to try opening herself up to them a second time, then decided against it. They could be waiting for her to do exactly that.

Silence fell between them again, and she just didn't feel right about breaking it with small talk. She checked her fish instead, and found the clay rock hard; that was a good indication that the fish inside was done, so she went ahead, raked it out of the coals, and broke it open. The skin and scales came away with the clay, leaving the steaming white flesh ready to eat without all the labor of skinning or scaling. She made fairly short work of it. As usual, it tasted like—not much of anything. Visceral memories of hot, fresh bread smothered in sweet butter, spicy meat and bean soup, and that incredible garlic and onion-laced fish stew that Jewel made taunted her until she drove them from her mind.

After that, they let the fire die down to coals and banked them with ashes to reduce the amount of light in the cave. If the hunters *were* going to try something tonight, there was no point in giving them the advantage of being able to see their targets clearly silhouetted.

She moved toward the barricade by edging along the side of the cave to keep herself in the shadows as much as possible. Tad did the same on the other side. The rain had indeed slackened off early for once; instead of illuminating a solid sheet of water in front of her nose, the intermittent flashes of lightning showed the other side of the river, with the churning, rolling water between.

There was no sign of anything *on* the other side of the river, and that wasn't good. Up until now, there had always been at least one lurking shadow in the bushes over there; now there was nothing. That was just one more indication that Tad's instincts and her reading of the hunters' impatience were both correct. They were going to try something tonight.

She glanced over at Tad; when lightning flickered, she could see his head and neck clearly, although he was so still he could have passed for a carving. He kept his eyelids lowered, so that not even a flicker of reflection would betray his presence to anything watching. His natural coloration blended beautifully with the stone behind him, and the lines of his feathers passed for rock-striations. It was amazing just how well camouflaged he was.

His ear-tufts lay flat along his head, but she knew better than to assume that meant he wasn't *listening*; the ear-tufts were largely decorative tufts of feathers that had nothing to do with his hearing. No, he was listening, all right. She wondered how much he could hear over the roar of the waterfall beside them.

But when the noise of his trap coming down thundered across the river, it was not at all subtle; in fact, it was loud enough that even the rock of the cave mouth vibrated for a moment. She jumped, her nerves stretched so tight that she went off-balance for a moment, and had to twist to catch herself with her good hand. She regained her balance quickly and moved to go outside. He shot out a claw, catching her good wrist and holding her where she was.

"Wait until morning," he advised, in a voice just loud enough for her to hear it over the roaring water. "That killed something. And they aren't going to be able to move the body."

"How much rock did you pile up?" she asked incredulously. How had he been able to pile up *anything* with only a pair of talons instead of hands, and with one bad wing?

"Enough," he replied, then chuckled with pardonable pride. "I didn't want to boast until I knew it had worked— but I used a little magic to undermine part of the cliff-face that was ready to go. I honestly didn't know how much was going to come down, I only knew it would be more than I could manage by stacking rocks."

"From the sound of it, a *lot* came down," she answered in awe. *What a brilliant application of a very tiny amount of magic!* "Did you feel it through the rock?"

He nodded. "There could be a problem, though," he added. "I might have given them a bridge, or half a bridge, across the river. There was that chance that the rock would fall that way."

But she shrugged philosophically. If he had, he had; it might well be worth it to find out just what, precisely, had been stalking them all this time.

"And the cliff could have come down by itself, doing the same thing," she answered. "There's no point in getting upset until we know. I doubt that we're going to see any further trouble out of them for tonight, anyway."

She was quite right; the rest of the night was as quiet as anyone could have wished, and with the first light, they both went out to see what, if anything, Tad's trap had caught.

When they got to the rock-fall, they both saw that it had indeed come sliding down into the river, providing a bridge about halfway across, though some of it had already washed farther downstream. But as they neared it, and saw that the trap had caught a victim, Blade was just as puzzled by what was trapped there as she had been by the shadows.

There had been some effort made to free the creature; that much showed in the signs of digging and the obvious places where rubble and even large stones had been moved off the carcass. But it was not a carcass of any animal she recognized.

If a mage had taken a greyhound, crossed it with a serpent, and magnified it up to the size of a horse, he would have had something like this creature. A deep black in color, with shiny scaled skin just like a snake or a lizard, and a long neck, it had teeth sharper and more daggerlike than a dog's. Its head and those of its limbs not crushed by the fallen rock were also doglike. They couldn't tell what color its eyes were; the exposed slit only showed an opaque white. She stared at it, trying to think if there was anything in all of the stories she'd heard that matched it.

But Tad had no such trouble putting a name to it.

"*Wyrsa*," Tad muttered, "But the color's all wrong. . . ."

She turned her head to see that he was staring down at the thing, and he seemed certain of his identification. "What's a *wyrsa?*" she asked sharply.

He nudged the head with one cautious talon. "One of the old Adepts, before Ma'ar, made things like this to mimic *kyree* and called them *wyrsa*. He meant them for a more formidable guard dog or hunting pack. But they couldn't be controlled, and got loose from him—oh, a long time ago. Long before Ma'ar and the War. Aubri told me about hunting them; said that they ran wild in packs in some places." His eyes narrowed as he concentrated. "But the ones he talked about were smaller than this. They were white, and they had poison fangs and poison talons."

She bent down, carefully, and examined the mouth and

the one exposed foot for poison sacs, checking to see if either talons or teeth were hollow. She finally got a couple of rocks and carefully broke off a long canine tooth and a talon, to examine them more closely. Finally she stood up with a grunt.

"I don't know what else is different on these beasts, but they aren't carrying anything poisonous," she told him, as he watched her actions dubiously. "Neither the teeth nor the claws are hollow, they have no channel to carry venom, and no venom sacs at the root to produce poison in the first place. Venom has to come from somewhere, Tad, and it has to get into the victim somehow, so unless this creature has poisonous saliva. . . ."

"Aubri distinctly said that they were just like a poisonous snake," Tad insisted. "But the color is different on these things, and the size. *Something* must have changed them."

They exchanged a look. "A mage?" she asked. "Or the storms?" She might know venom, but *he* knew magic.

"The mage-storms, if anything at all," Tad said flatly. "If a mage had changed *wyrsa* deliberately, he wouldn't have taken out the venom, he'd have made it worse. I'll bet it was the mage-storms."

"I wouldn't bet against it." Blade knelt again to examine the head in detail; it was as long as her forearm, and most of it was jaw. "Tad, these things don't *need* venom to hurt you," she pointed out. "Look at those canines! They're as long as my finger, and the rest of the teeth are in proportion. What else do you know about *wyrsa?*"

He swallowed audibly. "Aubri said that the bigger the pack was, the smarter they acted, as if part of their intelligence was shared with every other one in the pack. He also said that they were unbelievably tenacious; if they got your scent, they'd track you for days—and if you killed or hurt one, they would track you forever. You'd never get rid of them until they killed you, or you killed them all."

"How comforting," she said dryly, standing up again.

"And we've hurt one *and* killed one. I wish we'd known this before."

Tad just shuffled his feet, looking sheepish. "They might not connect us with the rockfall," he offered tentatively.

"Well, it's done and can't be undone." She caught something, a hint of movement out of the corner of her eye, and turned her head.

And froze. As if, now that she and Tad knew what the things were and the *wyrsa* saw no reason to hide, a group of six stood on the bank across from them. Snarling silently. Tad let out his breath in a hiss of surprise and dismay.

Then, before she could even blink or draw a breath, they were gone. She hadn't even seen them move, but the only thing across from them now was a stand of bushes, the branches still quivering as the only sign that something had passed through them.

"I think we can safely assume that they *do* connect us with the rockfall," she replied, a chill climbing up her spine. "And I think we had better get back to the cave before they decide to try to cross the river again."

"Don't run," Tad cautioned, turning slowly and deliberately, and watching where he placed his feet. "Aubri said that would make them chase you, even if they hadn't been chasing you before."

She tried to hide how frightened she was, but the idea of six or more of those creatures coming at her in the dark was terrifying. "What charming and delightful creations," she replied sarcastically. "Anything else you'd like to tell me?"

He shook his head, spraying her with rain. "That's all I remember right now."

She concentrated on being very careful where she walked, for the rain was getting heavier and the rocks slicker. It would do no one any good if she slipped on these rocks and broke something else.

Well, no one but the wyrsa.

"Has *anyone* ever been able to control these things?" she asked. "Just out of curiosity."

The navigable part of the track narrowed. He gestured to her to precede him, which she did. If the *wyrsa* decided to cross the river, he did make a better rear guard than she did as soon as he got turned around. "Not that I've ever heard," he said from behind her. "I suppose that a really good mage could hold a coercion-spell on a few and make them attack a target he chose, but that would be about the limit of 'controlling' them. He wouldn't be able to stop them once they started, and he wouldn't be able to make them turn aside if they went after something he didn't choose. I certainly wouldn't count on controlling them."

"So at least we probably don't have to worry about some mage setting this pack on our trail after bringing us down?" she persisted, and stole a glance over her shoulder at him. His feathers were plastered flat to his head, making his eyes look enormous.

"Well . . . not that I know of," he said hesitantly. "But these aren't the same *wyrsa* I know. They've been changed— maybe they are more tractable than the old kind. Maybe the poison was removed as a trade-off for some other powers, or it contributed to their uncontrollability. And a mage could have brought us down in their territory for amusement without *needing* to control them, just letting them do what they do."

"You're just full of good news today, aren't you?" she growled, then repented. *I shouldn't be taking our bad luck out on him.* "Never mind. I'm sorry. I'm just not exactly in a good frame of mind right now."

"Neither am I," he said softly, in a voice in which she could clearly hear his fear. "Neither am I."

Tad kept a watch all day as Blade concentrated on fishing. Once or twice a single *wyrsa* showed itself, but the creatures made no move to cross the river to get at them.

Of course not. Night has always been their chosen hunting-time, and that should be especially true of wyrsa *with this new coloration.* Swift, silent, and incredibly fierce, he would not have wanted to face *one* of this new type, much less an entire pack.

I wonder how big the pack is, anyway? Six? Ten? More?

Were they the sport-offspring of a single female? *Wyrsa* were only supposed to litter once every two years, and they didn't whelp more than a couple at a time. *If these are all from twin offspring of a single litter, back when the storms changed them—how many could the pair have produced? Four years to maturity, then two pups every two years. . . .*

There could be as few as the seven that they had seen, and as many as thirty or forty. The true answer was probably somewhere in between.

He and Blade ate in silence, then she banked the fire down to almost nothing while he took the first watch. As soon as it was fully dark, he eased several rocks into place to disguise his outline, then pressed himself up against the stone of the floor as flat as he could. He hoped he could convince them that he wasn't there, that nothing was watching them from the mouth of the cave. If he could lure one out into the open, out on the slippery rocks of the riverbank, he might be able to get off a very simple bit of magic. If he could stun one long enough to knock it into the river—well, here below the falls it *would* get sucked under to drown. Nothing but a fish could survive the swirling currents right at the foot of the falls. That would be one less *wyrsa* to contend with.

He didn't hear Blade so much as sense her; after a moment's hesitation, she touched his foot, then eased on up beside him.

"Couldn't sleep," she mouthed into his ear. He nodded. Stupid, maybe, but she had good cause for insomnia.

She pressed herself even farther down against the stone than he had; anything that spotted her from across the river would have to have better eyesight than an owl.

The rain is slacking off. That was both good and bad news; he had an idea that the *wyrsa* didn't much care for rain, and that they were averse to climbing around on rain-slick rocks. Like him, they had talons, but he didn't think that their feet were as flexible as his. Those talons could make walking on rock difficult.

On the other hand, as the rain thinned, that made visibility across the river better, especially if the lightning kept up without any rain falling.

Something moved on the bank across from his position. He froze, and he felt Blade hold her breath.

Lightning flickered, and the light fell on a sleek, black form, poised at the very edge of the bank, peering intently in their direction. And now he saw that the white glazing of the dead one's eyes had been the *real* color; the *wyrsa's* eyes were a dead, opaque corpse-white. The very look of them, as the creature peered across the river in their direction, made his skin crawl.

He readied his spell, hoarding his energies. No point in striking unless everything was perfect. . . .

He willed the creature to remain, to lean forward more. Lightning flickered again; it was still there, still craning its neck, peering.

Stay . . . stay. . . .

Now!

He unleashed the energy; saw the *wyrsa* start, its eyes widening—

But instead of dropping over, stunned, it *glowed* for a moment. Blade gasped, so Tad knew that she had seen it, too, as a feeling of faintness and disorientation that he had experienced once before came over him. He wheezed and blinked a few times, dazzled, refocusing on the *wyrsa*.

The *wyrsa* gaped its mouth, then, as if recharged, the creature made a tremendous leap into the underbrush that nothing wholly natural could have duplicated, and was gone.

And with it went the energy of the spell. If the *wyrsa* had deflected it, the energy would still *be* there, dissipating. It hadn't. The spell hadn't hit shields, and it hadn't been reflected.

It had been inhaled, absorbed completely. And what was

more—an additional fraction of Tad's personal mage-energy had gotten pulled along behind it as if swept in a current.

"Oh. My. Gods," he breathed, feeling utterly stunned. *Now* he knew what had hit them, out there over the forest. And now he knew why the *wyrsa* had begun following them in the first place.

The *wyrsa* were the magic-thieves, not some renegade mage, not some natural phenomena. They ate magic, or absorbed it, and it made them stronger.

Blade shook him urgently. "What happened?" she hissed in his ear. "What's the matter? What's going on?"

He shook off his paralysis to explain it to her; she knew enough about magic and how it worked that he didn't have to explain things twice.

"Goddess." She lay there, just as stunned for a moment as he was. And then, in typical fashion, she summed up their entire position in a two sentences. "They have our scent, they want our blood, and now they know that *you* produce magic on top of all that." She stared at him, aghast, her eyes wide. "We're going to have to kill them *all*, or we'll never get away from here!"

The Wyrsa Pack Leader

Nine

Tad hissed at the cluster of *wyrsa* across the river. The *wyrsa* all bared their formidable teeth and snarled back. They made no move to vanish this time, and Tad got the distinct impression that they were taunting him, daring him to throw something magical at them.

Well, of course they were. They had no reason to believe he had anything that could reach across the river except magic, and they *wanted* him to throw that.

Throw us more food, stupid gryphon! Throw us the very thing that makes us stronger, and make it tasty!

He'd already checked a couple of things in their supplies. The stone he had made into a mage-light and the firestarter he had reenergized were both inert again; if he'd needed any confirmation of the fact that these were the creatures that had sucked all of the mage-energy out of the carry-basket and everything in it—well, he had it.

I wonder what Father would do in a situation like this! But Skan would not likely have ever found himself in a situation like this one. Nor would his solution necessarily have been a good one ... since it likely would have involved a great deal of semi-suicidal straight-on combat and high-energy physical action, which he was not in the least in any

shape to perform. Skandranon was more known for his phys-
icality than his raw inventiveness, when it came right down
to facts.

*Oh, Tad, not you, too—now you are even comparing your-
self to your father. The real question is not what my father
would do, the real question is, what am I going to do in this
situation!*

He raised himself up as high on his hindquarters as he
could get, and gave a battle-scream, presenting the *wyrsa*
with an open beak and a good view of his foreclaws. They
stopped snarling and eyed him warily; with a little more respect, he thought. He hoped.

"I wish you wouldn't do that." Blade emerged from the
back of the cave where she'd been napping, hair tousled and
expression sour. "It's a bad way to wake up, thinking that
your partner is about to engage in mortal combat."

"They don't seem to like the look of my claws," he
replied, trying to sound apologetic without actually apolo-
gizing. "I was hoping I could intimidate them a little more."

He studied the knot of *wyrsa*, which never seemed to be
still for more than an eyeblink. They were constantly moving, leaping, bending, twining in, around, over and under
each other. He'd never seen creatures with so much energy
and so much determination to use it. It was almost as if they
physically couldn't stay still for more than a heartbeat.

They had come out of the underbrush about the time that
the fog lifted and the rains began; if the rain bothered them
now, it certainly wasn't possible to tell.

Then again, why should it bother them? That it did had
been an assumption on his part, not a reflection of what was
really going on in those narrow snake-like heads. They had
neither fur nor feathers to get wet and matted down. The only
effect that rain had on their scales was to make them shiny.

"On first blush, I'd say they don't look very intimidated,"
Blade pointed out. But her brows knitted as she watched the
wyrsa move, and her eyes narrowed in concentration. "On

the other hand—that's a very effective defensive strategy, isn't it?"

Tad gazed at the stalkers' glistening hides, the way it moved and flashed. The patterns they moved in knotted and reknotted, like a decorative interlace. "Is it? But it bunches them up all in one place; shouldn't that make it easier to hit one?" He watched them carefully, then suddenly shook himself as he realized that the creatures' constant movement was making him go into a trance! He glanced over at Blade. She lifted an eyebrow and nodded.

"Not bad if you can put your attacker to sleep, hmm?" she asked, then smiled slyly, which put Tad instantly on the alert. He'd seen that smile before, and he knew what it meant. Trouble, usually for someone else. "Well, let's see if we can take advantage of their bit of cleverness, shall we? Stay there and look impressive, why don't you? I need something to keep them distracted."

She retreated into the cave. The *wyrsa* continued their hypnotic weaving as Tad watched them, this time prepared to keep from falling under their spell, glancing away at every mental count of ten.

"Duck," came the calm order from behind him.

He dropped to the floor, and a heavy lead shot *zinged* over him, through the space where his head had been. Across the stream, one of the *wyrsa* squalled and bit the one nearest it. The second retaliated, and Tad had the impression that it looked both surprised and offended at the "unprovoked" attack. The weaving knot was becoming unraveled as the two offended parties snapped and hissed at one another.

Another lead shot followed quickly, and a third *wyrsa* hissed and joined what was becoming a melee. That seemed to be more provocation than the others could resist, and the knot became a tumbling tangle of quarreling *wyrsa*, with nothing graceful, coordinated, or hypnotic about it. Now most of the knot was involved in the fight, except for a loner who extricated itself from the snarling, hissing pack. This creature backed up slowly, eying the others with what was clearly surprise, and Blade's third shot *thudded* right into its head. It dropped in its tracks, stunned, while the rest of the group continued to squabble, squall, and bite.

Blade stepped back into the front of the cave and watched the *wyrsa* with satisfaction. "I wondered just how cohesive that pack was. I also wonder how long it's going to take them to associate a distance-weapon with us; I doubt that they've ever seen or experienced one before."

At just that moment, another one of the creatures emerged from the bushes, and uttered a cry that was part hiss, part deep-throated growl. The reaction to this was remarkable and immediate; the others stopped fighting, instantly, and dropped to the ground, groveling in submission. The new *wyrsa* ignored them, going instead to the one that Blade had brought down, sniffing at it, then nipping its hindquarters to bring it groggily to its feet.

"I'd say the pack-leader just arrived," Tad said.

The new *wyrsa* swung its head around as he spoke, and glared at him from across the river. The dead-white eyes skewered him, holding him in place entirely against his will, while the *wyrsa's* lip lifted in a silent snarl. The eyes glowed faintly, and his thoughts slowed to a sluggish crawl.

Tad felt exactly like a bird caught within striking distance of a snake; unable to move even to save his own life. It was a horrible feeling of cold dread, one that made his extremities feel icy. At just that moment, Blade stepped between them, and leveled a malevolent glare of her own at the pack-leader. In a calm, clear voice, she suggested that the *wyrsa* in question could do several highly improbable, athletically difficult, and possibly biologically impractical things involving its own mother, a few household implements, and a dead fish.

Tad blinked as his mind came back to life again when the *wyrsa* took its eyes off him. He'd had no idea Blade's education had been *that* liberal!

The *wyrsa* might not have understood the words, but the tone was unmistakable. It reared back as if it were going to accept the implied challenge by leaping across the river—or leaping into it and swimming across—and Blade let another stone fly from her sling.

This one cracked the pack-leader across the muzzle, breaking a tooth with a wet *snap*. The creature made that strange noise of hiss and yelp that Tad had heard the night one got caught in his deadfall. It whirled and turned on the others, driving them away in front of it with a ragged squeal, and a heartbeat later, the riverbank was empty.

Blade tucked her sling back into her pocket, and rubbed her bad shoulder thoughtfully. "I don't know if that was a good idea, or a bad one. We aren't going to be able to turn them against each other again. But at least they know now that we have something that can hit them from a distance besides magic."

"And you certainly made an impression on the leader," Tad observed, cocking his head to one side.

She smiled faintly. "Just making it clear which of us is the meanest bitch in the valley," she replied lightly. "Or hadn't you noticed the leader was female?"

"Uh, actually, no. I hadn't." He felt his nares flush with chagrin at being so caught in the creature's spell that he had completely missed something so obvious. "She's really not my type."

Her grin widened. "Makes me wonder if the reason she's keeping the pack here has less to do with the fact that we killed one of her pups, than it does with her infatuation with you. Or rather, with your magnificent . . . physique." Her eyes twinkled wickedly.

Whether or not she realizes it, she's definitely recovering. But I wonder if I ought to break something else, just for the sake of a little peace!

He coughed. "I think not," he replied, flushing further with embarrassment.

"Oh, no?" But Blade let it drop; this was hardly the time and place to skewer him with further wit, although when they got out of this, he had the feeling that she would *not* have forgotten this incident or her own implications. "You know," she continued, "if we had even a chance of picking her off, the pack might lose its cohesiveness. At the very least, they'd be spending as much time squabbling over the leadership position as stalking us."

He scratched the side of his head thoughtfully. She had a good point. "We have to be able to see them to pick one particular *wyrsa*," he pointed out. "And traps and rockfalls are likely to get the least experienced, not the most. But it does account for why they're being so persistent and tenacious."

"Uh-huh. We got one of her babies, probably." Blade sank down on the stone floor of the cave, and watched the underbrush across the river. He turned his attention in that direction himself, and was rewarded by the slight movement of a bit of brush. Since there wasn't a breeze at the moment, he concentrated on that spot, and was able to make out a flash of dark, shiny hide before the creature moved again.

"Interesting." Blade chewed on a nail, and regarded the brush with narrowed eyes. "I don't think we're going to see them out in the open again. They learn quickly."

That quickly? That was impressive; but he called to mind what Aubri had told him about the pack's collective intelligence. If there were many more than just the knot that he'd seen, it would mean that as a group, the pack might be as smart as a makaar, and that was pretty smart.

Regardless of what Father claims.

The bushes moved again, and he caught another glimpse of slick black hide. *A cross of greyhound and snake . . . I can't imagine anything more bizarre. But then, Blade would tell me that my imagination isn't very good. I wonder what kind of vision they get out of those strange eyes? Can they see in the dark? Could that white film be a screen they pull across their eyes to protect them from daylight? Can they actually "see" magic? Or scent it?*

"I wonder what we look like to them," he said, musing aloud. Blade shot him a sharp glance.

"I suppose I looked fairly harmless until I whipped out my sling," she replied. "But I suspect that *you* look like a movable feast. After all, you *are* burdened with a magical nature, and it might be rather obvious to them."

"You mean—they might be more interested in me than you as prey?" he choked. She nodded.

"Probably as someone they'd want to keep alive a while, so they could continue to feed on your magic as it rebuilt. They're probably bright enough for that."

He hadn't thought about that.

It did not make him feel any better.

Amberdrake stood beside the leader of their party and wrung more water out of a braid of hair. He waited for the fellow to say something enlightening. Fog wreathed around them both, and shrouded everything more than a few paces away in impenetrable whiteness.

"I wish I knew what was going on here," Regin muttered, staring at the pair of soggy decoys wedged up in the fork of a tree. "There's no trail from the camp, which looks as if the Silvers were trying to conceal their backtrail. But there isn't a sign of anything hunting them, either. And now—we find this." The ground beneath the tree was torn up, as was the bark of the lower trunk, but there was no blood. There *was* a deadfall rigged of wood that had been tripped, but there was no sign that anything had been caught in it. They might have passed the site by, thinking that it was just a place where some large forest creature had been marking his territory.

Except that there was a human-shaped decoy and a gryphon-shaped decoy wedged high in a tree.

That isn't very enlightening.

"They might have run into some sort of large predator," Drake pointed out. "Just because we didn't see any sign of a hunter, that doesn't mean they weren't being trailed. That would account for why they tried not to leave a trail. Maybe that's even the reason why they left their camp in the first place."

This was the first sign of the children that any of them had come across in their trek toward the river. Amberdrake took it as a good omen; it certainly showed that the duo had gotten this far, so their own party was certainly on the right track. And it showed that they were in good enough health to rig something like this.

"Maybe. But why decoys?" Regin paced carefully around the trunk of the tree, examining it on all sides. "Most forest predators hunt with their noses, and even in this rain, the trail from here to wherever they *did* spend the night would be fresh enough to follow. I wonder what we can learn from this."

"I don't know; I'm not a hunter," Amberdrake admitted, and let it go at that.

Skan didn't, however. "Whatever tore this place up is an animal—or at least, it doesn't use weapons or tools," he pointed out. "It might just be that the—that Blade and Tad wandered into its territory, and they built the decoys to keep it occupied while *they* went on their way."

"Maybe." Regin shook his head. "Whatever it was, I don't recognize the marks, but that doesn't surprise me. I haven't recognized much in this benighted forest since we got into it. And I'm beginning to wonder how anything survives here without gills."

With that, he shrugged, heading off into the forest in the direction of the river. Amberdrake followed him, but Skan lingered a moment before hurrying to catch up lest he get left behind and lost in the fog.

"I don't like it," he muttered fretfully as he reached Drake's side. "I just don't like it. It didn't look right back there, but I can't put my finger on why."

"I don't know enough about hunting animals to be of any help," Drake replied bluntly. He kept telling himself that the children were—must be—still fine. That no matter how impressive the signs these unknown creatures had left were, the children had obviously escaped their jaws. "All I know is that whatever made those marks must be the size of a horse, and if I were being chased by something that size, I probably wouldn't be on the ground at night. Maybe they put the decoys up one tree and then climbed over to another to spend the night."

Unless, of course, they're too hurt to climb trees. But in that case, how did the decoys get up in one?

"Illusion!" Skan said suddenly, his head coming up with a jerk. "That's it! There's no illusion and no traces of one on those decoys. Tad's not a powerful mage, but he's good enough to cast an illusion, and if I were building a decoy I'd want to make it look as much like me as possible! So why didn't he put an illusion on it?"

"Because he couldn't," Drake said flatly. "If mage-energy got sucked out of the basket and everything else, it could have gotten sucked out of him, and it might not have built up enough yet for him to do anything."

"Oh." Skan was taken a bit aback, but finally nodded his acceptance of Drake's explanation. Amberdrake was just as glad, because he could think of another.

Tad can't work a simple magic like an illusion because he's hurt too badly.

On the other hand, those decoys were soggy enough to have been here for a couple of days, so that meant that the children made fairly good progress for two people trying to hide their backtrail, So that in turn meant that they couldn't have been hurt too badly. Didn't it?

He also didn't want to think about how having mage-energy drained from him might affect Tad in other, more subtle ways. Would it be like a slowly-draining wound? Would it affect his ability to work magic at all? What if he simply was no longer a mage anymore? Gryphons were inherently magical for good reasons, and Urtho would not have designed them so otherwise. Although the Mage of Silence had made many mistakes, the gryphons were considered his masterpieces. Magic collected in their bodies with every breath and with every stroke of the wings. It stabilized their life systems, cleaned their organs, helped them fly. Amberdrake had never heard of what would happen if a gryphon were deprived of mage-energy completely for an extended amount of time; would it be like fatigue poisoning, or gout, or something even more insidious, like a mental imbalance?

The rescue party was moving along in a tightly-bunched group to keep from getting separated in the mist. *We're on the right track at least; the children certainly came this way,* Amberdrake reminded himself. *They're moving right along, thinking, planning. If they're in trouble, the best place for them is the river. There's food there that's easy to catch, and maybe caves in the cliffs. They're doing all the right things, especially if they're having to deal with large predators.*

Maybe this was why the rescuers hadn't found much in the way of large game. They'd tried to send on their findings by teleson, so that the other two parties out searching knew to turn back to the river. The mage Filix *thought* he'd gotten everything through clearly, but without local mage-energy to draw on, he couldn't be certain that all the details had made it over. Still, whether the children went north or south when they encountered the river, *someone* should run into them now. Their own party was going to try to the north, mostly because they did know for certain that Ikala's would be coming up from below them, also heading north.

This damned fog. It makes me more nervous than the rain! If—when—we all get out of this, I am never leaving the city again, I swear it. Not unless it's to visit another city. So far as I'm concerned, you can take the "wilderness experience" and bury it in a hole. He'd never forgotten the hardships of the trek to White Gryphon, and he had been all too well aware of what this mission would involve. He thought he'd been prepared for it. *Except for one thing; I'd forgotten that now I'm not as limber as I used to be for this sort of thing. Judeth and Aubri certainly didn't volunteer to traipse through the woods, and now I see why. They probably think I'm a fool, forcing myself to go along on this rescue, trying to do a young man's job. Maybe letting me go was Judeth's way of getting revenge upon me for threatening her!*

But Blade wasn't Judeth's daughter, nor was Tad Aubri's son.

No, I'd rather be out here. At least I know that I'm doing something this way. Zhaneel and Winterhart must feel the same, or they wouldn't have insisted on coming either.

But the fog was doing more than just getting on his nerves; he kept thinking that he was seeing shadows flitting alongside them, out there. He kept feeling eyes on him, and getting glimpses of skulking shapes out of the corner of his eye. It was all nonsense, of course, and just his nerves getting the better of him, but—

"Drake," Skan whispered carefully, "we're being paced. I don't know by what, but there's something out there. I can taste it in the fog, and I've seen a couple of shadows moving."

"You're sure?" That was Regin, who had signaled for a halt and dropped back when he heard Skan whispering. "Bern thought he might be seeing something, too—"

"Then count me as three, because I saw large shadows moving out there and behind us," Drake said firmly. "Could it be whatever tore up the ground back there?"

"If it is, I don't want to goad it into attacking us in this fog," Regin replied. "Though I doubt it will as long as we look confident."

"Most big hunters won't mess with a group," Bern confirmed, nodding. "They like single prey, not a pack."

Drake must have looked skeptical, because Regin thumped him on the back in what was probably supposed to be an expression of hearty reassurance. It drove the breath out of him and staggered him a pace.

"There's too many of us for it to want to contend with—" Regin pointed out with confidence, "And *we* aren't hurt. I don't care if it paces us, as long as it doesn't come after us, and it won't. I'm sure of it."

Amberdrake got his breath again, and shrugged. "You're the leader," he said, keeping his uncertainty to himself.

Regin grinned, as if to say, "That's right, I am," but wisely kept his response to a grin and waved them on again.

Drake continued to feel the eyes on his back, and kept thinking about beings the size of a horse with talons to match—the kinds of claws that had torn up the earth to the depth of his hand. Would a party of seven humans and one gryphon look all *that* formidable to something like that? And what if there was more than one of those things out there? The way the ground had been dug up certainly suggested that there were several.

"You won't like this," Skan gryphon-whispered, which was as subtle and quiet as a human's normal speaking voice. The gryphon glanced from side to side apprehensively. "Drake, I think we've been surrounded."

All the muscles in Amberdrake's neck went tight, and he shivered reflexively. He no longer trusted Regin's self-confidence in the least.

At just that moment, Regin signaled another halt, and Bern took him aside to whisper something into his ear.

The leader looked straight at Skan. "Bern says we're surrounded. Are we?"

"I think so," Skan said flatly. "And I don't think whatever it is out there is just curious. I also don't think it's going to let us get much farther without a fight."

Regin's face darkened, as if Skan had challenged him, but he turned his eyes to the shrouding fog before replying. "The General always says the best defense is a good offense," he replied in a growl. "But there's no point in lobbing arrows against things we can't see. We'll lose ammunition without impressing them."

"The rains are going to begin as soon as the fog lifts, sir," Bern pointed out. "We *still* won't be able to see what's out there, and you can't shoot with a wet bowstring."

Regin leveled his gaze on Filix next. "Is there something you can do to find out what's following us? Maybe scare it away? I don't want to waste time better spent looking for Silverblade and Tadrith."

The mage shrugged. "Maybe. I can try. The best thing would be to try to stun one so that we can see what it looks like. I don't have to see something to stun it, I just have to know in general where it is."

The leader spread his hands, indicating his full permission. "You're the mage. Try it, see what happens."

Amberdrake opened his mouth to object, but closed it again; after all, what did he know? Nothing about hunting, predators, or being stalked. If their stalkers were only curious after all, stunning one wouldn't hurt them; if they were thinking about making a meal of the rescuers, well, having one of their lot fall over without a mark on him should make them back off for a while. At least, it certainly seemed to him that it should work out that way. And by the time the hunters regained their courage, the rescue party would probably be long gone.

Skan opened his beak, and Amberdrake thought he was going to object as well, but it was too late. Filix had already spotted something, or thought he had, and had unleashed the spell.

The result was not what any of them had expected.

A dark shadow in the fog glowed suddenly—Amberdrake got an odd, unsettling feeling in the pit of his stomach—and Filix and Skan cursed together with heartfelt fluency.

"What?" Regin snapped, looking from one to the other. *"What?"*

"It ate my spell—" Filix began, but Skan interrupted him. waving the teleson he'd been carrying around his neck.

"It ate the teleson!" the gryphon roared. "Damn! Whatever's out there is what pulled Blade and Tad down, and you just fed it everything it wanted!"

Skan was just glad that they had alerted the other parties that they had finally found signs of the missing children *before* the teleson became a pretty piece of junk. By the time they camped that night, it was evident that, not only had the creatures out there "eaten" the teleson—or rather, drained away all of its mage-energy—but they'd "eaten" the energy from every other magical device the party had.

Why they'd waited so long to do so was a matter of con-
jecture at this point. Maybe they'd been screwing up their
courage to do so; maybe they just been biding their time until they had a certain number of their lot in place. Maybe the
things were staying in hiding until something was thrown at
them, as a form of cover.

"It wasn't my fault!" Filix kept protesting. "How was I
going to know?"

He couldn't have known that some bizarre animals were
the cause of the trouble, of course, but since they *had* known
there was something out here that ate magic, it seemed to
Skan that lobbing spells around indiscriminately was obviously a bad idea. He had been about to say just that when
Filix had lobbed the first one.

Well, what the search party had to deal with now were
the results. In the short term, that meant the tents had to be
put up by hand, and using freshly-cut poles and ropes; fires
had to be started with the old-fashioned firestriker, and any
number of other problems, both inconvenient and possibly
hazardous, suddenly arose to confront them.

In the long term—having gotten a taste, the strange and
possibly hostile creatures that had stalked them through the
fog and rain might now be looking for a meal.

The tents were keeping the rain out, but were not precisely dry anymore. They weren't keeping bugs out, either.
Skan wondered how long it would take until it occurred to
Regin that the waterproofing and bug-protections on their
rations might also have been magical. Serve him right if he
had to eat soggy, weevil-ridden ration-bread!

The two tents shared a canvas "porch;" it lacked a canvas
floor and one wall, but gave protection to their fire. They
gathered in the two tents on either side of the fire, with the
flaps tied back. Regin called them for a conference as the
light began to dim in the forest outside. Rain drummed
down on the canvas, but Regin had pitched his voice to carry
over it.

"We're doing fine," Regin decreed, as they sat, crowded

into the two tents meant for a total of four, not eight; at least this way they all had space to get in out of the wet, even if it was not completely dry beneath the canvas. "We have nothing to worry about. Canvas still keeps out rain, wood still burns, and we still have the north-needle, which is, thank the gods, *not* magical. We've found the river, and it's only a matter of time before we either run into the missing Silvers or one of the other parties does. If they do, they'll try and notify us, realize what happened when they don't get our teleson, and come fetch us. If we find them first, we'll just backtrack along the river until we meet one of the other parties, then get back to the base camp. Not a problem."

Skan was hardly in agreement with that sentiment, but Regin *was* the leader, and it was poor form to undermine confidence in your leader when it was most needed by others.

This is not a wartime situation. And now we know that the magic stealers are just some kind of strange wild animal, not an enemy force. If we're just careful, we should get out of this intact and with the children. At least, that was what he was trying to tell himself.

"For tonight, I want a double watch set; four and four, split the night, a mage in each of the two watches." Regin looked around for volunteers for the first watch, and got his four without Skan or Drake needing to put up a hand.

Skan did not intend to volunteer, but Filix seemed so eager to make up for the mistake that cost them all their magic, that it looked as if the younger mage had beaten the gryphon to volunteering. Skan wondered what the young man thought he was volunteering *for;* he was hardly a fighter, and the idea of throwing magic at something that *ate* magic did not appeal to the gryphon.

I am not lobbing a single spell around until we lose these menaces, he resolved. *If these things eat magic, it stands to reason that magic makes them stronger. And the stronger they are, the more likely they are to attack us physically.*

Well, Filix could use a bow, at least, even if he didn't possess a gryphon's natural weaponry.

He might do all right at that—provided he thinks before he acts. He wanted to take Filix aside and caution him, but an earlier attempt had not been very successful. Filix clearly thought that Skan was overreacting to the situation. One of the biggest problems with the younger mages—youngsters who had come along after the Cataclysm—was that they thought magic could fix everything. They had yet to learn that magic was nothing more than another tool, and one that you *could* do without if you had to. Maybe things wouldn't be as convenient without it, but so what? *Snowstar ought to force them to spend a year* not *using magic.*

Regin nodded with satisfaction at his volunteers. "Right. Close up the watch right around the camp; there's no point in guarding a big perimeter tonight. If you get a clear shot, take it; maybe if we make things unpleasant enough for whatever is out there, it'll get discouraged and leave us alone."

And maybe you'll provoke them into an attack! Skan reminded himself that he was *not* the leader and kept his beak clamped tightly shut on his own objections. But he resolved to sleep with himself between Drake and the tent wall, and to do so lightly.

Somehow he managed to invoke most of the old battle reflexes, get himself charged up to the point where nerves would do instead of sleep, and laid himself warily down to rest with one eye and ear open. In his opinion, Regin was taking this all far too casually, and was far too certain that they were "only" dealing with a peculiar form of wild animal. And he was so smug about the fact that he had brought nonmagical backups to virtually every magical piece of equipment except the teleson that Skan wanted to smack him into good sense again.

Bringing backups isn't the point! he seethed, as he positioned himself to best protect Drake in an attack. *The fact that there is something out here that can eat magic and is clearly hostile—that's the point! What good are our backups going to do if these things decide that they want more than just a taste of us from a distance?*

The rains slowed, then stopped. The fire died, leaving them with nothing but glowing coals for a source of light. Just as the camp quieted down for the night, the "wild animals" proved that they were not intimidated by a party of eight.

Skan came awake all at once with the sound of someone falling to the ground, followed by cursing and a bowstring snapping practically in his ear. But it wasn't Filix taking the shot—the mage was lying on the ground, just outside the canvas wall nearest Skan, gasping for breath.

The other three humans not on watch scrambled up, but Skan was already on his feet, ready for trouble. A moment later, Regin hauled the half-conscious mage into the tent. "What happened?" Skan asked harshly, as the other two fighters scrambled outside, leaving himself, Regin, and Drake alone with the disabled mage. Amberdrake went to the young mage's side immediately and began examining him.

The leader shook his head. "I don't know," the young man admitted, looking pale and confused in the light from the single lamp that Drake had lit. "He saw something out there, and I think he was going to work some magic on it— he muttered something about his shields—and then he just fell over. I took a shot at something moving, but I don't think I hit it."

"He's been drained," Amberdrake said flatly, looking up, with his hand still on Filix's forehead. "I saw this once or twice in the war, when mages overextended themselves."

I remember that; it was on the orders of an incompetent commander.

"The only difference is that this time, Filix didn't overextend himself, he was drained to nothing by means of the spell he cast," Drake continued. "My guess is that those creatures out there were able to use his previous magic to get into his shield-castings, and then just pulled everything he had out of him, the way they pulled the mage-energy out of the teleson. And probably Tadrith and Silverblade's basket as well."

"Stupid son of—" Regin bit off what he was going to say. "Is he going to be all right?"

"Maybe. Probably. As long as he doesn't give whatever is out there another chance to drain him." Drake looked angry and a little disgusted, and Skan didn't blame him. "I'll do what I can for him, but you should be aware that it isn't much. Lady Cinnabar herself couldn't do much for something like this. What he needs is rest, rest, and more rest. We're going to have to carry him for the next few days. He probably won't even regain consciousness until tomorrow, and his head will hurt worse than it ever has in his life for several days."

"Well, we'll go short one this shift." Regin shook his head again. "Stupid—" He glanced at Skan, who drew himself up with dignity.

"*I* know better than to try anything magical," he retorted to the unspoken rebuke. "I'll use a more direct method of defending this camp, if I have to use anything."

Stupid fool thought that if he cast shields, he'd be safe against this, Skan fumed. *Never bothered to remember that magical shields are themselves magical, did he? And since shields are spun out from your own power, they are traceable directly back into your own mage-energies. He probably didn't think it was necessary to cast anything more complicated, and figured his shields would block anything coming in. . . .*

The result had clearly been immediate, and had certainly been predictable.

He pulled Drake back into the tent they had been trying to sleep in. "We'll stay here," he told Amberdrake. "Leave him in the other tent with Regin."

"With just one man to watch him?" Amberdrake asked. Skan shook his head.

"Does it matter?" he replied. "There's nothing you can do for him, and if something comes charging in here, we're going to have more important things to think about than defending an unconscious mage."

There it was; hard, cruel, war-truths. This *was* a war, whether or not Regin realized it yet.

Evidently Drake did; he grimaced, but didn't protest any further. He remembered. He knew that the two of them must make their priority that of finding the children. And he knew all about cutting losses.

Which was just as well, because a few moments later, the second attack came.

There was no warning. They hadn't even blown out the lantern or tried to lie down again. The rain must have covered any sounds of approach, for there certainly was nothing outside the tent walls to indicate anything was wrong. All that Skan knew was that Bern shouted, then screamed, and something dark came ripping through the canvas of the tent, knocking over the lantern in the process, plunging them into darkness until the spilled oil flared up. *He* knocked Drake to the ground and stood over him, slashing at whatever came near in the darkness.

He ignored anything outside the tent to the point where it simply didn't exist for him, concentrating fiercely on tiny currents of air, sounds, movement, and what little he could see reflecting from the burning spilled oil. His talons connected several times with something that felt like snakeskin, tearing through it to the flesh beneath, and he clenched any time he was able to, so that he might rend away a chunk of meat. But his opponents uttered nothing more than a hiss, and they dashed away through the double rents in the tent canvas as if his fierce opposition surprised them. The fight couldn't have lasted for very long, for not only was he not tired, he hadn't even warmed up to full fighting speed when the attacks ceased, and the attackers vanished, silent shadows sliding between the raindrops.

He stood over Drake a while longer; the *kestra'chern* had the good sense to stay put and not move the entire time. When Amberdrake finally moved, it was to pat the flame out with the edge of a bedroll and then right the lantern.

"Are they gone?" came the voice from between his feet.

"I think so," Skan replied, shaking his head to refocus himself. Only then did he hear the moans of wounded, and the sound of Bern calling his name.

"We're here!" Drake answered for him as he relit the lantern with a smoldering corner of the bedroll. "We're all right, I think."

"That's more than the rest of us can say," the scout replied grimly, wheezing and coughing. "Can you get out here and help me? If I let go of this rag around my leg, I'm going to bleed myself out."

Drake swore, scrambled for the medical kit in the darkness, and pushed through the ruined tent wall. Skan followed slowly.

When the lantern had been relit so that Drake could see to treat wounds, and everyone had been accounted for, they discovered that Regin and Filix had been killed by more of the things. They had probably died instantly, or nearly so. Amberdrake reached for the bodies, and could only locate so many pieces. *At the very least, they got the mercy of a quick death.* There wasn't much left of them. Blood was spattered everywhere, and it was difficult to tell what part belonged to whom.

He left the tent quickly, reminded all too forcefully of some of Hadanelith's victims.

And of Ma'ar's. . . .

I'm supposed to be hardened to this sort of thing, but maybe I've just seen too much death, too much suffering. Maybe I am not as tough as I thought I was, or wish I could be, even after all this time. It was one thing to think about cutting losses—another thing to lose people like this. We were caught unprepared, despite my hoped-for lessons of experience.

Amberdrake remained for a few moments longer, and when he came out, he surprised Skan by the thoughtful look of concentration he wore. Finally, as the other men bundled the two bodies hastily in the remains of the tent, he drew Skan aside.

"Are these things animals, or not?" he asked.

Skan blinked. "They certainly fought like it," he replied cautiously. "*Extremely* efficient predators. They didn't have weapons, just talons and teeth, and . . . and speed. I don't think I've ever seen anything that fast since the last makaar died. *Fierce* predators; no wonder we haven't seen much game, and all of it small. They must have emptied out the forest around here, of ground-based game at least." He shook his head. "We should have figured that out, and assumed they'd attack us for food. They must be half-mad with hunger by now; they can't live long on rabbits, snakes and bugs, not as big as they are."

Drake nodded, as if he had expected Skan to say that. "In that case, tell me this; why didn't they drag their prey off with them to eat? Why didn't they try and kill more of us?"

Skan opened his beak to reply, and shut it with a *click*.

Why didn't they, if they're just big hunters with an incidental ability to eat mage-energy?

"Maybe we don't taste good?" he suggested lamely.

"Maybe. But that hasn't stopped lions from becoming maneaters when they're famished. Shalaman showed us that, remember." Amberdrake chewed on his lower lip a moment. "I have a feeling . . . that these things are planning something. And that they don't intend to let us get away. Skan, they're a lot worse than they seem."

"They seem bad enough already to me," Skan grumbled, "But I see your point."

He didn't have time to think much more about it, however, for Bern, as acting leader, decreed that there would be no more rest that night.

They spent the rest of the dark hours in the open, sitting in a circle with their backs together, facing the forest with weapons in hand.

It was a long, cold, and terrifying night. Every time a drop of water fell from a leaf, someone started. Every time a shadow seemed to move, they all got ready to defend their lives. Skan had never spent a night as frightening as this one, not even during the war, and he prayed no one else would ever have to, either. Stelvi Pass had been a summer day compared to this unending, wet, cold waiting. He didn't know how Amberdrake was managing to bear up; it was bad enough to endure this knowing that he *could,* if there was no other choice, escape by flying into the treetops. Even in a fight, he could defend himself against fairly stiff odds. But Drake couldn't escape and he wasn't a fighter, and in his place, Skan knew he'd have been babbling with fear.

As soon as there was any light at all beneath the trees, Bern ordered them to move out, down to the river that they had heard all night long. The flood-swollen river, which roared at their feet, with nothing on the other side but a rocky cliff-face and a scrap of path.

"You two aren't fighters, so you get across the river and hold it for us so we can cross," he ordered Drake and Skan. Skan took one look at the swollen, raging waters, and seriously considered mutiny.

But Amberdrake just picked up a coil of rope from the wreckage of the camp, and gestured to him to follow down to the rocks at the edge. There he rigged a harness of rope for himself, while Bern and the rest stood nervously with their backs to the water, facing the forest, bows and swords ready. Soon enough, the fog would rise, and when the shadow-creatures came back, the besieged rescuers wouldn't be able to see them until it was far too late.

Drake, the expert in ropes and knots, moved far more quickly than Skan would have thought possible under the circumstances. His fingers fairly flew as he put together a harness it would be impossible to get out of without undoing at least half of the knots. It must have seemed to the four injured fighters that he was taking a ridiculous amount of time, however. He was even making sure that it would fit over his pack—the precious pack that had what was left of their medical kit, and the oil and oil lamp.

"Hurry up!" Bern shouted, his voice pitched higher with strain and nerves.

Drake ignored them, and turned to Skan. "You can't carry me over, but you can tow me through the water," he pointed out. "There's no way I'm going to slip out of this."

He fastened the loose end of the rope to a tree at the water's edge, without elaborating anything, but his plan was obvious to Skan. The harness was rigged so that Drake *could* swim freely, but could also be towed along easily, which is what he meant Skan to do, flying above the river. Once he got Drake to the other side, the *kestra'chern* could fasten his rope to a boulder or spike of rock, and the others could plunge in and drag themselves across.

Providing, of course, there weren't more of those things on the other side, waiting somewhere.

If that last thought occurred to Amberdrake, he didn't hesitate for a second; once he had the end of the rope tied off, he plunged immediately into the river, almost before Skan had hold of the end fastened to his harness. Caught off-balance for a moment, Skan held on against the tug of the current, then launched himself into the air.

Amberdrake sputtered and submerged once, then steadied. He called out, "It's drier in here than in the forest!"

Once there, he was utterly grateful that Drake was a good swimmer, and he allowed himself a brief, tension-relieving smile at Amberdrake's quip. His friend was able to keep his own head above water, so that Skan's only task was to pull him onward.

Only! This is like playing tug-of-war against five teams of draft horses!

It was obvious within a few moments that this was going to be a great deal more difficult than it looked. They weren't even a single length from the shore, and Skan wanted to quit.

The gryphon's wings beat laboriously, the muscles in his back and chest burning with pain, as he pulled against the current and the weight of Drake's body. Below him, Amberdrake labored against the current trying to pull him under, and occasionally lost the battle. But he had honed his swimming ability in the powerful surf below White Gryphon; between his own strength and Skan's, his head always popped back above the surface again, long enough for him to get another lungful of air. Ten heartbeats later, they were out of time.

"Hurry!" Bern shouted again, his voice spiraling upward in fear. "They're coming!"

Skan ignored him as best he could, concentrating every fiber on getting a little more strength out of his wings. Drake was not doing well down there; the treacherous currents kept pulling him under, and each time he rose to the surface it took a little longer.

They were about halfway across when the sounds of battle erupted behind him; short screams and cries that echoed above the roaring river. He ignored those, too, as best he could.

His world narrowed to the face of his friend in the water below, the rope in his front talons, the pain of his laboring body, and the farther shore.

His lungs were on fire; his forelimbs ached with all the tortures of the damned from the strain of holding Drake and pulling him onward. His vision fogged with red, as it had only a few times in the past, when he had driven himself past his limits.

The bank was only a few lengths away—but he was out of energy, running out of strength, and just about out of endurance.

He wasn't going to make it. He could drop the rope and save himself, or they would both be dragged under.

No! He was *not* going to surrender with the goal so close! *Come on, gryphon. If he can do this, so can you. You're a team, remember! He's counting on you not to let him drown.*

Think of what Winterhart would do to you if you did! Think of what Gesten would do!

Amberdrake has been with you all your life, gryphon, all your life. He's had his hands in your guts and your blood in his hair, putting you back together from pieces. He didn't leave you then, he wouldn't leave you.

From somewhere came another burst of strength, and with a cry that was half a scream of defiance and half a moan of agony, he drove himself at the bank.

He made it by mere talon-lengths, dropping down on it with all the grace of a shot duck, and landing half on the bank, half in the water. With a groan, he grabbed the rope in his beak and dragged himself and Drake, talon over talon, onto the bank and safety.

He wanted to just lie there, panting, but there were still four more people on the other side. Somehow he pulled himself up to a standing position on shaking legs, just as Drake got to his hands and knees, and both of them turned toward the far bank at the same time.

All they saw was torn foliage, the slashed end of the rope hanging off the tree Drake had tied it to, splashes of red that weren't likely flowers—and the empty shore. They watched, panting and slumping down against each other until the fog closed in, leaving them staring at blank whiteness.

They were alone.

It could not be much longer before whatever it was that had attacked them found a way to cross, unless it took a long time—to eat.

For a moment, he felt stricken, numb, frozen with shock. But he had been in too many fights, and lost too many comrades, for this to paralyze him now.

Mourn later, find safety now!

Drake looked at him from beneath a mat of hair that had become a tangled, dripping mess, his clothing half torn from his body by the fight of last night, and a strange look of hope in his eyes. For one stark moment, Skan was afraid that he'd gone mad.

"Blade—" he began hoarsely, then coughed, huge racking coughs that brought up half a lungful of river water. Skan balled his talons into fists and pounded his back until he stopped coughing and waved Skan off.

"Blade—" he began again, his voice a ruin. He looked up and pointed north along the riverbank. "She's that way. I can feel her. I swear it, Skan!"

With one accord, they dragged themselves to their feet and stumbled northward over the slippery rocks and wet clay of the bank below the cliff face. North—where their children *must* be.

Tad inspected the last of the traps with no real hope that he would find anything at this one that differed from all the rest. The first *wyrsa* they had killed had been the last; none of the traps worked a second time. In fact, the *wyrsa* seemed to take a fiendish delight in triggering the damned things and leaving them empty.

So far, they had not dared the last one, another rockfall that he or Blade could trigger from inside the cave. He suspected, though, that it was only a matter of time before they did. On the other hand, they would not be able to disarm it without triggering it, so perhaps they were all even.

As he had expected, this snare lay empty, too. He decided that the rope could be better used elsewhere, and salvaged it. It certainly would have been nice if *this* one had worked, though. His nerves were wearing thin, and he was afraid that the *wyrsa* might be able to drain mage-energy from him constantly now, since they were so close. He didn't dare try shielding against them; shields were magical too, and they could surely be eaten like anything else magical.

When they had first found the cave, he had thought that the noise of the river and the waterfall would cover the sounds anything approaching made, but over the past few days he had discovered to his surprise that he had been wrong. To a limited extent, he had actually gotten used to the steady roaring, and was able to pick out other noises beyond it.

But the very last sound he had been expecting was the noise of someone—a two-legged someone—scrambling over the rocks at a speed designed to break his neck. And panting.

Especially not coming *toward* him.

Those were not *wyrsa* sounds, either, not unless the *wyrsa* had acquired a pair of hunting-boots and put them on!

He had barely time to register and recognize the sounds before the makers of the noise burst through the fog right in his face. He hadn't heard the second one, because *he* had been flying, and his wingbeats had *not* carried over the sound of the falls. Tadrith looked up to find his vision filled with the fierce, glorious silhouette of the Black Gryphon.

"Father!" he exclaimed, in mingled relief and shock. "Amberdrake—"

"No time!" Skandranon panted, as Amberdrake scrabbled right past him without pausing. "Run! We're being chased!"

No need to ask what was chasing them. Skan landed heavily, then turned to stand at bay to guard Amberdrake's retreat. Tad leaped up beside him, despite his handicap. With two gryphons guarding the narrow trail, there wasn't a chance in the world that the *wyrsa* would get past!

But they certainly tried.

The fog was as thick as curdled milk, and the *wyrsa* nothing more than shadows and slashing claws and fangs reaching for them through the curtain. But they couldn't get more than two of their number up to face Skan and Tad at any one time, and without the whole pack able to attack together, their tactics were limited. They *were* fast, but Tad and Skan were retreating, step by careful step, and that generally got them out of range before a talon or a bite connected.

Step by step. And watch it. Slip, and you end up under those claws. Thank Urtho for giving us four legs. They retreated all the way to the shelf of rock in front of the cave, and that was where their own reinforcements stepped in.

"Duck!" came the familiar order, and this time when he and his father dropped to the ground, not only did rocks hurl over their heads, but a pair of daggers hummed past Tad's ear like angry wasps. They both connected, too, and one was fatal. The *wyrsa* nearest the water got it in the throat, made a gurgle, and fell over, to be swept away by the rushing torrent. The second was lucky; he was only hit in the shoulder, but gave that familiar hiss-yelp, and vanished into the fog. Skan and Tad took advantage of the respite to turn their backs in turn and scramble into the cave itself.

There they turned again, prepared for another onslaught, but the *wyrsa* had evidently had enough for one day.

Tad sat down right where he was, breathing heavily, heart pounding; his father was less graceful and more tired than that, and dropped down into the sand as if he'd been shot himself, panting with his beak wide open.

"I always knew those throwing-knives were going to come in handy some day," Amberdrake observed.

He looked nothing like the Amberdrake that Tad had known all his life. His long hair was a draggling, tangled, water-soaked mess; his clothing stained, torn, muddy, and also sodden. He wore a pack that was just as much of a mess, at least externally. At his waist was a belt holding one long knife, a pouch, and an odd sheath that held many smaller, flat knives, exactly of the kind that had just whizzed over Tad's head.

"Yes, but—you had to—learn how—to throw them—first," Skan replied, panting. "You and your—bargains!"

"They *were* a bargain!" Amberdrake said indignantly. "A dozen of them for the price of that one single fighting-knife that *you* wanted me to get!"

"But you—knew how to—*use* the—fighting-knife!"

Blade brought her father and Skan a skin of water each, and they drank thirstily. She looked from one to the other of them, and carefully assessed their condition. "I don't think I'm going to ask where the rest of your group is," she said quietly. "I'm pretty certain I already know."

A tiny oil lamp cast warm light down on Amberdrake and his patient. Blade sat at her father's feet while he examined her shoulder, as Skan and Tad kept watch at the mouth of the cave. "You did a fine job on Tadrith's wing," Amberdrake murmured. "I only wish he had done as good a job on your shoulderblade."

Well, that certainly explained why it wouldn't stop hurting. "You're not going to have to rebreak it, are you?" she asked, trying not to wince. He patted her unhurt shoulder comfortingly, and it was amazing just how good that simple gesture felt.

"Not hardly, since it was never set in the first place. Immobilized, yes, but not set. I'm astonished that you've managed as much as you have." He placed the tips of his fingers delicately over the offending bone. "It's possible that it was only cracked at first, and not broken, and that somewhere along the line you simply completed the break. Hold very still for a moment, and this *will* hurt."

She tried not to brace herself, since that would only make things worse. She felt his fingers tighten, sensed a *snap*, and literally saw stars for a moment, it hurt so much.

When she could see again, *she* was still sitting upright, and *he* still had his hands on her shoulders, so she must have managed not to move. She sagged gratefully against the rock he was sitting on, and wiped tears from her eyes, weakly.

"Now, stay still a moment more," he urged. "I haven't done this for a long time, and I'm rather out of practice."

She obeyed, and a moment later, felt the area above the break warming. The pain there vanished, all but a faint throbbing in time with her pulse.

I'd forgotten he still has some Healing ability . . . not enough that he ever acts as a Healer anymore, but enough that he could in the war. In fact, he was first sent by his family off to train as a Healer, but his Empathic senses got in the way. In the war he was supposed to have been very good, even on gryphons.

Amberdrake finally lifted his hands from her shoulder and sighed. "I'm sorry, dearheart, I can't do as much as I'd like."

It was far more than she'd had any hope of before they arrived!

"You did a great deal, Father, believe me. I hope you saved plenty of yourself for Tad," she said. "Especially since you did specialize in gryphon-trauma during the war!"

"I did," he replied as she twisted around to look up at him. He combed his hair out of his eyes with one hand, and grimaced. "I'll keep working on you two as I recuperate, too. But I never was as competent at Healing as I'd like, and accelerating bone growth—well, it's hard, and I never did learn to do it well. Maybe if I'd gotten the right training when I was younger. . . ."

"Then *you'd* have been a Healer, Lady Cinnabar would have been *your* lady and apprentice instead of Tamsin's, and I wouldn't be here," she interrupted. "I love you just the way you are, Father. I wouldn't change a thing."

And suddenly she realized that she meant exactly that, probably for the first time since she had been a small child.

She knew that he had needed to extend his empathic sense in order to Heal, and he still hadn't barricaded himself; he felt that, and his eyes filled with tears.

He wanted to hear that from me as much as I wanted his approval! she thought with astonishment. *How could I have been so blind all this time! Thinking only the child could want approval from the parent—how stupid of me— the parent wants approval from the child just as much.*

"Blade—" he said. She didn't let him finish. She reached up for him as he reached down for her, and they held each other while his tears fell on her cheeks and mingled with hers.

It was he who pulled away first, not she; rubbing his nose inelegantly on the back of his hand as he sniffed, and managing a weak smile for her. "Well, aren't we a pair of sentimental idiots," he began.

"No, you're a pair of *sensible* idiots, if that isn't contradictory," Skandranon interrupted. "You two were overdue for that, if you ask me. And, if you don't ask me, I'll tell you anyway, and I am right, as usual. Drake, what can she do now, if anything?"

"I've strengthened and knitted the bone a bit," Amberdrake replied, looking at her although he answered Skan. "And I've done something about the pain. I wouldn't engage in hand-to-hand, but you can certainly throw a spear, use a sling, or do some very *limited* swordplay. No shields, sorry; it won't take that kind of strain."

"We don't have any shields with us, so that hardly matters," she replied dryly. "Nor bows, either; we had to concentrate on bringing things we could use."

"Well . . . I know how to make a throwing-stick and the spears to go with it, if you know how to use one," Amberdrake admitted. "That should increase your range. There ought to be *some* wood in here straight enough for spears."

He knows how to make a weapon? She throttled down her surprise, and just nodded. "Yes to both—now let me go replace Tad at the front and you can work your will on him."

She almost said *magic,* but stopped herself just in time. Since the *wyrsa* hadn't come calling when her father began his Healing, evidently they did not eat Healing-energy. Which was just as well, under the circumstances. Perhaps it was too localized, or too finely-tuned to be sucked in from afar.

She stood up, hefted a spear in both hands, marveling at her new freedom from pain, and smiled with grim pleasure at the feel of a good weapon. Tad retreated to the back of the cave, and she took her place beside his father.

"So, what exactly are those nightmares?" Skan asked. "Have you any idea?"

She stared out into the rain—the rain had begun early, which meant that the fog had lifted early. That was to their advantage; with four enemies in the cave, she didn't think that the *wyrsa* would venture an attack in broad daylight.

"Tad thinks they're some kind of *wyrsa,* maybe changed by the mage-storms," she told him. "They're about the size of a horse, and they're black, and I suppose you already know that they eat magic."

"Only too well," Skan groaned.

"Well, to counter that advantage, they seem to have lost their poison fangs and claws," she said. "I don't think they're going to try entrancing us again after the first time, but if they start weaving in and around each other, they can hypnotize you if you aren't careful."

"The *wyrsa* I used to hunt were better at it than that," Skan observed, watching the bushes across the river tremble. "So they've lost a couple of attributes and gained one. Could be worse. One touch of those claws, and you were in poor shape, and that was with the hound-sized ones. A horse-sized one would probably kill you just by scratching you lightly."

"I suppose that counts as good news, then." She sighed. "I think this is a pack of youngsters led by one older female, probably their mother. We don't know how many there are; two less than when they started, though. I don't know if you saw it, but Father got one; Tad got one a couple of days ago, with a rockfall. The problem is, no trap works twice on them."

"*Wyrsa*, the size of a horse," Skan muttered, and shook his head. "Terrible. I'd rather have makaar. I wonder what other pleasant surprises the mage-storms left out here for us to find?"

She shrugged. "Right now, this is the only one that matters. It's pretty obvious that the things breed, and breed true, so if we don't get rid of them, one of these days they'll come looking for more magic-meals closer to our home." She turned her gaze on Skandranon for a moment. "And what *did* happen to your party, other than what I can guess?"

Skandranon told her, as tersely as she could have wished. She hadn't known any of the Silvers well, except Bern, who had been her tracking teacher, but it struck her that they had all acted with enormous stupidity and arrogance. Was it only because when they didn't meet with any immediate trouble that they assumed there wasn't anything to worry about?

"Between you and me, my dear," Skandranon said in an undertone, "I'm afraid the late Regin was an idiot. I suspect that he assumed that since you were a green graduate, probably hurt, and female to boot, you got into difficulties with what to him would have been minor opponents. He was wary at first, but when no armies and no renegade mages appeared, he started acting as if this was a training exercise."

She tried not to think too uncharitably of the dead Silver. "Well, we *don't* have much experience, and it would be reasonable to think that we might have panicked and overreacted," she said judiciously. "Still. I'd have thumped that Filix over the head and tied him up once I found the wreck and *knew* there was something that ate magic about. Why attract attention to yourself?"

"Good question," Skan replied. "I wish now I'd done just that." His mournful expression filled in the rest; she could read his thoughts in his eyes. Or was that *her* empathic sense operating? *If I had, they might still be alive. I should have pulled rank on them.*

She turned her attention back to the outside, for she felt distinctly uneasy having the Black Gryphon confess weakness, even tacitly, to her. And yet, she felt oddly proud. He would not have let her see that, if he were not treating her as an adult and an equal.

"Well, what it all comes down to is this," she said grimly. "No one is going to get us out of this except ourselves. We have no way to warn anyone, and what happened to you is entirely likely to happen to them, unless they're smarter than Regin was."

"Oh, that goes without saying—the closest team to us is led by Ikala," Skan said—rather slyly, she thought.

And she clutched her hands on the shaft of the spear as her heart raced a little. *Ikala—if I was going to be rescued by anyone. . . .*

She shook her head; this was not some fanciful Haighlei romance tale. "They're still in danger, and we can't warn them," she repeated. "Remember, these damned things get smarter every time we do something! I think they may even get smarter every time they eat more magic. I doubt that they're native, so Ikala won't know about them. The best chance we all have to survive is if we four can eliminate these creatures before anyone else runs afoul of them. If they *do* get nastier every time they eat something, everyone out there could become victims. For all we know—if they share intelligence as Aubri said—they may share their power among each other as they die off. The fewer there are, the more powerful the individuals might become."

She was afraid that Skan might think she was an idiot for even *thinking* the four of them could take on the *wyrsa* pack, as ill-equipped as they were, but he nodded. "Are you listening to this, Drake?" he called back into the cave.

"To every word, and I agree," came the reply. "It's insane, of course, to think that we can do that, but we're used to handling insanely risky business, aren't we, old bird?"

"We are!" Skan had actually mustered up a grin.

But Amberdrake wasn't finished yet. "And what's more, I'm afraid that trait runs in both families. Right, Tad?"

A gusty sigh answered his question. "I'm afraid so," the young gryphon replied with resignation. "Like father, like son."

Skan winked at her. "The basic point is, we have four excellent minds and four bodies to work on this. Well, between your broken bones and our aching ones, we probably have the equivalent of *two* healthy bodies, rather than four, but that's not so bad! It could be worse!"

Blade thought about just a few of the many, many ways in which it *could* be worse, and nodded agreement. *Of course, there are many, many ways in which it could be better, too. . . .*

"So, while those two are back there involved in patching and mending, let me get my sneaky old mind together with your resilient young one, and let's see if we can't produce some more, cleverer tactics." He gryph-grinned at her, and to her surprise, she found herself grinning back.

"That's it, sir," Tad said, from back in the cave. "That's all the weapons we have."

"Blade?" There was surprise in her father's voice. "I thought you said that you didn't have a bow."

"I did!" She left Skan for a moment and trotted back to the fire, to stare at the short bow and quiver of arrows in surprise. "Where did *that* come from?"

"I brought it in my pack," Tad said sheepishly. "I know you said not to bring one because you couldn't use it, but—I don't know, I thought maybe you might be able to pull it with your feet or something, and if nothing else, you could start a fire with it."

"Well, she still can't use it, but I *can*," Amberdrake said, appropriating it. He looked up at Skan and his son. "You two get out there and start setting those traps before the sun goes down; we'll get ready for the siege."

There would be a siege; Blade only hoped that the traps that the other two were about to set would whittle down the numbers so that the inevitable siege would be survivable. If the mother *wyrsa* had been angry over the loss of a single young, what would she be like when she lost several?

Tad and Skan were going out to set some very special single traps—and do it now, while the *wyrsa* were at a distance. They knew that the *wyrsa* had withdrawn—probably to hunt—because Blade and her father had used their empathic abilities to locate the creatures.

It had been gut-wrenching to do so, but it had at least worked. They hoped that the *wyrsa* would be out of sensing range of small magics, because that was what they intended to use.

The bait and the trigger both would be a tiny bit of magic holding the whole thing together. That was why it needed Skan and Tad to do the work; they were physically stronger than Blade and her father. When the *wyrsa* "ate" the magic holding everything in place—

Deadfalls would crush them, sharpened wooden stakes would plunge through them, nooses would snap around their legs and the rocks poised at the edge of the torrent would tumble in, pulling them under the water. And for the really charming trap, another huge rockfall would obliterate the path and anything that was on it.

They would have to be very, very clever; the magic had to be so small that the *wyrsa* would have to be on top of it to sense it. Otherwise it would "eat" the magic from a distance, triggering the trap without its killing anything.

Meanwhile, Blade and her father gathered together every weapon in their limited arsenal for a last stand.

It has to be now, she kept telling herself. *The* wyrsa *are nibbling away at Tad and they'll do the same to Skan. The more they eat, the stronger they get. We have to goad them into attacking before they're ready, and keep them so angry that they rely on their instincts and hunting skills instead of thinking things over. If we wait, there's a chance the next party will bumble right into them. . . .*

That would be Ikala and Keenath—and the idea that either of those two could be in danger made a fierce rage rise inside her, along with determination to see that nothing of the kind happened.

Spears; the long ones, and the short, crude throwing-spears that Amberdrake was making, with points of sharpened, fire-hardened wood. Those were hers, those, and her fighting-knife, which was just a trifle shorter than a small sword. Amberdrake would take the bow, his own fighting-knife, and his throwing-knives. She still had her sling, and that could be useful at the right time.

There wasn't much, but it was all useful enough. When she had divided it into two piles, hers and her father's, she sat down beside him at the fire to help him with the spears. He made the points, she fire-hardened them, until the pile of straight wooden stakes was all used up. Then she took a single brand from the fire, and he put it out.

She went all the way to the back of the cave and started a *huge* new fire there, one of the objects being to make the *wyrsa* believe that they were farther back there than they actually were. She piled about half of their wood, the wettest lot, around it. This wood was going to have to dry out before it caught—and she thought she had that timed about right.

It's too bad this cave is stable, she thought wistfully. *It*

*would be nice to arrange to get them inside, then drop the
ceiling on them.*

Well, in a way, they were going to do that anyway.

She helped her father drag all of the rest of the driftwood
that they had collected to the front of the cave and arrange it
along the barricade. There was quite a lot of it, more than
she remembered. Tad had certainly been busy!

*And this had better work, because we are using up all of
our resources in one attempt. What was it that Judeth always told us? "Never throw your weapon at the enemy!" I
hope we aren't doing that now.*

But being cautious certainly hadn't gotten them anywhere.

*Strange how it was the younger pair that was so cautious,
and the older willing to bet everything on one blow.*

Periodically, she or her father would stop, close their eyes,
and open themselves to the *wyrsa* to check on their where-
abouts. It was Amberdrake's turn to check when he cut his
"search" short, and put his fingers to his mouth to utter the
ear-piercing whistle they had agreed would be the "call in"
signal. Skan came flying back low over the river, with Tad
running on the trail a little behind him.

At that point, the gloom of daylight had begun to thicken
to the darkness of night, and they were all ready to take
their positions. Blade sent up a petition to the Star-Eyed One
that this would all work. . . .

*The Star-Eyed only helps those who help themselves, and
those who have planned well don't need the Star-Eyed's
help. Always remember that, Blade. If you haven't done
your best, you have no reason to hope for the Star-Eyed's
help if it still goes bad.*

She crouched down behind a screen of rock and dead
brush, away from their safe haven of nights past and waited,
her spear-thrower in one hand, three spears in the other. She
hadn't had time to practice, and she only hoped that she
could hit somewhere in her targets, instead of off to one side
of them. From where she crouched, she wouldn't have to
make a fatal hit, just a solid one, and they would probably go

into the river. There was nowhere for them to hide, even in the darkness, because it wasn't going to *be* dark, not completely. Skan had made a quick sortie across the river before they went off to set traps and had returned with rotten wood riddled with foxfire. Any time she saw one of the chunks of foxfire vanish, she was supposed to throw.

They had planned as well as they could. Now it was just a matter of waiting. . . .

And I never was very good at waiting!

She kept quiet, tried not to fidget, and listened for sounds up the trail.

Skan had an advantage over all of the others; he knew where each trap was, because he felt the mage-energy. And he would know as they were triggered, because he would sense that, too. Under any other circumstances, the tiny bits of energy he and Tad had invested in the triggers would have vanished in the overall flows of energies, but with *nothing* around to mask them, they "glowed" to him like tiny fires in the distance.

And he tensed, as he felt the first of them "go out."

That was the strangling-noose. . . .

He wished he had Drake's empathic ability as well. It would be nice to know if their trap had gotten anything.

They had been careful to set things that worked differently—though hopefully the pups would venture over here slowly, and would be so greedy to get at the bits of magic that none of them would realize that the magic-bits and the traps had anything to do with each other.

The next one is the set of javelins, and if there's a group, it should take out several. And they'll be cautious after they spring that one.

The javelins, hidden under brush, were far enough away from the trigger that he was fairly certain that the pups would make no connection between the two.

And there it goes! In his mind's eye, another little glowing "fire" went out.

Two down, two to go.

One trap working from above, one from in front. One takes out a single pup, one takes out several. No pattern there, and nothing in the way of a physical trigger to spot.

The next trap would take out a single pup again; and it worked from the ground. That would be the foot-noose. He felt his chest muscles tighten all over as he "watched" that little spark of energy, and waited for the pups to regain their courage. He knew that at least he and Tad were safe from detection tonight; they'd used up all but a fraction of their personal energies making the traps. There was nothing to distract the pups from the bait.

Time crawled by with legs of lead, and he began to wonder if he and Tad had done their work a little too well. Had he discouraged the pups? Or would the loss of several more goad them into enough rage to make them continue?

Only Blade and Amberdrake knew the answer to that question, and only if they had opened themselves up empathically again.

Just when he was about to give up—when, in fact, he had started to stand, taking himself out of hiding—the third "spark" died.

He crouched back down again, quickly.

They all heard—or rather, felt—the fourth trap go. It was the one that had originally been set with a crude string-trigger that went into the cave. When it went, it would not only take several *wyrsa* with it—hopefully—but it would have the unfortunate side-effect of spreading rock out into the river, widening the shelf in front of the cave. But that couldn't be helped. . . .

The rocks under him shook as the *wyrsa* triggered the last trap—and he didn't need to be empathic to know that this final trap totally enraged them. Unlike the cries that they had uttered until now, their ear-piercing shrieks of pure rage as the remaining members of the pack poured over the rocks were clearly audible over the pounding water.

More than four— But it was too late to do anything other

than follow through on their plan. With a scream of his own, he dove off the cliff, right down on the last one's back.

The head whipped around and the fangs sank into his shoulder, just below where the wing joined his body. He muffled his own screech of pain by sinking his own beak into the join of the creature's head and neck.

The thing wouldn't let go, but neither would he. It tried to dislodge him, but he had all four sets of talons bound firmly into its shoulders and hindquarters. In desperation, it writhed and rolled, and sank its fangs in up to the gumline. He saw red in his vision again, but clamped his beak down harder, sawing at the thing's flesh as he did so. He jerked his head toward his own keel, digging the hook of his powerful beak even further through hide, then muscle, then cartilage.

The spine . . . he had to sever the spine. . . .

Amberdrake stood up on his tiny shelf of rock and fired off arrow after arrow into the one *wyrsa* that had been unfortunate enough to cross *his* blob of foxfire. The arrows themselves had been rubbed with phosphorescent fungus, so once the first one lodged, he had a real target. He'd throttled down any number of emotions as the *wyrsa* came closer and closer, but—strangely enough, now that he was fighting, he felt a curious, detached calm. His concentration narrowed to the dark shape with an increasing number of glowing sticks in it; his world constricted to placing his next arrow somewhere near the rest of those spots of dim light. Sooner or later, he would hit something fatal.

He knew that he had, when the shape bearing the sticks wobbled to the edge of the water, wavered there for a moment, then tumbled in.

He chose another as it crossed a blob of foxfire, and began again.

Tad was close enough to his father that he saw the difficulties Skan was in. At that point, it didn't matter that it was not in the plan—he surged out of hiding and pounced, sinking *his* beak into the *wyrsa's* throat, and his foreclaws into its forelimbs. A gush of something hot and foul-tasting flooded his mouth, and the *wyrsa* collapsed under Skan's weight.

He let go, spitting to rid himself of the taste of the *wyrsa's* blood, as Skan shook himself free of the creature's head and staggered off to one side. Tad guarded him as he collected himself, keeping the other *wyrsa* at bay with slashing talons.

Then he wasn't alone anymore; his father was fighting beside him. "Good job," Skan called. "I owe you one."

"Then take the one on the left!" Tad called back, feeling a surge of pleasure that brought new energy with it.

"Only if you take the one on the right!" Skan called back, and launched himself at his next target.

Tad followed in the same instant, as if they had rehearsed the maneuver a thousand times together.

Blade's weapon was not as suited to rapid firing as her father's, and she had to choose her targets more carefully than he. He had a great many arrows; she had a handful of spears, and not all of them flew cleanly.

But when she *did* connect, her weapon was highly effective. She sent three *wyrsa* tumbling into the river, and wounded two more, making them easier targets for Skan and Tad.

Just as she ran out of short spears, she saw—and sensed— the moment that they had all been waiting for. The bitch- *wyrsa* was herding her remaining pups before her into the cave the two humans and two gryphons had abandoned. She obviously intended to reverse the situation on her attackers, by going to ground in what should have been *their* bolt-hole.

"She's going in!" Blade shouted. She seized the longer of her two spears and jumped down to the ground. A moment later, her father joined her, and with Tad and Skan they formed a half-circle that cut off the *wyrsa* from escape.

The pups had clearly had enough; now that they were all in the cave, they were silhouetted clearly against the fire at the rear. The pups, about three of them, milled about their mother. They didn't like the fire, but they didn't want to face the humans and gryphons either.

The *wyrsa*-bitch, however, was not ready to quit yet. She surged from side to side in the cave, never presenting a clear target, and snarled at her pups. It looked to Blade as if she were trying to herd them into something. She and Amberdrake edged up farther into the cave, following the plan. In theory, with the two weakest members of the party in plain sight, the bitch should do what they wanted her to.

"She's trying to goad them into a charge!" Amberdrake shouted. "Get ready!"

Blade grounded the butt of her spear against the rock, hoping against hope that she wouldn't have to use it—

"Now!" Drake shouted, as the bitch herded her pups up onto the brush and rock barrier.

And at that signal, Skan and Tad used the last of their mage-energy, and ignited the oil-soaked wood of the barricade with a simple, small fire-spell.

With the fire already going at the back of the cave, there was a good draft going up the chimney. The flames swept back, and merged with the second fire at the rear. The cave was an oven, and the *wyrsa* were trapped inside.

The *wyrsa*-bitch turned and heaved herself at the barricade nearest Blade. Her dead-white eyes blazed rage as she stared at the human, and Blade felt her hatred burning, even without being open empathically.

Amberdrake dropped his spear; it clattered to the ground as he seized his head in both hands. His knees buckled and he fell in a convulsing heap.

Without hesitation, Blade picked up her own spear, aimed, and threw.

The bitch-*wyrsa* took it full in the chest and continued forward, screaming defiance. She heaved up into the air, towering above all of them for a moment—and Blade was certain she was going to come over the barricade anyway. Blade's heart pounded in her ears—only that sound, and the sound of the *wyrsa's* scream, louder than anything she had felt before.

The *wyrsa* fell forward, but didn't leap. The spear jutted from her chest, only a quarter of its length in. She stumbled forward in shock. Her forelegs crumpled—and the butt of the crude spear struck the ground and drove itself in deeper.

Blade fell into a crouch without hesitation and groped for her fighting-knife, but she could not take her eyes off the vision of the black *wyrsa* pitching backwards, to be consumed in flame.

"We won," Tad said, for the hundredth time. As the rain washed *wyrsa* blood from the rocks, he locked his talons into another body and dragged it to the river, to roll it in. Blade hoped that something in there would eat *wyrsa*, and that the blasted things wouldn't poison the fish.

After the flames had died down, they had all moved back into the cave to see what was left. Not much was recognizable compared to the bodies outside the cave, but the skulls of the charred *wyrsa* were easily broken off for later cleaning. The families of those people the creatures had killed were entitled to them, perhaps for a revenge ceremony during mourning, so the grisly task was done with solemn efficiency. Inside, the rock was nicely warmed, and the two exhausted fathers had a good, comfortable place to lie down and get some rest.

Meanwhile she and Tad dragged their own weary bodies out into the rain again, to clean up the mess.

"This is the last one, thank the gods," Blade said, as she hauled the last of the beheaded bodies to the river's edge. Together, she and Tad shoved it in, and together they turned and walked back to the cave.

"Drake is burning some fish for you, Blade," Skan greeted them as they climbed over the rock barricade. "Zhaneel would not approve. By the way, *both* the other rescue-parties are near enough for Mindspeech with me, so we won't have to eat fish much longer."

Blade's heart surged with joy—and then her throat tightened, as she realized just *how* close the others must have been last night.

They could have walked right into the same kind of trap that my father did, she thought soberly. She had been wondering ever since yesterday evening if they were doing the right thing by trying an all-or-nothing last-stand. Now she knew they *had* been.

"When will they get here?" Tad asked eagerly, as Blade accepted fish from her father with a smile of thanks.

"Tomorrow, probably. Your mother is thrilled, Blade. Tad, your mother and brother would be flying in here now if it weren't raining." Skan gryph-grinned at all of them. "I promised them that we would do our best not to melt before they got here."

"That was probably safe," Blade agreed. "Did you tell them anything other than that we were all safe?"

Skan ground his beak and dropped his head. "I confess; I told them everything while they were still far enough away that your mothers couldn't flay us alive for risking all our necks last night." He coughed. "I know my Zhaneel, and I suspect Winterhart will react the same. Weary by the time they reach us, they will be so grateful that we are all right that they will probably have forgotten that we took on all those *wyrsa* by ourselves."

Amberdrake winced. "Maybe Zhaneel will—but Winterhart won't," he said guiltily. "And she'll *never* forgive me for acting like a hotheaded young fighter and standing on a ledge in the dark, firing arrows into the damned things! And if I actually admit that I—well—I was *good* at it—"

Blade patted his knee, and smiled as a rush of love filled her heart.

"Don't worry, Father," she said fondly. "I'll protect you."

For the first time in days, if not weeks, Tad lay on a ledge in the open, sunning himself. Finally, *finally*, the rains had lessened last night, and although the fog had appeared on schedule, the rain had not chased it away. It looked as if the weather was getting back to "normal."

Tad whooped, and leaped off his ledge to gallop toward his

brother. Keeth arrowed in for a landing down on the recently-added stretch of rock-and-gravel beach in front of the cave. A moment later, as Tad and his brother closed on each other for the gryphonic equivalent of a back-slapping reunion, the "mothers' party" appeared around the curve of the trail.

Now it was Blade's turn to launch herself off her ledge and run straight into the arms of her mother, while Amberdrake brought up the rear. Tad grinned to his twin as they watched his Silver partner hugging her mother and even shedding a few tears. She was acting just as any normal human would in the same situation, and about time, too!

Things settled down a little, and Winterhart paused to wipe a couple of happy tears, as the second party rounded the bend. With a gasp, Blade broke off her conversation with her mother to run straight for the leader of the party.

Ikala looked surprised, but extremely pleased, when she threw her arms around him—and it would have taken an expert to determine if she kissed him first, or he kissed her.

Tad took a quick look at Amberdrake and Winterhart; they looked stunned, but gradually the surprise was being replaced by—glee?

Probably. Now they're finally going to get their *wish, after all!*

"What is *that* all about?" Keeth gurgled. "She's never done *that* before!"

Tad laughed. "Oh, it has been a complicated mess, but I think I can explain it. Drake sees her as a real person now—not just as his daughter, his child. They've fought alongside each other. Now she's—well, now she knows who *she* is; that she's not a reflection of Drake or her mother, and that she doesn't have to work so hard at being their opposite. It's—well, she's free, free to be herself."

"And you?" Keeth asked shrewdly.

Tad laughed. "After seeing Father in action, I can't say I mind being the son of the Black Gryphon anymore. And now he has fought beside me, and he knows there is more to me than obstacle courses and fatherly pride. Word will get around, and then he will have to cope with being referred to as 'the father of that brave Silver.' I guess that's justice."

Keeth grinned and leaned against his brother. "That should give us all some rest and freedom."

Freedom, he thought with content. *That's what it is all right. Freedom.*